Praise for
Reaper's Justice

"Intense, edgy, and passionate."
                                                    —*RT Book Reviews*

"Exceptional . . . [A] hands-down winning tale that is not to be missed."
                                                    —*Romance Reviews Today*

"Those familiar with this author know she's the queen of writing fresh, sensual Westerns with characters that will remain with you long after the last page is turned."
                                                    —*A Romance Review*

Caleb

"A terrific thriller."
                                                    —*Genre Go Round Reviews*

Promises Reveal

"Few writers can match the skill of Sarah McCarty . . . The fast-paced story line hooks the audience."
                                                    —*Midwest Book Review*

"Entertaining, and kept this reader turning the pages."
                                                    —*Romance Reader at Heart*

"Titillating, sizzling, and realistic . . . I don't know ho does it, but I want more and more and more. You will, too, this fantastic tale."
                                                    iews

"A must-read . . . Enticing and erotic . . . I e!"
                                                    Junkies

"Highly entertaining . . . Plenty ste mpliment to the series."
                                                    Romance Review

"A delightful tale with lots of intense pass Outstanding! Not to be missed by fans of historical Westerns w enjoy a strong dose of erotic fiction."
                                                    —*The Romance Readers Connection*

continued . . .

Running Wild

"[Sarah McCarty's] captivating characters, scorching love scenes, and dramatic plot twists kept me on the edge. I could not put it down."
—*Night Owl Reviews*

"Sarah McCarty entices and enchants . . . and has taken paranormal romance to a whole new level." —*Romance Junkies*

"You are going to love this . . . Entertaining and passionate . . . Fast-paced story lines and super-hot sex scenes . . . Sarah McCarty definitely takes you on a wild ride and . . . weaves a fascinating paranormal."
—*Lucrezia Magazine*

"This one is a scorcher. If you're looking for a romance to raise the temperatures, then look no further than McCarty's *Running Wild*!"
—*Romance Reader at Heart*

"Provide[s] werewolf romance fans with a strong, heated collection. Fans will be *Running Wild*." —*Midwest Book Review*

More praise for the novels of Sarah McCarty

"[A] pulse-pounding paranormal." —*Road to Romance*

"Masterfully written." —*The Romance Readers Connection*

"Powerfully erotic, emotional, and thought provoking."
—*Ecataromance*

"Has the WOW factor . . . Characters that jump off the pages!"
—*Just Erotic Romance Reviews*

"Toe-curling." —*Fallen Angel Reviews* (recommended read)

"Ms. McCarty is a genius!" —*Romance Junkies*

Titles by Sarah McCarty

RUNNING WILD
WILD INSTINCT
PROMISES REVEAL

The Shadow Wranglers
CALEB
JARED
JACE
SLADE

The Shadow Reapers
REAPER'S JUSTICE
REAPER'S VOW

⊰ THE SHADOW REAPERS ⊱

REAPER'S VOW

Sarah McCarty

BERKLEY SENSATION, NEW YORK

THE BERKLEY PUBLISHING GROUP
Published by the Penguin Group
Penguin Group (USA) LLC
375 Hudson Street, New York, New York 10014

USA • Canada • UK • Ireland • Australia • New Zealand • India • South Africa • China

penguin.com

A Penguin Random House Company

This book is an original publication of The Berkley Publishing Group.

Library of Congress Cataloging-in-Publication Data

McCarty, Sarah.
Reaper's vow / Sarah McCarty—Berkley Sensation trade paperback edition.
pages cm— (The shadow's reapers)
ISBN 978-0-425-24770-9 (pbk.)
1. Werewolves—Fiction.   I. Title.
PS3613.C3568R43 2014
813'.6—dc23   2013043329

PUBLISHING HISTORY
Berkley Sensation trade paperback edition / March 2014

PRINTED IN THE UNITED STATES OF AMERICA

10 9 8 7 6 5 4 3 2 1

Cover art by Phil Heffernan.
Cover design by George Long.

For those who've fought their way back from the physical or emotional brink, and all those who supported them. Welcome home.

REAPER'S VOW

⊰ 1 ⊱

THEY WERE OUT THERE. COLE PATTED HIS BIG PALOMINO, Rage, on the shoulder and listened to the breeze rustle through the leaves, the low rasp joining the warning tingle creeping up his spine. Finally. The ones who'd kidnapped his cousin Addy were within reach. Untying the leather thong keeping his rifle in the scabbard, he smiled in anticipation. Demon wolves. Reapers. Outlaws. He didn't give a shit what fanciful names anyone called the men who'd torn up the town and stolen his cousin. He was getting her back. No matter how long it took. He'd been tracking their sorry asses for two months. Two long months in which he'd been led down more false trails than he'd care to admit. Addy's kidnappers were clever. He grazed his fingers over the hilt of the knife riding his hip. But cleverness wasn't going to save them. Nothing was. He had the tenacity of a badger when it came to family. And his brothers and Addy were all the family he had left.

Let her go.

Reese's order rippled along his consciousness. Normally, he valued his younger brother's opinion, but this time the echo of Reese's voice wasn't something Cole wanted to hear. Reese had the asinine notion Isaiah was good for Addy. What she wanted. The answer to a prayer. Cole snorted. Yet at the same time Reese believed Isaiah was a legendary Reaper. One of the demon spawn, the stories said, that haunted the mountains surrounding their valley, protecting it from outsiders with strength and reflexes that outdid a normal man's tenfold. A man capable of turning into a wolf. A monster. Cole shook his head. This was the man Reese thought was right for their cousin Addy? Shit, his brother had to have lost his mind to believe that Reapers were anything but humans with a fanciful reputation or to believe that Addy's request to leave with Isaiah had been anything but coerced.

A trickle of energy came at Cole from the right. Edgy and stealthy. The knife-edge pulse of power a hunter put out. Cole had no doubt who was the prey. Shit. The Reapers were now hunting him as much as he'd been hunting them. Which wasn't quite how he'd planned on things going. Reaching down, he slid his rifle free of the scabbard. After two months he was finally close enough to Addy's kidnappers to get their attention. Another tingle went down his spine. Different. Familiar. Addy. She was near. Instinct said call out. Common sense kept him quiet. If Addy was anywhere nearby, she was dangling as bait.

A curse ripped through his mind right along with another surge of bad energy. Trouble.

He spat the bad taste from his mouth, scanning the hills and ledges sporadically dotted with trees that made up the high mountain landscape, feeling the battle coming. With a smile Cole rested his rifle across his lap. It was about damn time.

The fuckers might have stolen Addy, but he'd get her back. He'd done it before, and he'd do it again. And if the Reapers had harmed one hair on her head, there'd be no mercy. Not like before. Before he'd been so horrified at the way he'd found her, he hadn't thought of anything except getting Addy home. He levered the shells into the chamber of the Spencer. This time he'd hunt their sorry asses down and gut them. Make them pay. Every single last one of them.

Against the backdrop of the current tension in the air, Cole saw again the way Addy had looked at him in that Indian camp. The terror in her eyes. The shattered lightness that had been her soul. Because he hadn't been home when the attack had come fifteen years ago. Hadn't been able to protect her. He'd promised himself right then he'd never see that look in her eyes again. Yet here he was back on her trail, same as before, worry riding tandem with anger, in all likelihood about to face the same shattered look. Only this time he didn't know if Addy could recover. There was only so much a body could take. And Addy had already had her fill. Hell, for that matter, so had he.

Goddamn. It wasn't fair this should happen to her twice in one lifetime. Addy was fragile. She always had been, but her time with the Indians had left her broken. It'd taken her years to rebuild her world. He'd watched her do it, every step forward anchored by a new ritual. Every ritual anchored in her worry stone. She never went anywhere without her worry stone, but she didn't have it now. Cole reached into his pocket and touched it. He'd found it lying in a pool of blood in the remnants of the battle like a plea. Or a warning.

He shook his head again. Before she'd been a child, but now she was a woman grown, and there were ways a man could hurt a woman . . . Cole jerked his hat down as the old knot of dread in his stomach flared. He didn't want to think about that. Steering the big palomino off the path into a small cut in the rise, he pushed back the memories and focused on the increasing tingle along his spine that forecasted the trouble that was coming.

Closing his eyes, Cole traced the energy. The ability was a gift he'd been born with and one he'd honed over the years. It'd saved his life more times than he could count. The surges were coming at him from two, no, three directions. He frowned. They were flanking him. Driving him forward like a sheep to the slaughter. He looked around. Steep hills surrounded him on either side. No way out. He had two choices: to go back or to ride into a trap. There was no good place to take a stand here. And there wouldn't be where they waited, but there was a chance he could find a spot between here and there. The only good news was they probably weren't aware that he knew what they were doing. That warning tingle had always been his advantage. The thing that kept him alive. That and his reflexes. He had very good reflexes.

With a press of his knee Cole urged Rage forward. The horse, surefooted and stable, responded. Rage was always Cole's choice when he went to battle. A man needed someone steady by his side when things got hairy, which maybe explained why he'd never gotten married. Women were a liability. Sweet and sexy and satisfying to dally with, but they tended to the emotional. He had enough responsibilities. He didn't need the challenge of one more. Truth was, he was getting tired. The tingle got stronger snaking down his spine. He looked around. And careless, if his current predicament was anything to go by. He'd wanted to find the Reapers, but on his terms, not theirs.

Ahead the path twisted through the rocky hillside. The trees were getting sparse. The palomino nickered. Cole patted Rage's shoulder three times, the way he did when he wanted to let the animal know trouble was coming. The horse tossed his head in anticipation, and the energy rippling through his muscles spread to Cole. Cole contained it with ruthless determination. He wasn't an excitable man, but it was hard not to respond to those primitive surges. Not to let his own restless need override the hard-won lesson of patience. He'd been waiting a long time for this confrontation, and he had a lot on the line. Too much to go off like a kid.

Ahead the path split around a copse of trees, but there wasn't a goddamn clue as to what lay beyond, either. Which meant they had the advantage. He paused. It was natural for man and horse to go to the right. He touched the reins to Rage's neck, directing him left.

From the bushes came a low growl. Dropping the reins and whipping out his revolver, Cole took aim. But there was nothing at which to shoot. Goddamn. The Reapers were like fucking ghosts. There but not. Energy snapped around his head. He snapped around with it, expecting to see a Reaper, but there was nothing. The growl came again, this time from the other side. Rage spun and crow-hopped two steps, taking them down the other path. The growling stopped. Cole leaned back, directing Rage to stop; Cole's senses flared, searching for a clue. Had that growl been deliberate? Was he being driven right? What the hell did it matter? To stand and fight here would be a fool's game. He was exposed on all sides. Rage nickered and backed up two steps until Cole patted his neck. "That's not an option."

At this point his options were limited; whichever way he went, trouble was waiting. He saw a gray shadow slip through the low brush. It disappeared before he could get off a shot. If that was a wolf, it was damn quick.

Man. Wolf. Whatever form they take, Reapers are lightning fast.

Reeses's description whispered through his mind. Cole swore. The one thing he didn't need right now was nonsense flitting through his head. From above and to the right, a pebble tumbled down the wall, the slight noise sounding as loud as a gunshot in the unnatural silence. He glanced up, squinting against the morning sun. The pebble gathered speed and company, sending a spray of dirt sliding down the hill.

Along with scent of dust came the same frustration he'd had fifteen years ago when he'd hunted for Addy after everyone else had given up. The same feeling of chasing shadows, not substance. The same impatience. He pushed the emotions aside, forcing his muscles to relax. He might not have the advantage, but he was ready.

"Come on, fuckers."

A surge of energy whispered around him like smoke blown on the wind, raising the hairs on the back of his neck. Energy like nothing he'd ever felt before. Not good or evil but . . . powerful.

Demons.

Reese's claim about Reapers whipped through his mind. Cole shook his head, scanned the trail, and pulled his hat down over his eyes. Shit! Now he was getting as fanciful as his brother. On edge from too little sleep, too much coffee, and too much worry, he was giving too much credit where credit wasn't due. Isaiah Jones might have a bit more speed, a bit more presence than most, but was as human as he. He'd seen his eyes, touched his skin, and seen him bleed.

Felt his power.

The insidious thought pricked his practicality. Cole shrugged that off, too. Some men were just better at giving off energy, like himself. It didn't mean they were more than human, and for sure if Jones had been a demon, Addy would have seen through him from the get-go. Addy knew about evil. She wouldn't have made the foolish mistake of taking him into her home.

Into her heart.

Another unwelcome notion Reese had brought up. Cole wanted to spit the thought out; it left that bad a taste in his mouth. Damn Reese and his preaching. No way could Addy be in love with Jones. The man wore trouble the way some wore chaps. By all rights, one look at him should have sent sweet Addy running for cover. That it hadn't irked Cole to no end. It made no sense, and things that didn't make sense churned his gut, but the one thing Addy hadn't been afraid of was that man. And that took skill. Not magic. The same skill a cardsharp used in a poker game. Illusion and pretense. That was all the magic Jones possessed.

Cole remembered how Addy had stood in the curve of Jones's arm and defied them while Jones had looked . . . befuddled. Shit. Cole shook his head again at the instant of sympathy he'd felt for the man at the time. He urged Rage forward with a press of his knees. He didn't know what Jones had done to make Addy cuddle up to him like he was her favorite feather bed, but it wasn't going to work on Cole. And no doubt it'd stopped working on Addy by now. Jones might have had her walking around as if under some lovesick spell, but that had ended the night of the dance when all hell had broken loose. When the wolves had attacked. When Jones had . . . Cole frowned. He had memory lapses about that night due to his injuries, but he knew Isaiah had done something. Something that had put a look of horror and terror in Addy's eyes. Jones was going to pay for that. Cole had promised Addy she'd never have to be afraid again when he'd brought her home the first time. Now Jones had made a liar out of him. That score needed settling as much as Addy needed rescuing.

Another trickle of rocks signaled more movement above. Different pulses of energy flicked at him. Animal and human. One, two, five, ten. Too many too count. Too many too sort. All moving in from different angles, different distances. All centered on him. Farther down the trail Cole could see where the hills sloped toward each other and narrowed the path, the perfect place for an ambush. Looking over his shoulder, the path was just as narrow. There was no going back and no going forward. Ahead and again to the right, there was another cut in the bank. The space was just big enough to hold him. He patted Rage's shoulder, reached behind, and unbuckled his saddlebags.

"Looks like this is it." As if he understood, the horse tossed his head. "I'm going to hold them off while you make a break for it." Cole opened the flap of the saddlebags, grabbing bullets and stuffing them into the deep pockets of his duster. Now, he not only had Reapers to deal with but wolves. Rage snorted and sidestepped.

"Yeah. I feel it, too. There's a shit storm coming."

The warning tingles were climbing like ants up his spine. The Reapers didn't surprise him but the wolves? That did. Rainfall had been light of late but not that light. Certainly not enough of a drought to cause desperation. Which meant there was another explanation. And no matter what Reese thought, Cole didn't believe Reapers were wolves wearing a human disguise. More than likely the Reapers had a few wolves as pets, and folks in shock from battle had jumbled their memories into something much more fantastic. As the legend gave them power, the Reapers had been content to let the rumors grow to myth. Cole dismounted, listening to his senses. Not liking what they were telling him.

Dragging his saddlebags off Rage's back, he slung them over his shoulder. Tugging the horse's reins, he urged him forward. "Wait for me down the trail." Rage tossed his head and planted his feet. Cole slapped his flank.

"Not your fight today, friend."

Rage hesitated, tossed his head, nostrils flaring as he reared, his cream white mane catching the light. His front hooves made a staccato tattoo on the hard ground when he hit all fours again. It was a measure of Rage's loyalty that he paused when the scent of wolf had to be hanging so heavy in the air.

Cole slapped his flank again. Harder. "Go!"

With a snort, Rage gave in to the same nerves eating at Cole and galloped down the path. Cole fired two shots in rapid succession up at the ridge, providing what cover he could, cursing because the horse deserved better for his loyalty, but two bullets was all he could spare with an uncertain battle looming.

"Watch your back," he muttered after the horse, watching until the animal turned the corner. Cole felt the warning tingles grow to a steady crawl under his skin. No more pebbles tumbled through the silence. No snarls emanated from above, no voices broke the quiet, but they were out there.

"Fucking wolves."

And fucking Reapers. He levered two shells into the chamber of the rifle and cocked the hammers. They were out there, too. Every inch of his skin tingled, indicating the danger all around.

A short animalistic cough came from the right and above, followed by a sense of amusement. He whipped the rifle around. He couldn't see a damned thing down the sight except rock and dirt.

"Do that again you son of a bitch, and I'll give you something to laugh at."

No sound came. But the almost laughter lingered in his head.

"Reapers. I've been watching them. They're more than you think, Cole."

Damn Reese and his superstitious leanings. Reapers were men, and wolves were wolves. The only thing that gave Reapers an edge was the superstition with which men viewed them. Against his will, Cole remembered when he'd confronted Isaiah outside Addy's home. How Reese's certainty had resonated as firmly in his mind as his hand on his arm.

He'll kill you before you can pull the trigger.

No one's that fast.

Reapers are.

A chill went down Cole's spine. He looked up at the opposite ledge. If Reapers really shifted from wolf to human depending on their mood, a Reaper in a human body with a gun could pick him off like a fish swimming in a barrel right now.

"Fuck."

Again that cough that sounded like laughter from the ledge above. A little back and to his left now. Cole resisted the urge to fire at it. A fool wasted ammunition. A bigger fool stayed where he was. There was deadfall back the way he'd come, with an overhang offering some protection. If he could make it there he'd have a chance. A growl came from the direction he'd just come, then another, deeper, more menacing one. They wanted him to go forward? Fuck that. He was backtracking. Leaping to his feet, he fired two shots in the direction of those growls and charged back down the path.

On the first step, he felt the change in energy. They were coming up behind him fast, on the ridge. Lightning fast. Fuck. Tightening his grip on the rifle, he drove himself harder. He felt a surge of unified energy behind him as clearly as he heard the tumble of rock down ledges. A wolf leapt out in front of him. He brought it down with a bullet between the eyes and kept running, leaping over the body, all of his senses sharpening as he ran. Dirt crushed beneath his boots. Wind whistled past his ear. And those silent growls grew louder in his mind.

They were fast, but he only needed to be just fast enough. He just needed to make it to the deadfall and to the narrow clearing beyond, and he'd stand a chance. He was almost to the opening when he heard that coughing laugh again. Behind him claws dug into the earth scattering twigs and dirt and rock. They were coming.

Ahead was the downed tree and vegetation that made up the deadfall. With a shout of victory, he leapt for it arms wide, guns tight in his hands. Too late to stop his leap, he saw the three wolves standing shoulder to shoulder in front of him. Bigger than any he'd ever seen, they stood there with their hackles raised. Waiting. This was the real trap.

Fuck.

He whipped his rifle forward as he landed. The wolf on the right moved in a blur of fur and teeth, grabbing the barrel in incredibly powerful jaws and yanking it from Cole's grip, before dropping it to the ground and looking at him through eerily human green eyes. Common sense said his fancy was running away with his imagination, but in his gut Cole knew that wolf had known exactly what he was doing. The wolf had disarmed him as neatly as any human could have.

"What the hell kind of wolves are you?" he asked, keeping his revolver trained on the trio who watched him with nothing akin to the fear they should have had. The hairs on the back of his neck stood on end.

And again from behind him came that cough that sounded distinctly like laughter.

Looking over his shoulder, Cole understood one thing: the chances of him getting out of this alive were dangling around slim to none. Three wolves in front and three or more coming up fast behind him, and somewhere back farther, many more. And only six bullets in the chamber. Even if he emptied his guns, he couldn't kill them all. Addy's face flashed across his mind's eye. Dammit! He couldn't die here like this. She needed him. The wolves took a step closer. Cole didn't bother to step back. Where would he go?

"Come on, you bastards."

As they stalked forward, moving as one, another thought came hot on the heels of the first. If he died here, his brothers would have no idea where to find him. Their knowledge of his death would only come when he failed to return year after year. Fuck. He wouldn't wish that on anyone. Which only left him one option: staying alive.

Behind him a wolf snarled. In front of him two of the three gathered their muscles to jump. With a lift of his lip he snarled right back. There wasn't a Cameron born who knew the meaning of quit. And he certainly wasn't going to give it a definition now. Fucking wolves. Drawing his knife, he leapt forward, the Cameron battle cry cutting through the air as cleanly as the bullet fired from the barrel of his revolver. The wolf going for his throat dropped midair.

Twisting around Cole thrust upward with the knife, driving it into the gut of the one going for his unprotected back. Blood spilled over him like warm rain, obscuring his vision as he shoved the body away. Spinning on his heel, he faced the rest, heart pumping, battle fever clearing his mind of all but the fight.

With a twitch of his fingers he invited them in. "Who's next?"

⤚ 2 ⤙

THEY CAME AT HIM AS ONE UNIT, PERFECTLY COORDI-
nated in their attack. Four wolves, each weighing easily two hundred pounds, leapt toward him, lips drawn back, fangs gleaming.
Balancing on his toes, Cole waited. At the last second, he dove
under them, rolling to the left before coming up to his feet, ready to
make use of the knife. He blinked. They were right there with him,
stealing his advantage with reflexes as quick as his own. Maybe
quicker.

Damn.

One with a white mask lunged, snapping at his knife hand. Cole
jumped back. His boot slipped on a rock. Before he could recover,
the masked wolf was on him, knocking him backward. There was
no time to twist or do anything but fall. He hit hard. His breath left
him in a rush as his head slammed back. Pain gouged at him as the
wolf's huge feet dug into his biceps. He blocked the sensation with
the ease of practice, focusing his attention instead on the way the

wolf had him pinned to the ground. How the fuck had the animal known to do that?

The wolf's breath hit Cole's face like a fetid blow. Saliva dripped on his neck as the wolf lowered his head, his strangely human eyes holding Cole's, challenging him as his jaws opened wider. Emotion and energy hit Cole in discordant waves. Hatred. Purpose. Insanity. The wolf was insane, maybe even rabid. Shit. If the damn thing didn't kill him, he'd kill himself rather than force his brothers to do it when the rabies took his reason. Cole shifted his weight. The wolf growled long and low in his throat. Did it think a threat meant shit to a Cameron?

"Fuck you," he snarled right back at the animal.

Bold words from a man who was outnumbered and couldn't move. As if the wolf read his mind, its lips pulled back farther into what Cole swore was a grin. Cole managed to turn the knife in his hand, aiming the point at the beast's paw. The animal snarled again. Cole ignored the warning.

"Let's see how well you do missing a foot."

Wrenching his arm up, he jabbed at the wolf's paw. A blur of motion out of the corner of his eye was the only warning he had before teeth sank into his knife arm.

Agony shot up his arm and horror infected his soul. Another wolf. Likely as rabid as the first. The knife dropped to the ground. He gritted his teeth against a moan. Rabies. His head hit a rock so hard he saw stars. The horror solidified to determination as the first wolf lowered its head a fraction more. So close its breath seared his skin. Fuck. Wolves he could fight. Rabies there was no cure for. He heaved up to no avail, straining fruitlessly against the horror.

A tremendous wave of energy exploded across his torso, and the weight abruptly lifted off his arms. The loss of tension left him jerking pointlessly. Before Cole could react, the earth shuddered under the force of bodies hitting the ground. A quick turn of his head to the right revealed the small space teaming with wolves, the new colliding with old within vicious battle, their claws tearing up the ground around him as they strained for supremacy. The din of bloodcurdling snarls filled his ears. The musky scent of churned dirt filled his nostrils as he rolled to the left only to come up against a wall of legs. Fuck, there was nowhere to turn. Digging his fingers into the dirt, Cole waited for his chance.

It never came. The battle was short and vicious, and at its end yet another wolf stood beside Cole. It was bigger than the masked one, with thick black fur tipped with silver. Its jaws gaped wide, showing off large, pointed white teeth dripping blood. As Cole watched, the wolf's face distorted. Blurred. Cole blinked and shook his head. He'd hit it going down, but he hadn't thought he'd hit it so hard that he'd be seeing things. The wolf dissolved, distorted, and reshaped, and—impossibly—became a man, but it was not just any man. Isaiah Jones, naked, blood on his face, squatted beside Cole where the wolf had just crouched.

Cole blinked to quell the mix of fascination and horror inside him. Shit, the rumors were true. Reapers could change shape. That was going to take some digesting. Cole blinked again and inched his hand toward the knife.

For a second Jones looked as dazed as Cole felt. Then he shook his head, and with a flick of his hand he indicated Cole's appearance. "You're a mess."

The tone rasped across Cole's nerves. "You're not looking that appealing yourself."

"Uh-huh." Jones shoved his hair off his face. "What the hell are you doing here?"

"I lost something."

"Your mind for starters."

Cole shrugged. "And you've lost all appearance of being human."

Isaiah narrowed his eyes. "A necessary consequence of saving your ass."

Cole moved his hand closer to the knife hilt. "Wasn't aware you were that fond of it."

Isaiah stared at him deadpan. "I'm not."

Cole smiled at the snap in his tone. "But Addy is."

And that had to gall the other man to no end.

"I wouldn't save your ass because of that."

Cole arched a brow at him. "No?"

Isaiah met his gaze with flat honesty. "You endanger with your presence everything I'm fighting to build."

Interesting. "So why?"

"You saved Addy's life." Isaiah stood. "That's a blood debt."

Anything with the word blood in it was serious. "Good to know monsters have honor."

Isaiah held out his hand. Cole didn't take it. Isaiah narrowed his eyes but didn't withdraw the offer of assistance. "You shouldn't have come here."

"You shouldn't have taken Addy."

Isaiah snorted. "You don't know her well if you think any man could 'take' that woman."

"Addy is fragile."

"Not anymore."

He hated that Isaiah knew that before he did.

"So you say."

"So I do." Isaiah crooked his fingers. "You want to lie in the dirt all day or do you want to get moving?"

Cole sure as shit didn't want to be lying in the dirt at the feet of this man.

Spotting his hat, he grabbed it off the ground. The knife gleamed dully in the churned-up ground to his right. The urge to reach for it rode him hard.

"You wouldn't make it."

The way Isaiah spoke with the calm of a man whose words were supported by cold, hard fact aggravated the shit out of Cole. He should have stayed home, which he could have done had Isaiah left Addy alone.

Isaiah cut him a glance. "I would never leave Addy."

Search as he might, Cole couldn't see any signs of the wolf in the man standing before him. Around them other naked men milled about checking bodies, donning clothes. There was no common look of family between them beyond well-developed physiques. They were blond and brunette, dark and light skinned. To all intents and appearances, they were just men now. Hard to believe a few minutes ago they were wearing fur and snarling like animals.

"We call that our inner beast."

Cole's gaze snapped back to Isaiah's. "You read minds, too?"

Isaiah shrugged. "It wasn't hard to read that thought."

Cole remembered another reason he didn't like Jones. The man didn't like to give a straight answer.

The men formed a line. Waiting. For him, Cole realized. He took Jones's hand, resentment and anger surging through him. A kidnapper's hand. Isaiah's eyes were watchful as he helped Cole up. Cole didn't have any goddamn option but to say thank you.

"Had you stayed where you belonged, there'd have been no need for this battle."

No doubt Jones would like Cole to believe that. Cole looked around at the bodies on the ground and the hard, determined expressions of those that had survived.

"Then why do I get the feeling this battle would have happened whether I was here or not?"

Isaiah just stared in that steady, provoking way he had.

Dusting his hat off he asked, "Not answering?"

Isaiah grunted. "The battle would have happened. But it would have happened at a time and place of my choosing and not because we had to waste energy rescuing you."

"So these aren't friends of yours."

"No."

Short and to the point. That answered that.

"If you're that unhappy with it, why did you bother?"

Isaiah's lip lifted in a snarl. "You are cousin to my mate."

The word choice hit Cole wrong. "What the fuck do you mean by 'mate'?"

Isaiah didn't answer. Just started walking away. Cole slammed his hat on his head, swore under his breath, and followed. Every step annoyed the hell out of him. He wasn't one to follow. But this man knew where Addy was. With a sharp motion of his hand Isaiah communicated with someone behind Cole. Cole turned. A tall man with shoulder-length blond hair and dressed in brown wool pants and a black vest went into the trees. A second later he came out leading Rage. Cole was pleased to see the horse whole.

Isaiah pointed down the mountain. "Your home is that way."

Rage tossed his head when Cole got close. Cole knew exactly how the horse felt. He didn't like this, either. He took the reins and patted his neck. "That it is."

Another Reaper tossed him his rifle. He caught it. Rage didn't flinch.

"Where you want to go, you're not welcome," the Reaper that had fetched Rage informed Cole.

As if he cared. Cole nodded up the path. "Is that where Addy is?"

Isaiah came alongside Cole, leading a buckskin gelding. "Thank you, Dirk."

The two Reapers shared a glance before Dirk nodded and walked away.

"She is by my side always," Isaiah informed Cole.

"And you're heading which way?"

Jones jerked his chin to the left.

Cole nodded and looped the stirrup over the horn of Rage's saddle before checking the cinch. "Then that's where I'm going."

Isaiah paused, his hand on the horse's opposite shoulder. "I can't guarantee your safety."

Cole looked back at the bodies and pressed his palm over the bite on his forearm. There wasn't any point worrying about it. He wouldn't have much time if that wolf had been rabid. Cole lowered the stirrup. "I don't recall asking you to."

Isaiah smiled. "Reapers don't get rabies."

Only long practice allowed Cole to keep his surprise hidden. "You read minds as easily as you shed fur?"

Isaiah swung up on his horse. "Your thoughts aren't that complicated."

He nodded at Cole. Two men immediately rode up and flanked him. Dirk was one. There was something about that Reaper that commanded attention. Something that had nothing to do with his energy and everything to do with the way he carried himself. As if he expected death itself to step aside. He bore watching.

Cole mounted his own horse. Rage tossed his head. Isaiah shook his. Another motion of Jones's hands and Dirk bound Cole's hands behind him before he could even react. Fuck, these Reapers were fast. He yanked at his hands. And thorough. He wasn't going to be getting out of these any time soon. He snarled at Dirk. Dirk smiled back, an even white baring of teeth.

"Scared?" Cole taunted.

"Cautious," Dirk countered calmly. "You have a reputation." He glanced at Cole out of the corner of his eye. "Some have wondered."

"What?"

"Whether Reaper blood flows in your veins."

The hell it did. "I'm not a fucking monster."

Dirk smiled and backed his bay up. "Well, whatever you are, you won't be escaping any time soon."

"I wasn't aware I was trying to."

Isaiah turned his gelding around, filling the space Dirk had just left with his presence and his energy. "It's a precaution in case you go getting nervous."

"I'm not the nervous type."

"And we're not monsters."

Cole remembered the moment when Jones had gone from beast to man. "In whose opinion?"

With a twist of his lips that could have constituted a smile, Jones's shot back, "Addy's."

Shit. "My cousin sees what she wants."

Jones stared at him for a second and said with flat honesty, "She sees you."

Yes, she did. In a far more flattering way than he deserved.

"And she's anxiously awaiting your arrival," Jones finished.

"She knows I'm coming?"

"I promised her I would bring you home if that's what you wanted."

"It's not my home." The claim bounced harmlessly off Jones's back as he started up the trail.

"But it is Addy's," drifted back over the Reaper's shoulder.

Cole gritted his teeth. "Not for long."

There was a silence, and then an older man with a full beard and bushy hair said, "Addy will be happy to see you."

The grudging admission took Cole by surprise, especially coming from a man who looked like he wasn't far from animal. A peace offering? Cole looked around at the stony-faced men and felt the radiating hostility. Probably not. Shifting deeper in the saddle, he smiled, taking satisfaction at the collective displeasure. If Addy was happy to see him, Cole thought, she'd be the only one. And the perverse part of him that always had her shaking her head . . . smiled.

AN hour later Cole's amusement over being an annoyance wore thin. As far as he could determine, they were heading due east. The only thing east was a cliff face. Maybe Jones was toying with the idea of throwing Cole off it?

"Where is this place?" he asked Isaiah, leaning back in the saddle, signaling Rage to stop.

The horse stopped immediately. The man didn't give any response. From behind Cole came a growl. He looked over his shoulder, and Dirk jabbed him in the center of his back with a rifle. Cole clenched his fists. The rawhide bonds cut into his skin.

"Do that again and I'll kill you."

Dirk smiled a half smile that didn't reach his eyes. Cole could see the intent in the man's cold gaze even before he raised the muzzle of the gun. "You make it so easy."

"Enough!" Isaiah snapped.

After a heartbeat, Dirk lowered the gun.

Cole smiled at the man's reluctance.

"He would kill you, you know," Isaiah informed him.

"Maybe, maybe not."

Isaiah shook his head. "You don't understand Reapers."

Cole wished his hands were freed to tip his hat down. Instead, he shrugged. "Maybe you just don't understand me."

"Your arrogance is irritating."

What was irritating was being helpless amid these Reapers. "So I'm told."

Isaiah didn't answer. The rhythmic sound of multiple hoofbeats was all that could be heard for a few minutes. The silence grated as much as being helpless did. "Where are you taking me?" he asked gruffly.

"To Addy."

It wasn't like Jones to be so obliging. "Why?"

"Because she'd have my head if I didn't."

That was interesting. "You're afraid of Addy?"

No response, but the energy coming off the other man was softer. Whatever Isaiah Jones was, Cole realized, the man cared about his cousin.

"Is she all right?" he asked grudgingly.

Isaiah didn't turn around. "She could be better."

That snapped him to attention. "What do you mean?"

With a wave of his hand Isaiah dismissed the question. He stopped in front of a sheer cliff base and half turned. "I'm going to release you now. I'd really appreciate it if you'd escape."

He wasn't going anywhere without Addy.

Isaiah gave a jerk of his chin. There was an immediate shift in the energy behind Cole. Before Cole could spin around, he felt a tug on his arms, and then his hands were free. He rubbed at his wrists. Dirk tucked his knife back in his boot.

A smile ghosted Isaiah's lips. "Now's your chance to escape."

Cole looked around. As far as he could tell, the only option any of them had was to head back the way they'd come. As if reading his thoughts, Dirk stepped back. And following him, each of the ten other Reapers did the same, opening ranks in an open invitation. Cole tipped his hat down. He wasn't making it that easy.

"Yeah, I gathered that."

"But you're not taking it."

It was a statement, not a question. "Nope. So what are we doing now?"

Isaiah sighed. "We're going up."

Up looked like a sheer rock wall.

"Reapers have wings as well as fangs and claws?"

Isaiah shook his head. "Nope."

Dismounting, Isaiah approached the wall. Without a word he reached for a spot above his right shoulder. His finger seemed to sink into the stone. Interesting. Cole dismounted and tossed Rage's reins to Dirk. Two steps closer he could make out the subtle changes in the rock face.

"You created a ladder."

"Of sorts."

The big man started climbing, before pausing and calling down. "Pay attention, and put your hands and feet where I do mine."

Cole looked up. The Reaper was already ten feet up. "What happens if I don't?"

"Just do as you're told, and you won't find out."

"Figures there'd be a hitch," Cole muttered and started climbing. Halfway up, he couldn't find the spot. He reached for what looked like an obvious ledge.

Isaiah snapped, "No! I told you. Where I put *mine.*"

Cole eyed the ledge. Was the ledge a trap? More interesting.

"And where would that be?"

"Six inches down and to the right."

He found the fingerhold. "Thanks."

He'd have to pay more attention.

Jones grunted. "Addy'd cry for a week if I only brought her a body to bury."

Cole thought of about ten retorts, but he didn't have the breath to spare to spit them out. The pace the Reaper set was brutal, and Cole wasn't used to this kind of work. He settled for swearing under his breath. When he got to the top of the ridge, his legs and arms were burning, and his breath was soughing in and out of his lungs. To his disgust, Jones hadn't even broken a sweat.

"Hell of a path home you've got there."

"Keeps out the riffraff," Isaiah said, motioning to a boulder for Cole to sit. "Usually."

Pride was the only thing that kept Cole standing. Isaiah did nothing but cock an eyebrow at him before taking a seat himself.

From up on the top of the cliff the whole valley could be seen. Cole wasn't surprised to see a sentry positioned strategically to the left. It's what he would have ordered. Isaiah gave the sentry a nod. The sentry gave Cole a dirty look. Cole shot him one right back. He brushed his hands off on his pants and settled his hat back on his head. With a wave of his hand he motioned toward the stretch of rough land before them.

"What are you waiting for?" he asked Isaiah.

With that inquiry, the man's lip twisted with a smile. "For you to catch your breath."

Cole hated to be considered weak. "It's caught."

If he discounted his shaking legs.

Isaiah smiled. "We'll wait a bit longer."

Cole put his hands on his knees. "The hell we will."

With a cock of his eyebrow Isaiah asked, "You know where to go?"

It took everything Cole had not to cast his energy out and find Addy, but there were some things he didn't want this Reaper to know, and Cole had a feeling this man would know if he searched for Addy that way.

"No."

"Then we'll go on my time."

Cole had no choice but to let the Reaper be in charge. He sat on a convenient boulder. Dirk handed him a canteen. He was the type that would blend into the crowd except for that feral air about him, which was enhanced by those distinctive green eyes. He might look like any other to most, but Cole had a feeling Dirk had tricks up his sleeve. Cole took the canteen cautiously, sniffing the water.

"The water's not drugged," Isaiah said. "Dirk can be trusted."

Not from where Cole sat. As if Dirk could read Cole's mind, the blond man smiled before walking away.

"I seem to be a source of amusement for your men," Cole commented, watching Dirk and finding his utter lack of energy . . . interesting.

Cole had never met a people so capable of controlling and flexing energy in his life as the Reapers.

"It's your attitude," Isaiah said. "It's a lot of bravado for one man to toss about."

Cole rolled his stiff shoulders. "It's not bravado if you can back it up."

Isaiah shook his head. His tone was almost pitying. "Yeah."

Cole finished drinking and capped the canteen, but he didn't contest the doubt. If the Reapers wanted to underestimate him, he could adjust. He wasn't so winded now, though his arms and legs still ached. Climbing cliffs wasn't something he did every day.

With a jerk of his chin, Isaiah prodded Cole on. "Let's go."

Cole memorized every step of the path. It wasn't going to be easy to get Addy out of here, and he'd prefer any path to this one, but if he had to drag her kicking and screaming down the cliff, he was going to free her. The hold the Reaper had on Addy would be broken. In the center of a small clearing, Isaiah stopped. Cole stepped forward and saw the hole in the ground. Isaiah squatted beside it.

Comprehension came quickly. Cole swore. Son of a bitch, he hated dark places.

Isaiah looked up. "Not afraid of the dark, are you?"

Cole smiled. "Not any more than you."

Isaiah grunted. "Then you're not going to like this one bit."

With a start Cole realized the man had admitted to a weakness.

"Shit, we're going in there?"

Isaiah nodded.

The ranks of the waiting Reapers broke. The big, rough-looking man with shaggy brown hair and an equally shaggy beard stood at Isaiah's shoulder.

"I'll go first."

Isaiah shook his head but didn't look away from that hole. "It's all right, Gaelen."

Gaelen sighed but didn't budge. "I'm in a hurry to get home to my bed. Don't feel like waiting for you to poke along."

The sound that came from Isaiah could only be described as a growl. The hairs on the back of Cole's neck rose. Gaelen took a step back, but he still hovered.

"Don't tell me the big bad Reaper is afraid of the dark?" Cole needled.

Isaiah's mouth set in a hard line as he sat at the edge. "Bad times. Bad memories." He slid his feet into the gap.

Cole's stomach twisted as the ground seemed to swallow the other man's legs, memories of his own rising to choke him.

Bad times. Bad memories. No shit. He watched as Isaiah disappeared into the hole, a shiver snaking up his spine as the other man's hat disappeared. Cole had spent ten days in a Mexican jail, a structure that was nothing more than a hole in the ground with bars set over the top. Some experiences left their mark on a man.

"Your turn," Dirk ordered, coming up behind Cole.

Cole's fingers curled into a fist at the mockery in the other man's tone, but he didn't move.

Dirk's lips twitched at the corner. "What's the matter?"

"Fuck you."

"You're not my type."

Cole stood and spun, rage driving his fist toward the other man's smirk. Dirk caught Cole's fist in his hand. Cole blinked at the strength it took to do that. He'd underestimated Dirk.

Bravado.

Fuck!

"We don't have time for this shit," Gaelen muttered, forcing his shoulder through the opening and dropping into the hole. "The boss doesn't like tunnels."

"He's right," Dirk said, releasing his fist. "So either start climbing, or I'm going to knock you out and drop you in."

"On my head?" Cole mocked. "That won't make Addy happy."

"Head, ass, back, I don't care. My job is just to get you there. No one gave *me* any specifics as to how you had to arrive."

The dead or alive was implied. Damn Reapers. Since he couldn't help Addy dead, Cole set his jaw and stepped down, finding the ladder with his foot. Five rungs down the dank scent of the earth rose up to surround him, bringing out old memories, old fears. He fought them back.

Ahead he could hear Isaiah's breathing, tight and controlled, like that of someone battling demons. His own breath was taking on the same pattern, he knew. He didn't want to have anything in common with the Reaper, but apparently they both had a dislike of being buried alive.

A torch flared, and the scent of kerosene blended with the dankness. "Sorry, Isaiah," Gaelen said from around the corner. "Someone forgot to refresh the torches."

Isaiah's response was a snarl Cole wanted to echo. A torch now did little to dispel demons already wakened.

Shadows danced on the walls as Gaelen came around the corner. From farther back Cole could hear the other Reapers descending into the cave. Gaelen waved the torch. "We've got light now."

Isaiah nodded. "Good. Let's go."

"How long do we travel this way?" Cole asked Isaiah.

"Too fucking long."

After a minute Cole had to agree. The torch only gave off so much light, and the dark pressed in from the surging shadows. He concentrated on counting his footsteps, measuring the distance as they traveled. He figured they'd gone about three hundred yards before he could see a lessening in the darkness. Between the cliff, the tunnel, and whatever else Jones had set up as a deterrent, it really wasn't going to be easy to get Addy out of here.

The tension in his chest loosened the closer Cole got to daylight. Finally, the tunnel took a hard bend to the left, and the end was in sight. As they got closer to the opening, the tunnel widened until it was big enough that they could exit it four abreast. He looked out. Beneath them stretched a valley surrounded by ridges and cliffs, totally enclosed, or so it would appear. He could see a river meandering through the center. The valley was huge, miles and miles of forest and streams. In a nearby clearing, he could make out the gray-white of canvas tents. He looked at Isaiah.

"How'd you find this place?"

"I didn't."

Which could mean anything. Cole was getting sick of word games.

They set off to the right, taking the rocky footpath down. No effort had been made to hide this one. Hell, why would they? The chances of anyone getting this far were slim to none. As they got closer to the valley floor, Cole could hear the faint sounds of hammering and smell smoke. A world inside a world, hidden away from prying eyes.

"I see being with Addy hasn't loosened your tongue."

"Hasn't loosened my brains, either." Jones shot him a look. "You'll be tolerated here, Cameron, not welcomed."

Cole hid a smile. Jones wasn't as calm as he'd like Cole to believe. "Your hospitality needs work."

"Not to my way of thinking."

"But then, you're not the best judge, are you?" There was another sentry posted at the foot of the path. Cole eyed the pistols slung low on the man's hips, the rifle resting in the crook of his arm, and the pack at his feet, no doubt holding ammo and other necessities. The casualness of the man's posture didn't hide the hostility in his gaze. "He there to reinforce your hospitality?"

"Nah," Isaiah said dryly, nodding to the man. "He's just there to make sure a few understand its limits."

Meaning Isaiah would kill Cole if necessary, Addy's love notwithstanding. The same way Cole would kill Isaiah if it came to that. Cole tipped his hat to the hard-eyed sentry.

"Good to know we understand each other."

3

COLE DIDN'T KNOW WHAT HE EXPECTED WHEN HE WENT into the encampment, but the Reapers' settlement looked no different than any other mining or lumber settlement he'd ever been to. Dirty tents flapped in the breeze, half-constructed houses sat alongside what one day were obviously intended to be streets. One significant difference was there was no store or church looming over it all as symbols of hope and permanence. Things were built sometimes just because settlers plain needed a visible hedge against the odds of failure.

A lot of people toted their dreams westward. A huge chunk lost them along the way. He wondered if the Reapers were an ungodly people or if perhaps this was just a temporary stop. A combination of both would suit him. He didn't want to like monsters. And he didn't want them hanging around his cousin or his town. He opened his mind just a bit, scanning for Addy's energy. He didn't find it, experiencing his own sense of failure. She was here somewhere, and he knew it. Which meant she was shielding her energy, or someone was. Isaiah grunted. Too late Cole felt the other man's energy touching his. Easing his mind closed, he pretended he hadn't noticed.

Cole cocked an eyebrow at Isaiah. "Nice place you've got here."

Isaiah didn't respond; he just kept striding forward like a man on a mission. And looking ahead, Cole knew why. Sitting outside a tent set against a half-constructed house, a pile of fabric in her lap, was Addy. He'd expected her to look downtrodden, shattered, but the woman that looked up and saw them was . . . glowing with health and—he growled under his breath—happiness. The way Cole always dreamed his woman would glow, assuming he ever found one. Just one more thing to hate Isaiah Jones for. He'd stolen Cole's fucking cousin.

Addy's smile faltered when she saw Cole. That falter struck Cole like a blow. In all the months he'd searched for her, he'd never doubted that she'd be happy to see him. Her need had been what had driven him at a killer pace through the goddamn mountains and lousy weather. And her smile fucking slipped? He pulled his hat down over his eyes and caught up with Jones.

Wiping her hands on her apron, Addy stood and set aside her sewing. And that glowing smile spread to include him. It irritated the crap out of Cole that he was the afterthought when he'd always been the one Addy depended on.

"Things change," Isaiah said as if he'd read Cole's thoughts.

Cole growled, "Not that much."

Isaiah shook his head. "You are one stubborn son of a bitch."

"So I've been told."

Isaiah smiled mockingly. Sheer force of will kept Cole from punching him as Addy gathered up her skirts and came toward them, practically running, ankles exposed to any that cared to look. If the blatant display of emotion from the always controlled Addy wasn't shocking enough, the way Jones checked it with a subtle shake of his head was downright jaw-dropping. Like a trained dog, the ever-defiant, stubborn-to-the-core Addy slowed to a sedate walk.

"Fuck. What the hell have you done to her?" Cole asked.

"Watch your language. And not a damn thing."

Cole snorted. "Does she sit on command, too?"

He never saw the fist that connected with his jaw, but he saw the stars as he hit the ground. When his vision cleared, Jones was above him with his hands clenched.

"You show her respect."

Rubbing his jaw, Cole retorted, "I don't need you to tell me how to treat my cousin."

"You need something," Isaiah muttered too low to carry.

"You don't need him to tell you what?" Addy asked.

She stood beside Jones, wringing her hands together, anxiety putting a pleat between her brows. Cole was used to seeing Addy anxious. But this was different. Her fear wasn't of change, dirt, or Jones. It was of him. Shit.

"Nothing." Cole stood brushing the dirt from his pants. "Just talking nonsense."

Addy looked first at Isaiah, then at him, and then back to Isaiah. "So much nonsense you had to strike him?"

Cole answered before Isaiah could. "Yes."

She shook here head, studying him with familiar concern. Many a time he'd returned from a job to be treated to that look.

"You shouldn't have come, Cole."

Not once had he come home from a job to hear that. "So everyone keeps telling me."

She clenched her hand in her skirt. "I told you I was fine."

"You left a hastily scribbled note that you were fine. Not the same thing as seeing it for myself."

She shook her head at him. He was familiar with that expression, too. There was no one more stubborn than Addy when she was set on a course. And from the way she reached for Isaiah's hand, she was still set on Isaiah.

"Well, you can see for yourself now. I'm fine." She smiled up at Jones who stood there too smug and confident for Cole's taste. "And not only that, I'm happy."

"Could be fever," Cole offered just to see the familiar twist to Addy's mouth. Too much had changed too fast. When she grimaced the way she always did when he was perverse, a bit of his "normal" settled back into place.

"Do I look sick to you?"

Addy looked happy, but that didn't mean Cole had to acknowledge it.

"Hard to tell the way you're blushing."

"I am not."

"He's just looking to get a rise out of you, Addy girl."

"Stay out of it, Jones."

"Why?" the other man asked in that irritatingly logical way he had. "When you started it in my presence?"

He had him there. Addy reached out as she had so many times in the past. Cole didn't meet her halfway. Tracking her across the country didn't put him in the sweetest of moods. And truth be told, now that he'd finally caught up to her, he wasn't feeling anything he'd expected. Which was a unique experience unto itself. He was used to being in complete control. Of himself, the situation, and all those in it.

It was Isaiah who took Addy's hand, slipping his fingers between hers, giving her the support Cole refused. "As I said earlier, things change."

"Shut the hell up."

"Watch your language."

"Oh for Pete's sake! Enough." Addy motioned to someone behind him. "Gaelen will show you to your house."

Gaelen made a sound under his breath that sounded distinctly like a growl. "I've got work to do." He in turn motioned impatiently to a petite brunette gathering wood at the edge of the meadow. "Miranda can show it to him."

The woman straightened at hearing her name, her arms full of kindling. She didn't say anything, just froze in place, a tantalizing statue of feminine promise. Against his will Cole's energy reached for hers.

"You know Miranda doesn't—"

Gaelen cut Addy off. "Miranda can handle one human male."

The same sense of shock Cole saw in Miranda's eyes went through him as their gazes met. Only along with his came a deep-seated sense of recognition. Search as he might, he couldn't find any reason for it. A woman like the woman before him, he'd remember meeting. Dressed in a man's wool shirt that hung off her slender frame, she looked sweet, lost, and desirable. Her hair was a dark autumn brown. She wore it pulled back in a long braid that should have been severe but only served to enhance the delicacy of her features. She had big, round brown eyes framed with thick lashes, a tiny nose, and a rosebud mouth. She looked for all the world like one of those china dolls he'd seen in the dry goods store. Delicate. Beautiful but broken. Because now that she'd turned, he could see the scars that cut deep slashes down one side of her face. She ducked her head when she felt his gaze. And in the next second he felt the addictive whisper of her energy. Hotly feminine and tempting, it tugged at him from beneath a current of fear. He liked the seductive pull. The fear he could do without.

"It's all right." He tipped his hat, attempting his gentlest smile, everything in him wanting that fear gone from between them. "Just point the place out. I'll get myself settled."

Miranda looked to Addy. Addy sighed and glared at Gaelen's retreating back. "Some people have no appreciation for order."

"But they still have value," Jones reminded her.

Addy snorted and reached into her pocket. Cole knew what she was reaching for. He'd seen that same move too many times to have a doubt. She wanted her worry stone. Cole reached into his own pocket. Before he could hand it to her, Jones reached over and gave her his hand, and damn if she didn't rub his fingers the way she used to rub her stone. Just . . . well, damn.

"Just because we don't have a finished house doesn't mean we can't be hospitable," Addy said.

Cole shrugged, watching Miranda make her escape out of the corner of his eyes. "I'm not really a guest."

"Well, you're certainly not a prisoner! You're family."

"If Jones had his way, I'd be dead family."

"That's not true. Is it?" Addy looked over at Isaiah.

Jones shrugged. "There was a time when I would have wished it."

Addy elbowed him in the side. He obliged by grunting. Against Cole's will he had to like the man for indulging his cousin.

"But not now?" she asked.

"He's got some skills with a gun and a knife. It's always helpful to have somebody like that around during trouble."

Cole looked around the little valley with its idyllic setting and feeling of bustling hope. "What kind of trouble could you have here?"

Addy licked her lips. The hold on her energy slipped. The hairs on the back of Cole's neck stirred at the touch of apprehension that stole from her to him. Was she the one doing the shielding? "You'd be surprised."

Jones cut in. "We can talk about it after dinner."

"Oh my God! Dinner!" Addy spun on her heel.

"What about it?"

"It's burning!" she gasped and bolted.

Cole frowned. "It's not like Addy to burn a meal."

"She's having a harder time than expected building rituals here."
Jones sighed. "Nothing's familiar. Her rhythm's off."

"If she was home, she wouldn't have any trouble."

"If she was home," Gaelen retorted, coming up with Cole's saddlebags draped over his shoulder, "she'd be dead."

Cole snapped, "What the hell does that mean?"

At the same time, Isaiah growled, "Not now, Gaelen."

Cole turned to Jones. "Somebody better tell me something fast. That's my cousin."

"And my mate."

"What the hell happened to wife?"

"There's a lot you don't understand," Gaelen interjected.

"I thought you had work to do," Jones snapped.

Gaelen patted Cole's saddlebags, smiling and revealing slightly longer side teeth that looked remarkably like canines. "I'm doing it."

Cole couldn't look away from those teeth. "Just what the hell are you?" Cole asked, his senses jangling all over again.

Gaelen's smile faded. He tossed Cole's bags at his feet. "Don't you remember? We're Reapers."

He couldn't forget. Cole picked the bags up in his good arm. While it felt like most of his stuff was in there, he was sure the more pertinent items like weapons were not. "And what exactly is a Reaper?"

"You know as well as anybody else."

That wasn't saying much. "I know what I've seen."

And didn't want to believe.

He looked at Jones. "Let's talk now."

Jones's expression went to that carefully blank state that, Cole knew from their first encounters, meant he was planting his feet. Shit.

Someone hollered to Isaiah from across the compound.

"Later," Isaiah repeated quietly.

Cole wanted to grab Isaiah's arm and yank him back as he turned to answer the call.

"Won't do you any good, human," Gaelen said. "There isn't a soul alive that can make Isaiah speak before he wants to."

"Until now."

"Uh-huh." Gaelen folded his arms across his chest. "You think mighty big of yourself."

"Maybe," Cole threw back, watching Isaiah interact with the man who'd called him over. There was a deference in the other man's attitude. Attentiveness in Jones's. Whatever he was, Jones wasn't a bully. More puzzle pieces that didn't fit the image Cole had nursed over the last few months. "Or I might just be tired of chasing your asses all over creation looking for answers."

Gaelen shrugged. "Well, Isaiah might not be answering your questions because he doesn't like you, or he might not be answering because it's a long story and right now too many other people need a piece of him. Hard to tell."

Nothing worse than getting a sensible answer when a man wanted a reason to throw a punch.

Cole hoisted his saddlebags up onto his shoulder. "You still too busy to show me where I'll be bunking?"

If he had to wait, he might as well do it in comfort.

"I should be, but I suppose if I don't, you'll go poking around under the pretense of searching for a bed."

It was Cole's turn to smile. "I do have that tendency."

"That's what I thought." With a jerk of his head Gaelen ordered, "This way."

HIS bunk was a one-room cabin with loose-planked sides that let in sporadic beams of sunlight. There wasn't anything strictly feminine about the place, but it had a feminine feel that went beyond the makeshift curtains dressing up the narrow window.

The space consisted of a small table, two chairs, a bed in the corner that was too short for his large frame, a roughly hewn trunk at the foot of the bed, and shelves against the wall on which dishes and pots were stacked. And a smaller bed catty-corner on another wall. Not much went on inside this small space except sleeping, but it was spotless. He wondered if they'd cleaned for him. He didn't know how he felt about that.

He tested the mattress with his hand. It was thin but firm. From the feel of things a layer of material covered the husks beneath. The sheets and blanket looked clean. He set his saddlebags down. He'd certainly stayed in much worse places.

Taking his makings for a smoke out of his pocket, he went outside. Sitting on the stump to the left of the door, he dragged a sulfur across the axe propped against the side of the house. The soft hiss of the flame whispered across his nerves in an unnecessary warning. He was in the enemy camp, living on the mercy of a man who bore him a grudge, buying time for . . . ? Cole pushed his hat off his brow and took a drag on his smoke. Hell, he wasn't even sure anymore. He'd come for Addy, but the Addy he'd come to rescue bore little resemblance to the confident, apparently happy woman who'd greeted him.

Too weary to dwell on that, Cole leaned back, pulled his hat down over his eyes, and observed the comings and goings from under the brim. It always paid to know your enemy. And nothing said more about a group's philosophy than how they went about setting things up. Like with all growing settlements the initial impression was chaos, but as he sat and smoked and watched, he could see there was order behind it. The camp was divided up into four sections. From what he could tell there was a married section, a single male section—he didn't see any identifiably single women beyond Miranda—a cooking section, and a bathing/personal business section. Everybody seemed to have a job and know what needed to be done. He could say a lot of things about Reapers, but

that they were lazy wasn't one of them. They didn't have much to
spare for him, except the occasional curious glance.

He saw Miranda appear out of one of the houses, a child by her
side. They were too far away for him to discern if the child was hers,
but their coloring was similar. He reached for her energy. Before he
could touch it, he felt the rise in Isaiah's. *Fuck.* Isaiah *could* sense
his tests. That was going to complicate things. He settled back to
observing.

Miranda went about her business with calm efficiency. From
what he could tell, she wasn't one for idle chitchat. She said "hi" to
no one, and no one said "hi" to her. But there were no signs of ani-
mosity. It was simply as if the others were respecting her wishes.
Interesting. A woman who wanted to be left alone.

It was definitely going to take a little while to figure out the ways
of this place, but as much as he'd anticipated looking down on anything Isaiah did, Cole was grudgingly impressed. There was mud,
of course, because it'd just rained and the ground had been dug up,
but there wasn't filth. Everything had its place. Everyone had his
job. Whatever Jones was doing, it was organized, including changing Addy. Cole didn't like change. Especially in the ones he loved.
And he especially didn't like it in Addy. She'd always relied on
him, and her rituals. She'd built them slowly and steadily over time,
and Addy being here was . . . he shook his head. All wrong.

The temperature dropped as the sun set. As dusk fell, Jones
crossed the compound, coming toward Cole with long, firm strides.
The man might be crazy, but he was confident. Cole stood. There
was an air of tension about the other man. As he got closer, he took
off his hat and ran his hand through his thick brown hair. Cole
always remembered Jones's hair as being too long, but it was neatly
trimmed now. Addy's doing, no doubt.

Son of a bitch. Cole didn't want to accept Jones in Addy's life.
Reese's voice echoed in his mind. *Like it or not, she loves him. So*

why don't you give him a chance? Cole shook his head. Didn't look like he was going to have a choice.

"You ready to listen?" Isaiah asked.

"It depends on whether you're ready to talk," Cole answered.

"I'd rather kick your ass out of here and get back to my life."

That was honest enough. Cole took out fresh makings. "If any ass kicking's going to be going on, I'm going to be the one doing it."

Isaiah's attention was on the makings. "Uh-huh."

"From the way you're looking, I'm guessing you haven't had a smoke in a while."

Isaiah shrugged. "It pisses Addy off."

Cole passed over his makings.

Isaiah's lips quirked and took them. He set about rolling the cigarette with his usual efficiency. "You don't know your cousin too well if you think being mad at me is her foot out the door."

Cole sighed. "Used to know her." He passed Isaiah a sulfur. "It seems she's changed some, though."

"For the better."

Cole looked at him and took a drag of his cigarette. "Yeah, well, that would be according to you, and you've got an interest in me seeing her as happy."

Isaiah lit his smoke. "She is happy."

"But she's not safe." Cole hazarded a guess.

Isaiah took a drag of his own cigarette and blew the smoke out, looking up at the hills and the ridges as if he could see what was coming in the landscape.

"No, she's not."

"And why would that be?"

"Reapers have laws."

"And one of these laws affects my cousin?"

Jones nodded again, took another drag of his cigarette. "One of the laws is, Reapers are forbidden to take up with human women."

That sounded serious.

"What's the penalty for breaking that law?"

"Death."

"To you?"

"To both."

"Shit. And they sent somebody out after you?"

"There've been a few."

"But that's not the biggest problem?" Cole hazarded another guess, looking at Isaiah's expression. Smoke curled around his face casting an air of mystery. As he narrowed his eyes, Cole could see what Addy saw in him. The man radiated strength and power.

"There are those that think that Reapers are in a position to take over this country now that it's in such disarray after the war."

"Fuck, they want to go into politics?"

Isaiah shook his head. "No. They want power. A lot of power. They see themselves as superior, but the hitch in the giddyup is Reaper law.

"So how does Addy play into this?"

Jones shook his head. "Shit. We need whiskey for this."

"I don't have any more, do you?"

Jones shrugged. "Just one of the many things on the to-do list."

"Setting up a bar?"

"At this point we'd settle for the sufficient contents for the bar, but yeah. Liquor is scarce."

"Then I guess we'll have to make due with cigarettes. So spill it."

"Reapers are different. You've seen it yourself."

Monsters whispered through his mind.

"Make your point."

"It's not an easy one to make to a human."

"I'm getting damn tired of people calling me human with a sneer in their voice."

Isaiah took another drag on his cigarette, shook his head, and flicked off the ash. "Anyone ever tell you for a man who is living on borrowed time, you've got a lot of attitude?"

"I've been told a lot of things."

Isaiah looked at him from the corner of his eye. "In this case, you ought to listen."

Cole knew what Isaiah meant, what he was trying to tell him. He was in charge of this band, but his control was not absolute. At any time Cole could find himself under attack. As if he didn't know it. The energy humming under his skin was a constant warning.

"Noted. Now, get on to telling me what's going on with Addy."

"She's making her home here."

"So I noticed."

"You don't approve."

"No."

"She can't go back with you."

"So you say."

"It's the way it is."

"Why?"

"She's Reaper now."

"Even if that marriage you held is legal, she can be un-Reapered in the time it takes for a judge to hit his gavel on the stand."

Isaiah's lip lifted in a snarl, and his eyes took on a strange glow. The energy that pulsed out from him pummeled Cole with hard, invisible blows.

"You will not take her from me."

Cole was beginning to get that impression. "And you can't keep what's not yours."

"She's my mate. There is no part of Addy that doesn't belong to me."

Cole didn't like the images that came with that. "Being with you will only get her hurt—"

"You saw her," Isaiah cut in. "Does she look hurt?"

"No." Dammit, she didn't. She looked like Addy, yet different somehow. "Not yet."

In a wink the other man's energy disappeared, and his face became a flat, expressionless mask. Cole wasn't impressed.

"You'd do well not to rouse the beast in us."

"I'll do whatever it takes to get answers."

Isaiah took another drag on his cigarette, the tip glowed bright orange in the deepening gloom. Around them the crickets stilled. His energy seethed.

"Even if those answers don't exist?"

"They exist. It's just a matter of hunting them down."

"Addy said you were persistent."

"I showed up here, didn't I?"

"I told her you would. She wasn't happy about it."

"Why?"

Isaiah stubbed out his cigarette on the sole of his boot. "She worries you'll judge her."

If she'd worried about that, she wouldn't have left him with just a note. She would have told him personally rather than running. "What does it matter if I do or don't?"

Isaiah looked at Cole from under the brim of his hat as he straightened. "You matter to her."

Bullshit. Before the word could follow the thought, he heard familiar footsteps behind him. Addy.

He turned around, and she was standing there. He wanted to hold on to his anger, but she kept walking right on up to him, slid her arms around his waist, and made mincemeat of his intentions.

She looked up at Cole, those big blue eyes so familiar and full of love. "Why is it so hard for you to understand, Cole? You're both my family."

Jones's energy snapped aggressively as he hugged her back; he couldn't help it. "It's more a matter of accepting, not understanding." He shrugged. "Jones is not the man I would have chosen for you."

"But he's my choice."

This close Cole couldn't miss the contentment in his cousin. "So you keep telling me."

But she was more than telling him. She was showing him. In ways he couldn't ignore.

Isaiah growled again and caught Addy's hand, tugging her back to his side. She went easily, sighing as she melted into Isaiah's side as if she belonged there.

"Cole, you've treated me like I don't know my own mind ever since you brought me home when I was eleven," Addy said in that soft, controlled voice she used when she was about to lay down the law.

Cole cut her off before she could finish. "You were fragile."

"And you made me strong," she countered just as quickly.

He didn't like the way she was standing up to him. He didn't like the sting of truth in her words, and he really didn't like the way Isaiah wrapped her hand in his as if Cole was a threat from which she needed protection.

"And now you're both my family," Addy finished.

Addy and Isaiah stood there united, their energy so blended, their contentment so strong, Cole couldn't even fire back. They were a couple. Whatever else was going on, that was the truth. And Addy was happy. Another truth. And he was going to have to like it. Fuck. That was the worst truth of all.

Cole took the last drag on his cigarette, the acrid smoke burning his lungs, before throwing it on the ground and grinding it out with the toe of his boot.

"You sure can pick 'em, Addy." A Reaper. A goddamn Reaper.

"Yes, I can, and if you'd stop being so mad at yourself, you'd probably figure out there's a lot to like in Isaiah."

That was asking too much. "I'm never going to like that son of a bitch, and he's never going to like me."

Addy looked between Cole and Isaiah, and Isaiah shrugged. Her face fell and then took on that stubborn look Cole knew so well. He'd seen it in the mirror often enough.

"You could at least try."

Cole didn't want to notice the way Isaiah's fingers stroked down Addy's cheek in a comforting gesture. He didn't want to see how it seemed to settle the distress within her. He didn't want to see any of this. He wanted Addy back where she was safe.

As if she read his mind, she said, "Cole, you can't protect me anymore."

"The hell I can't."

"That scared woman is never who I wanted to be and not who I am now." She hesitated, glanced at Isaiah, and ventured cautiously, "And there are complications."

That snapped his head up. "That's the third time someone's suggested you're in danger. Don't you think it's about time somebody told me what's going on here?"

"There are people that want me dead."

"Dammit, Addy," Isaiah swore. "I told you we'd ease into that."

Addy patted Isaiah's hand. "Cole doesn't need protecting, either. It drives him crazy not to know the way of things."

That was the truth.

"Who wants to kill you?"

"Other Reapers."

"There are more of you? How many?"

"We don't know."

"What do you mean 'you don't know'?"

"Ten, twenty, could be a thousand. We don't know."

"That's one of the problems," Addy said.

"One of what problems?"

"It's not something Isaiah likes to talk about."

"Tough." If others were trying to kill Addy, Cole wanted to know about it.

She sighed. "Cole. You don't need to know everything tonight."

"I've been on your damn trail for two months, Addy. You think I want to wait one more minute for the answers to my questions?"

"I think you need to," Isaiah interrupted.

"Why?"

"Because we need to discuss it."

"You and I?"

"No." Isaiah stated calmly. "The council and I."

"Discuss what?"

"How much to tell an outsider."

Son of a bitch. "I've got to wait on a bunch of Reapers to come to agreement?"

"Yes."

"Is that as impossible as it sounds?"

A smile quirked Isaiah's lips. "Pretty much."

"Then someone better get me a drink."

4

HE HAD TO WAIT FOR THE WHISKEY IN THE SMALL CABIN they'd assigned to him. It took only twenty strides to get from one end to the other. He knew because he'd done it seven times now. He was about to measure off the other directions when a knock on the door interrupted his plans. He opened the door.

"That'd better be my whiskey."

It was, though it was only half a bottle and was thrust at him with disgruntled charity by a scowling Gaelen.

"You'd damn well better savor that."

Cole took the bottle. Liquid sloshed inside the container. "I intend to."

Gaelen let it go reluctantly. Cole could understand. Sometimes the only thing standing between a man and pure loco was the balancing burn of whiskey. He stepped back and motioned to the dark interior. "Care for a shot?"

Gaelen pushed past him, heading straight for the mantel. When he turned, he had two tin cups in his hand. Clearly, he'd been here before.

"Damn nice of you to offer me my own whiskey."

The cups clanked together as he set them on the too short, wobbly table.

Cole pulled the cork and poured a double measure in each cup. "I'm feeling downright charitable."

Gaelen tossed back the whiskey and slammed the cup on the table. "I don't care how you feel as long as you don't get comfortable."

Cole sipped his whiskey more slowly. And not only because it had the raw taste of liquor rushed to the bottle, but because Gaelen was a man who had the answers Cole wanted. It was just a matter of prying them out of him. Cole favored the philosophy that all he needed to get the right answers was the right prod. From the way Gaelen was guzzling that whiskey, Cole might have already found it.

"Not much chance of that."

He poured the man another glass. Gaelen took it without a thanks. "I've heard you're a stubborn son of a bitch."

"So everyone keeps telling me."

Gaelen cocked an eyebrow at him. And Cole realized under the shaggy hair and beard the man wasn't as old as he'd assumed.

"What would you call it?" Gaelen prodded.

"Doing right."

"You think it's right to chase down your cousin and drag her home whether she wants to go or not?"

Cole placed his cup on the table and let his energy whip out. "Yes. Addy's a Cameron."

Gaelen didn't even flinch. "We just fought a war over that issue. One soul can't own another."

Interesting phrasing. Cole swirled the whiskey in his cup. "Addy's family."

"Mine, too."

"She didn't even know you until three months ago."

"She's Reaper now."

"So are the guys that tried to kill you back on the trail."

Gaelen tossed back his drink. "Every family has its bad apples."

Cole poured him another and probed carefully. "Seems like your whole tree's plum bad."

"Uh-huh." Gaelen tossed back that drink, too, and held out the cup. Cole filled it with the last of the bottle. As the last drop hit the cup, Gaelen smiled. "Things are not always as they appear."

"What the hell does that mean?"

The other man stood and tossed back the last shot of the whiskey as steadily as he had the first. "It would appear you're not only not getting my whiskey, you're also not getting any answers." He turned. Right before he got to the door, he threw over his shoulder, "Reapers don't get drunk."

Cole watched the door close behind him and looked at his near-empty cup. "Well, hell."

He could have mentioned that earlier.

COLE took the empty whiskey bottle and spun it on the table. Addy was a Reaper. He shook his head. His sweet, shy, scared-to-the-toes-inside, completely-composed-on-the-outside cousin a Reaper. Whatever the hell that meant. He stopped the spinning bottle with the flat of his hand.

What had Addy gotten them into? Christ, he was beginning to believe even the Reapers themselves didn't know what being Reaper meant. If that were the case, how was he supposed to protect her? How could Isaiah protect her? How could anyone protect her?

Fuck. Cole grabbed his cup and pushed back from the table. He needed air and space in which to think. He needed to release the energy whipping around inside him. He needed to ride hard until exhaustion gave him peace. He opened the door. Short of that, he needed a good brawl.

No guard challenged his exit. A gust of wind charging before the upcoming storm whipped his hat to the side. He caught it, resettling it with a wry smile. Clearly, Isaiah wasn't set on preventing his leaving. Hell, the man was probably hoping Cole would hightail it out of here before the storm blew over. That wasn't going to happen. Cole closed the door behind himself. Until he knew Addy was safe, Cole wasn't going anywhere.

Raindrops hit his hat in fat plops. Energy pulsed on the breeze, and a sense of foreboding peppered him along with the rain. A ride was out, but might be he could pay Rage a visit if the Reapers had brought him here. Only one way to know.

Cole headed for the barn. Large and well built, it was clearly the first thing they'd put together. That was interesting. Apparently for Reapers as well as humans, a good horse meant survival.

The barn door swung silently open on well-oiled hinges. The scent of grain and horse wrapped Cole in a familiar hug. As a boy, he'd always gone to the barn to think, and as an adult, he still found the familiar scents and sounds soothing. He looked up and debated the empty hayloft, but he didn't want to be stuck up in a loft if trouble came calling.

He whistled for Rage. A horse nickered. Another stomped its foot, but Rage's familiar snort was nowhere to be heard. Damn.

To the right there was a wooden box up against the wall, probably for tack. Wandering over, he took a seat. Leaning back against the wall, stretching out his legs, he let the day's weariness seep out. He wished it was as easy to relax his mind. When he'd left the ranch, his goal had been simple: to find Addy and bring her home. He'd found Addy, but simple was long past gone.

He lifted the cup to his lips, listening to the rain. Such a calm, peaceful sound in the middle of chaos. He tried to concentrate on it. And failed. The whiskey hit his tongue in a smooth flow of flavor, the bite coming on the back end as he swallowed, reminding him that with all things in life, you had to take the good with the bad.

He stared through the crack in the boards at the falling night beyond. Addy had found happiness with a monster. How the hell was he supposed to make peace with that?

They'll hunt her.

They could hunt all they wanted. They'd never get her. Even as he thought it, he knew that was a promise he couldn't keep. He'd fought Isaiah and lost. If ten Isaiahs came after her? They'd get her. Of all the unknowns, that was the one truth.

"Shit." The word echoed softly. Outside raindrops fell harder, thundering on the roof, almost, but not quite, covering up the sound of a gasp. His senses snapped to attention. He wasn't alone. Somebody was hiding behind him, tucked away in the corner between the post and the building. There was a certain pitch to the exclamation and a shortness to the breath that made him suspect he was dealing with a child. He pretended to take another sip of the whiskey.

As a test, he said "shit" again. There was a rustling as if the person moved. He smiled.

"I shot an eavesdropper once. Bullet went in one ear and out the other." He pretended to take another pull on his whiskey, listening for the response. "Can't abide people that sneak up on me to listen to what I say."

There was a little thud as if something soft hit wood, another gasp, and he could feel the panic coming out of the corner. It served the kid right. The only reason he'd be out in the barn at suppertime would be because he'd been up to no good earlier. Cole smiled, remembering the few times he'd hidden out in the barn in the hope of escaping his father's wrath. Barns were friendly places with lots of hiding places. A good place to wait out a parent's anger. As long as the offense wasn't that bad.

Cole took another sip of his whiskey. The time he'd dipped little Tilly Taylor's pigtail in the inkwell, he'd gotten a licking all right, but it hadn't had much heat, and the lecture afterward about how to properly seduce a woman had been invaluable. Well, to be fair, at the time he hadn't realized his father was teaching him how to seduce a woman. He'd just been talking about how to treat her properly. But Cole had figured it out eventually. That had been the thing about his pa. Everything he said had layers. He'd been a good man, a good husband, and a good father. He'd taught Cole everything he knew. He'd died trying to protect his family. Cole drained the cup. That's how he wanted to go. Making a difference.

An "I was here first" cut through his reverie.

He arched his brow. Someone was packing a hell of a lot of belligerence.

"So?"

"You can't say bad words around me."

Cole smiled a bit at that reprimand delivered in a high, sweet voice. His eavesdropper was a little girl. One that brought back memories of the days of sparring with Addy when she was little. She'd packed a lot of the same attitude.

"I can't?"

"No," the voice said, and he could just imagine little arms folded across a small chest. He wondered if the girl was a blonde or brunette. For some reason his mind flashed back to Miranda. He'd bet she'd been a beautiful child. She was a stunning woman, mesmerizing in a way he still didn't understand. He added finding out about her to his list of things to do—right after he took care of his eavesdropper.

"Who's going to make me?"

"Mister Isaiah will."

That was said with a great deal of satisfaction and confidence. "I don't see Mister Isaiah here."

"He'll come if I tell him to."

Cole bet he would. The big Reaper seemed to have some soft spots.

He decided to call her bluff. "Why don't we go get him?"

There was silence.

"Ahh, that kind of barn time, eh?"

That rustle could have been a nod.

"You want a drink of my whiskey?"

"I'm not allowed whiskey." He heard the implied "you dolt" at the end.

Cole bit back a chuckle. "You're not, huh?"

"I'm too little." As if he didn't already know that.

"I don't like it anyway," she added.

Interesting. "How do you know you don't like it?"

"I tried it."

Not when anyone was looking he'd bet.

"I see." He bit back a smile. "Well, I like it."

"Well, you're stupid."

That brought his eyebrows up. He couldn't remember the last time someone had called him stupid.

"You're packing a lot of attitude for somebody hiding in a corner this hour of the night."

"I'm mad."

"Why?"

"I don't like Jenny Hastings."

Ah, now they were getting to the root of the matter. "Jenny pis—" He caught himself just in time. "Jenny ticked you off, huh?"

"She's stupid."

"Stupid" seemed to be her preferred insult.

"I see."

He didn't, but it couldn't hurt to agree.

"And she wets the bed."

"So, because Jenny Hastings wets the bed, you're hiding here in the barn?"

There was a rustling he took to mean she was nodding in agreement again.

"It's all because of him."

"Who's 'him'?"

"The bad man."

She had his full attention now. He asked very casually, "Is someone hurting you, honey?"

He'd kill the son of a bitch, and fuck whatever that did to any Reaper law.

"I'm not going to let him hurt me."

That was good. "Is he threatening to hurt you?"

Another rustling indicating another nod of her head. He tapped the whiskey cup on his knee and said, "I see," when he really didn't.

There was a disgruntled huff and then, "Dolly and me have to sleep with Jenny Hastings because of him."

"Why?"

"Because they gave him our house. He wants to steal Miss Addy away, and now he's got our house."

Shit. Cole blinked. The bad man was him.

"And you have to sleep with Jenny Hastings who wets the bed because this man took your house?"

She nodded.

"Maybe he really doesn't want to steal Miss Addy away. Maybe he loves her."

"If he loved her, he wouldn't make her sad."

"What makes you think she's sad?"

"I snuck into the barn the other day, and I saw her crying."

"Did she see you?"

She shook her head. "Nope. I can sneak real good."

He wished he could see her face. If her expressions were anything like her energy, she had a very expressive face. "How'd you learn to sneak so good?"

"I can't fight with Mommy, so when I get mad, I come here."

"Why can't you fight with Mommy?" He'd fought with his parents all the time.

"Because she's sad."

"Your mommy's sad?"

Another rustle that he assumed meant another nod.

"She doesn't know I know, but me and Dolly know."

Dolly? "And you don't like to make her sadder."

She nodded.

Nice kid. "Is this your secret place?"

"Used to be."

He smiled at the accusation in the three words. "I won't tell."

"Yes, you will. Grown-ups always tell."

He shook his head. "I won't."

"Why not?"

"Because I had a secret place in the barn when I was a boy, and I know how special it is."

There was a long, pregnant pause followed by a very aggressive, "If you tell, I'll make you sorry."

He could just imagine.

Without turning, he put his hand over his shoulder with his little finger crooked, remembering Addy's favorite thing.

"I'll even pinky swear."

The tension that came from that corner was immediate. A pinky swear was a powerful thing, but she had to touch him to pinky swear, and Cole imagined that was a pretty scary thing.

There was another rustle, the scent of hay intensified, and then a small finger curved around his.

Damn, how little was she?

"Done."

Immediately she slipped back into her corner.

"Why's your mommy sad?"

"She doesn't want to marry."

"Then she shouldn't."

"I think she misses Daddy, too."

That was understandable.

"And I'm not always as good as I should be."

"I'm sure your mom thinks you're the best thing ever."

A little hesitation.

"I try to be good."

"Everyone slips up now and then."

"Do you?"

All the time. He thought it but didn't say it. Instead, he pointed out, "You just heard me swear."

"Two times you said bad words."

He nodded.

"You're not supposed to say bad words around me. I'm little."

Convenient how she trotted that out now when just a minute ago she was threatening him.

"I didn't know you were back there."

"Mama says you can't use that as an excuse. How you behave when no one else is around is your character on parade."

Lord, her mom sounded like a stickler.

"Speaking of your mother, is she going to be looking for you soon?"

There was another one of those silent rustling nods.

"Hadn't you better be getting on home?"

"I can't go home. The bad man has my house. He's probably sleeping in my bed." She said that last as if it would be a permanent contamination. He was actually a bit offended.

"Why'd they put him in your house?"

If he'd known he'd be displacing a woman and a child, he would have just slept in the barn.

"Miss Addy said he had to have a house."

Addy would say that.

"And yours was the only available?"

"Everybody else lives with somebody."

So her mother was unattached. Again Miranda's face flashed through his mind.

"And you don't?"

"No. I think the dreams scared my daddy away."

She'd lost him there. "Dreams?"

"People don't like it when Mommy dreams."

From that he deduced her mother had nightmares.

"Do you?"

"No."

"What do you do when she dreams?"

"I hold her close and stroke her hair. Sometimes she wakes up."

"And when she doesn't?"

"Then she screams."

"Why?"

"Bad men chase her in her dreams," she whispered.

Cole felt that tightening in his gut. "I'm thinking maybe you shouldn't be telling me this."

"Everybody knows everything here. Can't get away with nothing."

And there was that fresh bit of resentment.

"You going to be in trouble when you go home?" he asked.

"Yes."

"Well, did you do the wrong?"

Another silent nod that was indicated by the rustling of hair on wood.

"Then I guess you have to take the punishment when you do the wrong, don't you?"

A long sigh. "That's what Mommy says."

"You don't agree?"

"I hope she makes Uncle G punish me."

"Why?"

"It doesn't hurt when he spanks."

Cole bit back a laugh. He just bet it didn't. "Uncle G is special to your mom?"

"Uh-huh. When mama's so mad she can't talk, she sends me to Uncle G to spank."

"What does Uncle G do?"

"He gets a real mean face."

"And?"

"He says things in a quiet voice."

"And?"

"He spanks me."

"But it doesn't hurt?"

She shook her head. "He thinks it does, I think."

She said it as if that was a good thing. Cole couldn't imagine spanking a little girl. He couldn't imagine tolerating anyone making the attempt. Especially this little girl. There was something so . . . familiar about her energy.

He stood and tucked the cup in his coat pocket. "Well, it might be time to head on home, honey. It's raining, and your mom will be worried. Does she know where you hide?"

"No. This is my new spot."

So her other one had been found. He put the cup in his pocket. "How 'bout I give you a ride."

Silence.

"The longer you wait, the more trouble you'll be in."

This time the response was a snort. "Me and Dolly aren't afraid."

"But I bet your mom is worried though."

The snort faded to a sigh. "I don't want to sleep with Jenny Hastings."

"We all have to do things we don't want to. Besides, maybe Jenny has outgrown that problem."

"I'm never that lucky."

It was such an adult thing to say it made him smile. "Neither am I. Now, do you want a lift or not?"

There was a shuffling of feet, a sound of something skimming wood, her hand as she came around the corner of the stall. He couldn't see much at first in the gloom beyond that she was tiny.

He lit a match, giving her light, and when she came around the corner of the box, he almost dropped it. A tiny, delicate, fae little creature with big brown eyes, long lashes, a round face framed by fat brown ringlets, and a cherub's mouth came toward him. She was dressed in a faded blue smock that did nothing to diminish her impact. Fairy child, that was all he could think. At first. After the shock, came anger.

Damn. She shouldn't be five feet from the front door without a guard, let alone out in the barn by herself at dark. Her mother should know better.

As she got close enough to touch, he saw she clutched a rag doll in her arms. The doll sported an equally faded but pretty blue dress and a fancy painted face. Dolly, he presumed.

Cole's first impulse was to scoop her up and away from the dirt of the barn floor. She looked too angelic to be real. She frowned up at him.

"You're going to burn your fingers."

In the next instant he did. He quickly snuffed the match, not dropping it on the floor, but wetting it to make sure it was extinguished before putting it in his pocket.

He struck another one. The impression of a tiny fairy child lasted into the next flame. Her mother had to be worried to death.

"You ready to go home?"

She shook her head and took a step back. And another. "You're the bad man."

"Yep, I'm the one that took your bed. But that doesn't mean I would have done it had I known."

She didn't look soothed. "You're Miss Addy's cousin?"

He nodded.

She scowled at him. "You've come to take her away from us."

He shrugged. "I came to see that she was happy."

"Why?"

"Because she's my cousin and it's my job to look out for her."

"I don't have cousins."

What could he say to that? "I'm sorry."

She cocked her head to the side. Her pigtail slid across her face. She blew at it. "You don't seem bad."

"No one's all bad, honey."

"Miss Addy says you love her."

"I do."

"She says sometimes you do wrong things in the name of love. And when people do, you have to forgive them."

She didn't look on the verge of forgiveness. If a fairy could look hostile, he was seeing it.

He cocked an eyebrow at her. "I suppose you do."

The little fairy child stood there as the match burned closer to his fingertips, studying his expression, not answering. And not the least bit rushed by the flame's journey to his fingertips.

"Taking Miss Addy away from Mister Isaiah would be very bad."

"I'm stewing on it."

"Mister Isaiah keeps her safe. He makes her laugh. She laughs a lot." The last was accompanied by a glare.

Cole couldn't remember the last time Addy had laughed.

"She does, huh?"

The kid nodded. "He loves her, and that's a gift Mama says."

"I agree."

Making shooing motions with her hands she said, "You're going to have to just get along."

She said that with the wisdom of a much older person, which made him think it was something she'd heard before.

"What makes you think I can?"

"Mama says you just have to want to, and it happens."

"Maybe I don't have a lot of wanting in me."

The match burned down; he wet his fingers and snuffed it out, putting that one in his pocket, too.

Before he could light the next one she said, "You're not supposed to light matches in the barn."

"We'll make a concession tonight because it's hard to see."

"The rain makes everything dark."

It did that.

He took off his coat and held it out. She couldn't see. He could see her slightly though. He'd always been able to see in very little light. Another advantage he'd been born with.

"Take three steps forward," he told her. It was too much to expect instant obedience.

"Why?"

"Because you're cold, and I took my coat off, and I'd like to wrap it around you."

"It'll be too big."

"Think of it as a large blanket."

She shivered. "Is it stinky?"

He'd had enough. He took a couple steps forward, wrapped her in his coat, and picked her up.

"You tell me."

At first she sat very stiff and quiet, and then, "You smell good."

He couldn't imagine why his coat smelled good. Must be that

dunking in the river, before he'd met up with the Reapers, that had taken out the worst of the stench.

"I do, huh?"

"Like horse and the woods outside."

He'd never been described that way.

"Dolly likes it," she declared as if that decided everything.

"She does, huh?"

He rubbed his hands up and down her back as she shivered again.

"You should have gotten dressed before you left."

"My coat was in the room with Mommy."

"So how'd you get out?"

"Jenny's house has a real window."

He made a note that if he ever had kids, no windows in their room.

"Her mama insisted on it in case there's a fire."

He changed his mind. He wanted windows in his kid's room.

"Good point."

He tucked her closer as she shivered again. She was such a tiny thing. He couldn't remember Addy ever being this delicate. And there'd been plenty of times he'd held her while she cried or laughed or just drifted off because the day had gone on too long and she couldn't stay awake. He definitely remembered her having more substance.

"What's your name?" he asked.

"Wendy."

"Hello, Wendy." He hitched her up. "I'm Cole."

She grabbed his neck. "It's very nice to make your acquaintance, Mister Cole."

Manners were obviously something her mother had instilled deep. He liked that.

"How about we get you home, Miss Wendy?"

Her head bobbed against his shoulder in a nod. He might smell of outdoors and horses, but she smelled like cotton and . . . vanilla?

"All right."

The answer ended on a yawn. Someone was getting tired. The rain pounded harder on the roof. The storm was turning into a real drencher.

"Which house is Jenny's?"

She jerked her head in a direction that could mean anything. He rolled his eyes. They were standing inside the barn for shit's sake.

As if she sensed his impatience, Wendy muttered. "I can walk."

Not a lot of enthusiasm accompanied that statement. Clearly Miss High and Mighty liked being carried.

"Really? Because I thought we'd have a race."

"Oh." She perked up. "A race?"

"Yeah, we're going to race raindrops."

She smiled. And even with all that weighed on his mind, he felt an answering tug of his lips. She looked so familiar.

"Hold on tight."

Her arm clamped around his neck as he headed for the door. Her doll slipped. He caught it before her gasp could fade.

"Best hold tight to Dolly, too."

She wedged the cloth doll into the hollow of his throat. He gave it another tuck as he explained, "It's been a while since I raced the rain. Might be a bumpy ride."

She nodded. He opened the door. Cold, wet wind blew in. Wendy pointed to the right.

"You go out and go that way three houses."

He squinted through the failing light. "The house on the right or the left?"

She checked her right hand, her left, and then her right again before deciding, "On the right."

This time his smile was full bore. "How many raindrops we gotta beat?"

"A hundred."

"We have to get there before a hundred raindrops touch us?"

She nodded.

"What happens if we don't?"

"The thunder god will get us."

"The thunder god?"

"He's very mean. He makes your bed shake and gives you nightmares."

She was afraid of storms. No wonder she was clinging like an opossum to his neck.

"All right. We're going to hit that door running. You've gotta do your part though."

"What's that?"

"You gotta hold on real tight, and you gotta say 'go, go, go' as fast as you can."

"Why?"

"Because I'm going to run as fast as you say go."

She perked up at that, clearly pleased to be in charge of the pace. "All right."

"Are you ready?"

Her muscles tensed, and her lip slid between her teeth. "Yes."

"You count. We go on three."

She nodded and started counting. On three he sprinted into the rain.

⚜ 5 ⚜

AS SOON AS COLE STEPPED OUTSIDE, THE DROPS HIT HIM like pellets of ice. He pulled Wendy closer. It might be coming up on summer, but that rain felt like winter. He jogged down the street, which was quickly turning to mud. In his ear Wendy chanted. "Go. Go. Go."

He didn't need the encouragement. He hated getting soaked. As soon as he dropped Wendy off, he was heading back to his house and a warm fire and dry clothes.

He jerked his chin at the next house up. "Is that it?"

Wendy pushed the coat aside. He pulled it back up. She pushed again.

"I can't see."

He didn't suppose she could. This time he let her push it down. When she saw where they were, she nodded.

Cole stopped at the front of the door. Light glowed from the inside. Water dripped off the roof. He knocked and took a step back. The jacket moved.

"Just go in, silly."

Silly. He could imagine the reception he'd get, a strange man walking into a Reaper's house. Reapers were many things but defenseless wasn't one of them.

"I'll wait for your mom."

He heard her hair rustle as she shook her head.

"She won't be there."

"She won't? Why not?"

The child seemed to duck deeper into the coat.

"She might be looking for me."

So much for getting to dry clothes and a warm fire any time soon. Now, he'd have to go in search of the mom. "It's not nice to worry your mother."

Wendy shrugged.

He knocked on the door again. The noise and the voices within dropped off.

He didn't knock a third time. The energy seeping out from the structure was tense. Anger mixed with fear. Wendy shoved the coat off. With the innocence of youth she said, "It's all right. You can go in."

He didn't think so. Keeping his focus on those threads of energy he asked, "Who lives with you?"

"Miss Cindy, Jenny."

"Is Cindy Jenny one person or two?"

She giggled. "Cindy is a woman. Jenny's a girl."

That would be two, and that wouldn't explain the tension from within.

"Do your mom and Cindy get along?"

"Mama says they do."

That would be a no, and that would explain the tension. But not the fear.

Footsteps approached the door. Soft and light. A woman. He relaxed slightly. When the door opened, it was the perfect china doll who packed a prizefighter's punch to his sense standing there. Miranda. Her energy wrapped around his with a taut, wary twist. He wanted to reach out and pull her closer. Before he could, the connection cut off. He swore under his breath, barely suppressing the urge to charge after it. For a second she simply stared at him, making him believe, almost, that she felt it, too. Was it possible?

"Do you need something, Mr. Cameron?"

"Cole, will be fine, ma'am."

"Can I help you, Mr. Cameron?" she repeated.

He ignored the hint and studied her face, the softness of her lips, the intelligence in her eyes, the pale, creamy curve of her cheek. Everything about the woman was perfect. Every feature a delight to his senses. And her energy . . . he caught a mental whiff of it again. Lust surged in his blood, and his cock thickened. Son of a bitch, her energy was hot like molten steel melting over his, surrounding it . . .

From the vicinity of his chest Wendy piped up. "Hi, Mommy."

That explained the sense of familiarity he'd felt about Wendy. Her energy resonated with the same timbre as Miranda's. He shifted the little girl higher. "I believe I have something for you."

Wendy waved timidly at her mom from the confines of the coat.

"You, young lady, were supposed to get some water and come straight back," Miranda snapped. The edge to her voice could have been annoyance, but when she looked over her shoulder, the hairs on the back of Cole's neck rose.

Wendy's "I know" was guilt soft.

Miranda looked at him, then Wendy, and then back over her shoulder again. "We'll talk about it later."

It only took a split second to note the lines of tension beside her eyes, the tightness of her mouth. When Cole looked down, Miranda's fingers were white-knuckled on the door. Something in that house had Miranda scared.

"Thank you for bringing her home." She reached out. She had

elegant hands with long fingers and neatly trimmed nails. It was easy to imagine her reaching out to touch him with those hands. To feel them sliding over his skin in a soft caress. Too easy. He didn't need this now.

"She shouldn't be out unsupervised." His tone was harsher than he intended. Both Miranda and Wendy jumped.

"She normally isn't—"

The door opened farther, cutting off the explanation. Miranda's energy flared in a hot panic. A man with dark blond hair and pale gray eyes stepped up behind her. He didn't look happy. Meeting Cole's gaze, he put his hand on the jamb above Miranda's head. It was a clear statement of possession.

Cole's response was just as clear. Like hell. The denial howled through Cole like a high wind, pushing against his control. Trailing the gust of emotion came a whisper of truth. Miranda would never belong to this man.

The certainty soothed a bit of the anger prowling beneath his surface calm. Behind the stranger Cole could see a thin woman standing with her hands on the shoulders of an equally thin child with big, fearful blue eyes. Jenny, he assumed, and the woman had to be Cindy. She looked like all the fight had left her years ago.

Cole nodded to the man. "Evening."

"Can I help you?"

It was a challenge clear and simple. Wendy stiffened. Miranda's energy flicked out and then pulled in tight before she whispered, "He was just bringing Wendy home, Clark."

The man looked down. Cole didn't need to see Miranda's shoulders stiffen to know she tensed. Her energy telegraphed her fear in staccato pulses.

"It's almost supper time; why wasn't she home already?"

It was a simple question, but the timbre in which it was asked implied so much more. And all that threat packed in it ticked Cole off. A man didn't bully women and children. Cole answered before Miranda could.

"Because she was with me."

"This is none of your business."

"I'm making it mine."

"He's—" Miranda began.

Clark cut her off. "I know who he is."

Cole shifted his grip on Wendy. "I'm more interested in who you are."

Mighty interested.

"The name's Clark. Clark Hastings." His hand dropped to Miranda's shoulder. She jumped, and Wendy jerked and clung to Cole. He stared at that hand and rubbed Wendy's back.

"Good to know."

"This is my house." Clark continued. "These are my women."

Beyond Clark, Cindy looked down. Her discontent filled the room. Cole gritted his teeth. He'd seen many a broken-down horse sport that same look. He glanced back at Clark. And many a bully wear that same smug expression. "That's a whole lot of claim for one man."

"To a human maybe."

Cole was getting damn tired of that attitude. Clark reached for Wendy.

"I'll take her."

"No," Miranda gasped.

"No," Wendy echoed with a heck of a lot more force.

They needn't worry. Cole shoved a smile at Clark. Clark wouldn't get his hands on the little girl. "No need, I think I can make the few steps into the house."

Cindy gasped and grabbed the bowl off the table. Was she expecting a brawl or planning on starting one?

Clark looked over his shoulder. "Put the goddamn bowl down, Cindy."

Instead, Cindy clutched that bowl in one hand harder and her daughter harder still.

Cole elbowed past Clark. Miranda followed so close he imagined he could feel her breath on his back. He liked that thought. "Seems to me your women don't care for your temper much."

"They're going to."

"Uh-huh." The house wasn't big. It was basically one room with what looked to be a lot of bedrolls piled in the corner. It only took a few steps to get to Cindy. "Are you all right, ma'am?"

After a couple blinks Cindy nodded. "It was my mother's bowl," she whispered as if that explained everything.

"I see."

"You don't see shit," Clark snapped.

Cole turned and caught Miranda's hand, and with a tug he kept her right on moving until she was behind him with Cindy and Jenny. "I see a man comfortable with bullying women."

"No one here is any concern of yours."

"Well now, Wendy here is a friend of mine so she is my concern.

Clark's energy sharpened. Cole's sense that he was a man looking for a fight honed to a certainty.

Cole patted Wendy's back. "Honey, it's real important now you let me go and go to your momma."

If the speed with which Wendy released him was any indicator, Wendy was as scared as her mother. Cole set her on the floor. Instead of going for her mother, she went for Clark. As hard as she could, she kicked the other man in the shin.

"You leave us alone, you big bully."

"You goddamn brat," Clark snarled and drew back his hand.

"Wendy!" Miranda gasped and lunged.

Cole blocked her lunge, caught Wendy by the back of the dress, and tossed her behind him, and in the same flow of movement punched Clark in the throat.

He dropped like a stone.

Cole pulled his revolver and took aim dead center between the bastard's eyes. Behind him there were more gasps. The only one not wheezing the way he wanted was Clark. Reapers recovered with impressive speed.

"Where I come from, grown men don't beat on little girls."

"You're not where you come from," Clark rasped as he sprang to his feet.

Cole took a step forward, slammed a hand into the man's chest, and drove him back.

"I'm here now."

"Fuck you."

"Watch your mouth."

"Stop it!" Miranda snapped.

"I will as soon as he does."

Clark snarled.

Cindy gasped.

Miranda groaned. None of which did a thing to lessen Cole's anger.

"If you don't stop it, I'm going to report this to Isaiah," Miranda snapped.

Sounded like a damn weak threat to Cole, but surprisingly, he felt a twitch in Clark's energy.

Clark snarled, and that wildness peculiar to Reapers filled the room.

"You say anything, and I'll make you pay for it."

An answering wildness surged from Miranda. This was going south fast. She stepped around Cole. He caught her arm. Clark grabbed the other. She stood between them like a wishbone at Thanksgiving, her head whipping side to side.

"Let go of me, both of you."

If Cole let her go, Clark would have her. Fuck that.

"Get over here," Clark ordered, tugging hard.

"I believe she said she's not interested in your company."

Wendy came flying past, foot drawn back for another kick. "Don't you hurt my mama again."

Again?

Surprisingly, it was Cindy who snatched Wendy, feet kicking the whole way, out of danger. And the small drama broke the tension. Clark released Miranda.

Cole shook his head and looked at Miranda. "There's a lot of fire in that girl."

Miranda shook her head. "I don't know where she gets it from."

"Doesn't matter where it comes from. It needs to be curbed," Clark growled. "Such disrespect won't be tolerated."

"Seems to me it's not your call," Cole growled back, letting Miranda step back.

"I've made it mine. So has the council."

"That hasn't been decided," Miranda countered.

"It's as good as done, and it's time you settled into the idea."

"No."

From across the room, Cindy caught his eye. There was a plea in her gaze he didn't understand until she looked at Miranda and then the door. Still holding his gaze, she released Wendy. Cole caught the child before she could tear into Clark again.

"Easy now."

She glared up at him and folded her arms across her chest. "I don't like him."

Very aware of Clark poised to strike, Cole edged the little girl farther back. "Doesn't appear anyone does."

"Miss Cindy does."

"Miss Cindy," he said, watching as Wendy slid protectively up to her mother. "She's married to him."

"He wants my mommy, too."

"So I gathered."

"Wendy, hush."

Wendy paid no mind to her mother, finishing with her now familiar glare, "He wants everything."

"Just because a man wants, doesn't mean he gets."

"The council—"

Miranda slapped her hand over Wendy's mouth and pulled her back against her. "Hush."

"Even the child knows it's a done deal, human."

"Uh-huh." Cole waved his hand dismissing that argument. "Do you have anything you value here?" he asked Miranda. She pointed to the corner. "Go get it."

"She's not going anywhere," Clark snapped.

Miranda hesitated.

"Go," Cole repeated. She did, quickly gathering up a blanket-wrapped bundle.

Jenny began to cry. Everyone froze. Clark snapped to Miranda. "Put that shit down and take care of the kids."

Cole reiterated, "Keep walking, Miranda."

Wendy tugged on Miranda's arm when she hesitated. "Come on, Mommy."

Cole didn't want to know how scared a woman had to be to think going off with a stranger beat staying with someone she knew, but that split second of hesitation was all Miranda wasted.

Cole smiled at Clark.

"It appears to me we have a few choices here. One, I can take Wendy and Miranda back to their house. Two, we can find Isaiah and discuss this, and then I take Wendy and Miranda back to their house. Or three"—he pulled out his other revolver and aimed it between the other man's legs—"I can kill your sorry ass right now and take Wendy and Miranda back to their house. One way or another, Miranda and Wendy are leaving your care."

"The hell they are."

Cindy found her voice. "Please, Clark, not tonight. Isaiah will throw us out if there's another incident. Please, let the council handle it."

Miranda stood still, clutching her blanket-wrapped stuff to her chest, and backed toward Cole, stopping halfway, looking at Clark as if the bastard had any say in anything. It ticked Cole off.

"Miranda, get over here."

She didn't move.

He looked at her and cocked an eyebrow. "Please?"

She hesitated a second and then came over. Her energy was just as wild as Clark's but for a different reason. He was flat-out crazy. She was simply terrified.

Cole stopped her before she could pass.

"Go behind me please." Miranda looked at the pistols, swallowed, and then nodded.

"This isn't over," Clark muttered as she and Wendy inched past.

The words yanked Miranda up short as she opened the door. The wild in her energy flared, riding the gust of cold, wet air that blew in. Cole grabbed her arm and pushed her out into the rain before the impulse could explode into words. The door slammed shut behind them. The storm raged around. Wendy whimpered. Lightning crackled across the sky. It was nothing compared to the emotion flashing in Miranda's eyes. A fighter like her daughter.

Her lips parted. Cole put his hand over her mouth. Holding her gaze, he quietly took over her war.

"It's over as far as you're concerned."

BENEATH his palm Cole felt the hard edge of Miranda's teeth. The storm thundered and crackled. It was nothing compared to the energy seething around them. Anger spiked with fear. Her fear of Clark. Of him. He shook his head.

"If I wanted you hurt, I would have left you with him."

He looked down at Wendy who was huddled against her mom, shivering. "And the kid, too."

Wendy frowned at him. He shook his head. Always so ready to fight, this one. When he picked her up, Miranda turned on him, her big brown eyes catching his, her lips pulling back from her teeth in a feral threat. Her canines were slightly longer, like Isaiah's. And getting longer by the second. *Reaper.* The knowledge went through him on a shiver. It should have been one of repulsion. But it wasn't. Son of a bitch, what was it about this woman?

He gentled his voice.

"She's getting soaked. I can keep her drier in my coat."

Miranda blinked. Her mouth opened and then closed. She watched him the way one watched a coiled snake as he tucked the little girl against his chest.

"I want to go home," Wendy whispered wearily against his chest.

"We're heading there."

She shook her head. "Not there, our real home."

"Where's that?"

"I can't tell."

"Why not?"

"It's a secret."

"Why's that?"

If he was hoping to get past a six-year-old, he was doomed to failure. She just shook her head and locked her lips closed.

"It's none of your business," Miranda answered for her, pulling the coat a little tighter around her daughter. This close Cole could smell the faint sweetness of Miranda's soap. Clean and flowery, it made him think of summer and sex.

"In case you haven't noticed, I've been making it mine."

"I've noticed, and you've done enough."

"That doesn't sound like gratitude."

She started trudging through the mud. Looking back over her shoulder, she muttered, "Probably because it's not."

Making sure Wendy stayed wrapped up, Cole followed. Behind him he heard the door creak open. Creeping along with the light came Clark's energy. Tainted. Reckless. Frustration spiked with imbalance. Cole looked back. Clark was nowhere in sight, but framed in the doorway Cole could see Cindy huddled back against the wall, her children clutched in her arms. Fresh blood trickled down her chin. He cursed under his breath. The bastard had hit her. Isaiah needed to do something about him. A man like Clark was trouble and no benefit to anyone. He needed to go.

"I don't like him, either," Wendy whispered.

Had he said something?

"Did he ever hurt you, pumpkin?"

She nodded. "Once."

Fuck telling Isaiah. Cole would kill him himself.

Miranda was far enough ahead to be out of earshot. "What happened?" he asked.

She stirred in his arms. "Momma hurt him."

"Your momma?"

Wendy nodded. "She can be mean."

He found that hard to believe. The woman was all delicate femininity.

"But never to you." He hazarded a guess.

Wendy looked up, and her eyes were bright in the flash of lightning. Sure. "Of course not. She loves me."

"What did Clark do? When your mommy hurt him."

"I don't know." There was a pause and a shift. "I was hiding."

"Oh?" Ahead, Miranda looked back over her shoulder. He ignored the impatience in her stance.

Wendy shrugged. "I was little."

She was barely bigger than a minute now. "There's no shame in being little or being scared."

"You're not."

"Sometimes I am. I just don't give in to it."

"Me, either."

He shook his head. Someone had to teach her to check that spirit. "I noticed."

"Is everything all right?" Miranda called.

"Just fine."

"I'm getting wet," Wendy informed him. He took the hint.

"Then I'd better hurry."

It took just a minute to catch up with Miranda. You'd think it'd been hours from the worry in her expression.

"Was something wrong?"

"We were talking."

Her gaze ran over the bump that was Wendy in his coat. She cocked an eyebrow at him. "In the rain?"

Skepticism abounded. He opened the door and held it for her. "Your daughter likes to talk."

Her frown deepened rather than eased. "She can be a chatterbox."

He motioned her into the house. "She's charming, and you know it."

"To some people."

He didn't pretend to misunderstand. "Clark is plumb loco."

"We're home?" Wendy asked against his neck.

He looked around the small structure. Now that he knew to whom the home belonged, he could see evidence of both in the home. Miranda in the feminine neatness, and Wendy in the touches of chaos.

"What the hell was Isaiah thinking kicking you out of your home and putting you in that mess?"

Miranda shook her head again.

"It wasn't his choice."

"What the hell do you mean it wasn't his choice? He's boss here, isn't he?"

She licked her lips. "It's complicated."

Wendy wiggled. He let her slide to the floor. "How complicated?"

Miranda's gaze met his. "None of this is any of your business."

"We've already been over that ground. I made it my business about an hour ago."

"What you made was an enemy you didn't need to." She dropped the bundle on the floor by the bed. "You should have left when I told you to at Clark's or just stayed away."

"And left your daughter in a barn where anything could happen to her and anybody could find her?"

She turned, backing up a step until her calves hit the bed. If she were a whore, he'd take that as an invitation.

"She's safe here."

"I've got news for you, sweet doll, no one's safe anywhere. There's always somebody willing to invade your little world and tear it apart."

Miranda wrapped her arms around her waist, then as if realizing what the motion betrayed, snapped them down to her side. Her clothes were soaked and sticking to her curvy little body in a way that had his cock twitching and his conscience smarting. The place was cold, and she was chilled, and he was debating points he'd long since settled.

Cole strode over the fireplace he'd prepped earlier and stacked some kindling over the pile of twigs before reaching into his pocket and taking out a sulfur, striking it, and setting it to the pine needles beneath. They crackled and burned immediately, the bark and twigs above catching fast. Behind him he could hear Wendy moving about, the lightness of her steps betraying her location, but as far as he could tell, Miranda hadn't budged. She was stuck like an opossum to that bed.

He watched the flames devour the kindling. "That man was going to hurt your kid."

"I know."

As the flames licked at the first log, he glanced over his shoulder. "And what the hell did you think you were going to do about it?"

Her fingers curled into her palms, and her lips drew back again, revealing those sexy little canines.

"Kill him."

Taking in her small size and slight stature, Cole just shook his head. "Uh-huh. You may be Reaper, honey, but so is he."

The fire had caught. He stood and added, "You're not safe here."

Wendy walked over to her mama, Dolly in her hand. "He wants to be my papa."

Cole didn't miss the betraying way she leaned against her mom. "Seems to me he's already somebody's papa."

"I don't want him to be mine."

"Understandable." He glanced at Miranda. It was hard to ignore the way the wet blouse adhered to her shape, revealing the hard points of her nipples, but he gave it a hell of a shot. "Where's your husband?"

"Gone. Where's your wife?" she shot back.

"I've never had one."

"I can see why," she muttered.

It was such a woman-type retort, he couldn't suppress the smile tugging his lips.

"Yeah, I am a bit rough around the edges."

Wendy left her mom and came over to the fire, Dolly held before her like a shield. He blocked her before she could step too close.

"Gotta be careful around fire with skirts, little one."

She looked down at her skirts, then at the fire. "Oh." She immediately took two steps back. Her mother gave every impression she'd like to follow suit, but she held her ground.

Cole lost his smile. "I won't be staying here tonight."

"But where will you go?"

The protest was halfhearted at best. He didn't take offense. "I'll be sleeping in the barn."

Miranda was shaking her head before he finished the sentence. "Isaiah said—"

He cut her off. "I don't give a rat's behind what Isaiah said. I don't put a woman and child out of their bed for my comfort."

"You're Addy's family."

"Cousin to be exact."

She nodded.

"But that doesn't change a da—darn thing."

"We all know what you did for her."

He wondered which tale they were talking about. "Then you also know I mean what I say."

A shiver preceded her nod.

Hell, the woman would probably catch pneumonia while he wasted time arguing with her.

"You need to get into something dry."

She didn't move. "I will."

The "after you leave" hung silently between them.

"Then I'll get going and let you get to it."

He grabbed his saddlebags and headed for the door. With his hand on the knob he looked back.

Miranda was still standing by the bed, fingertips on the coverlet, tension in every line of her body. Wendy stood by the fire. Both of them looked at him with identical big brown eyes. Both of them looked lost and scared. Hell, even Dolly looked scared.

It's complicated.

Cole had the incredible urge to go back and gather them close. To tell them it would be all right. He shook his head at his own foolishness. What the hell was he thinking? It likely wasn't going to be all right. They weren't his responsibility. Still the urge pressed. Still he resisted. With an inaudible "hell" he opened the door.

A softly whispered "Be careful" stopped him dead in his tracks.

Cold air rushed past him, sending goose bumps chasing over his skin as he turned. "Why?"

Miranda licked her lips. She looked scared to death but determined. "Clark's not . . . right. He won't take well with you interfering in his plans."

Cole shrugged. "Won't be the first time someone's taken exception to my decisions."

"He won't fight fair."

"He's sneaky," Wendy piped up.

"I'll keep that in mind." But he was still sleeping elsewhere. Tipping his hat to both, he ordered, "Drop the bar on this door when I leave."

He had barely cleared the stoop when he heard the board thunk. At least the woman knew how to take an order. He remembered the way the rain plastered her dress to her chest and the full breasts it revealed. And those beautiful steal-your-soul eyes. And that courage that came out of nowhere, backed by the same fire so much more visible in Wendy. It was an intriguing combination. Adjusting his position he smiled. And the lady wasn't married, which meant there wasn't any reason she couldn't take any order he cared to give. He pulled his hat down over his brow, letting the rain run off the brim. She just might be his type. And his time here might not be as tedious as he'd thought.

A pulse of energy came out of the storm. The hairs on the back of Cole's neck stood on end. His smile slipped. Clark. Cole could only think of a few reasons the Reaper would be out in the storm. None of them good. *Shit.*

Continuing on his path, Cole tracked Clark's energy, which paced him. Cole loosened the tie down on his revolvers. Entering the barn, he took his saddlebags and put them down in a pile of clean hay in the corner. Clark's energy held steady. Cole untied his slicker from the bags, a little late but better late than never. Drawing it on, he buttoned it closed.

As he felt Clark slip away, he followed, tamping down his own energy, not wanting to project the way the Reaper was. A bit short-sighted of the man to think he was undetected, but Cole was used to men overestimating their abilities and underestimating his. In a fight it didn't matter as much who was bigger as it did who was meaner and more skilled, and he had a lot of skills.

Cole followed Clark until he went back to his house. Miranda seemed to think her association with Isaiah was protection. He wasn't so sure. A man like Clark didn't take "no" well, and the appearance of another man in his woman's vicinity had to put his temper on edge. Clark didn't seem like he had ahold of much—his sanity or his temper.

Cole took up a position at Miranda's door, bracing his rifle against the side so it'd be protected from the rain by the overhang. He sat down on the rock stoop and pulled his hat down over his brow. Whatever the ass had in mind for Miranda, it wasn't gonna happen tonight.

Cole sat there with the rain falling around him, the chill nipping at his skin, and focused most of his energy on the women. When not terrified, Miranda's energy was soft and sweet, sliding over his with a velvet kiss. He loved the way she felt. So seductively feminine, so hotly sexual. He knew he should pull back, but that velvet touch was stronger than steel and he needed . . . more. Much more.

The soft strains of a lullaby crept through the door. Cole closed his eyes and listened. Miranda had a high, sweet voice, pure on some notes, raspy on others. Sex wrapped up in sound. And she was only singing a lullaby. What would that voice do to him if she sang a love song?

Cole shook his head, flexed his fingers, and forced himself to pull back, feeling as if he peeled layers off his insides as he did. Miranda made him feel exposed and vulnerable with a need that had nothing to do with sex. For the first time since he'd set out after Addy, he felt truly threatened.

Fuck.

6

HE WAS OUT THERE. MIRANDA COULD FEEL COLE IN THE vibration of the thunder, within the flashes of lightning. Her pulse skittered, and her nipples hardened. He felt like a threat. Like a promise. Reaching under the mattress, she touched the handle of her husband Michael's sword. It didn't give her the peace she expected. Cole Cameron was a potent force. And he drew her. That was so dangerous.

She looked to where Wendy slept, a frown pleating her brow. Miranda wanted to reach over and smooth that frown away. Six was too young to have worries that haunted your sleep. She hadn't wanted this life for herself, definitely not for her daughter, but life wasn't big on choices. It certainly hadn't offered her any.

Memories pushed at her mind. Snarls leaping out of the darkness, tearing her from her husband's arms, tearing at her skin, tearing her from her hopes and dreams. And now they were trying to tear at her daughter. Leaning over, she pulled the covers up over Wendy's shoulders and kissed her hair.

"I won't let them have you, baby. I promise you." She just wouldn't. And as hard as it was to accept, keeping that promise was going to require a strong man to keep the predators away from her daughter. But it was also going to take a man Miranda could control. Because when she came of age, Wendy was going to have options. No one was going to force her into a life she didn't want.

Rain lashed the windows. Lightning crackled in an earsplitting cacophony. Miranda jumped. The energy she felt from Cole stayed steady. She clung to it. Just because it felt good—even for a second—to have something to anchor her panic.

Wendy stirred. "Shhh, baby. Everything is fine. You're fine."

With a murmur Wendy settled. So sweet and innocent to believe Miranda saying something made it so. Miranda remembered Clark drawing back his fist. The helpless moment when she'd known she couldn't get to her daughter in time. And the overwhelming relief when Cole had stepped in. Another burst of wind and rain pounded the roof. Her conscience slammed her with equal force. Whoever he was, Cole had saved her baby, and she'd repaid him by letting him sit out in a storm getting soaked.

She might be Reaper now, but she'd been raised better. Grabbing her shawl to wrap around her nightgown, she stood and headed for the door.

Being raised right didn't make it any easier to open that door. There was something about Cole Cameron that both drew her and scared her. As if there was more to him than met the eye. She didn't like secrets. She lifted the bar. It felt so much heavier than it was. As if lifting that bar changed everything.

She opened the door slowly so it wouldn't squeak. Light from the interior spread out over the wet ground, highlighting the ripples of raindrops in the puddles. Cole looked at her from the stoop. Water dripped off his hat. Shadows caught on his whiskers and haunted his eyes. He looked like anything but a safe place. She clutched the doorjamb. It took two tries to find her voice.

"You'll catch your death sitting there."

"I'll be fine."

Men always said that, human or Reaper. It didn't make it true. "You're not Reaper."

He looked at her. A cold, steady stare from beneath the brim of his hat. It heated her from the inside out.

"No, I'm not."

"You'll catch cold."

"This isn't the first time I've sat in the rain."

She glanced over her shoulder. Wendy still slept.

"Close the door. You're letting the heat out."

And be on what side of it? She wasn't dressed for the rain. And she still owed him.

"You don't know what you're doing here."

"I know exactly what I'm doing."

She tried again "There are things you don't understand happening here."

He cut her off. "Maybe. But I recognize a bully when I see one. And that man you're stuck on is one miserable son of a bitch."

What could she say? Clark *was* a bully. "I'm not stuck on him."

"Set on him, then. Same difference."

No, it wasn't. But that wasn't the point. She tightened her grip on the doorknob. "If you tell Isaiah what just happened, things will get worse."

"Are you saying Isaiah would sanction Clark hitting a little kid?"

"No. It's just—"

Again he cut her off. This time she didn't mind, because she had no idea how she was going to finish that sentence.

"I have my share of problems with Isaiah," Cole growled, "but there's no way he'd countenance anyone beating on a child."

Pain in her fingers warned Miranda that she was clutching the door latch too tightly. She forced herself to relax. First her fingers, then her arms, and lastly her voice.

"It's not as simple as that."

"It's not?" Wind blew the rain, splattering the front of her night-gown, the little droplets hitting it here and there, creating specks of transparency. One landed just to the right of her nipple. His gaze dropped. His mouth thinned, and the air between them thickened with tension as her gaze followed his to where her shawl had slid down. That wet clinging spot was almost, *almost* big enough to show the color of her nipple.

Miranda crossed her arms over her chest and jerked the shawl back up. Heat crept up her cheeks. She wanted to slam the door shut. She didn't. His gaze met hers. She never knew hazel eyes could burn so.

"You need to go inside."

Prudence agreed. Pride kept her feet planted as she asked, "You're determined to do this?"

"I'm not leaving you unprotected."

That's what she'd figured. Sighing, she stepped back and opened the door wide. "Then come inside."

He didn't move. "That's not going to do your reputation any good."

"No worse than having you stand guard in front of my house."

"If I'm sitting in front of your door, people will know I'm not sleeping with you."

He wasn't Reaper. He wouldn't understand the drive for a mate. She shook her head. "A claim is a claim is a claim."

He got to his feet, shaking the water off his shoulders. "Interesting way of putting things."

"As I said, there's a lot here you don't understand.

"Uh-huh."

More raindrops hit her nightgown. At this rate she'd be all but naked in a few minutes. She stepped back. "For the love of Pete, come in."

"I'll get your floor wet."

She rolled her eyes. "As if that's the problem I'm going to be worrying about right now."

She motioned him in. This time he went. A few steps past the door, he stopped.

"You made coffee?" He kept his voice as low as hers as he took off his hat.

It was the last of her small stash, but he didn't need to know that. She shrugged and held out her hand. "You'll be needing something warm in your stomach."

He handed the Stetson to her before cocking an eyebrow at her. "I hear an accent. Irish?"

She shook her head. "Scottish."

"Nice."

The way he said "nice" sent a totally unexpected shiver down her spine. It'd been so long since she'd felt such emotion it took her a second to recognize it for what it was. Desire.

"I'm not going to jump you, ma'am."

Thank goodness he thought she was just nervous. "Thank you."

He cocked that eyebrow at her again. She took his coat, holding it away from her. "A man who was planning on assaulting me wouldn't be sitting out in the cold on a miserable night, guarding me from another one who feels it's his right to do just that."

What was it about his look that made her feel like a bug in the open?

"Which brings us back to my question: why does he feel it's his right?"

She draped the coat over the chair by the fire. Water dripped onto the rough wood floor, slipping between the cracks and disappearing like she wanted to. How was it possible to be jealous of water? "According to some, we're to be mated."

He didn't look shocked. He just grabbed the towel hanging on the hearth and took the plain enameled pot off the fire. "How about according to you?"

She shrugged. "It's complicated."

He poured a cup of coffee. "I've got nothing but time."

She supposed he did. She rubbed her hands down her nightgown. "There are not many women who are suitable. The law says when there is a match, it has to be honored, no matter what."

"Even if the hombre's already on the hook?"

"That hasn't happened before."

"So they're experimenting with you."

"Yes."

He cocked an eyebrow at her. "And you're fine with this?"

"I have been discussing it with him."

"Discussing, huh? He doesn't seem the talkative type."

"I have to think of my daughter."

"How does Wendy play into this?"

She tugged her shawl around her, vividly aware of how worn it was, how worn out she was, as those too-knowing eyes of his traveled from her head to her stockinged feet.

"Clark is a bully and a brute."

How dare he sit there in front of her fire, drink her coffee, and pick apart her life? She glared at him. "But strong enough to hold what's his."

He stared at her for the longest time before responding. "You're afraid of him."

"I am not."

It was a lie. Clark scared her witless. The whole Reaper community scared her. Especially her position within it.

He took another measured sip of the hot coffee. "He was going to hit Wendy tonight."

She would have killed him if he had. "She provokes him."

"Even I don't believe that's justification, and I'm human."

Was that a touch of amusement in his tone? It caught on her frustration and pulled it to the front of her control. Her fingers tightened on the voluminous folds of her nightgown. Memories she wanted buried chased the frustration.

"You have no idea what you're up against. You don't know what they can do to you with just a lift of a finger, how it can change everything. Ruin everything."

"I've had a taste. But"—he stood—"Camerons don't go down easy."

She couldn't even remember feeling that invulnerable. Certainly not after that awful night her life had divided into two parts. Pre-Reaper and post-Reaper. "Camerons will go down just like everyone else. And when you do, there won't be anything left of you but the blood soaking the earth, and they'll laugh, and they'll go on as if nothing happened. But you won't." She felt again the claws ripping her face, the teeth tearing at her throat. She'd prayed so hard in those moments to live, which only proved panic made people foolish.

He took a step forward. The table was behind her. She couldn't take a step back. He reached out. She braced herself. She felt the beast rage as the memories howled. Her talons bit into the wooden surface. And all he did was run the back of his fingers down her scarred cheek. She wanted to duck and hide.

"Is that what they did to you?"

She shook her head. "I'm not going to talk about that."

"Why?"

She took a step back. "Because it doesn't matter."

His eyes narrowed. She felt his concern like a touch, wrapping around her in a firm, invisible hug, pressing her, demanding . . . something. She didn't have anything to give anyone, let alone someone like him who would demand everything.

His gaze cut to her daughter. "Wendy's human, isn't she?"

How had he known that? "Yes."

"Reapers hate humans." He didn't make it a question.

"Not all of them."

"How about the ones here?"

She licked her lips again. "They, for the most part, like her."

The look he gave her let her know he heard the evasion and didn't appreciate it. "For the most part. A human among Reapers. What's going to happen when she grows up?"

That was the big question. One she didn't want to answer. Taking a deep breath, she forced her beast back. Stepping past him, she took the cloth and grabbed the pot. He caught her arm. She wanted to lash out but held herself together. One glance and he let her go. Slowly. The sensation of his touch lingered.

"Not a place you want to go, huh?"

"No."

Grabbing a cloth at the fireplace, she poured a cup for herself and then refilled his. The only betrayal of her nervousness was the rattle of the pot when she put it back. She quickly squashed it. This was a man to whom one didn't give the advantage. When she turned, he was sitting at the table. She licked her lips.

"I have a little honey if you need it sweetened."

He shook his head. "It'd be a waste of honey to try and sweeten me up."

She didn't smile at the joke, but she did hand him the cup, being careful to keep her fingers out of contact with his. She didn't want to feel that jolt of desire. She couldn't afford to be weak.

"Take the chair by the fire, please."

He didn't argue. Just sat on one chair and put his feet up on the other. She pulled the third out but didn't sit.

"I have some milk."

Again, he shook his head. "Save it for Wendy."

It irked her that he knew how dear milk was and he thought of her daughter. She didn't want to like him. Liking him could go nowhere.

He caught her look. "I'm not a monster, you know."

"They said you took on four Reapers and defeated them."

"I had help."

"So you didn't do it?"

He shrugged. "There was a fight. I won."

He said that as if it were nothing.

"But you're human."

"I got lucky."

"You defeated four Reapers."

"Yes."

He had to be lying. Four. She studied him from under her lashes. He was big boned and lean, with well-honed muscles that flexed beneath his shirt. No doubt he was something in a fight with humans, but with Reapers? It just wasn't possible.

He set his cup on the table. "What do you want from me?"

She shook her head. "I just wanted to thank you for the favor you did me earlier."

He said something under his breath.

"What?"

"You can't negotiate and win with that man."

"I'm not trying to win. I'm just trying to—"

Cole knew what she was trying to do. It was written in every nervous stroke of her fingers over her arms. Telegraphed in the way they tangled in the wrap. The woman was between a rock and a hard place.

"Negotiate a better position?"

She nodded.

"Have you talked to Isaiah about it?"

Her eyes flashed to his. Her "no" wasn't a surprise. She'd already said she didn't think Isaiah could help. And Clark was too confident to feel threatened.

He sighed and wrapped his hands around the cup. The heat from the coffee spread to his hands, warming them. He looked at the black liquid, the lamplight glinted off the surface, and he shook his head.

A cup of coffee in payment for risking his life. Damn. Even he didn't hold it that cheap. He took a sip.

"You can't do this alone."

"I don't have a choice."

No, he supposed from where she sat she didn't. "You need help."

Anger flashed in her eyes. A hint of red heated the deep brown. *Reaper.*

"I'm fine."

He'd heard Addy speak those words in that same cold, flatly determined yet hopeless tone too many times not to know it for the lie it was. She wasn't fine. Without help she was, quite simply, fucked.

"Saying it doesn't make it so."

She jumped, and coffee spilled from her cup. She grabbed the cloth and dabbed at the back of her hand. He watched, feeling the frantic flick of her energy.

"Miranda . . ."

Across the room Wendy whimpered. Miranda latched onto the slight sound like a cat on a June bug, hurrying to the bed, whispering soothingly, pulling the blanket up over the child's shoulders the way mothers did. As if the weave were a magic shield that nothing could penetrate.

Cole pushed his coffee away, watching them both, frustration battling with disbelief. What had he been going to say? That he'd help her? He had no position here. Hell, Miranda was right. He didn't even have a clue as to what was going on, and he was going to get in the middle of it? He had enough problems without borrowing a stranger's.

Wendy's whimpers grew stronger. Fear, pure and simple, spread through the room. Cole gritted his teeth. There was something seriously wrong when a little girl's dreams held that much terror. Little girls should dream about sunny days braiding daisy chains and skipping through fields and Christmas and puppies and kittens and all the things that fascinated children. Wendy cried out.

"Leave my mommy alone!"

Anger lashed through the fear. Miranda cast him a glance. Hopeless. Desperate. She didn't want him to see this, but it was far too late. Energy pummeled him in relentless waves. Hers. Wendy's. And all of it was filled with the bite of horror. What in hell had happened to these two?

Wendy thrashed and cried out again. Her fist caught Miranda on the cheek. She flinched and whispered faster. Cole slowly brought the cup of coffee to his mouth and watched as the tension in him tightened. No amount of fast talk could halt memories that strong. Someone had hurt that little girl. Deeply.

In a routine that bordered on ritual, Miranda managed to get Wendy settled back into a quiet sleep. The energy in the room eased but didn't totally calm. Cole nursed his coffee as Miranda hovered by the bed. He knew from Addy's nightmares Wendy would sleep now. Miranda had to know it, too. Which meant she was stalling. No big surprise why.

"Your coffee's getting cold," he told her.

She shrugged and looked over her shoulder. Instead of flashing fire, her gaze just telegraphed defeat. He knew that feeling, too. Nothing like holding someone you love as they relive a horror to make a body doubt everything.

"I don't feel like it anymore."

No, for sure she didn't need coffee. What she needed was sleep.

"Why don't you go lie down and get some sleep, too, while I stand guard?"

She looked at him and the door. Outside the rain still poured.

"I'm not tired."

As if to make a liar out of herself, she yawned.

"You going to stick to that lie?"

She shook her head and stroked her fingers over Wendy's shoulder. "It doesn't matter if I lie down, I won't sleep."

It was probably the first bit of unvarnished truth she'd given him. The woman spun half-truths with the intricacy of a spider spinning a web.

"Too much on your mind?"

She nodded again, and her attention wasn't on his face but much lower. There was no telling what she was thinking from that look, but the way her tongue touched her lower lip, a hint of deeper pink on pink, gave him ideas.

He reached for his gun belt. "You want me to take them off?"

He would give a pretty penny for this woman to ask him to take off his guns, his boots, and his pants, until it was just the two of them skin to skin.

Shit. His cock twitched.

Her eyes flew to his. Shock, horror, and *son of a bitch*—it had to be his imagination that tacked desire onto the list of emotions he read in her expression.

Her gaze dropped down, then just as quickly jerked back up. Fresh tension laced the air. "No, I was just—"

With a slash of his hand he cut her off. He couldn't do anything about his cock, but he could put an end to her fear.

"Do us both a favor and crawl into that bed and pretend to sleep."

"I didn't mean . . . I mean I can't—"

He cut her off again. "Just because I appreciate a beautiful woman doesn't mean I forget who I am."

She licked her lips. His cock twitched again. He thought she'd retreat, but she didn't. That chin came up and those soft, tempting lips pressed ever so slightly together. The woman had guts.

"And who are you?" she asked as if it mattered.

"Cole Cameron."

He stood. She put her hand on his arm. Frissons of electricity skittered up under his skin.

"And what does that mean?"

He tipped her chin up, adding a bit more tension to the taut energy between them. "It means you and your daughter are church-pew safe with me."

Questions he didn't want to answer filled her eyes.

"Go to bed, Miranda. I promise I won't touch you."

"There's no point."

He stroked his thumb across her lips. In a subtle experiment he brushed his energy across hers, siphoning off some of the stress spiking within her. She didn't blink or otherwise acknowledge the touch, but she did relax. "Tonight it's safe to sleep."

She blinked. Her energy withdrew, but she didn't. "Because you're here?"

The words formed against his skin in an intimate caress. She was challenging him. Showing him she wasn't intimidated. He smiled and pressed his thumb a touch harder. He tugged her shawl up with his free hand, covering her breasts "Yes."

It was the truth.

She dropped her hand from his arm, eyeing his smile as if it were a bad thing. Shit. Had it been so long since he'd smiled that he couldn't do it anymore?

She stepped to the side, squeezing out from between him and the table. "Thank you."

"You're welcome."

As soon as she was clear, she took one step and then another and another until the bed was at her back. The whole distance she didn't take her eyes off of his. Like he was a rattler prepared to strike.

He didn't like the comparison. "I told you I wouldn't hurt you."

"I know."

But she didn't believe it, and that just pissed him off. "Then act like it."

She fussed, her hands moving over her arms and the skirt of her nightgown in a graceful dance. It was also as arousing as hell. He turned his back. "Just get in the bed."

"You could go back outside."

Thunder rumbled; it was not as close, but the rain was still steady. "In case you haven't noticed, it's pouring out there."

"You didn't mind before."

Before she hadn't looked at him like he was a rapist. Now he had something to prove. He wasn't a threat to her. "I mind now."

Her energy snapped with annoyance, and then there was a rustle as she slid into bed. When he turned back, she was watching him cautiously from under her lashes.

A twinge of something that could have been guilt flicked his conscience. Cupping his hand around the chimney, he blew out the lamp. Miranda's energy jumped and focused. He pulled his hat down over his brow, slumped a bit down on the chair, and acted like he was going to sleep. He felt a little of the tension leave her energy, but it still seethed around him in wary twitches.

After ten minutes of lessening tension, she asked softly, so softly if he'd been asleep he wouldn't have heard, "Did you really kill four Reapers?"

"Yeah, I really killed four Reapers."

There was a rustle of the sheets. Was she turning on her side or her stomach? His imagination wouldn't let go of either image. On her side he'd be able to follow the curve of her hip with his hand, over the fullness of her thighs, indulging in a bit of play in the hollow of her waist before wandering up to her breasts. On her stomach, that fine ass would be sticking up.

Shit. His cock thickened and strained against his pants. He'd been too long without a woman.

This woman.

He pushed the thought away. From across the room her breathing quickened. "What are you so damn afraid of, woman?"

"Losing control."

That made twice she'd been honest. He gentled his voice. "Of what?"

"Everything."

"Why?"

Her energy gathered. "Why do you have to ask so many questions?" she snapped.

"Because no one will give me any answers," he snapped right back.

There was another long expulsion of breath. "You don't know what you're asking."

"So tell me."

He could hear her hair rustle on the sheets, feel the flare of her energy as she denied him.

"I'm not allowed to talk about it."

"Says who?"

"Says Isaiah."

"The same man that's letting this Clark fellow bully you."

"He's not 'letting' anything. I'm the one that agreed to the union."

"Why in hell would you agree to anything like that?"

"I told you."

"Yeah, I heard you last time. You need a strong man to protect your daughter."

"Yes."

"Protect her from what?"

He felt the flex in her energy that preceded the evasion.

"What every mother's afraid of. The wrong time. The wrong man. The wrong place."

"Reapers."

So soft he almost didn't hear. "Yes."

In the wake of that truth the silence was deafening. He waited, but she didn't say more. Wendy murmured in her sleep. Thunder rumbled in the distance. He could push for more or let it go. He opted for the latter. The woman was strung out tighter than a kite string in a high wind.

"Where you from, Miranda?"

Her energy swirled in a flurry of panic. A reaction he was more used to in criminals than in a woman. But still she answered.

"Virginia."

"Not much of a drawl for a Virginian."

"Northern Virginia."

He made note. "So how'd you end up out here in the back of beyond?"

"My husband, Wendy's father, wanted to come west to start over. There wasn't much left of our home after the North's act of aggression."

"You mean the war."

"I call it like it was."

"So you're a Southerner."

"You just got done saying I didn't have an accent."

Did she think she could confuse him? "Yes. One more piece of the puzzle that is you."

"I'll thank you not to see me as a puzzle or a challenge."

"Are you telling me or asking me?"

There was a rustling that indicated a shrug. "Both."

He smiled. He did like a woman with a bit of fire.

"So you've got Southern sympathies but no Southern accent; you were married but have no husband; you obviously come from culture, yet you're stuck in the back of beyond in this territory in some of the harshest terrain with a group of monsters called Reapers."

"It's none of your business what I am."

"May not be my business, but there's enough to you to make a man curious."

"I'll thank you not to be curious."

"Too late."

"My life is no concern of yours."

"Not unless I choose to make it so."

And he just might. The woman intrigued him on all levels for no particular reason he could put his finger on beyond the fact that she had the most delicious energy that'd ever rubbed against his. He'd seen prettier women, he'd seen more voluptuous women, but he'd never met a woman that made his cock hard just thinking about the touch of her fingers on his. Add to that the fact that she had sass and fire and she was in a bit of a pickle, and well, she was downright irresistible.

"I can feel you thinking over there."

"What kind of feel?"

"I can just feel it, and I'm not your concern, and I don't want to be your challenge, and I don't want to be the puzzle that you have to fix. I have enough problems without adding you to the mix."

"More problems than just Clark?"

"If it were just Clark, I could have solved it myself."

Interesting. "How's that?"

"I'd kill him."

The woman was getting more intriguing by the second.

She flopped over and sat up in the bed. Wendy stirred.

"Careful, you're going to wake your daughter."

She huffed at him for the helpful hint.

He smiled, knowing she couldn't see it in the shadow from his hat.

"Is it just me you enjoy provoking, or is it a general habit?"

"Might be generalized. But I'm pretty much focused on you tonight though."

"Because you think I owe you?"

"Because you're there and I'm here, neither one of us is sleeping, and I'm curious."

"My God, it's a wonder nobody's shot you before now."

He broke out laughing at that. "A few have."

"You need enemies with better aim."

"If I had enemies with better aim, little Wendy would be sporting a broken jaw."

That shut her up quick.

"I'm not a threat to you, Miranda."

"You are. You're just too stupid to know it."

"The only other person that's accused me of being stupid is your daughter."

"I'm surprised more haven't. I thought it would go hand in hand with a bullet in your ass."

"Language, language."

"I stopped worrying about the basic courtesies a long time ago."

"Right about the time you hooked up with the Reapers?"

She didn't bother to deny it. "Yes."

"Since we're on the subject, how did you come to be with the Reapers?"

"It wasn't by choice."

"Kinda figured that. Were you always a Reaper and just didn't know it? Were you hiding out among humans?"

"I can't tell you."

"Why the hell not?"

"They'll kill me."

That truth hung between them. *Fuck.*

"You really are in trouble, aren't you?"

"Yes. And you're not helping. So, please, come morning pack your stuff, get out of my house, get out of this village, and disappear."

"That would make you happy?"

"Yes."

"Then I'll think on it."

He pulled the hat down a little bit lower on his face and settled in the chair. He could feel her glaring at him, probably plotting a way to demand a promise rather than a "think on it."

His smile grew a little broader as she slumped down in the bed. He stretched his long legs out and crossed his feet at the ankles, letting the fire warm the soles of his boots.

His stay might just be getting a little interesting after all.

⋰ 7 ⋱

INTERESTING WAS THE NEXT MORNING WHEN WENDY bounced out of bed at the crack of dawn, ready to make a mad dash for the outhouse, and he was feeling about a hundred years old from sitting in the chair all night.

She froze, her nightgown swirling around her legs when she saw him. Her eyes, so like her mother's, grew as big as silver dollars. He stood.

"Mommy?" she whispered.

He couldn't blame her for the fear. Between the trip here and the night in the chair, he was as stiff as a board and not moving with his usual ease. He might just be getting old.

"It's all right," he told her with a smile that felt more like a grimace and likely looked like one, too, if her reactions were anything to go by.

Wendy took a step back and that chin of hers came up.

"You leave my mommy alone."

It seemed to be the child's battle cry. "Your mommy will always be safe with me."

She looked at him, and her lip slipped between her teeth as she absorbed that.

"I've go to go potty."

That's what he'd figured from the way she was shifting from foot to foot.

Miranda moaned and rolled over but didn't wake. He wasn't surprised. She'd spent most of the night, arm draped over the side of the mattress, watching him.

"Let's not wake your mommy. She's tired."

For a second more Wendy hesitated, but with a grimace she nodded. He knew what that grimace meant. They were running out of time. "Do you think you can make it?"

She shook her head.

"Where's the chamber pot?"

She shook her head again and started to bob. There was no more time for discussion. Scooping her up, he made a dash for the door.

He got her to the outhouse in the nick of time. Or so he thought, but when he put her on the ground, she didn't go in.

"What's wrong?"

Standing, legs crossed, tears in her eyes, she just looked at him. "What?"

To his horror she started to cry. Big, fat tears that ripped at him. "Dammit, what?"

"You're not supposed to swear."

"And you're not supposed to pee your pants."

"I didn't!"

Yet. The "yet" was imminent.

"Then what's the problem?"

She opened the door and pointed inside. It took him only a

minute to spot the problem. There was a big ass spiderweb on the ceiling. And even he had to admit the occupant didn't look friendly.

"That is one ugly spider."

She nodded.

"I can see why you're afraid."

"I'm not a scaredy-cat!"

Obviously a sore subject. He grabbed up a stick off the ground. "Only a fool is never afraid."

She jumped back as he leaned into the outhouse and scooped the spider, web and all, onto the stick.

She screamed when he came back out, the spider dangling. "Kill it! Kill it!"

He looked at her. "Go get your business done while I send this fella off to better parts.

She didn't move.

"Unless you want me to put him back?"

She was in the outhouse in a flash, braids dancing, the door slamming behind her. He chuckled and walked the spider off into the tall grass.

"Sorry, fella. But you wore out your welcome."

He lobbed the stick deeper into the brush.

It would be nice if he could take care of all his problems so easily. And for the first time in his memory it wasn't Addy's face that flashed into his mind but Miranda's. *Shit.*

From the far edge of the village came the sounds of raised men's voices and grunts. And cheers. Not a battle then. The outhouse door banged.

"Mister Cole?"

He turned back to Wendy. "Right here."

She held up her arms as he approached.

"Feet cold?"

She nodded.

It was as natural as anything to pick her up. "How long has that spider been there?"

"A week or so." She curled her arm around his neck. "Why didn't you kill it?"

"Because it didn't do anything wrong."

"It scared me."

"I know." He shifted her higher and headed back to the house. "But you could have asked your mom to remove it."

"She's afraid of them, too."

Miranda was afraid of a spider, but she thought she could handle Clark? He set Wendy down on the stoop. "Isaiah, then."

"Mommy says we can't bother him all the time."

"Interesting."

The door opened. Miranda stood there, looking sleep tousled and relieved, her shawl tucked tightly around her as she frowned at them both. "Mommy also said you aren't supposed to leave the house without telling her."

"It was an emergency," Cole explained.

Wendy nodded. "I had to go pee."

Miranda caught her daughter by the shoulders and drew her close. "We don't speak of such things in mixed company."

"Oh."

"It's all right," Cole said.

Miranda shook her head. "No, it's not."

Wendy leaned back against her mom and looked up. "He got rid of the spider."

"Huh?"

"The spider in the outhouse."

"Is that why you've been having . . . problems?" She shook her head. "You should have told me."

Over Wendy's head, Miranda mouthed a thank-you.

"You told me we couldn't be scaredy-cats."

All the weight of the world settled into Miranda's expression. "When it comes to real things that scare you, it's not being a scaredy-cat."

"Mr. Cole says only fools aren't afraid."

Miranda looked at him, her expression a mixture of anxiety and—hell, he didn't know what the "and" was. But it made something he didn't recognize inside him curl in pleasure and the weary stiffness of the night disappear in a heartbeat.

"Thank you."

"You're welcome."

"He also says you can't kill something just because you're afraid," Wendy continued.

Miranda didn't have anything to say to that. Cole ruffled Wendy's hair.

"If you're all set here, I'm going to see what all the hubbub's about over there." With a jerk of his chin he indicated the direction of the noise.

Miranda's gaze went past him down to the end of the village where he could hear raised male voices.

"You're not seriously thinking of joining the practice, are you?"

Maybe. "Practice?"

"Training," she corrected hastily. "They train."

He'd like to see that. "I might. It's been a while since I had a good tussle."

"It's only pretend fights," Wendy piped up.

Miranda shook her head. "Pretend fights in which bones get broken."

Her concern was touching.

"Remember me? The man who took down four Reapers?"

"You said you got lucky."

"Well, there was some skill involved."

It ruffled his pride that she thought he was no match for a Reaper. They were, after all, just men with good reflexes.

"They're not, you know," she said, stepping back so Wendy could go into the house.

That snapped him straight. He knew damn well he hadn't said that aloud.

"What?"

"Everybody thinks that, but it's not true," she explained, as if nothing out of the ordinary had happened.

"Thinks what?"

"That Reapers are just humans with better skills."

So he was realizing. Apparently some of them could read minds. "What are they?"

"I don't know, but they're more than that."

How could so many people be something and not know a thing about it? "Maybe it's time someone found out."

"Isaiah won't be able to protect you."

Son of a bitch, did she think he was a boy in short pants? "Who asked him to?"

She bit her lip, and this time he had no trouble reading the fullness of her expression. Terror. She was terrified for him. The knowledge soothed some of his earlier irritation.

"Don't go."

He brushed her hair back from her cheek. "Are you really worried about me getting hurt, or are you worried I'm going to start talking to some people and figuring some stuff out?"

"There's no mystery here."

The woman was full of mystery, full of fear, full of passion. And she wasn't pulling away from his touch. He wondered if she realized that as much as he wondered if she knew she'd read his mind.

"China doll, there's nothing but mystery here."

Her eyes searched his. "Why do you call me that?"

"I'm guessing for the same reason you're not backing away from my touch."

She closed her eyes slowly and shook her head. "Then we're both fools."

"I've been called worse."

She did step away from him then. "I'm sure. And by better people than me."

He took in her sleep-tumbled disarray. The softness of her mouth, the sweet tension of her energy. He'd like nothing better than to push her back into that house, lay her down on that bed, and slip his cock into her hot pussy with slow and easy strokes as he woke her up with kisses just as slow and easy. "No. I don't think so."

With a shake of her head she grabbed the door. Before she closed it, she muttered with a complete lack of heat, "Go get yourself killed already."

He smiled and shook his head. Nothing was ever that easy.

COLE tipped his hat to a couple of women working outside as he passed. They lowered their eyes and ducked into their houses as if just acknowledging the gesture could get them killed. There weren't that many women here. He'd expect them to be valued, but each one, with the exception of Addy, looked scared as shit. Addy didn't look scared at all. Just another thing that needed explaining.

When he reached Addy's house, the door was open, letting in the fresh morning air. There was a fire out front with a coffeepot sitting on it. He walked up to the door and rapped on the doorjamb.

"Addy girl, you in there?"

There was a rustling and then, "Coming!"

Addy came to the door, a piece of cloth and needle and thread in her hand. The stitches were uneven. She'd never been much of a sewer.

"I see your skills haven't improved."

She blew her hair off her forehead. "Well, they're going to have to. There's no money for store-bought clothes, and Wendy needs a new outfit."

"Why not have her mother make it?"

"That's a proud woman."

He couldn't argue with that.

"Too proud to accept help?"

She sighed. "Miranda didn't come to us under the best of circumstances, and her position now is rather tenuous."

"Her position is fucking dangerous."

"Watch your language."

"I'll do that just as soon as I don't feel like I'm sitting on top of a keg of dynamite and everybody around me has a sulfur."

She sighed. "Cole, you're not one of us."

"Us? What the hell is that? Did marrying that Reaper suddenly put you outside of our family?"

"No, but it brought up complications."

She pointed to the pot. "Pour yourself some coffee."

"Why?"

"Because you're always testy until you've had some, and I'm going to answer your questions."

"Trust me, coffee isn't going to help my mood as much as answers."

But he poured himself a cup anyway and took a seat on the log bench. Addy sat beside him with a sigh.

"There are things you don't know, don't understand." She pushed her hair off her forehead. "Things even I don't understand that affect all of us."

There was only one thing he wanted to know. "Are you in danger, Addy?"

"You know I am."

"From other Reapers."

He didn't make it a question, and she didn't pretend it should be. "Yes."

"Because you married Isaiah."

There was the barest of hesitations before she responded, "Yes."

The same kind of hesitation Miranda had given him.

"We promised no secrets between us, Addy."

Her hand over his was warm and familiar, but not comforting. "I know. I just don't know where to start."

And as he sat there, the pieces of the puzzle started to scramble in his mind with the chaos of leaves strewn in the wind, but then they began to settle. He focused on one fact at a time, and from that, order took shape. Addy had grown up human; he knew that as well as he knew the back of his hand. She claimed now to be Reaper. Something Isaiah had done to her had brought that about, but it stood to reason that if Addy could be turned into a Reaper, then so could Miranda.

"Maybe I can help. Miranda wasn't born Reaper, was she?"

She shook her head.

"No one's born Reaper."

"So no Reaper was ever born."

"As far as we know."

"Seems like you don't know much."

She stood, dropping her hand to her hip and taking up that hip-shot stance that always meant she was out of patience.

"I'm betraying my husband by telling you this, Cole, so listen up, because if you're going to stay here, there are some things you do need to know."

He took a sip of coffee. "I'm listening."

"Not all Reapers are cut from the same cloth, just like all men aren't cut from the same cloth, but what they all have is a tremendous amount of power, a certain amount of madness, and no understanding of their capabilities."

"Explain."

"I want to." Her hands wrung together before the right one reached into her pocket. Looking for the worry stone she thought she'd lost. The one he held.

"Just spit it out, Addy."

She bit her lip. Took a breath. The stone in his pocket weighed heavier than it should. There was a time when he would have given it to her without hesitation, but now . . . Now everything was different. Addy was different. Just how much he wasn't sure. Just another piece of the puzzle to be put together. He waited for one minute. Two. Finally she sighed and straightened her skirts.

"Not everybody can be converted to Reaper. If an attempt is made—"

"How is someone made?"

"Through bites."

"Bites." An image of Isaiah sinking his teeth into Addy's fair skin turned Cole's stomach. "You let that son of a bitch bite you?"

She shrugged and blushed, her gaze skirting his. "I didn't mind at the time."

At the time—his mind revolved around that and then recoiled as the meaning sunk in.

"Son of a bitch, he bit you *then*?"

She blushed deeper but didn't deny it.

He took his hat off and ran his hand through his hair before shoving it back on his head.

"I'll kill him."

"No, you won't." She folded her arms across her chest and leveled him with that superior look that worked so well for her. "You had to suspect some of this."

He had. But not *that*. It was going to take some getting used to. "Fine. I won't kill him." *Yet.* He motioned her on. "Keep talking."

"Reaper passion is very violent, much more so than humans. All their drives—a Reaper is stronger physically and mentally, his passions are stronger. Human women don't tend to do well with that."

"Meaning?"

"They get hurt, or they die, or they get bit and become mad."

"So you're telling me Reapers have a hard time finding a sexual companion."

She nodded. "It's forbidden for Reapers to associate with human women."

"So Isaiah told me. Under penalty of death. And yet he's still alive."

"Blade had a lot to do with that."

"Who's Blade?"

She sighed and sat back down. Her posture was proper as always. It was good to see she hadn't changed completely. "No one's really sure of that, either, except everyone knows he's a very powerful Reaper."

"Figures."

She eyed him sternly. "He saved my life."

"I'll keep that in mind." He finished his cup of coffee in one long pull. Taking the cup from his hand, she refilled it.

The pot rattled as she set it back on the coals.

"There are some that believe Reapers and humans should never mix. And others . . ."

Taking the cup from his hand, she took a sip, fanning her mouth when the hot liquid scalded her.

"Careful, it's hot."

She glared at him. He smiled back and prompted, "And others?"

"They believe that if a woman can be converted and mated, then she can breed Reaper children."

Hearing the word "breed" coming from his cousin's mouth in regard to herself and other women just didn't set well.

"So you're telling me that you, Miranda, and the other women here are targets for a bunch of locos that want to have babies with you?"

"Just Miranda, Cindy, and I. The other women haven't been converted."

"Lovely. And Jenny?"

"Clark says she was born Reaper."

"Says?"

"There's some doubt to that but others are willing to believe it's true so they are willing to bend the mating law."

Which explained why Clark felt he was entitled to two women.

"Isaiah's downright open-minded."

Addy shook her head. "It's not Isaiah but the council. Isaiah doesn't believe the laws are well thought out."

"No. I don't suppose he would, seeing as obeying them means he would lose you." He got a glare for the observation. "Just what is this council?"

"Every pack has a group of men who make decisions and interpret the laws handed down by the national council."

"A Reaper court, in essence."

She nodded. "Clark has influence with the council."

"The same council Isaiah asked what to do about me?"

She nodded. "They're leaving you to Isaiah's discretion, by the way."

"Counting on the hostility between us to settle things?"

Addy smiled slightly. "Probably."

He could work with that. "So why the hard shove for Reaper children?"

"Some feel the children will be superior."

"And what do they intend to do with these 'superior children'?" He had an idea, but he wanted to hear it.

"I don't know. I assume they think it will give them an advantage and that they'll be able to gather some power. I mean it's what men always want—power. It's what the people that kidnapped me wanted. It's what the men that converted Isaiah wanted—power. Everything's all about power."

"And what do you want, Addy?"

"I want peace and quiet and time to enjoy the man I love."

"That ship sailed."

She nodded. "I know."

Leaning against him, she hugged him. Regret permeated her energy.

"You shouldn't have come after me, Cole."

"You knew I would."

She sighed. "I'd hoped you wouldn't."

"I promised you that you'd never be taken again, Addy."

"And I wasn't taken this time. I walked away."

"With him."

He glanced down the street to where he heard Isaiah's voice raised above the others.

"Yes"

"Even knowing what he is, what being with him could cost you?"

"Yes."

"He's really worth all that to you?"

She nodded. "And more. He lives for me. He'd die for me, and he makes me happy."

And she'd do the same for Jones. Cole could read it in her face, feel it in her energy, An energy that used to be a lot weaker.

Reapers. He cocked an eyebrow at her.

"Did you become stronger when you converted, Addy?"

Had he really asked his cousin that, as if being converted was a normal thing?

She licked her lips and took a step back. "I became a lot of things, but yes, I am stronger."

"You don't need your worry stone anymore."

She shook her head. "I've got Isaiah."

She really did love him. Reese was right.

"You're being foolish, you know. You'd be safer back at the ranch."

She shook her head again. "No, I wouldn't. That's still in Reaper territory, and the rumors are out. They would look for me there, and they'd kill everybody to get to me. You, Reese, and Ryan. And I'd be in a worse position than I am now."

"Do you really believe that?"

"I really believe that you would die trying to protect me from something of which you have no comprehension."

"How much comprehension do I need?"

"Close your eyes and think back to when you were very, very young and there were bumps in the night and monsters under your bed and gargoyles in the closet, multiply your fear by ten, and then you might just have an inkling of what you'd be up against."

"Shit, Addy, and you're one of them?"

"Not them. Not the crazies. But yeah, I'm Reaper, and I love my husband, and I'm going to make a life with him even if it's hard."

"How about if it's impossible?"

"Nothing is impossible. You taught me that."

He slapped his hand against his thigh, his fingers rubbing up and down the holster of his revolver.

"I might have steered you a bit wrong there."

"No, you didn't. I knew you were going to come for me, Cole. The whole time when I was captured by the Indians, I knew you were going to come for me, and I did just what you said. I stayed alive, and I believed. And when those other men kidnapped me, I did everything you said. I remembered their faces. I did what I had to do to stay alive, and I came home. Nobody's ever given anyone a better gift than that faith you gave me."

Threading her fingers through his, she brought his hand to her cheek. He wanted to yank it away before she could say what she was going to say. He'd been taking care of Addy for twenty years. To the point she was more daughter than cousin. He knew her like the back of his hand, which meant he knew all the wishing in the world couldn't stop a determined Addy. But he tried anyway.

"Don't say it."

Tears moistened her eyes as her gaze met his. "It's time for you to let me go, Cole. Time for you to stop worrying about me and start making your own life."

"I've got a life."

She patted his arm. "You're thirty-five years old, Cole. You're famous as a bounty hunter and rancher. You've created so much from so little, but you've got nothing for yourself. You have no woman, no wife. Your house looks like a barn without a single nicety."

"Three men live there."

She let him go and shook her head. "You haven't built your life to have a future. You've just built a . . . space."

She moved her hands up and down her thighs, her fingers rubbing unconsciously on the stone that she no longer carried. Cole couldn't look away. He was so used to seeing her with that worry stone. He'd given it to her, and now it was gone. She didn't need it though, and she was trying to tell him she didn't need him.

"I like my life just fine."

"Then it's my turn to tell you, you're being a fool. You need to find a woman that makes your heart beat faster, a woman who you'd die for and who'd die for you. You need to have kids. You need to have a real life."

"Fuck, Addy."

She stood. "I can't be the reason you stay alive anymore, Cole. You saved me, you healed me, and for whatever guilt you feel, whatever debt you think you owe, I absolve you of it."

She was tearing the rug out from under his feet. Addy was fragile. She'd always needed him. "Addy . . ."

She opened her arms to include the whole dilapidated village. "This is my life now. I'm happy."

"As a Reaper."

"Don't say it with such disgust. Through you and then Isaiah and then by becoming a Reaper, I found that person that was lost so long ago. I don't regret anything. I'm me again."

"And if they kill you?"

"Then I'll die with no regrets." Standing on tiptoe, she straightened his hat before brushing his hair off his forehead.

"Can you say the same, Cole?"

He wanted to rail at her, but the energy coming at him was just as calm and as focused as he'd ever felt from anyone. Addy meant what she said. She was comfortable in the middle of this chaos, trying to build something from nothing, living hand to mouth, being hunted.

She was happy.

"Son of a bitch, Addy."

"What?"

He took a step back. "I think I'm jealous."

She smiled at him. "You should be. More than that, you should be looking for the same kind of love for yourself. Now"—she pointed down the way—"the men are training down there. You might want to join them."

"Aren't you worried I'm going to get my butt kicked?"

She shrugged. "You probably will, but that's never stopped you before."

"Because I'm a hardheaded son of a bitch?"

She said, "Because you're a Cameron and a force to be reckoned with."

"I do need to talk to Isaiah."

She rolled her eyes. "Not about me, I hope."

"Nope, Addy girl, for once you're not on the menu."

She smiled as if he'd just given her a gift. "Thank you."

THE village wasn't that big. It didn't take Cole any time to get to the empty field at the edge. In the muddy grass, men were fighting hand to hand. No weapons. They moved with the ease and grace of well-trained warriors. Another thing not to hate about Isaiah. The man believed in being prepared.

It didn't take long for Cole's presence to be noticed. One by one the men came to a halt. One young kid stopped midfight. His opponent's blow hit him in the side of the face. Blood sprayed from his nose as he went down.

Cole cocked an eyebrow at the boy. "Don't ever let down your guard, son. The fight's not over until the other party can't stand up anymore."

"Who the hell are you to tell me anything?" the kid snarled, getting to his feet.

"The one that can put you back down there again if you don't keep your mouth shut."

Isaiah came up. "I see you're being as charming as ever, Cole."

"This is one of my good days."

"Uh-huh."

There was a cut on the other man's cheekbone and a bruise on his chin.

"What brings you to this edge of town?"

"You're training. Thought I'd join in."

Isaiah's eyes narrowed. "These are Reapers. You're human."

"Everybody keeps telling me that."

"You'll get hurt."

"Seems to me if Reapers are going to be my enemy, it stands to reason that I ought to learn their strengths and weaknesses."

"Everyone's different."

"But I'm sure there are certain consistencies."

"Yes." Isaiah looked at him. "Are you ready for what you'll see?"

Cole remembered Addy's comment about the gargoyles in the closet.

"It's been mentioned."

"That's not an answer."

"Do you think anything you can tell me is going to prepare me for the reality of what you're afraid to show me?"

"No. I also can't promise you they'll"—he pointed to the field—"remember that you don't regrow parts."

"Then I guess I'd better keep my guard up."

Isaiah shook his head and sighed. "You should probably do that regardless."

"You gonna let me train?"

Isaiah didn't look happy about it. "Addy's going to have my head for this."

If Isaiah didn't know Addy had sent him down here, Cole wasn't going to enlighten him. "I know."

"You don't seem upset."

"I owe you, Isaiah. A lot of sleepless nights, a lot of stress, and one punch in the jaw."

"And this is going to make up for it?"

"Well, watching Addy take a strip off of you if I get hurt, knowing you might not find your bed so warm tonight, would ease a bit of the sting."

"You're a hard man, Cole Cameron."

"It's a hard country."

Isaiah looked up to the mountaintop. "It's gonna get harder."

"Then all of us have to be in the best shape that we can be."

Isaiah didn't deny it. Some things didn't need repeating.

THE training wasn't just rough; it was brutal. For the first fifteen minutes Cole went hand to hand with some of the younger Reapers. What they lacked in skill they made up for in speed and agility. By the time he'd been out there twenty minutes, Cole was sweating and getting a real appreciation for the battle potential of a Reaper. They not only had lightning reflexes, but hitting them was like hitting a brick wall, and damage that normally would have dropped a human merely made them grunt. Cole had to change his whole style. He had to fight the way he'd once told Addy to fight—with cunning rather than muscle.

It was, he decided as he went down for the tenth time, his ears ringing and his vision blurring, a humbling experience.

This time when he went to get up, Dirk put his hand out, those green eyes of his showing a grudging respect.

"You don't have to keep doing this. You can just stay down."

"And miss the fun? I don't think so."

"You don't have anything to prove."

"But I've got a hell of a lot to learn."

At that Dirk tugged, pulling Cole to his feet, and the flatness of his gaze was replaced with a touch of approval.

"There's a lot of Addy in you."

"I'm older than her. There's a lot of me in her."

"I prefer to think of it the other way around."

"Why?"

"I like Addy."

Cole smiled and then winced as the cut on his lip split again. Isaiah called a break. Everybody headed for the water barrels. The day was warming up.

"That's one advantage you'll have," Dirk said.

"What?"

"Reapers are susceptible to dehydration."

"More so than people?"

"Our bodies work much faster, which burns more liquid. It's not the heat that gets us; it's the exertion."

Looking around, Cole did notice that while he was thirsty and taking a drink, the Reapers were guzzling water.

"So there is a vulnerability."

"There's a couple. There are other things you've gotta watch out for." Dirk took the dipper passed immediately to him when he reached the barrel. Apparently, even in Reaper society, skills were admired and deference was shown to those of higher rank.

Dirk dipped the dipper in the bucket and passed it to Cole; a couple of the young men frowned, and others made note. How anyone felt about the big Reaper showing friendship to Cole was kept under control.

"The Reapers you'll likely be fighting?"

Cole said, "Yeah?"

"They're excitable. Get their goat, and they get sloppy."

Cole nodded. "Anything else I should know?" he asked as he handed the dipper to the next in line.

"Yeah. Clark's not real happy with you."

"Clark can kiss my ass."

"He's more likely to rip out your throat."

Cole fondled his knife. "He's welcome to try."

"He has mating rights over Miranda."

"Well, I'm claiming squatter's rights."

Dirk smiled. "You like the widow?"

"More than that, I don't like to see any woman backed into a corner."

"Well, neither do I."

"Then why aren't you doing something about it?"

Dirk shrugged. "My hands are tied."

"Reaper law?"

"Reaper law."

"It's Clark's bad luck then that I'm not Reaper."

"The thought had crossed my mind." Dirk's grin faded as he watched the men regather on the field. "Providing you survive practice."

8

BY THE TIME TRAINING WAS OVER, COLE FELT AS IF HE'D been trampled in a stampede. Every bone in his body ached, his muscles were bruised, he was bleeding from a half dozen scrapes and sporting a split lip, and one of the young pups had come damn close to breaking his nose. The only thing he wanted was a long, hot soak in a bath, a bottle of whiskey, and a bed.

And for all that he was really no closer to understanding the origins of the Reapers than he had been that morning. But there was one thing he did understand about them. They were damn dedicated fighters. And disciplined. Even the youngest ones had control, and that he attributed to Isaiah's leadership. For a man rumored to be crazy, he ran a tight outfit.

Cole adjusted his hat to block the sun and winced again. Damn, he was going to hurt when he got up tomorrow. As soon as the thought passed, he realized that he didn't have a place to sleep. He'd given Miranda and Wendy back their house, which left him homeless. Ah well. It wouldn't be the first time he'd slept with the live-stock. But first, he'd have to swing by Miranda's to get his things. Pain in his lip alerted him to the fact he was smiling. For no other reason than he was going to see her.

You need to find a woman that makes your heart beat faster . . .

Fuck. That was the last thing he needed. Jamming his hat on his head, he walked faster. Determination kept his resolve steady right up until two houses from hers when he felt the first touch of her energy. Sweet, hot, and seductive, it slid over his with no intent, just an instinctive reach that sank deep. His heart beat faster. His breath quickened, and his cock throbbed.

Dammit. He didn't need this, but need it or not, as soon as he saw Miranda through the open door, he knew his protests were too late. Even standing at the table, a tan apron tied over her dress, with her hair pulled back in a braid and flour smeared on her cheek, she was the most compelling woman he'd ever seen. His steps slowed as he took in the view and the sensation. Her moves were smooth and efficient as she rolled out the dough, then grabbed a metal cup. For sure she was making biscuits. He took off his hat. Did the woman have to be that perfect?

He knocked on the door. She didn't jump. Had she sensed him as he had her?

"Afternoon."

She nodded and looked him over from head to toe. If he'd gone by her expression, he wouldn't have thought she gave a shit. But as connected as he was to her energy, there was no mistaking the stress of well-concealed worry.

"You survived training."

Her tone matched her expression.

"You didn't really think Isaiah was going to let anybody kill his wife's cousin, did you?"

She shrugged. "I didn't think so, but I also wasn't sure how aggravating you intended to be."

"No one *intends* to be aggravating."

"You do."

He motioned with his hat. "You've got flour on your face."

She rubbed her cheek against her shoulder, spreading the flour farther.

He shook his head and walked over. "You're just making it worse."

She took a step back. Catching her arm, he put a halt to her flight, and with the sleeve of his shirt, he gently wiped the flour from her cheek, replacing it with a streak of blood.

"Damn."

"What?"

He caught her hand before she could touch the spot.

It bothered him more than he cared to admit to see her bloody from his touch.

"You can't get it off?"

He chose a clean section of his sleeve and wiped. "I got it off."

His response was harsher than he intended.

She shifted uncomfortably and put her other hand over her scarred cheek.

"Don't."

Her gaze snapped to his. "Then stop staring."

"Stop telling me what to do."

"Why?"

He caught that hand, too, and pulled it away, revealing her insecurity and the perfection of her imperfections.

"Because I told you to."

"And who are you?"

"The man who thinks you're beautiful."

She blinked. Just blinked.

"Don't fucking cry."

"I'm not."

The hell she wasn't. "Ah, hell."

He pulled her into his arms, cradling her against his chest. She stood stiffly. He didn't care. She felt damn good in his arms. Tiny. Soft. Right.

There was a sniff and then, "You swear too much."

"I know." She rubbed her cheek against him.

"In case you missed it, I'm sweaty and covered in grime." His conscience demanded he tell her that.

"I know."

She didn't move, and he didn't mention it again. He just held her, and she . . . well, she just held on. It was peaceful with her energy smoothing along his, but then that peace started to stir restlessly and a subtle heat built and spread. His cock twitched. Before she could notice, he broke the silence.

"Lunch smells good."

"Thank you. Isaiah dropped off a rabbit."

His stomach rumbled loudly. "Rabbit stew is my favorite."

He felt her smile against his chest. "Are you angling for an invitation?"

"Are you offering?"

"I wasn't planning on company."

"I just came by for my things."

"I put them over there." She stepped back and pointed to the side of the door. His arms immediately felt empty. But at least the grime on him hadn't dirtied her. "It didn't take much packing."

He couldn't tell if her tone was censoring or approving. "I travel light."

He grabbed up his saddlebags and opened the flap.

"It's all there," she said, pouring water into the washbowl to clean her hands.

He supposed it was, but the checking seemed to irritate her, and since he was irritated she hadn't invited him to lunch, he continued his inspection.

Wiping her hands on a towel, she frowned at him as she went back to the table. "I wouldn't steal."

"Never thought you would, but you might have missed something."

"In a place this small?"

"Things happen."

Just then his stomach chose to rumble again. She sighed and cut out another biscuit before flipping it onto the pan.

Brushing a tendril of hair off her cheek with her shoulder, she asked, "Would you like to stay for lunch?"

"Yes."

"That was quick."

"I'm hungry."

"So I noticed."

"And you're a soft touch."

Another sigh. "I'm working on it."

"Don't work too hard on my account."

This time a half-amused roll of the eyes accompanied her sigh. "Where's Wendy?"

"Addy's teaching her how to sew at her place."

"That ought to be interesting considering Addy doesn't know one end of the needle from the other."

"We're all learning new things here, and right now the big challenge is threading the needle."

"I see." He put the saddlebags down and winced.

She sighed and looked at his face and made a bow out of the last of the biscuit dough before putting it in the pan with the others. "Sit down before you fall down."

She turned and dusted off her hands. Heading back to the basin, she rinsed them off before carrying the basin to the door and tossing the dirty water outside. Setting the basin on the table, she motioned him over.

"Sit down here. Let me tend to your cuts."

"Giving orders now, are you?"

Getting the pitcher, she poured fresh water into the basin. "You're going to bleed all over my house."

"I'm not dripping anymore, am I?" He checked his lip and winced again.

She shook her head and pulled out a chair. "Sit down, will you?"

"It's all right."

She snapped the towel at the chair. "Sit. And don't be worrying I'm going to think you're weak. You just spent four hours battling with Reapers, and you're still alive. I think weak is a moot point."

He sat in the chair, feeling awkward and strange. Taking his hat from him, she set it on the spindle of the adjacent chair.

"Just sit still and let me take care of this."

He eyed her warily. He was pretty sure the cut on his lip needed a stitch. "You have a lot of experience patching up men?"

"Fair to middlin'."

"Your husband was the brawling kind?"

She shook her head. "No, but on the wagon train out, there were several boys, and they were always getting into one scrape or another."

She dipped the rag in the water and dabbed at his cheek. He winced, just for show. Her touch got gentler, smoother, so when she dabbed at the other cheek, he winced again. She stopped and looked at him. He looked up at her, keeping his expression blank.

She dipped the cloth in the water; red ran outward from the cloth. This time she held it against his lip tenderly. She had to stand in front of him to do it. Her breasts were inches from his face. All he had to do was lean in, and he could take the point of one in his mouth, nibble it through the cloth of her dress, roll it across his tongue. Fuck. His breath caught. Her energy twitched, became more sensual. She was aware of him, too.

"Hold that against your lip," she said.

"You're going to soak the scab off."

"I want to. It needs some salve. Maybe a stitch."

"I'm not putting salve on my lip, that stuff tastes like"—he caught himself before he could say "shit"—"crap."

"It'll scar."

"What's one more scar, honey? I've got tons of them already."

That got a frown out of her. "Are you hurt anywhere else?"

He lifted his right arm, checked the scrape. It wasn't too deep. "No, I'm good."

She grabbed his wrist, lifted his arm, and checked the same scrape. "No, you're not."

She lathered some soap on the sponge and worked at his arm, soaking the dirt out of the scrape. It stung like hell. His breath hissed in.

"Hey!"

"Don't be such a baby," she told him. "That blow to your lip hurt much more than this."

"Yeah, but that I wasn't doing to myself."

"Well, you're not doing this to yourself, either. I'm doing it to you."

"Why?"

"So you won't get an infection."

"Do Reapers get infections?"

She shook her head. "No."

"Why not?"

"I don't know."

"Seems you all don't know much about anything."

"That's the truth."

"And yet somebody's out there making laws."

She nodded.

"You realize that doesn't make any sense."

"I realize that, but I'm not the one making any decisions."

"Isaiah is?"

She shook her head again, "No. The council has the decision-making skills, and it makes the laws that pertain to us within the framework of the original laws."

He wasn't fond of anything that set itself up as a council. "They changing them as they find more facts?"

"We hope so. Isaiah is sending a petition through Blade."

"Who's Blade?"

"Addy knows him."

Blade was clearly a man he had to meet. "I know but I haven't had the pleasure. Who is he? To the people here."

"Enforcer. Rule breaker." She shrugged. "Nobody knows for sure, but he's a very powerful Reaper."

"More so than Isaiah?"

"Isaiah is, I guess . . . what you'd considered an outlaw among the Reapers."

"Because he took Addy as his wife?"

"That's part of it, but mainly because"—she shrugged again—"he's a good man. He doesn't believe having power gives a body the right to exploit it."

" 'Exploit.' That's a big word."

She dabbed harder. "Not so big you didn't understand it."

"My ma was big on book learning."

"So was mine."

"You like to read?"

She nodded. He looked around. There weren't any books, which wasn't a surprise. Books were heavy and fragile. Both aspects made them a luxury ill afforded by many.

As if reading his mind, she said, "I miss them. More than that, I miss them for Wendy."

"A kid should have books."

"I'm working on it."

She seemed to be working on a lot of things.

"Isaiah said he'd try to get some for the children." Tilting her head she studied his lip. "I actually think this will heal without a stitch."

"Good." He growled under his breath. "I'm going to have to stop thinking of Isaiah as a monster, aren't I?"

She nodded. "Especially as there aren't that many Reapers that care about good."

He looked around. "But some do."

"Yeah."

"And Isaiah is gathering them up, trying to make something out of nothing."

"Yes."

"In a society that doesn't have much value for him."

"Yes."

Shit. That was such a human thing to do. Every town that'd sprung up here in the West was a case of someone trying to make something decent out of chaos.

"How did you end up with him?"

She blinked and jerked. "He found me."

He winced for real this time. "Found you?"

She nodded and resumed her dabbing at his scrape. "Our wagon train had been attacked. I was taken prisoner."

"Indians?"

"Rogues."

"Rogue Reapers or humans?"

It was scary how he was beginning think of Reapers as normal.

"Reapers." Her fingers touched her scarred cheek the way they did when she felt uncomfortable. Addy had her worry stone. Miranda had her scars. "I wasn't well. He brought me here and took care of me."

"What about Wendy?"

"When I was better, he fetched her for me."

"From where?"

She looked at him and didn't answer. Just rinsed the soap from his arm.

"I asked you a question."

"And I don't want to answer."

That was blunt. "What if I insist?"

She looked up. "Then I'm not going to give you lunch."

"You strike a hard bargain."

She shrugged and inspected the scrape for any bits of dirt. Her fingers lingered on the puncture wounds from his own battle with the Rogues.

"This isn't from today."

"No. I got that before I got here." Her nail caught at his skin, and he winced.

"I'm sorry"

"No problem."

She looked at him. "Are you staying for lunch?"

He nodded, accepting the price. "I'll stop poking about."

Not because she ordered him to but because he kinda liked the way she fussed over him. Liked the way her hair smelled. Liked the way her fingers lingered on his skin in a subtle caress. He'd never been one for being fussed over, and quite frankly there'd never been much of an opportunity for anybody to fuss. If stitching needed to be done and he couldn't do it himself, he went to the nearest town, or his brothers took care of it. But it was different being cared for by a woman. Her touch was gentler, soothing, less offhand. He could see how a man could get used to it.

He couldn't resist adding, "For now."

That "for now" got another wary glance.

He reached up to brush her hair off her cheek. It was a thought-less gesture backed by nothing more than instinct. She jerked back. His senses snapped to attention at that flick of fear. He wanted to ask what exactly happened on that wagon train, but it didn't take a genius to figure out what could have happened to a beautiful woman after the lust of battle.

"I'm sorry," he told her, keeping his voice as gentle as he could. It still sounded pretty rough to him. "You've got flour on your cheek again."

"Oh." She rubbed at it with her shoulder.

He took the cloth from her hand; picking a clean corner, he dabbed at her face, and then he handed it back.

"There."

Her skin was white and creamy, not tanned like he would expect. He wondered if that was because she was a Reaper or if she just didn't do much in the sun.

"What's it like for a woman to be a Reaper?"

She shrugged. "What's it like for anyone to be anything?"

"You're evading the question."

"Yes, I am."

"Why?"

She wrung the rag out. "I don't want you to get to know me, and I certainly don't want to get to know you."

"Why?"

"Because you're a threat to everything I've planned."

"Why?"

"You know why."

He did, but he wasn't above a lie when it served his purpose. "No, I don't."

"Because we're attracted to each other, and if we act on that attraction, you're going to get killed, and then after they kill you, they're going to come after me."

"You're attracted to me."

"That was not the important part of my statement."

He dismissed that. "Someone's always trying to kill me."

She huffed and dropped the rag on the table. "I can see why, but in this case it's better you just let this go."

"What if I don't want to?"

"What part of they're going to kill us did you not understand?"

"They won't touch you."

"Says you?"

"Yeah." He'd kill everyone and burn the fucking compound down around the corpses if anyonee tried to hurt her.

"And when you leave?"

"I'll take you with me."

Her breath caught, and her energy flickered with a hope that was snuffed out as soon as it flared. "That won't be safe."

"For whom?"

"You."

This time he did brush that tendril of hair off her cheek, and he didn't pull his hand back, just let it rest against the softness of her skin, absorbing her heat and her tension. "China doll, I'm in the back of beyond, living in a nest of Reapers, half of which would like to kill me, learning to fight a whole new way because I get the impression there are other Reapers coming to threaten mine. What of any of the facts you know about me makes you think I'm interested in being safe?"

She shook her head. "I can't explain."

"You can say anything you want to me."

Her energy pushed with the desperation of a cornered animal. "There's no taking back some things once they've been said."

"Who's asking you to?"

"Addy will."

"This doesn't involve Addy."

She dropped the rag into the basin, and water splashed over the side. "I owe her. You're her cousin."

"You owe me more."

Grabbing the rag back up, she slapped it dripping wet into his hand.

"Clean the rest of your cuts yourself. I'm going to put the biscuits on the fire."

She marched outside, biscuit pan in hand. He thought about following, but he hadn't gotten this far in life by pushing past the point of results, and it wouldn't be productive to push Miranda any more. She was clearly a woman at her limit.

A woman who was attracted to him. He smiled and scrubbed his knuckles. A man could work with that.

AFTER a tense lunch Cole grabbed up his saddlebags.

"Thank you for the hospitality."

Beyond a "You're welcome" Miranda didn't say a word. Pretending a grumpiness he didn't feel, hiding a smile he couldn't quit, Cole strode out the door, taking the right to Addy's house. With any luck Isaiah would still be there.

As soon as he reached Addy's, he knew Isaiah was home. The energy from inside the small building was intense, sexual. The ass was bedding his cousin. Cole knocked on the door harder than he needed to.

"Addy?" he called out.

There was some swearing and then a "Go away" from Isaiah.

Cole had no intention of going anywhere. "I've got a question to ask."

"Ask it later."

The hell he was going to ask it later. There was too much satisfaction in asking it now.

"Can't wait."

"Why not?"

"Because apparently not knowing the answer is going to get me killed."

He heard a gasp, distinctly feminine, and a curse, distinctly masculine. He'd figured that would work. From the thump he bet Addy had all but pushed Isaiah out of bed.

"Just a minute."

Leaning against the side of the house, he smiled and asked, with a touch of feigned unease, "Think I got that long?"

The door opened. Isaiah walked out, his jeans pulled up but not buttoned, his cock clearly shoved hastily inside. The exact image of a perfectly frustrated man.

Cole grinned.

Isaiah closed the door slowly.

"This had better be good, or I'm going to kill you myself."

"Is that any way to talk to your new cousin?"

"My soon to be dead cousin if he doesn't get on with it."

"What kind of attraction could a Reaper woman feel for a human that would get him and her and her daughter killed?"

The question landed between them like a bomb. Isaiah's energy came to a pinpoint. Cole felt a tickling in his mind. With everything in him, he thrust back. Isaiah's eyebrows went up.

"You're an interesting man, Cole Cameron."

"I'm not interested in being interesting to you. I want an answer to my question."

Isaiah looked around and stepped slowly away from the door. With a flick of his fingers he motioned that Cole should follow.

"Where are we going?"

"Out of earshot."

Cole looked around. He couldn't see anybody nearby.

"Reaper earshot," Isaiah explained.

They went to the edge of the woods. Isaiah stopped just inside the trees. Cole felt Isaiah's energy spread out. He'd always wondered if the man could read minds. He no longer doubted the answer to that was "yes."

"Who are we talking about here?" Isaiah asked.

Cole turned slightly so the sun wasn't in his eyes and leaned against a tree. "Who do you think?"

"Miranda."

"And what makes you think she has an attraction for you?"

"She asked me to leave, and when I dawdled—"

"If you forced her—"

"You want to be eating your teeth?" Cole interrupted.

Isaiah straightened in that deceptively slow way he had. "You think you've got what it takes?"

Cole pushed off the trunk. "Yeah, I do."

Isaiah tilted his head to the side as if assessing Cole's potential. This time when Cole pushed against that tickle, it wasn't so easy to eject. With a nod Isaiah broke the connection, "I believe you just might. Someday. But today is not that day. So just answer my question so I can get back to my wife."

Cole wanted to snarl at that.

"Miranda implied her attraction to me wasn't an ordinary attraction. That it was something Reaper."

Isaiah whistled under his breath. "Mating potential."

Cole blinked. "Which is?"

"A bonding that is so elemental it goes beyond what the humans call love. Valued not only for the strength of the bond but because only bonded couples are believed to have the potential to produce children."

Cole knew the attraction he felt for Miranda was deep, but that deep? "What happens if Miranda and I have this mating potential?"

"Things get interesting."

"Why?"

"We thought that mating potential was a onetime thing."

"And?"

"If Miranda isn't lying, that was a mistake."

"You're saying the attraction she feels for me is the same attraction she feels for Clark?"

"I don't know. We would have to analyze it."

"Analyze it how?"

Isaiah ran his hand through his hair before buttoning up his jeans.

"I don't fucking know."

Cole was getting sick of "I don't knows."

"What *do* you know?"

"Apparently less every day."

Despite himself Cole had to feel for the man. His frustration consumed his energy. "How did you become Reaper?"

"I was kidnapped, and somehow they made it happen."

"Somehow? They?"

With a wave of his hand, Isaiah dismissed the questions. "That's not important. I'm more concerned about this attraction Miranda feels. You haven't encouraged it?"

"I haven't exactly *dis*couraged it."

Isaiah's gaze snapped to his. "You feel it, too."

"She's a beautiful woman."

"She's average looking at best."

"She's fucking beautiful."

Isaiah shook his head. "This is going to complicate everything."

He didn't look unhappy. "What?"

"Clark has petitioned to have you removed."

"The boy doesn't like humans?"

"The man doesn't like *you*. I was wondering why, but now I know. Without you here he had a clear shot."

"Life is rough."

Isaiah ran his hand through his hair again and shook his head again. "Hard to believe, but you just might be the answer to a prayer, Cameron."

"Oh yeah?"

"Yeah. No one wanted Miranda marrying Clark, but my hands were tied."

"Because of the mating attraction." Cole hated the thought of Miranda being attracted to that brute.

Isaiah nodded. "But what you may not know is she didn't have one to him."

"Then how the hell did that get approved?"

Isaiah shrugged "The council thought a one-way thing was enough, but if your attraction is mutual, that decision can be challenged."

"It shouldn't exist in the first place."

"But it does."

Cole ground his teeth. "So she has to marry Clark, whether she wants to or not, put up with his moods, and share him with another woman because a bunch of men decided a one-way attraction fit the law?"

Isaiah shrugged. "Reaper law is far from perfect."

"If it's anything, it's permanently flawed." The thought of Miranda with another man pissed Cole off.

Isaiah's eyebrows went up. Cole wasn't used to anyone being able to read him the way he could read others. It was damn irritating.

"Shut the hell up."

An equally irritating smile ghosted Isaiah's lips. "I haven't said a word."

"She's not marrying that ass."

"She doesn't have an option."

"He's a brute."

"He'd be controlled."

Like hell. Cole ground his teeth, picturing Wendy and Miranda stuck with Clark, little more than slaves in his home, cowering beneath his anger.

"You said there has to be a mating attraction for a wedding to be recognized?"

"Yeah."

"And mutual trumps one-sided?"

"Yup."

Cole jammed his hat down on his head. "Then she's fucking got an option."

❧ 9 ❧

THE ONE THING ABOUT TOSSING OUT DYNAMITE WAS
that it didn't always explode when you wanted. Sometimes it just
sat there, fuse hissing, dragging on your nerves. At least that's how Cole
felt ever since he'd staked his claim on Miranda earlier that afternoon.
Now, hours later, Cole was sitting in front of the barn whittling on a
stick, wishing he could turn his mind away from the potential as easily
as Isaiah had shaken his head and turned away. But the thought was in
his head and wouldn't budge. Every time he saw Miranda that subtle
little sense of possession flowed past his control, whispering "mine" in
his head, and that sexual pull he'd been fighting just got stronger until
watching her walk down the street caused his cock to get hard.

He imagined coming up behind her, sliding his hands around
her waist, pulling her back against him, leaning down, kissing the
side of her neck, sliding a hand up to her breast through her clothing, flicking his thumb across the nipple, hearing her gasp, feeling
her melt back against him and that soft nub harden to his touch.

Damn. He shifted his leg. He had it bad. For a woman who was determined to give herself to another next week. Digging the knife into the stick, he gouged off a bump. Maybe. If he let the son of a bitch live.

As if the thought conjured the bastard, Clark came out of one of the houses and caught up with Miranda. The snarl started in his gut as Clark grabbed her arm. There was nothing in Miranda's body language that said she welcomed the other man's advances. Nothing to say she rejected them, either. She just stood there looking at him. That is until Clark tugged her arm again.

Miranda took a step back, obviously not liking whatever Clark had said. Clark immediately crowded her back against the nearby house. Inside Cole the snarl built.

"He makes her cry," a small voice said from around elbow height. Goddamn, Wendy was sneaky.

He looked down. She was looking at the couple. All he could see was the neat part in her hair. "Your mom know you're out here in the barn again?"

Wendy shook her head. "I'm supposed to be taking a nap before supper."

Supposed to be. He cocked an eyebrow at her. She wasn't paying him any mind. She was frowning at Clark.

"You're going to get a whipping."

The quick glance she cut him afforded him an excellent view of her outthrust lower lip. "I don't care."

"Uh-huh." He had to fight back a grin at the bravado. He continued whittling. "That's mighty big talk from a mighty small person."

She was back to glaring at Clark. "Mama says he's going to be my new daddy."

So Miranda had broken the news to Wendy.

"I take it that's not settling well?"

She shook her head. "I don't want him to be my daddy."

What was he supposed to say to that?

"Sometimes you need to give people a chance."

"He hurts Mommy."

Except when it came to that. Still, there was a chance Wendy had misunderstood. Adults making love could look like a fight to a kid. Cole approached even more gingerly.

"Things aren't always as they appear."

She turned and gave him a pitying look. "She has bruises on her arms. And when he thinks no one's looking, he'll pinch her real hard so she'll do what he says."

The snarl built to rage. The knife cut deep. The stick snapped in two. "You see an awful lot."

"Mommy doesn't want me to, but I peek."

He bet. "You, little girl, do a lot of things you're not supposed to be doing. Rules are made to be followed."

"I don't like the rules."

Neither did he, but he wasn't a fairy child.

"It's a not a matter of you liking them or not; it's a matter of keeping order and doing what needs to be done."

"I won't follow any of *his* rules." She stuck out her lip farther. "Ever."

She was back to glaring at Clark. Across the way Miranda was back to retreating. Her flight was hampered by a large wooden barrel. The smile on Clark's face when she realized she was trapped had Cole straightening. He dropped the stick but kept the knife out.

"Your mama's doing what she thinks is best for you, and you don't help her any by breaking the rules."

"I don't want her to marry him. He's mean," Wendy added.

Yeah, he was. Meanspirited, mean hearted. Just flat out mean.

"Is there anybody you *would* like to see with your mom?"

She looked at him out of the corner of her eye. "You don't have a wife."

"No, I don't."

"My mama's real pretty."

Clearly, six-year-olds didn't waste much time on subtlety.

"Yeah, she is. But I'm not." He ruffled her hair. "If you scoot, you can get back into bed before your mom knows you were out."

"I'm too old to take naps; she was just worried 'cause I sneezed."

"You're not too old if your mom says so."

She didn't have a ready comeback for that. But after a second she came up with, "I can't go back now anyway."

"Why not?"

"*He'll* see me and get mad, and they'll fight."

"You're probably right." Clark didn't look any too happy at the moment. Whatever Miranda was saying was not what he wanted to hear. And knowing the woman's way with words, it was probably time for Cole to mosey over.

"Why don't you go back to playing in the barn?" he told Wendy. "Your mom will come looking for you soon enough when she's done with Clark."

She pouted. "She never gets to be done. He's always there."

An irritating revelation. "It just seems like it now."

Keeping his eye on the escalating confrontation, he reached over and pulled the door open. "Go on inside now. I think that orange and white momma cat had some kittens in the back corner."

"She did?"

"Be very careful, though. You can peek but don't touch. The mama will abandon them if you touch them."

"Why would she leave her babies?"

Clark swore loud enough to carry. "I don't know. Cats aren't people."

"My mama would never leave me."

He ruffled her hair again. "No, honey, she sure wouldn't." There was no end to what Miranda would do to keep her child safe.

"Mr. Clark would leave me. He doesn't like me."

"Well, we don't like him, either, do we?"

She smiled at him, revealing a missing front tooth. "No, we don't."

"Go on in now."

She walked slowly through the door, stopping to look back when Clark raised his voice again. The words weren't distinguishable, but the anger was.

He hurts Mommy.

"And don't worry about Clark. He's not going to be a problem."

"Promise?"

"Yes."

"Pinky swear?"

He eyed the tiny digit offered and shook his head. She needed to understand he was a man of his word. "I just said so."

She eyed him right back. "Some people make promises and then forget."

"Well, I'm not one of them. I keep my promises." He started to close the door, giving her no choice. "Now, scoot."

Whatever the argument was about, it looked like it was about to end. Miranda took another step back, and this time Clark didn't follow. It didn't help ease any of the aggression surging inside Cole. He didn't like that man being within a hundred feet of Miranda. Shit, he didn't like that man, period.

Wendy was right. Clark would always be around if something wasn't done about him. She was damn perceptive for a six-year-old.

Picking up a fresh stick, Cole went back to whittling, forcing himself to ease the strength of his stroke and to cloak his energy. That bit Isaiah let loose today about others listening was disturbing. He just might have been a little cocky to think he was the only one in the world that could sense people's energy. It was an advantage he'd taken for granted. It was still an advantage since Reapers saw humans as so unskilled, but it wasn't going to be much of one if he flashed everything he thought and felt. He had to work on banking his emotions. He remembered his encounter with Addy this morning. He might ask her how she did it. She'd gotten real good at hiding her energy from him and likely from others, too.

He was still working on the technique ten minutes later when Miranda came back down the path. He could tell from the length of her stride that she was not a happy woman. He kept whittling, pretending he didn't notice her approach. She kept coming, pretending she didn't know he was sitting there while her anger snapped around him. It ticked him off that she thought she could brush him aside so easily.

"Have you seen Wendy?"

"Good evening to you, too."

He felt her anger spike before she grabbed hold of it, controlled it, and banked it. She might have even managed to hide her response with anyone else but him. She ran her fingers down her braid before flipping it over her back wirh a long-suffering sigh.

"I'm sorry. Have you seen Wendy?"

He nodded. "Yeah."

"Where is she?"

"She asked me to talk to you about something first." That wasn't strictly the truth, but he wasn't above spinning a lie to bring about a good.

"I don't need you to speak for my daughter."

"She doesn't like Clark."

"I know."

"She's afraid of him."

"I can protect her."

He shook his head, jabbed the knife into the post behind him, and straightened. Catching her hand, he held her put while he unbuttoned her sleeve. He felt her energy tense a second before her muscles.

"Don't." She snarled, a short, feminine warning, backed by her equally fierce, "Let me go."

"Did you tell Clark to let you go?" He started rolling her sleeve up. She jerked on her arm. "Yes."

He held her arm still and looked in her eyes. "Did he?"

He took the second snarl as a "no."

"Then what makes you think you can make me?"

Her energy fluctuated wildly. "I can . . ."

Not before he saw what he wanted to see. He raised the sleeve up over her elbow. Small, dark ovals marred the inner curve. Fingerprints. He touched one lightly before looking in her eyes. Panic and anger warred for dominance in her expression. "You don't heal like a Reaper."

Her lips pulled back revealing her canines. "I kill like one."

He caught her other hand as she swiped at his face. She was strong. Very strong. But not stronger than him. Interesting.

He held her gaze. "Do you want me to kill him for you?"

She blinked. "What?"

"Clark." Releasing her, he asked again, "Do you want me to kill the son of a bitch for you?"

The "yes" was so strong in her face, in her energy, he was actually taken aback when she said, "No."

"Once you bind yourself to that man, by pack law you're out of options."

She licked her lips. "I have a plan."

What was she going to do? Run around the bed until the man wore out? "You can't stall him forever."

"Long enough."

"For what?"

"None of your business."

"China doll, I'm the best friend you have right now."

"Are you?"

"And I'm not going to let you let that bastard win."

She shook her head and her eyes glistened. "You have to."

That wasn't fair. "Don't you dare cry."

She blinked rapidly. "I'm not."

She was. On the inside. And had been for a long time. Damn.

He let her go. Satisfaction settled in his gut when she didn't take a step back like she had with Clark. He took her braid in his hand, ran his fingers down it. It was thick and warm from the sun. Her hair was probably beautiful when it was down, framing her face. He slid the braid up her arm, over her elbow, her shoulder, and down her back, and he kept going, tugging on her braid, pulling her head back.

She gasped. Her fingers pressed against his chest. Her eyes opened wide. Awareness flared between them.

Hell, no wonder he was hard every time he was around her. The woman made love to him just by looking at him.

"You've got no business marrying that man or even thinking about it. Not when you look at me like that."

She turned away. "I don't have an option."

He turned her back. "I'm your option."

Taking a step forward, forcing her back up against the barn wall, he saw the memories flare in her soft brown eyes as her palms pressed against his chest, but she didn't need to worry. He was nothing like Clark. He didn't want to take. He wanted to give. Everything she wanted. Everything she needed. Everything he had. Her energy embraced him. Her lips softened. Beckoned.

Cupping her wrists in his hand, he slid her palms up. "Put your arms around my neck."

She did, her protest token at best. "We're in plain view, and everyone—"

"Good." He wanted everyone to see him stake this claim.

He leaned in, and her breath caught. Her lips parted. He smiled.

Hell yeah, she wanted him. He slid his knee forward and kicked her feet apart. She sighed, a slight expulsion of breath.

"Yes," he answered the unasked question in her eyes. "I want this."

Another tug on her braid tilted her head back farther; her nails bit into his chest. Desire bit deeper still. His cock throbbed. Invisible lightning flashed around them. Her energy, his energy, all blended together. The world faded until there was only this moment, this woman, this kiss. This damn kiss.

He leaned forward, or maybe she stood on tiptoe, or, hell, maybe they just met in the middle. Who knew? Who cared? Her mouth was under his, and it was sweet, powerful. Unmistakable.

Mine. The word whispered through his conscience, through his mind, stronger now, blending with their energy, wrapping around it, pulling her toward him. He slid his knuckles down her spine, dragging her head back a little more, arching her into him so her hips rode his thigh and her breasts pressed into his chest.

He expected her to object, but instead her arms slipped farther around his neck, pulling him even closer, as she, too, felt the need to taste and to touch, the drive to be one. As if this kiss wasn't a beginning but a confirmation.

He hadn't meant for the kiss to get out of hand. He'd meant for it just to be a taste, a sampling. Just a little something to make her see *them*. Or, hell, maybe he'd just been fooling himself. There was nothing light or casual about the touch of his lips to hers. Nothing simple in the complexity of her taste. Nothing calm about the response of his senses. Where her fingers stroked his neck, his skin took fire.

She made a sound in her throat that went straight to his cock. He lifted her higher. She rose with him, her calf sliding up the back of his leg. Fuck yes, he wanted her legs around his waist, her body locked to his. She bit at his lips. Grabbing the folds of material, he dragged the skirt out of the way. She moaned and twisted against him, working her pussy against his shaft. Even through the layers of clothes, she burned him.

This is a mistake.

The warning whispered through his mind. His lust drove it back. He didn't care. Right, wrong, whatever. This is what had to be. This is what was. This is what he wanted, what he'd been searching for, only he hadn't known what it was. But now that he had it, he wasn't letting it go.

He pinned her harder into the wall, pressing every inch of her against him. This time she whimpered.

Too hard.

"Damn, I'm sorry," he groaned into her mouth, relaxing his grip a little, easing back—just a little, just enough so he wasn't crushing her but not enough to interrupt the pleasure.

"Kiss me again," she whispered back.

Hell, he hadn't stopped. He'd breathed the words into her mouth the same way she'd breathed them into his.

"Open for me."

"I am."

"Wider. I want all of you."

Her legs wrapped around his waist, her arms around his neck. Hitching herself up, she did as he demanded. Total and complete surrender. Shit.

Reaper. The thought whispered through the last bit of his remaining reason, but this time it wasn't a curse. It was an endearment.

She took all he had to give, taking his passion, his lust, his kiss; making it hers; giving it back in a way no woman ever had been able to. Wildly. Without inhibition. Matching him. Her energy blending with his to a level he'd never experienced with anyone else. It was as if she'd been made for him.

Mate. A foreign concept, but it lingered. Somehow so much more than a wife, so much deeper, and she was his.

He drew back just far enough to growl, "You're not going to marry Clark."

She didn't answer, just bit at his lower lip, begging him for more.

His hand went to the buttons on her blouse. He had five undone before a tickle of awareness snapped him to his senses. Now was not the time. This was not the place. For Pete's sake, they were in plain view of everyone.

He lifted his head. Her teeth scraped his shoulder, sank through the cloth into his skin. He felt the sting, the pressure, the utter perfection. He pressed her closer. The euphoria spread outward from the bite. *So right.*

Another trickle of awareness. People *were* watching. And the energy wasn't positive.

"Fuck." He gave her head a tug, separating her teeth from his shoulder. She growled in her throat, a threateningly sexy sound.

"You can growl all you want in private. This is a bit too public for what I'm going to do to you."

She opened her eyes, stared at him uncomprehendingly for a few seconds. And then he watched horror replace passion. Instead of digging into his chest, her fingers pushed.

After claiming him so thoroughly, it'd be a cold day in hell before he'd allow her to pretend it was a mistake. Sheer perversity made him hold her close so that she slid down his body. As soon as her feet hit the ground, she ducked to the left. He slammed his hand into the wall, making a barricade with his arm, stopping her cold. They needed to get something straight.

"You're not marrying Clark."

"I'm not?"

"No." Catching her chin on his finger, he tipped her face up to his. He kissed her again, a hard, quick press of his lips to hers, tasting her again. Letting her taste him. Because he needed it. "You're marrying me."

DINNER at Addy's that night was by command. The table was set with mismatched plates, but everything was properly aligned, and everything was in its place.

The hut was impeccable, more so than usual. Spotless. Not surprising. Addy was always at her most precise when she was most distressed.

Leaning back in his chair, Cole broke the ice. "I see you heard what happened this afternoon."

"Heard? There was a stampede to my door," Addy huffed, checking the meal.

"What's the verdict?"

"Nobody's reached a verdict. Right now it's just a lot of 'can this be, will it be allowed, what will the repercussions be?' Nobody's gotten around to what are they going to do with you."

He looked at Isaiah at the head of the rough plank table. "And on your side?"

"Same place I was this morning when we talked about it."

That didn't tell him anything. "She's not marrying Clark."

"She can't mate with you," Addy exclaimed, ladling stew into a bowl.

"Who says?" Cole asked, taking the bowl and handing her another.

"The law."

Cole brought the bowls over to the table. "Seems to me, based on what you've said, you've got two laws working here. One that says mating law takes precedence over everything, and the other that says Reaper men can't associate with human women." He placed one bowl before Isaiah and the other in the spot to his left. "But there's no law that says a Reaper woman can't associate with a human man."

Addy brought her own bowl over. "That's because no one even considered it a possibility."

"Doesn't change the fact that mating law still fits her and I better than her and Clark."

Isaiah took a roll from the basket before passing it around. "That has occurred to us."

"Miranda has never been formally promised to this man, has she?"

"No. The council was scheduled to discuss it next week before the wedding."

"That's cutting it close, huh?"

Isaiah shrugged. "There wasn't much chance of it being disapproved. There are so few women that are compatible with a Reaper, some things are just assumed."

"I bet that causes a lot less chaos."

Isaiah shrugged. "You've got a lot of men with a lot of appetites and very few outlets."

"And Clark laying claim to two didn't cause a bit of jealousy?"

"That is another issue that needs to be dealt with."

Addy poured coffee into the mugs. "This talk can wait until after dinner."

"Or it can take place during dinner, Cole countered."

Addy shot him a warning glance. "It'll upset your digestion."

"My digestion isn't that easily upset." Cole took the coffee. "Especially when I'm looking at a home-cooked meal." Taking a roll, he passed the basket to Addy. "So what are you going to do?"

"I don't have an answer for you."

"Why not?"

Isaiah caught Addy's hand and kissed the back. "Because Addy doesn't want you dead, I don't want insurrection, and no one wants to see Miranda unhappy."

"So give her to me. I'll make her happy."

"She'll be a widow in a day."

Cole looked at him over the rim of his cup. "I don't think so."

"Be that as it may, whatever my preference, this is a council decision."

"Is Clark a member of this council?"

"He is. He won't have a vote, but he'll have a say."

"I want to be present."

"I don't think that can be arranged."

"Then Clark can't be there."

Isaiah hesitated. Addy stroked his cheek. It always surprised Cole to see the big Reaper soften at Addy's touch. He'd always thought of Addy as practical and cold, like fine porcelain. But to Isaiah, she was the heat to his soul. At Addy's "That's only fair," Isaiah grunted.

"I suppose that could be arranged."

"When will the council have this meeting?"

"A couple of them are out on patrol, so in a couple days."

"And in the meantime?"

"A smart man might see it as time to convince Miranda he's a better bet."

"Does she have a say?"

"She'd better," Addy cut in.

Isaiah glanced at her. She folded her arms across her chest. This was clearly a long-standing argument. Isaiah sighed.

"There are some pushing for that."

"Who has a final say on that?"

"I will."

"How?"

Isaiah grabbed his cup. Addy squeezed his shoulder. It was a fleeting gesture, casual to anyone else, but in that moment she wasn't shielded, and the amount of love contained within her energy made Cole blink. He remembered his kiss that afternoon with Miranda. He was beginning to understand why Addy had given up everything to be with the Reaper.

"I formed this pack to give Reapers a home. Not to turn it into another prison."

"Blade won't be happy," Addie muttered.

"Blade will have to change his plans."

Cole perked up at the mysterious Reaper's name. "What plans?"

Isaiah answered. "On the surface, to unify Reaper law with the better understanding that we now have of what we are."

Addy asked the question that was on Cole's lips. "On the surface?"

"Blade has his own agenda. I'm not sure what it is or how much it involves us, but I don't trust it."

"Or him?"

"I'd trust Blade with my life, but with my pack?" Isaiah shook his head. "I'm not sure."

That was honest. "And until you are?" Cole prodded.

Isaiah held out one hand to Addy and the other to him. "Until then I'll let him enjoy our hospitality and I'll enjoy this nice meal."

Praying before a meal was one of Addy's rituals. Cole was surprised Isaiah had adopted it. The Reaper hadn't struck Cole as the religious sort, but he guessed if anybody had reason to be in contact with God, it would be a man who didn't know what he was, where he was going, or what he was doing. Cole completed the circle with a resigned acceptance. Like it or not, the Reaper was family now.

The prayer was a reflection of the man making it, straightforward and honest and to the point. At the end Addy added, "And dear God, thank you for answering my personal prayer and sending Miranda to Cole. Please guide them through the rough days to come."

Well, Cole thought, looking at Addy. At least one Reaper was on his side.

"Amen."

⇥ 10 ⇤

THE CALM FROM DINNER DIDN'T LAST LONG. HALFWAY back to the barn, pleasantly full and itching with a restless energy, Cole paused to roll a smoke. He needed something to take the edge off. A stiff drink or—Clark stepped out from between two buildings and into Cole's path—a good fight.

Cole smiled. "Evening."

Clark didn't return the smile.

Cole struck his sulfur on his boot. "Not indulging in the pleasantries?"

Clark's energy cracked like a whip. "I heard you paid a visit to Miranda today?"

Cole lit the smoke and took a draw. "Is that what you heard?"

"I don't want you around her."

He blew out the smoke. "That and two bits won't get you shit."

Addy would say he was playing with fire. He didn't care.

"She's going to be my wife."

"I heard you were whining for that."

A snarl rumbled deep in the Reaper's chest. Cole took the punch of energy without flinching. Clark's hands balled into fists. He had big hands. Cole remembered them lifted against Wendy, grabbing Miranda. It took everything he had not to release the rage burning in his blood.

"She's mine," Clark snarled.

"Seems to me you're supposed to be leaving her alone until the council convenes."

"What the fuck do you know?"

"Enough to know you're courting a shitload of trouble right now."

Clark's head lowered like a bull before the charge. "The council has no right to come between me and my wife."

Cole took another draw on his smoke, letting the acrid fumes smooth through him, balancing him. "You've already got a wife."

"Miranda will be my mate."

"Funny, I thought she was going to be mine."

Clark spat. "A Reaper married to a human? I don't think so. How could someone like you protect her?"

Cole smiled. "I'll endeavor to come up with something."

Like ripping off the bastard's head or cutting off his balls and shoving them down his throat. There were a whole lot of ways Cole wanted to settle this one.

The hair on the back of Cole's neck lifted. He stilled, searching for the cause. Clark snarled and looked around.

Dirk strode out from between the buildings.

"If I were the enemy, you'd both be dead."

Clark snarled again. Cole flicked his cigarette into the dirt. "Maybe."

Dirk ground it out beneath his boot. "There's no maybe about it. The pack can't afford the distraction of you two."

"I've been nothing but downright civil." Cole motioned to Clark. "Just ask your council member."

"Fuck you."

Cole palmed his knife. Dirk stepped between them.

"Fighting here in the street isn't going to solve anything."

Clark drew his lips back, exposing some impressive canines. "I have a right to challenge."

Dirk didn't even blink. "Then you take it before the council," he snapped back.

"The council is stalling."

"The council has a lot of things to do other than settling your petty disputes."

"Especially for a man who already has a wife," Cole interjected.

Clark took a step in. "There's no law saying I can't have two."

Cole followed suit. "There is no law saying you can, either."

Dirk slammed his hands on both their chests, holding them apart. "Both of you shut the fuck up."

"The hell I will," Cole growled.

"The hell you won't," Dirk countered.

"Miranda is Reaper," Clark reiterated. "She belongs with a Reaper."

Cole pushed Dirk's hand off him. "She belongs with me."

Dirk stepped back but not away. "Both of you stay away from her until the council makes its decision."

Cole met Clark's eyes over Dirk's shoulder. "I'm not going to leave her helpless."

"Well, I'm not going to leave her. Period. She's mine," Clark snapped before spinning on his heel and heading down the street. Toward Miranda's house.

Grabbing Dirk's wrist, Cole spun him. "Get out of the way."

The Reaper kept turning with the momentum, spinning them both around. "No."

"He's going to Miranda's."

"He won't get there."

The anger in Cole didn't subside, but the tension did.

Dirk met his gaze calmly. "Miranda is one of us. She enjoys the same protection as all."

Understanding came slowly. They'd put a guard on Miranda. "It'd better be a damn good guard."

"Gaelen considers Miranda family."

If it came to a fight between Clark and Gaelen, Cole's money was on Gaelen. Cole stepped back and spat the bad taste from his mouth. "Where were you when she needed you with him?"

Dirk didn't flinch. "Waiting for her to ask for help."

Only Miranda hadn't asked for it. Because she had a plan. Cole sighed. The woman had no trust.

"Does Clark know the pack is against him?" he asked Dirk.

Dirk didn't smile or otherwise change his expression. "There are some things it's better one find out for oneself."

In other words, no. Cole didn't get the impression Dirk liked Clark too much, but there was such a thing as loyalty among thieves, or Reapers, as the case may be.

"And if Clark kicks up a fuss?"

That twitch of the other man's lips might just be humor. "He is, of course, free to take it up with the council."

Cole started back toward the barn. "When they convene."

Dirk fell into step beside him. "Yes. But between now and then, you'd better watch your back, human. You won't always have somebody around to protect you."

Cole rolled his eyes. "Who said I needed protection?"

Dirk sighed. "I'm talking to a dead man."

"Everyone's always informing me it's my turn to die, yet I'm still standing here." He reached for Miranda's energy. He couldn't find it. "I'm not as weak as you all assume."

"No, but neither is Clark."

"He's welcome to fight me any time he wants."

"Clark knows the rules. If it's not a sanctioned fight, the prize can't be won."

"Sanctioned?" Cole tried again. Nothing. No sense of Miranda permeated the evening calm. His shoulder heated and burned where she'd bitten him. "What the hell is that?"

"If two Reapers wish to fight over a possession, the council has to rule that the dispute is valid and sanction the prize."

Fuck. They were barbarians. "We're talking about a woman here, not a piece of property. Our country just fought a war to settle matters of that nature."

"Human law is not Reaper law. And we're very aware of that war."

Cole remembered the conversation with Isaiah. "Didn't Isaiah say something about you all being part of that conflict?"

"Another reason others might want you dead is you know too much. With that in mind you might want to talk less and listen more."

Cole rubbed his shoulder, remembering Miranda's passion. Her fear. He needed to see her. He headed to the left, toward her house. "If you send an assassin, send more than one."

Dirk fell into step beside him. "You are a stubborn man, Cameron. And where are we going?"

Cole pointed to Miranda's house as the came around the slight curve. "There."

Dirk stopped. Cole didn't. "Why? There's nothing for you there."

Miranda was there.

"There's answers," he told Dirk.

"To what?"

"Whether I'm gonna be held accountable for breaking Reaper law."

He expected Dirk to try to stop him as he had Clark, but he didn't. And when he looked back, the man was just watching him, arms folded across his chest, a speculative expression on his face. Cole didn't know if Dirk was friend or foe. And he didn't care. Right now, he was just grateful to him for stepping aside. Clark he would have killed easily, but he had no beef with Dirk.

He rubbed his shoulder again. The spot itched and burned with a subtle irritating heat. Despite the fact it'd been hours since he'd seen her, the memory of Miranda's kiss lingered. Running his tongue over his bruised lower lip, he imagined he could still taste her kiss, addictively sweet yet spicy. His palms tingled with the urge to curve around her back, to press her close. The woman did drive him crazy. By the time he reached her house, his cock was hard, and his breath was coming harder. Of Gaelen there was no sign.

He knocked on her door. He felt the leap in her energy, excitement, and fear. And then a gathering pause.

"Who is it?" Miranda asked.

"You know who it is."

She opened the door, just a crack. Enough that he could see the creaminess of her skin, the deep brown of her eyes. As if her thoughts mirrored his, her tongue peeked out to moisten her lower lip.

Cole put his palm against the door. It was cool from the night air. The wood heated as his hand rested against it. The same way she'd heat if his hand rested on hers, but the heat in her wouldn't come from him. It would be in response to him and, damn, if that didn't make his cock jerk in his pants.

"Why are you so jumpy?"

"Clark was here."

Fuck. "Did he hurt you?"

She shook her head. "Gaelen talked to him."

As Dirk had promised. "Did you open the door for him?"

"No."

"But you did for me." The knowledge sank deep, satisfaction spreading outward, blending with his lust. The spot on his shoulder where she'd bitten him tingled.

She sighed and rested her forehead against the edge of the door, frowning at him. "Would you just go away?"

"Apparently not."

"You're ruining everything."

"Doesn't look that way to me."

"Of course it doesn't. It never looks that way to men. They get in their head what they want, and it's the only thing they can see."

He caught her chin in the edge of his finger and lifted her face up, bringing her gaze to his.

"Don't go lumping me in with everybody else you know."

Her eyes were dark with worry. "Why not? You're acting just like them. Only concerned with what you want, paying no attention to what I want."

"I'm paying attention to what you want. But more than that, I'm paying attention to what you need."

He drew his thumb across her bottom lip, taking that touch of moisture for himself. Letting go of her chin, he rubbed his fingers together, working that bit of her into his skin. He wanted to lick the woman from head to toe, drink in her kiss, her pleasure. Take her so hard, so deep, he'd breathe her scent on his deathbed.

Passion spiked between them. Miranda's breath caught. Her energy twined with his, blending in perfect harmony. His cock strained his pants. His breath strained his lungs. Miranda moaned and leaned against the door. Fuck, he wanted her. Now.

"No." Her voice was so sultry he didn't even hear her denial for what it was. It took the slamming of the door to do that. And even then he couldn't quite absorb it.

He blinked and breathed deeply, inhaling her lingering scent.

Through the door, she said, "If you want to give me what I need, go hunting. I'm out of meat."

The bar dropped down with a thunk. Cole didn't think he'd ever had a woman slam a door in his face before. Especially not one he'd been in the middle of seducing. Miranda had hidden depths. Strengths. He smiled. He liked it. Resting his shoulder against the door, he offered a bit of logic.

"It's evening."

"So?" The thickness of the wood did nothing to dull the soft stroke of her voice over his senses.

"Damn tough to hunt in the dark."

"I'll ask Clark."

The hell she would. "You do that, and you're going to find yourself over my knee."

That got a quick, "Hush. Wendy will hear."

He smiled because that jump in her energy had been excitement, not fear. "She sure will if I get to tanning that ass."

"Cole!"

He liked the way she said his name, all breathless and airy. Even through the door, it sounded good. He'd like her to say it like that when she climaxed.

"Did Wendy hear that?"

There was a pause and then, "She sneaked off to see those kittens again."

"That girl needs a better corral."

"She has so little fun here . . ."

He sighed. That was true. "I'll send her home when I get Rage."

"Thank you."

"And I'll get your damn meat."

"Venison?"

He shook his head. At least the woman wasn't afraid to ask for what she wanted. If that tendency extended to bed, they'd be good.

"I'll see what I can do. And Miranda?"

"What?"

"When I come back, we're going to have a chat about your habit of slamming doors."

"What if you don't come back?"

"I'll always come back to you."

Whether she knew it or not, it was a promise.

SOMETHING was wrong in these woods. Cole stopped at a stream, set his rifle against a rock, and knelt down, letting the cold water run over his hands. He'd been hunting now for three hours. It wasn't unusual to hunt for three hours and not find anything, but it was unusual to hunt for three hours and not find any signs of anything.

Something had spooked the game to the point it'd all gone to ground. Not much could cause that. An upcoming storm, if it was going to be a doozie, could sometimes. But not for three hours. And not so thoroughly.

A ripple in the energy around him set the hairs on his neck to rising. He shook the water off his hands and with apparent nonchalance sat back on his heels, drying his hands on his pants before grabbing his rifle, spinning around ready to shoot. Except there was no one there. Nothing. Just the ghost of a sensation in a forest gone quiet.

He knew that feeling. He'd had it for the last two months while hunting Addy. He'd had it strongest right before that last battle. Only Reapers could trigger his alarm with that invisible presence.

Clark. Had he followed Cole? He wouldn't put it past the man. Clark wanted him dead, and the Reaper didn't seem the type to be content with the council's ruling.

Grabbing his hat up off the ground, Cole stood. That feeling of something being wrong intensified as he stared around the woods. Dense and thick, they should have rippled with life, instead no birds sang and no squirrels chattered. It was as if everything around him could feel what he did. The danger lurking.

The spot on his shoulder itched. He rubbed at it, feeling the heat through his clothes. He pulled his shirt aside and looked at it. The wound had healed very quickly, already barely more than a few dark brown marks on his skin. There was no redness to show infection. He shook his head, sliding his fingers over it again, remembering that tight little body against him and the soft breasts melting into his chest. His cocked twitched in his pants. He licked his lips as he thought of the taste of her kiss. The urge to get home hit him hard. He shook his head and put his rifle over his shoulder. Since when had a Reaper camp become home?

He headed down the mountain toward the meadow where he'd left Rage. The farther down the hillside he went, the more his shoulder burned, and the stronger that sense of not right became. He started walking faster. The tickle grew stronger, the burn hotter, and soon he was running. When he got to Rage, he heard it. The first gunshot echoing off the hills. There was no way to tell which direction it came from. No way to tell how far away it was. The sounds were just an echo bouncing over and over. But he knew. Down in his gut where it mattered. He knew. Shortly after that first shot came another. And then another.

In his mind he heard a scream.

Addy!

Shortly after that scream came another. Pinging between gunshots, the voice echoed in his head in a high, desperate cry. Pushing through his consciousness. Tearing a place for itself from his mind. High-pitched, young. Fuck. Wendy.

From Miranda nothing. The camp was under attack, and the one who should be screaming his name was silent. Fuck.

Rage snorted and tossed his head. Grabbing the reins off the ground, Cole leapt onto his prancing horse's back, spun him around, and kicked him hard.

"Go!"

Something was very wrong in the Reaper village.

Rage gave Cole everything he had. Stretching out into that ground-eating gallop that had saved their asses so many times. Not flinching at the roughness of the terrain. Just recklessly plunging down hills, weaving through trees, charging up the rocky terrain. Giving Cole all he demanded and then some.

It wasn't enough.

The spot on Cole's shoulder burned like fire. He put his hand on it, focusing harder. Then he could feel it, like a blink, a knot of tension so tightly controlled as to be barely discernable. He poked at it.

Miranda.

No answer. He tried again, urging Rage to go faster, but the horse was already running flat out, flecks of sweat flicking off his neck, his breathing labored but not faltering. Just pushing forward with that heart that was so much of him.

The thundering of the hoofbeats blended with the sound of gunshots. They echoed through the hills, one on top of the other, resonating with the panic inside Cole.

Miranda.

Dammit woman, answer. And then, jaw tightening, he sent another thought to her. Just in case she couldn't.

Live.

One word, carrying all the force of his personality behind it. An order he wanted obeyed. He felt the flinch of her energy. She was alive, but for how long? And what condition was she in? For once he was glad she was Reaper. A Reaper could stand a hell of a lot without dying.

Hold on, Miranda.

Despite every instinct telling him to find Addy, to get to Miranda and Wendy, when he got close to the village, Cole pulled back on the reins, slowing Rage. Charging in and getting himself killed wasn't going to help anyone. He didn't regrow body parts. He couldn't afford to be reckless.

Pulling Rage to a stop by a copse of trees at the foot of a small rise, Cole jumped off and led the tired horse beneath the cover. Dropping the reins, he climbed the ridge.

The mark on his shoulder burned as hot as his rage. His clothes were too tight; his skin was too tight. He wanted to rip them off. He wanted to . . . He didn't know what, but the compulsion inside was strong to do something. Something he didn't understand, but he could feel it simmering. The need . . . the potential. Something just . . . more. Lurking.

More shots sounded. This close he could hear the shouts and snarls, which meant all were not fighting as wolf. Interesting. It would be a lot more interesting if he knew whether that was an advantage or disadvantage. As he started climbing the rise, the cold coherence of prebattle surrounded him like an old friend as he blended into the shadows, casting out for energy. So much came at him at once it was almost a blow. Unlike with humans whose energy was weak and easy to sort through, Reaper energy was different. They were individually strong, yet their energy was cohesive. The threads blended together as if on some level they thought with one thought, but the strands shone through with varying levels of clarity. As if some hid or overpowered others. Cole stored the information for later.

Scouting cautiously from the top of the ridge, he could see bits and pieces of the Reapers' village through the trees. There were flashes of light in the gloom, random movements, and smoke. A lot of smoke. They were setting things on fire. It was impossible to tell more than that. He checked for Miranda again.

Miranda.

Nothing. Dammit!

A flicker of panic whipped his attention around. He focused hard on that thread. *Miranda?*

As soon as he thought it, he knew it was wrong. The energy was too weak. Too scattered. Too . . . young.

Wendy. Weaving his way through the clamor in his head to that single thread, he pulled it close. Panic, pure and simple, came at him. And not the kind of panic that came from worry, but the kind of panic that only being in the face of danger inspired.

I'm coming, Wendy.

Goddammit, he was coming. Plunging down the hill, he mentally ran over his options. They were few. He could ride Rage in with guns blazing. That was the fastest. An option with humans. Not an option with Reapers.

Fuck.

Hold on, little bit. Just hold on.

He had the impression of heat. And choking. And surrender.

Oh shit. His gut went cold. She was in the fire. He didn't let his panic slip past his control, just channeled his fear and frustration into an order.

You will hold on!

He ran faster, picturing that fairy-child face, those big brown eyes so like her mother's. That incredible spirit.

Hold on! he mentally barked again. Hoping she could hear. Demanding she hear.

And then he did the hardest thing he'd ever done. He let her go. He needed all his senses to get to her.

Controlling his breathing, his senses strained outward for danger, as he skimmed the edge of the trees heading to the village. When he got close enough to smell supper cooking on the outskirts, he spotted a Reaper standing guard in the shadows. Not one of Isaiah's men. Cole blocked his own energy, slipped inside the man's mind, and, coming up behind him, slit his throat. Then Cole brought the blade across the man's neck again, cutting off his head.

Regrow that, bastard.

He moved forward, the scent of smoke stronger in his nostrils. When he came around the corner, he could see what was burning.

Flames nibbled up the side of the barn while smoke billowed all around in a thick cloud.

Wendy.

Dread settled like a ball of ice in his gut. Wendy was in that barn. He knew it as well as he knew his name. The impression of heat and choking took on an all-too-vivid significance.

Caution was no longer a concern. Cole ran through the battle, ignoring the bullets pinging at his feet, the shouts of the men he knocked over, and the claws tearing at his clothes. The only thought he had was getting to Wendy.

Hold on.

A Reaper leapt out in front of him, teeth bared in a horrific grin. Without breaking stride, Cole shot him four times and watched him go down, knowing he'd get back up again. Eventually. But eventually wasn't now. And Cole just needed the Reaper down for now. Cole leapt over the body. It was a clear shot to the barn.

When he got to to the door, the heat drove him back in a hard shove. A Reaper might be able to survive such a fire, but Wendy wasn't Reaper.

Son of a bitch.

Wrapping his bandana around his hand, Cole grabbled the latch and threw open the door. Outside the battle raged. Inside the fire devoured everything in sight with a dull, constant roar of satisfaction.

Nothing could survive that. Nothing. Not even a Reaper. Why the fuck couldn't the little girl be a Reaper?

He searched for her energy. There was a flicker of something. It could have been her; it could have been his imagination. The fire roared a challenge. A hay bale in the corner burst into flame. It was hell pure and simple, and going inside was nothing short of suicide.

Pulling his hat down tight over his brow, Cole whispered, "Fuck" and charged for the door.

⇥ 11 ⇤

MIRANDA WAS THERE BEFORE HIM, COMING OUT OF NO-
where, screaming Wendy's name, her skirts flapping about her legs,
coming too close to the flames. Grabbing her by the back of the
shirt, he yanked her away. Not fast enough. A tiny lick of fire caught
the hem of her skirt and started to spread. He beat at the flame. She
turned to him wildly.

"Dammit, woman, hold still." The skirt still smoldered. He ripped
it off.

She strained against his grip. "Wendy!"

He shook her to get her attention. When her gaze met his, her
energy locked with his, and he told her. "I'll get her, but you stay
here."

She looked at him and shook her head. "You can't."

Out of the corner of his eye he saw a movement. He shoved her
behind him, whipping out his revolver, not relaxing when he saw
that it was a bloody Clark.

Miranda threw herself at him. "Wendy's in there. Get her. Please."

Clark caught her shoulders, gave the burning barn one look, and shook his head.

"If she's in there, she's dead," he told her.

Miranda screamed. Cole swore and dipped his bandanna in the water trough to the side of the door before tying it around his face. Didn't that son of a bitch know that would just send her back into the fire? Couldn't he feel how much she loved her daughter? That she'd burn with her rather than leave her alone?

As if on cue, Miranda jerked out of Clark's arms and headed back in. Cole grabbed her again by the shoulders, shaking her. Using all his energy to drag her gaze to his.

"I'll get her for you."

The fire roared in the background. Clark swore. Bullets fired. Men died. None of it mattered, not in that moment. Only Miranda mattered. When her energy wrapped around his and clung, he repeated, "I'll get her."

Before she would answer, Cole shoved Miranda back at Clark.

"Hold on to her. Do *not* let her go."

"Fuck you."

Cole turned back to the fire. He probably was fucked. In the brief time they'd been arguing, the flames had spread; there was only a small corner to the left of the door where they hadn't reached. Taking a breath and reaching mentally for Wendy, he dove forward, clinging to the trail of energy that was the little girl. The happy little sprite who was so terrified right now her energy stuttered in and out.

Over the roar of the flames he hollered, "Stay where you are, Wendy! I'm coming."

He didn't know if she could hear him. Hell, it didn't even matter. Thinking she could kept him pushing forward as the heat seared his lungs and burned his skin. He followed the trail of her energy through the smoke, bumping into objects he couldn't see. Feeling his way around, pausing only when forced to regain his bearings. The smoke was so thick he felt like he had to part it with his hands to pass, but when he did, there was just more smoke, more blindness, more heat. He coughed and choked. His eyes watered.

Get down.

The command came out of nowhere before crystallizing in his mind. Harsh and masculine the order repeated. The taste of ash coated his tongue. Cole spat. Shit, he wasn't even sure which way was down. He dropped to his knees. The smoke wasn't so dense. He supposed he owed whoever had invaded his head a thanks. And he would right after he found Wendy. He had to find Wendy.

He started crawling. The scream of horses joined Miranda's scream. He could hear her chanting in his head.

Please, please, please, please . . .

He didn't know if she was begging him or praying to God. In the end it didn't matter, because without God's help there was no way in hell anybody's ass was getting out of here.

He kept going, digging through the smoke. He got back by the tack room where the water trough was. This far back in the barn, the fire wasn't so intense. The bastards must have set fire to the front and sides but left the back. Still, he didn't see how little Wendy could be alive. He leaned back against the wooden trough. In his mind Miranda chanted. He wanted to swear and curse. He wanted to pray. He didn't have the breath for anything but another hoarse call of Wendy's name.

There. That might have been someone.

"Wendy," he called her name again, and this time there was a cough and a splash and an answer.

"Here!"

He blinked and sat up. Son of a bitch, she was in the water trough. Smart little girl.

He crawled up onto his knees and reached into the trough. She was right there, shaking, coughing. Her face was streaked with black ash, her hair was a wild tangle, and her big brown eyes were bloodshot and terrified.

"You, Wendy, are one beautiful little girl," he told her. "What do you say we get out of here?"

She nodded.

"Then dunk under that water and get your hair really good and wet," he told her. "Then we're going to leave."

"But the fire . . ."

"Isn't going to touch you," he finished for her.

He wouldn't let it.

For a split second she hesitated, but then she pinched her nose closed and went under the water. Before she could pull herself up, he grabbed her dripping out of the trough and held her against his chest. Her arms crept around his neck as she coughed and shook.

"I knew you'd come for me."

"Good girl."

She pulled the bandanna down off his face.

"I heard you."

He nodded and looked around.

"How did I hear you?"

That wasn't something he needed to go into right now. "Save your breath."

While he figured out how to save their asses. One thing was sure. They couldn't go back the way he'd come in. The front of the barn was a wall of living, breathing fire. Arms of yellow and orange snaked out of the black, wrapping around fresh wood, pulling it into the conflagration, creating more smoke. More destruction. More death. Cole closed his eyes for a second. The horses had stopped screaming. Such a waste.

"Are we going to die?" Wendy whispered hoarsely, her gaze following his.

"Not today," he told her, standing. The devil wasn't taking her today.

She clung tighter. Yanking the bandana from around his neck, he dipped it in the trough.

"Lift your face up." The order came out a croak. He tied the fabric around her face. She tugged at it. He couldn't stop coughing long enough to tell her to leave it be, so he just shook his head at her and held it in place before heading to the back wall, bracing his back against it and lying down.

He sent a thought to Addy as hard as he could, picturing the back wall of the barn. He didn't know if it were actually possible to transmit thoughts, and this was a heck of a time to find out. He waited in vain for a response. Above timbers creaked and sparks fell. There was no response. He sent the same image again. Unfocused. Just tossing it out there. He didn't care who the hell opened that back wall. Friend or enemy. He just needed to get out. This time there was a response. Masculine, calm, incredibly powerful.

We're coming.

Cole's body covered Wendy's. She cried out, her little arms going around his neck again; she was clinging to him, putting all her faith in him.

"Help's coming," he told her. He blocked her view of the flames with his shoulders, feeling the bite of the multitude of ashes peppering him through his shirt.

"We're just going to lie down here where the air is fresher and wait a bit." She coughed and nodded at him. He pushed her hair away from her face.

"You all right?"

His voice was more of a rasp, and the question ended in a cough. But she didn't seem to know what that meant. She started chattering in his ear. Nothing had ever sounded so good.

Hurry the fuck up, he told that energy in his head.

Already here, the answer came back, and they were.

Axes struck at the back wall, the thuds punctuated by gunfire and men's shouts. Whoever was standing there had bullets flying around him. The weakened rafters creaked another warning. The whole place was about to collapse.

He looked down at Wendy.

"Do you know how to pray?"

She nodded. She folded her little hands in front of her. He'd never felt so helpless.

"Then start." It took a lot to get those words out.

She did, "Now I lay me down to sleep."

He wanted to curse because he had enough bad luck without her putting ideas into anyone or anything's head with "And if I die before I wake." Instead, he stroked his hand over the top of her head.

"Don't get fancy. Just ask God to make that man on the other side of the wall strong and keep him safe. That's all we need."

He didn't add "and for him to hurry."

He could see the flames licking across the hay on the floor. It was a race now to see what got to them first. The fire, the smoke, or help. He put his hand on the side of Wendy's face before sliding it down and slipping his fingers behind her head to her nape, and then he pushed himself up so he could get leverage with the other while still hiding the approaching flames. It would only take a second to snap her neck. A horrible damn-him-to-hell second. But she wouldn't die screaming with fire eating at her flesh. God forgive him, if she had to die, she'd die by his hand before he let that happen.

The axe bit through the wood.

"Might wanna hurry it up," he yelled.

He didn't know if they could hear.

The blade bit through wood, again and again, chipping away at the wall when Cole needed the axe to break through. The heat of the fire seared through his boots. He kicked at it, pulling Wendy up. Finally an axe blade broke the rough wood beside his head.

"Now," he hollered. "Get us out now."

They had to get them out of there now. The wood splintered, and there was a roar. Nails screamed in protest as they were ripped from their foundations. Smoke billowed out ahead of Cole.

Arms reached in. Flames licked up. He rolled, taking Wendy with him, pushing her in the direction of those hands. She was snatched from his grip while the flames ate his shirt. Relief shuddered through him. She'd made it.

He coughed some more. He couldn't stop. Couldn't move. Couldn't take his eyes away from the flames consuming his clothing. But he didn't hurt. At least he didn't hurt.

Closing his eyes, he sent a message to Miranda.

She's out.

"Christ, he's fucking burning up! Somebody get some water."

He heard the cry, but he didn't feel anything. The world was a dark, smoky place. And Wendy was safe. It was a good day.

"Give me that bucket," somebody yelled.

Water hissed to steam. Another victim of the fire.

His lungs burned, and the darkness clawed at him. He pictured Miranda's smile when she had her daughter back. Pictured the relief and joy. And fell back into the darkness.

"I don't know what the hell you want me to do with him," Isaiah said. "A human can't survive these wounds."

They were just standing there. Clark, Blade, Isaiah, Addy. Miranda stared at Cole's unconscious body. Why weren't they doing something?

"Do something anyway," Addy snapped.

"You will save him," Miranda ordered, pushing anything but conviction away.

"He's burned badly," Blade said, his black eyes as flat as his expression as he relayed that information. "Probably his lungs, too."

Miranda didn't want to hear that. "He went into that burning building to save my daughter. You won't let him die," Miranda commanded.

"He's human. Put him out of his misery," Clark interjected.

"Isaiah?" Miranda said, moving to the bed, closer to her sword, placing herself between Cole and them.

"What, Miranda?"

"Kill him."

Addy gasped. "You bitch."

Isaiah grabbed Addy's arm and held her back. Blade just smiled. "You might want to clarify who you want dead."

Miranda didn't hesitate. "Clark."

She wanted Clark dead. He'd left her daughter to die as if she were nothing. She wanted him more than dead. She wanted him to suffer.

Clark swore.

"Oh." With a wave of her hand, Addy dismissed Clark. "Him you can kill."

"That might be premature," Isaiah countered.

Miranda looked at him. "You promised me once that anything I needed you'd give me."

"I did."

Addy glared at Clark. "Reapers keep their promises, husband."

"They do."

"I want him dead."

"Go to hell," Clark snapped at her.

Miranda wanted to slash her talons across his mouth. "You will no longer talk to me that way."

"I'll talk to my intended any way I want."

"You're a coward, a thief, and I suspect impotent." She all but spat those words, disgust pouring out of her until it felt like it filled the room. "I'll never marry you."

"That's where you're wrong."

"You left a child to die. *My* child."

"Shut up."

She lifted her chin. "Make me."

Clark waved his hand to include the others. "Do you think they'll save you? They're bound by mating law. I could beat you right here, and they'll let me."

"Is that true?"

Blade smiled a cold smile. "He could take a swing."

Isaiah went still. "He is that stupid."

Clark took a step back. "They won't always be there."

Miranda closed her eyes against that truth. Clark was right. Isaiah and Blade wouldn't always be there.

The whisper came strong but silent into her mind. A voice yet not a voice. A thought yet not a thought. Strong, masculine, and foreign. *Make your choice, girl.*

Blade was in her head. She looked at him. He stared calmly back at her. A choice. She had a choice. Placing her hand on Cole's shoulder, over the place where she'd left her mark in the wake of that incredible kiss, she finally understood. Even through the material of his scorched shirt, the contact made her palm tingle. Reaper or human. She had a choice.

Do it.

"I accept this man as my mate."

Clark snarled. "The hell you say!"

She faced him squarely. "I reject your suit, your interest." It felt so damn good to say this. "I reject *you.*"

"He'll never have you," Clark snarled, stepping in.

From Cole came a wild surge of energy in a room gone strangely cold. The first sign of life she'd felt from him since they'd brought him in, and it'd come in defense of her. She bit her lip, a sob fighting for freedom.

"Neither will you," Miranda snarled right back at him, dropping her hand to the mattress, closer to the sword hidden beneath, but it was Addy who yelled for Gaelen.

He poked his head in the door.

Addy waved to Clark. "Please escort Clark back to his home."

"I'm a member of the council, bitch. I don't take orders from you."

Isaiah grabbed Clark by the neck, his talons embedding just over the jugular and backed him toward the door. A trickle of blood spilled down Clark's neck.

"But you do take them from me."

There was nothing more intimidating than Isaiah when he went all cold Reaper. Miranda smiled as Clark's bravado slipped along with his gaze.

Gaelen grabbed Clark's arm. "Come along, boy. Puffing up now won't change history."

The whole village knew of his cowardice. Miranda had made sure of it.

The closing of the door blew fresh air into the room. Miranda took a deep breath. It filled her lungs, her spirit. She felt lighter, as if a weight had been lifted from her shoulders.

A 220-pound one.

Her gaze flew to Blade. Nothing in his expression reflected the amusement in that quip. Was he the one talking in her head, or wasn't he?

"About damn time you did that," Isaiah growled, coming back, wiping the blood from his hand with the rag she used to clean.

"I didn't realize I could."

It wasn't a mistake she'd make again.

"There's always a choice," Blade interjected.

Addy interjected. "He won't go away."

"He will if he has any sense."

Addy snorted. "There isn't a lick of sense in that Reaper's body. He's made of up pride and self-indulgence."

"Then he will be dealt with."

Blade didn't sound worried about the potential confrontation. But then again, Miranda decided, looking at the enforcer, if she had that much muscle backing that much confidence, she wouldn't be worried, either.

"What about Cole?" she asked.

Blade shook his head. "If I could work miracles, I'd walk on water rather than circling around rivers looking for a shallow stretch."

"That's not an answer," Addy snapped.

"If his lungs are burned, there's nothing to do."

"If?" Isaiah asked. "You think there's a chance they're not?"

Blade shrugged. "I'm just saying I can't give him new lungs."

"Convert him," Addy whispered. "Make him Reaper."

No!

The "no" echoed in Miranda's head. She looked down at Cole's completely still body and knew, just knew, her mind wasn't playing tricks on her. That was Cole's choice, voiced in her head. She ran her eyes over his body. Bits and pieces of his clothing still clung to his badly burned body. She tried to imagine how he must have felt, knowing the fire was consuming him as the hole opened in the wall. She tried to imagine how much self-sacrifice it took for him to shove her daughter through first. How much courage it had taken in the first place to charge through the flames to save a child that wasn't his. Placing her hand on the one spot on his forearm that was whole, she squeezed gently.

Thank you.

"Takes three bites spaced out, Addy," Isaiah said. "He doesn't have that much time."

"Then keep him alive long enough to find that time."

Addy took a step closer. Miranda didn't move from where she stood beside Cole. A snarl built deep inside her. She tightened her grip on his arm.

As one, Blade and Isaiah looked at her.

"I agree, converting him would be the sensible choice," Blade said in that calm, commanding way of his, his near-black eyes never leaving her. For once Miranda didn't care if he saw to her soul. Her daughter was alive with only a few burns and a cough thanks to this man. It was her turn to protect him.

"What do you know, Blade?" Isaiah asked.

Blade turned his attention to Isaiah, his shoulder-length hair falling forward, hiding his expression. Miranda didn't fool herself that he'd turned his attention away from her.

"By rights he should be dead, but he's not."

"He's always been strong," Addy interrupted.

Blade nodded. "But I suspect the reason he's not dead is he's already halfway to conversion."

"How is that possible?" Addy gasped.

"He's been bitten twice," Blade explained. "Once during the battle and once since."

As one, everyone looked at Miranda. She moved her hand back to that spot on Cole's shoulder. Almost but not quite touching. Her palm tingled. Coincidence? "It just happened," she confessed in a whisper.

A smile tweaked the sternness of Isaiah's expression. "It can."

"He's compatible?" Addy asked.

Blade nodded. "Always suspected the man had Reaper blood in him."

"How can he have Reaper blood if we don't even know how the hell we got it?" Isaiah asked.

"That would be what's called an interesting question." Blade grabbed a chair and set it down backward close to the bed before straddling it and resting his arms across the back.

Inside Miranda the snarling resumed. He was too close. "The other one will be what happens if we don't convert him."

"What's the danger?" Isaiah asked.

Blade shrugged. "A man with Reaper blood half converted is not the same as a human twice bitten."

Isaiah ran his hand through his hair. "You've seen this before?"

"Nope."

"Then what are you basing this on?"

"The man ran into a burning building through a wall of fire to save a little girl that logic said was probably dead anyway," Blade pointed out reasonably. "And came out alive. And, more importantly, the fact that he's lying there healing while we're debating what to do to save him."

Miranda closed her eyes. If Cole was healing, he'd live. The relief was overwhelming.

"Then that's a good thing."

"As long as being half converted doesn't drive him insane, yes."

"How will we know?" Miranda whispered.

"Considering the man's impulsive nature, that's another good question."

The joke fell flat.

"I would know," Addy snapped at Blade, reaching for Isaiah. And he was there, as he always was, giving her his hand and his support. Miranda envied Addy that.

"Maybe, maybe not. If it came on hard, yes, but if crazy snuck in, he might be able to hide it," Blade added.

"I take it you have a solution?"

Miranda could have kissed Isaiah for that. Please let the enforcer have a solution.

"He could be converted now."

"He doesn't want to be Reaper." Despite everything in her that said, "Do it," Miranda owed Cole better than to listen only to her selfish wants.

"I'm not sure his wishes matter in this," Blade continued. "The good of the pack has to be considered."

Cole's opinion mattered. Miranda sat on the bed carefully, sliding her hand under the sheet and beneath the thin mattress until her fingers touched the hilt of the sword.

"Do it," Addy whispered.

"You know how it can go, Addy girl. Conversion is not easy for anyone, even someone with Reaper blood. *You* almost died. As weak as he is, he darn well might."

Addy didn't take her eyes off Cole. Miranda could feel her love and desperation. "He's almost dead now."

"Do it," Isaiah ordered Blade.

Miranda tightened her fingers around the hilt.

"I can't."

"Why not?" Addy and Isaiah demanded as one.

Blade motioned to Miranda. "Hers was the last bite. Hers has to be the final bite."

So it was up to her. She released her grip on the sword. "No."

"Miranda?" Addy's gasp was part question, part shock.

Miranda shook her head against the plea in Addy's eyes. "He'll hate me."

"But he'll be alive."

"He might live anyway."

Addy turned to Blade. "Really?"

Blade shrugged. "Slim to none is still a chance."

"It's not enough," Addy snapped.

Miranda brought her hand back up to Cole's shoulder, feeling the tingle, the expectation. Hearing his "no" again.

Addy waved her hand dismissively. "He's my cousin. You owe him!"

Miranda did.

She looked at Blade. "It has to be me?"

"Anyone else and he'll die for sure."

All or nothing. Why was it always all or nothing?

"Looks like you're his only chance." There was no mistaking the sympathy in Isaiah's tone. She knew why. He'd made this choice himself. For Addy. But in much more dire circumstances.

"Would you do it?" Miranda asked.

He shrugged. "I honestly don't know."

Neither did she. She owed Cole so much. He'd given Miranda her daughter back. He'd given her hope. She owed him everything. No, she corrected herself as selfishness nudged her along. She owed him the right thing.

"Isaiah!" Addy gasped.

"It's not my choice, Addy."

No, it was Miranda's.

"Then you should lie!"

Isaiah pulled Addy into his arms, pressing her face into his chest.

Miranda heard him mutter, "You know I can't do that," as she leaned down and brushed her lips across Cole's brow, breathing a caress across his cheek and his neck, inhaling his scent before replacing her hand on his shoulder with her mouth.

Just a bite. One bite and he'd be in her world forever. The way it should be.

Her fangs ached and lengthened. She opened her mouth ever so slightly and set her teeth against his skin, tasting him. Familiar. Addictive. And human. So completely human. All she had to do was bite down and that would all change. Just one little bite.

Why did the right thing always have to be so hard?

❦ 12 ❦

COLE SHOULD HAVE LOOKED SMALLER SPRAWLED ON HIS stomach in the bed, but he didn't. To Miranda he looked as big as ever. As powerful. She remembered the way he'd stood there in the devil's light of that fire, his eyes reflecting the flames, his mouth set as hard as the grip on her shoulders as he'd promised her he'd get Wendy out. It'd been suicide but he hadn't hesitated. He'd just . . . She tugged the sheet up a little higher over his burned shoulders, letting it settle butterfly soft back on his skin. He'd just kept his word. The dull gray muslin wasn't what he was used to, she was sure. But she'd given him the best they had. It was so little in light of what he'd given her.

Touching her finger to the warmth of his skin, she trailed the nail higher until it touched the mark of her bite just visible over his shoulder. He was healing fast. After only three days the worst burns were no longer oozing. Some were but dark spots of memory. Was he Reaper? Or human? Or caught somewhere in between? She didn't know, wouldn't know until after he woke, though his scent seemed different. But that could be her imagination. Or wishful thinking. Opening her palm over the mark, feeling the heat and the immediate answering warmth stir inside of her, she felt the overwhelming weight of guilt. She hadn't bitten Cole the third time, but that second time? She curled her fingers into a fist, releasing him from her touch. That second time might have been in the heat of passion, but she'd known what she was doing. Somewhere inside, she'd known.

Brushing his brown hair off Cole's face, she traced her finger over a slight scar on his forehead, wondering not for the first time how he'd gotten it, feeling the desire for him well inside her. So much more than sexual. So much more than anything. God forgive her, she wanted him, and she'd done what she'd had to to have him.

She paused, fingertips just shy of his beautiful mouth. God forgive her. She curled her fingers into her palm. When had she started believing in God again? She'd thought she'd given that up a long time ago, when she'd given up on her marriage and her husband had died in her arms from self-inflicted wounds because he couldn't face what had happened. She was as good as dead to everyone in her past, but apparently belief, like Reaper blood, could lurk undetected beneath the surface. It was yet another sign that she was coming back to life inside. She didn't know how she felt about that. Or how Cole would. But Blade? Blade would be happy.

She remembered Blade's expression of satisfaction when he'd thought she'd made the decision to convert Cole. He wanted Cole to be Reaper. She didn't know why. Nobody ever knew why *that* one did what he did. He was an enforcer with mysterious powers. Always on the fringes, always showing up when the balance seemed to be breaking. Moving between the high council and their council. Playing games. Her lip lifted in a snarl. She didn't want to be part of his game. She smoothed her fingers over the fresh growth of Cole's eyebrows. She wouldn't let him involve Cole. Blade might think he knew her, might think he could use her guilt against her, but she wasn't hiding anymore. She owed Cole better. She owed Wendy better. She owed herself better.

Cole stirred beneath her touch, his energy gathering beneath his skin. He'd be awake soon. Hopefully sane. Blade had speculated it would take a couple of weeks for a full healing once Cole came to. But Blade had been unable to speculate as to when Cole would be clear of the threat of madness. As she brushed the back of her fingers down Cole's cheek, his beard rasped against her skin. A harsh response to a soft gesture.

"Sleep," she whispered, not really wanting him to wake too soon. She wasn't ready to face that particular judgment day just yet. Anything other than human and he'd never forgive her.

He didn't sleep, but some of that restlessness left him and he relaxed. Miranda wished she could follow her own order. She was so tired. Tired of fighting, tired of trying to survive, tired of trying to protect her daughter, tired of doing it all alone. When she'd agreed to follow her idealistic husband out West so many years ago, to set up a store, and to reap the riches of this wild land, she'd never dreamed just how high the price would be, how harsh her future would be. What her dream would cost her. But she'd learned and she'd stopped dreaming. Until Cole.

Standing, she put her hands in the small of her back and stretched the kinks from her spine. But now she had another dream. And this time the price might be higher than she could bear. She blinked back the silly tears. She needed some air. She was getting morbid. Before she could step away, strong fingers wrapped around her wrist, anchoring her in place. Her heart jumped. Her pulse stuttered, and beneath the dread the joy that always arose from Cole's touch spread through her. Looking down, she found Cole was staring up at her, those hazel eyes of his intense with emotions she couldn't decipher.

"Hi." Her voice sounded strained to her own ears.

"What are you doing?" he asked.

His voice sounded raspy, and utterly beautiful. She bit her lip as more tears welled. She'd been afraid she'd never hear his voice again. "Watching you."

"Why?"

"You don't remember?"

"No." He ran his hand over his chest, grimacing as he touched spots still working on healing. "Not yet."

Damn. She tugged at her hand. "You were hurt."

He didn't let go, just frowned, and he rubbed her mark on his shoulder. Her canines tingled and her nipples peaked. And she watched.

His gaze cut to hers. "How?"

She gave him the simple truth. "There was a fire. You were caught in it."

He looked around at the shadows darkening the room. It would be night soon.

"How long have I been out?"

"Three days."

He started to swear, then caught himself.

"Sorry."

"I think in light of everything that's happened, you can say whatever you want."

His thumb grazed the inside of her wrist. "A promise is a promise."

"You remember that?"

His smile was a quirk of his lip. "I remember everything up until I went hunting."

She envied him that amnesia. She remembered every bit of how she'd become Reaper.

"I'm sure you'll remember the rest in time."

He nodded. His gaze searched the room. She knew what he was looking for. There were scars all over his body. The marks of a warrior. A warrior was never far from his weapons.

"Your gun belt is on the chair by the head of the bed. Your rifle is propped on the wall behind you. Your knife is under your pillow."

His gaze snapped to hers. "Are they loaded?"

"I don't know."

He nodded and closed his eyes for a moment, letting her go. "I'll check in a minute."

"All right." She rubbed her hands down her thighs, wondering how much he already remembered. He'd been aware as they'd been discussing converting him. Would he remember that, too? "Are you in pain?"

"Fair to middling."

"I have some willow bark tea that might help." She couldn't bear the thought of him in pain.

He cracked an eyelid. "I'm not in that much pain."

Willow bark tea was bitter. "I could add some honey."

His smile was a shadow of its former strength but it was still a smile. "That just makes the bad nasty."

She wished she could find her own. "All right. But let me know if you change your mind."

He pushed up on his elbows and cautiously arched his back. "I won't."

She wanted to run her fingertips over the muscles of his chest, to pet him like one would a big cat. He had such sleek, well-developed muscles. As if he heard her thoughts, Cole shifted onto his side. The sheet slid to his waist, highlighting the tan of his skin, the laddered muscles on his stomach, the hollow of his naval, and the dark line of hair that thinned until it disappeared beneath the sheet. He was a man in his prime, and the old scars mixed with fresh wounds did nothing to diminish his impact. Miranda forced herself to look away. It took a lot of will. The man was beautifully made.

"Aren't you worried I might use them on you?"

It took her a second to realize he was referring to his weapons and not his muscles. She shrugged, hoping he wouldn't notice her blush. Hoping he would.

He noticed. He was Cole. He noticed everything.

Cocking an eyebrow at her, he asked, "Care to share what's got you blushing?"

"I'm sorry, but no."

"That's a darn cold attitude for a man's future wife to be taking."

She wanted to match him in the relief that made him happy despite his pain, but she just couldn't. All she had was guilt and remorse. "I'm sorry."

Cole ran his hand over his chest, testing and probing, occasionally wincing. "I'll take some water in the way of apology."

She fetched it immediately. He drank it straight down. It took three more cups before he was satisfied. She couldn't help but compare it to a Reaper's thirst.

He started to sit up. She put her hand on his chest.

"You need to stay down."

"The hell I do." He tugged the sheet free of the mattress. "But if you want to be useful, get me some clothes."

Walking over to the chest at the foot of the bed, she opened it and pulled out the spare pants, shirt, and drawers she'd found in his saddlebags and tossed them to him before turning her back.

She listened as he got out of bed, braced for the thud of him hitting the floor. There was no sound beyond his grunt. Looking over her shoulder she saw his back was to her as he sorted the clothes. The man had a mouth to make hers water. Her canines tingled. She'd like to bite it. Folding her arms across her chest, she stifled the thought. "We need to get you more clothes."

Clothing rustled as he dressed. "I'm used to making do."

She couldn't just stand there imagining him dressing, dreading him remembering. "Would you like some coffee?"

"I thought you were out."

"Addy sent some over."

"You've got enough?"

She headed to the fireplace.

"Of course." There was silence as she grabbed the rag to protect her hands.

"I remember the fire," Cole said in that careful way people did when they didn't have all the answers.

Damn. "I've been waiting to thank you."

"No thanks necessary. Is Wendy all right?"

She kept her back to him, fussing with the rag, getting it just right around her hand. "Thanks to you, she's all right. Her voice is a little rough and she's got a little cough, but she's fine." She wanted to turn around so badly. "Thank you again."

"It was nothing."

She did turn then. He stood there, shirt shrugged on but open, fastening his pants. Button by button, covering that intriguing line of hair bit by bit. Her breath caught. She ran her tongue over her suddenly dry lips to moisten them. If the hot wrap of his energy around her wasn't enough to tell her that he knew how she felt, the sudden softening of his beautiful mouth would. The way he made her feel was nowhere near decent. She sighed. She should turn back around. But they both knew she wouldn't.

Letting her eyes devour him, feeling the tension rising within him, she said, "It was everything. Clark would have let her die."

"And you were going to marry him."

She shook her head. He started buttoning the shirt. No matter how closely she looked, she couldn't see any sign of unsteadiness in his stance. Her stomach clenched. Another sign he'd changed. "It was a good plan at the time."

"Uh-huh." He shrugged gingerly into his shirt. The washed-out gray brought out the blue in his eyes. "You nursing that coffee or serving it?"

"Oh, I'm sorry." Grabbing a rag, she wrapped the handle of the coffeepot and took it off the fire. Fooling with the pot and the cups bought her a couple minutes. Cole was already at the table when she turned back. Pants and shirt buttoned neatly. Sighing, she brought the items over. He met her halfway, moving stiffly but determinedly.

He took the cups from her hand. The brush of his fingers over hers was as deliberate as his gaze when it met hers. "You don't give me orders."

It was a purely masculine correction that brought everything feminine in her tripping forward. Her "Would you please sit down?" came out soft and breathy.

He did. She didn't know if it was because she asked nicely or if it was because his legs were about to give out. But at least he was sitting and not towering over her. Pouring coffee into the cups, she pushed one toward him.

He took the coffee she passed him without a word.

She licked her lips. "We don't have any cream."

"I like it black."

She remembered. She remembered everything about him. She was just stalling.

He blew across the cup, eyeing her steadily. "Are you going to sit or are you going to stand there looking like a cat with its tail under the rocker?"

Sit. She was going to sit. She grabbed a chair on the opposite side of the table, pulled it out. He waited while she got comfortable, sipping his coffee patiently as she put sugar in hers, watched while she adjusted her skirts and her seat. When she'd run out of fiddle, he reached across the table, casually pried her fingers from her cup, and cradled her hand in his. She forgot to breathe as he rubbed his thumb across the back.

"Now tell me."

Damn him for making everything easier. Making her like him.

"I formally refused Clark."

"About damned time."

She licked her lips and tugged at her hand. He didn't let her go.

"Now just tell me whatever it is that has you think I don't want to hear."

You're going to be mad."

"So I'll be mad."

"Blade thought it was a good idea."

Oh why had she just blurted that out as if Blade thinking anything made it all right?

Cole sighed and she couldn't blame him for the weariness in it. "Blade again? For someone I never see he wields a lot of influence."

"Blade's . . ." She shrugged. How could she describe the big man with the dark eyes, dark hair, and deadly ways? She settled for the truth. "Blade is an enforcer."

"And this means?"

"He enforces Reaper law. He's on the high council. I think."

"You think?" She spread her hands wide before curving them around her cup of coffee.

"Reapers don't know much about themselves. But nobody knows *anything* about Blade. He's just"—she shrugged again—"Blade. And when he arrives, things change."

"And the council changed their minds about me because of him?"

"Blade said if you could accept the conversion, I could have you."

"Have me? Like a cow brought to market?"

She looked at him. She hadn't missed his internal start at the word "conversion." He was avoiding that aspect for a reason. "You were very vocal about wanting me. They merely granted you your wish."

"And yours."

The guilt washed over her, too hard and too fast to hide. Across the table Cole went still.

"And what did you do, Miranda?"

Miranda, not china doll. Oh God. She didn't want to tell him this. Cold sweat broke along her forehead, down her back. She felt light-headed, clammy, drowning in dread. She clutched the coffee cup so hard her fingers hurt.

"You'd already had two bites."

He stared at her.

"One from the wolves and one from me when we . . ."

His hand went to his shoulder. "When we kissed."

She wondered if it tingled like her palm did when she touched it. "Yes."

His hand dropped to the table. His fingers curved around the spoon like one grasped the hilt of a knife.

"Go on."

Her stomach dropped, leaving a black void where her courage should be. Inside, she began to shake. "Normally, it takes three bites to make a human a Reaper."

She waited for that to sink in. It didn't take long. Cole's expression didn't change, but his energy got cold and dark and seemed to contract inside him into a hard, scary ball of intensity. Everything in her said run. She braced her hands on the table, ready to jump. His hands slapped down on hers, grabbing her wrists, pinning her in place across the wooden surface.

"What the fuck did you do?"

His grip hurt but not near as much as it was going to when she confessed. She pulled her own energy in, walling herself up in her mind, trying to block out the world. She wouldn't stand a chance against him if he got violent. He'd kill her. And she'd let him, she realized. Because she deserved it. She'd betrayed him.

His grip tightened painfully on her wrists. "What did you do, woman?"

She couldn't help a gasp. Turning her arm over, Cole frowned when he saw the marks of his fingers. His grip loosened but not enough for her to get away. He grazed his thumb over the marks. Almost like an apology.

He asked her again but so much softer, "What did you do, china doll?"

"I had to make a choice."

"Miranda . . ."

It was a warning. She didn't want to heed it, but he didn't give her a choice. He stood, keeping one of her arms pinned to the table. He walked around until he towered over her. His hand circled her throat while his thumb pressed up under her chin. When he pressed up, she had no choice but to get to her feet. They stood hip to thigh, breast to chest. This close she couldn't miss his scent, that spicy, earthy smell that was uniquely his.

She should have been terrified, but that wild part of her that didn't recognize caution leapt to attention. Simmered. Cole held her there balanced on his hand. Her life was his to take. And it felt so damn right, she wanted to cry. She was his. He could have anything of her. Even the truth.

"I refused that time."

He relaxed slightly. "So they had someone else do it?"

"Nobody else could. Blade said the third time had to come from me."

He snorted at the enforcer's name. "But you didn't."

She shook her head. Not then, but when she'd bitten him that first time, she'd done it on purpose. Hedging her bets. She hadn't known that one time would be all it took, but it didn't matter. If she hadn't bitten him then, he wouldn't be Reaper now. She dragged her eyes up to his, feeling the stupid, pointless tears welling past her control. "With you it might have only taken two."

"You converted me?"

Knowing it wasn't going to make any difference she whispered, "Not on purpose."

NOT on purpose.

Cole wanted to spit at the paltry denial. Wanted to rage at the betrayal. At her. He tightened his grip on her neck, expecting her panic, feeling her acceptance.

It would be so easy to snap her neck, Cole thought, anger pounding at him, pushing him forward. Just a little pressure there, a little twist here and she'd be dead.

Reaper. She'd made him into a goddamn Reaper. Rage tore through him with unrestrained force, black and powerful, narrowing his vision until all he could see was his hand on her neck and the acceptance in her sad brown eyes. His hand actually shook, and she stood there, damn her, daring him to kill her. Was he going insane?

Fight me, damn you.

She didn't fight. She just stood there, sadness washing over his anger, sinking through the cracks, bathing him in understanding. He tightened his fingers a fraction more. Her face bleached white, the scars whiter still. But she didn't run.

It took a hell of a lot to scar a Reaper.

It took a hell of a lot more to stand and let a man kill you. Goddamn her. Just, goddamn her. His grip loosened.

"Were you born a Reaper?"

She shook her head.

"No."

His rage faded and his vision expanded. His hand still shook, but his thoughts cleared. "Did you do it for love?"

"God no."

Which only left one option. "Were you forced into it?"

She nodded.

"Did you enjoy the experience?"

"No."

He let her go. "Then why the hell would you do it to anyone else?"

She looked at him for the longest time, tears welling in her eyes. It tore his heart out that he'd wanted to tear her throat up. It tore him up more to know she knew he'd wanted to. Even for one blind minute before reason had returned.

She only said one thing.

"Wendy."

It pissed him off from a whole other angle that she kept waving her daughter's name in his face like a talisman. To keep from grabbing her he grabbed his coffee. He might be a Reaper. He might be going insane, but he wasn't that easily manipulated. He took a swallow, then another. He had to take a third to keep from snarling as he asked, "So you all just got together and decided your need gives you every goddamn right you want to take away my choice of whether I want to live or die?"

"Yes."

"You don't pull your punches, woman."

She didn't apologize, just whispered softly, "You had mating potential."

He swallowed the last of his coffee, put the cup down, and turned toward her.

"Which according to Reaper law says I can do whatever I want to you. Take my revenge in any way I want?"

She swallowed hard, and then in that even voice he hated, said again, "Yes."

"Because you feel you deserve it."

She nodded. He was close enough to see the pulse pounding

double time in her throat. He might not be able to feel the panic in her energy, but the woman was panicking. But she was also standing her ground, for some moral reason that made no sense.

He slid his fingers over her cheek, into her hair, clasping a handful of strands at the nape of her neck, tilting her face back as he brought himself all the way up against her. "So I could slap you if I wanted to?"

Her breath caught, her eyes widened, and her fingers clenched into fists. But she didn't move. He took it as acceptance.

"My own private whipping post."

She nodded.

"You're going to let me take my anger out on you any way I want?"

"But not on Wendy," she interjected.

"We're not negotiating."

Her eyes narrowed and her energy lashed out. "You won't touch her."

No, he wouldn't. "I don't beat up on little girls."

She licked her lips. "Clark does."

"I know."

And there was the crux of the problem. No matter how mad he was. No matter that the rage inside him leapt like a living thing, Cole got Miranda's point. She was a woman in the middle of monsters with a human child; she was stuck between a rock and a hard place. Converting him had been her only way out.

"Tell me something. Did you know when you bit me that it could potentially change me?"

"No. Two bites never did anything to anyone."

"And if you had known then?"

There was a potent silence before she confessed, "I don't know."

"Wrong answer."

"It's all I have."

Cole didn't want to feel sympathy. He didn't want understanding. He wanted an outlet. And damn it, he'd have one.

He walked over to the bed, dragging her with him. She wasn't doing so well hiding her energy now. The closer they got to the bed, the more her panic beat at him.

He sat down and dragged Miranda over his lap, throwing up her skirts. He felt her surprise. Before she could figure out his intent, he swatted her ass three times fast. She cried out. The pained exclamation cut to his reason, stopping his hand mid-swat. He'd never spanked a woman in anger, and knowing that she was a Reaper and any damage would heal didn't mitigate the guilt of losing control. Or give him satisfaction.

Taking a breath, Cole let his hand settle on Miranda's ass, rubbing the round curves through the muslin. Putting an apology in the touch. Feeling the heat, feeling her nails dig into his calf through his denims.

Reaper or human, there were some things that he refused to do. He sighed and rubbed her ass again. It was a very nice ass, wide and round and firm with a cushion of fat over the top. It would be soft against his cock.

The lust hit him stronger than the rage. Son of a bitch, what was it about this woman that made him ricochet between extremes? She lay on his lap, stiff as a board, while he struggled with a need to push her to the floor, come over her, in her, and fuck her hard. Claim her, he realized. He didn't want to rape her; he wanted to claim her. In the most primal way possible.

Cole shook his head. Maybe he was already crazy. Turning Miranda over, he pulled her up into his arms and sat her across his lap. There were tears in her eyes. From pain or fear he didn't know. She had those emotions buried deeper than a pussy willow's roots.

He propped her chin against the side of his hand. Stroking his thumb over the tears on her cheeks, he sighed.

"It's a crazy road you've sent us down, lady."

"I didn't have any choice."

"That doesn't make it any better."

"What would you have had me do?"

Admit that part of the reason she'd bitten him had been desire. He sighed, "Nothing different. But there is something you do need to do from here on out."

He tapped his finger on her mouth, pressing it against those soft, full lips.

"What?"

"Don't hide from me anymore."

"What do you mean?"

"What you're feeling. Like right now. Your ass is smarting, you're terrified, and . . ."

He realized he could smell her desire.

"Aroused."

She blinked.

"Don't hide what you're feeling from me. That's the debt I'm calling in. You owe me, and that's what I want in repayment."

"You want me vulnerable to you?"

She ought to sound horrified. He intended to take full advantage. "All the way, no holds barred."

"And if I don't agree?"

He pushed her off his lap. "Then I probably will go crazy. You, lady, are apparently my trigger."

"I don't want to be."

He grabbed his hat up and headed for the door. He didn't want to be a Reaper, but it was what it was. He opened the door. Dirk stood there, whether to keep him in or others out he didn't care. Looking over his shoulder at Miranda, Cole jammed his hat on his head.

"Tough shit."

⊰ 13 ⊱

COLE DIDN'T HAVE TO WONDER WHERE TO FIND JONES. The Reaper was exactly where Cole would have been, doing exactly what he would have been doing had the events been the same at the Circle C. Cole walked up to the burned-out remains of the barn. The stench of burned wood hung in the air. Smoke still spiraled off some of the beams. Not much of the barn was standing, just one corner and part of the frame. The corner in which he'd huddled with Wendy, he realized. Son of a bitch. Reaching up, he touched the spot on his shoulder.

We don't know what you are.

Well, there was one thing he knew. He wasn't dead. Whether that was a blessing or a curse had yet to be determined. But he was still breathing and sane. Men called to each other over the bang of wood as timbers were pulled way. Jones looked up as Cole approached. Cole felt the touch of the Reaper's energy. He blocked it.

"I haven't gone loco yet."

Isaiah straightened and took off his right glove, then his left. "There's nothing saying you have to."

"Nothing saying I won't, either, is there?"

"No."

"So there's a chance."

Isaiah tucked his gloves in his back pocket.

"Without a full-fledged conversion, there's always a chance."

That was news to him. "From the way Miranda's jumping around, I thought it was a certainty."

Isaiah leveled Cole a look as he stretched his back. "Did you hurt her?"

"No."

Again Cole felt the touch of the other man's energy, and again he pushed it back.

"And if I ever do, you have my permission to put my sorry ass six feet under."

Isaiah cocked an eyebrow at him. "You think I need your permission for that?"

"Yeah."

Someone hollered a warning. Men scrambled to get out of the way as a timber fell. Everyone watched as it hit the ground, bounced slightly, and lay still.

"Hell of a mess," Cole said.

"Could have been worse."

Cole thought of Wendy. "Yeah. How many men did you lose in that attack?"

"None but three are badly injured."

"And the attackers?"

"Five. One of those was on the outskirts." Isaiah looked at Cole out of the corner of his eye. "Your doing?"

"Yeah." Grabbing a set of gloves off the end of the timber in front of them, Cole put them on. "You moving this?"

Isaiah took the other end. "You helping?"

"Beats the hell out of standing around. And I figure we can talk while we work."

"Got some questions, huh?"

"A lot of them. Like number one, why does everybody keep asking me if I'm feeling all right?"

"I told you, some people don't take well to the change."

"But Miranda didn't give 'em that final bite."

Isaiah grabbed one end of the charred beam; Cole grabbed the other. They lifted. It didn't feel nearly as heavy as it should have been. Some of that Reaper energy coming his way, maybe.

"So just what exactly can I expect?"

"I don't know."

"When can I expect it?"

"I don't know."

Cole swung the timber to the left to put it on the pile to the side. He let go of his end, catching Jones off guard. Cole had the satisfaction of hearing Isaiah grunt before he was forced to release his end, too.

"You don't know a hell of a lot, do you?"

"Nope."

"Do you even know what the hell you might have made me?"

"Believe it or not, we don't know that, either."

"How the fuck is that even possible?"

"Because we don't know what we were made into."

And that was a hell of a note. Cole slapped his hand against his thigh, resisting the urge to haul back and punch Isaiah in the face. Cole lifted his hat and ran his hands through his hair before settling the hat back on his head. "How long do I have?"

"I don't know; there have been cases where it's been a slow descent into madness instead of an immediate change."

"So you're saying that the danger isn't over? That if I don't agree to a third bite, I could marry Miranda, take on being a father to Wendy, and then this time next month suddenly be loonier than a rabid dog?"

"Possibly."

"But not likely," an unfamiliar voice added.

Cole turned to face the stranger. He was big, bigger than even Isaiah. He was dressed all in black. The darkness carried to his skin and hair. His eyes were darker still. His features sharp. His energy just . . . blank.

"Who the hell are you?"

"Have some respect when you speak to the enforcer," Isaiah snapped.

"Pardon me, but right now I don't have much respect for any of you. And until I get some answers, I'm not in the mood to develop any."

"The name's Blade."

The lethal edge to the man's attitude more than the knives tucked into his boots made it clear why he was called Blade.

"I've heard about you."

"And I you."

"So what makes you an expert on my sanity?"

"My nose."

"Pardon?"

"To be more exact, your scent."

"My scent?"

"You're not full Reaper, but I'm guessing somewhere back in your bloodline there was a Reaper. It's in your scent."

From the way Isaiah's head snapped around, this was news.

"Reapers are made, not born."

Blade took a smoke out of his pocket. "You can't think it was happenstance that those men who made you were able to create their weapons, Isaiah. The source had to come from somewhere."

"You're saying that somewhere there are born Reapers?"

Striking a sulfur on his boot, Blade nodded. "Yes."

Isaiah swore. Not as hard as Cole wanted to.

"And you think I'm part of that source?"

Blade shook his head. "No, but I think the blood runs in your veins. You've always been faster than other humans, more mentally attuned than them." He blew out a stream of smoke. "And there's that minor detail of you taking out four Reapers. That just doesn't 'happen.'"

"I could just be that good."

Blade smiled. "You could be."

Cole sighed. "But you don't believe it."

"I already told you what I believe."

"Are you part of this bloodline, Blade?" Isaiah asked.

"What I am isn't important. What is important is what he's going to do with what he's becoming."

The sun was shining; the air was warm. His gloves were still hot from the burnt timber, but a chill went down Cole's spine.

Isaiah pushed his hat back and took a step forward. Blade didn't step back. The man had balls; Cole had to give him that. He had to be feeling the anger lashing out from Isaiah, the unsteadiness of his energy.

"These are my people, Enforcer. What do you know that we don't?"

"I'm not at liberty to say."

Isaiah took another step forward. His energy lashed out. "Find it."

Sometimes Cole wondered if Jones had ever been sane. Addy's presence in his life had stabilized him the way he stabilized her, but, right now, Isaiah was one inch from going for Blade's throat. Cole sighed. If anything happened to Isaiah, Addy would take it personally. Talk petered off as men noticed the building confrontation. Cole stepped up and slapped Isaiah on the shoulder as if it were all in good fun. He forced a smile at Blade while keeping his hand clamped down on Isaiah.

"I think you'd better talk, Enforcer."

Blade looked between the two of them and sent back an equally false smile. Stubbing out his smoke on the sole of his boot, he said, "Not here."

Isaiah snarled. "Here works for me."

Blade just looked at him.

"This might be a conversation better served by privacy," Cole pointed out.

With another snarl Isaiah shook off Cole's hand, barked out a few orders to the men, and turned back. With a wave of his hand he motioned them on. "Let's go."

Blade started out down the path to the river, but as soon as they were out of sight, he veered into the woods. They walked into the trees, making a path where there was none.

The scents of rotting leaves, wood, and summer surrounded Cole. It smelled good and natural, and on any other day, the combination would have soothed him, but today all he could focus on was the relentless waves of anger coming off Isaiah and the tension coming off Blade. Whatever they were going to say, it wasn't going to be good.

They reached a small spot between three trees. Camouflage, he realized. He swept the area with his senses and felt nothing.

"We're alone," Blade confirmed.

So the other Reaper could sense energy, too.

"I can more than sense it; I can read your mind."

Fuck. "A handy skill to have."

Blade nodded. "If it helps, though, I can't always hear the words. Sometimes it's just images."

Cole pictured himself squeezing Blade's neck between his hands, choking the life from him. He sent a thought, *Read that.*

Blade smiled. "You're going to have to do better than that if you want to top out Isaiah. He's got me gutted over a log."

Cole looked over. "I thought he was one of yours?"

Isaiah shrugged and cut Blade another glare. "He's an irritating sort."

"No argument there."

Blade leaned back against a tree. "Nice to be appreciated."

"If you want to be appreciated, tell us what you know," Cole growled, not wanting to like the enforcer. "Why are your own kind attacking you?"

"We're not the only ones of our kind," Blade answered quietly.

"No shit."

"But we are the only ones of our kind over here."

"Over here?"

"In Europe werewolves live in established clans."

"Werewolves?" Isaiah repeated.

"Yeah. Werewolves. That's their name for us."

Cole blinked. A cold, hard knot settled in his stomach. "That's just legend."

Blade offered Cole his cigarette makings. Cole took them. There was the slightest tremor in his fingers. Werewolf? It made sense. Yet absolutely didn't.

"Well, legend or not, now you're part of it, whether you want to be or not," Blade finished.

Cole pulled out a paper. He'd have rather poured a shot. Or two. Or three. "Because Miranda bit me?"

"Because you love your cousin and are mated to Miranda."

The enforcer was right. Dammit. He poured tobacco onto the paper.

"How do you know there are others?" Isaiah demanded. Cole handed Isaiah the makings, which he almost snatched from Cole's hands. The smoke Isaiah started rolling was heavy on the tobacco.

Blade merely cocked an eyebrow at the rudeness and handed Cole a sulfur.

"A few years back I went to Europe. Sailed on one of those fucking oversize canoes they call ships." He took the makings back and started rolling another smoke. "Thought I'd get away from here, and I found out the hard way that we are not unique."

"Explain 'the hard way.'"

"Werewolf culture in Europe is very well established. You belong to a pack. Packs have a hierarchy within a clan. Interlopers are not welcome."

"Got your ass kicked, huh?" Isaiah growled, striking a sulfur on the heel of his boot.

Blade shrugged. "A time or two, but I kicked a few asses, too. Important asses, which kept me alive." He lit his own cigarette, shaking out the sulfur when he was done. "There, as here, it comes down to strength, and if you've got the strength to make a place for yourself, you can have it."

"You made a place for yourself?"

"Yes. For a while."

"So why are you here?" Cole asked.

"Because an unfortunate result of my appearance in Europe was to alert those clans of Rogue Reapers here."

Isaiah shook his own match out and tossed it to the ground. "Rogue? We're fucking Rogue?"

The wind changed directions, sweeping in the stench of burned wood and destruction.

"We came about through aberration. Man interfering with the way things should be. To them we're monsters, things that shouldn't exist but do. And if we don't become what they need us to become, if we don't police ourselves, they will take over the job."

"From Europe?"

Blade nodded. "Yeah. They have the numbers and the determination to wipe us out. And they would. They'd hunt us to the very last one to remove the contamination to the blood."

"Contamination? Makes us sound like a breakout of small pox."

"To them we are."

"Uppity bastards," Isaiah growled, blowing out a stream of smoke that disintegrated on the breeze as soon as it appeared.

Would the Reapers be extinguished before they even got started? Cole thought of Gaelen. And Dirk. Of the men he'd practiced with. Each and every one a warrior. "They'd better come packing."

The glance Blade gave him was pitying. "Make no mistake, they will. You think Jones is a badass? They've got thousands of years of being badass behind them. And best I can tell, they live two to three hundred years. That's a lot of experience to come up against."

Isaiah sat for a minute, absorbing the information. He took one, two, three puffs on his cigarette. "Two to three hundred years would be a nice spell in which to get to know Addy. Can we expect to live that long?"

Blade looked at him. "Don't know. No one's ever taken Reaper blood to create Reapers until the asses that made us."

Isaiah swore. "And they didn't even have the grace to do it clean. They just tortured and punished us until we couldn't see past the pain to fight."

Blade nodded. "And then they started feeding us that drug."

Drug?" Cole asked. They were drugged?

Isaiah looked off into the horizon, his energy seething. "Once they'd made us their weapons, they needed a way to keep us compliant so we'd take out the targets they wanted."

"So they got us addicted to 'the cure.'"

Blade snorted. "Some cure."

Cole had seen men addicted to opium do without. It wasn't a pretty sight. "That bad?"

Isaiah grunted. "Worse."

"How'd you get free?"

Blade blew a smoke ring. He watched it float, expand, and as it dissipated said quietly, "The thing about weapons is, no matter how well you think you've perfected them, there's always a chance they'll misfire."

Isaiah nodded and flicked an ash off the stub of his cigarette. "In case you can't figure it out, Blade misfired first. Then he arranged it so the rest of us could, too."

Blade smiled. It wasn't a nice smile. "One by one. Piece by piece their empire came down."

"And at the end?" Cole asked, knowing the men, knowing the answer.

It was Isaiah who answered. "None of them were alive to complain. The Reapers made their initial laws that still control us, one of them being not to consort with humans, and disappeared into the wilderness."

"You banished yourselves?"

"As broken as we were, it seemed a good idea at the time."

It wasn't a good idea now. Reapers were human at their core. Humans needed other humans. Isaiah was right. Those laws needed to be changed.

"Takes a fucked-up mind to do something like that," Cole murmured, beginning to comprehend the enormity of what had been done to Jones and the others. To see past what they were to the lives from which they'd come. Shit. "Makes for a fucked-up life, too."

Isaiah shrugged and drew on his smoke. "I don't think my life was worth much before they got hold of me."

"None of ours were," Blade interrupted. "That's why they chose us. Made it easy to break us since we didn't have anything to hold on to."

"Easy?" Isaiah asked. "Is that how you remember it?"

"After the torture, I don't remember shit."

Cole tried to imagine that. Not remembering his brothers, his parents, his ranch, his life. Everything that made him . . . him. He couldn't. He realized he was still holding the unlit match and cigarette. He put both in his pocket. He'd sucked in enough smoke and ash.

"So?" Isaiah asked. "When you say we have to clean up our clan—because I'm assuming our pack is going to be our clan—does that mean we have to form our own societies? Do we set them up by werewolf rules? Do we do all that just to keep the European werewolves happy?"

"No," Cole cut in, understanding what Isaiah didn't want to. "We do all that to keep Reapers alive, no matter what the werewolves decide."

Blade nodded. "I'm thinking it will come to war."

"Does anyone else know this?" Isaiah asked.

Blade shook his head. "Until there is a central government among Reapers rather than a loose collection of half-baked laws, all telling people would do is spook them."

"At least we have the pack council and the high council."

"Except the high council is the one that made the laws that designed to keep you all separate. We need to come together."

"Damn." Even Cole could see that wasn't likely to happen. Not if the ones who created the original laws were attached to them.

Blade nodded and leaned back against a tree. "Those are my thoughts."

There were still some things Cole didn't understand. "I have a couple questions."

"Shoot," Isaiah said, flicking the ash off his smoke.

"Who exactly made you Reaper?"

Blade answered. "During the war a group of opportunists, businessmen as they liked to call themselves, occasionally needed leverage in certain situations. They created us to be assassins and to provide them with that leverage."

"Where did they find you?"

"The streets, pretty much."

"They stripped away who we were and put in place what they wanted," Isaiah tacked on. "They liked the Reaper madness the process created. It gave them something to build on."

Isaiah said that with the dispassion of someone talking of a stranger. Hell, maybe it felt like that to him. Cole hoped so. Everyone had memories they didn't want to live with. Reapers apparently had more than most.

"And they used those assassins to what end?"

"For whatever they needed," Isaiah filled in. "If they needed a businessperson removed so they could buy what they wanted, they sent a Reaper. If they needed to change the course of politics in whatever direction they desired, we did it. We were point-and-shoot weapons with teeth and claws. We worked quietly. We worked quickly. We worked efficiently."

"We hunted," Blade growled.

The way the European werewolves would hunt Reapers, Cole realized.

"They controlled us with the cure," Isaiah added with the same dispassion as before. "Built our dependence on it and then made it the reward."

Rage whipped around Cole. Isaiah's. Blade's. Pushing at him like a spring storm. Wild and violent.

"We were animals," Blade snarled.

"But you're not now," Cole pointed out, breathing slowly to control his reaction to the emotional maelstrom catching him up. "Push came to shove, and you found your way out."

Isaiah looked up. His eyes glittered. His smile took on a feral edge. "Even the most beaten dog will turn on its master."

For the first time Cole felt the full power of the man that was Addy's husband. It was . . . impressive.

And Addy's protector.

The thought slipped into his mind with the smoothness of speech. He looked at Blade. Blade stared back. Cole acknowledged the truth with a nod. And protector. There was something to be said for having someone like Jones sitting watch over Addy. The woman did have a penchant for trouble. Another thought hit him.

"Can the werewolves in Europe have children?"

"Not frequently," Blade answered, "but they do, and the children are cherished."

"So women here, if they can have children, would they be valued in Europe?"

"I don't know. Bloodline matters a hell of a lot in clan hierarchy over there."

Isaiah grunted. "Cliquish bunch, aren't they?"

"Very."

Isaiah straightened and put out his smoke against the tree. "Then we need to become cliquish, too."

"Very," Blade agreed.

Isaiah looked over. "How long do we have?"

"Not as long as you'd think. Part of the deal of my being released to return to the U.S. was I was supposed to spy on your progress here and then report back."

"When?" Cole asked.

Blade didn't look concerned. "About six months ago."

"You didn't make it." Isaiah didn't make it a question.

"No."

Isaiah simply asked, "Why?"

"Because I didn't think it mattered what I had to report. My impression before I left was that the decision had already been made.

It was just a matter of gathering the forces. Any information I supplied would have been used for enhancing an attack."

The hair rose on the back of Cole's neck. Werewolf genocide. And Addy and Miranda were caught in the middle. "So they sent you back here to lull us into a false sense of security?"

"Apparently."

Isaiah straightened, looking off into the woods as if he could see beyond. "And you're sure they're coming?"

Blade nodded. "I'd bet the farm on it."

"And they're not going to be happy?"

"Nope."

Settling his brown Stetson on his head, Isaiah grunted, "Then this fighting we're doing among ourselves has got to stop. Or else we need to disappear."

Cole agreed. "If we separated out, blended into society, they'd have a damn hard time finding us all."

Blade looked at him. "True, but that would only delay things. They would hunt us relentlessly, track us down, and kill every man, woman, and child until there wasn't a shimmer of Reaper energy out there."

Isaiah swore, "Fuck that. We'll fight."

Cole agreed. "If I'm going down, I'm going down fighting, not cowering in the corner like a beaten dog."

Blade shook his head. "Bad analogy."

"Bad choices."

Cole turned to Isaiah. "What's the first thing we've got to do?"

"Get you married."

It wasn't a question.

"And then?"

"I haven't a clue."

❧ 14 ❧

COLE ARRIVED BACK AT MIRANDA'S LITTLE HOUSE AS dark was falling. It was of ramshackle construction that no amount of whitewash could improve. It still only sported one narrow window. It wasn't as nice as the lowest shack on the Circle C. Yet walking up to the door, he felt the same as he did when he rode up to his ranch. It felt like coming home.

Keeping his energy banked, Cole looked in through the window at the reason. Miranda and Wendy. They were sitting at the table. Wendy was making marks on the wooden surface with chalk. Miranda was teaching Wendy her letters, he realized. In the middle of the chaos, in the middle of the disaster yet to come, Miranda had found a moment of normalcy. He wanted to keep that for her.

Miranda looked up. He knew she couldn't see him. The light from inside would block his image, but she stared as if he were as clear as day. Damn. He felt the touch of her energy as a light caress against his senses. His cock stirred. He was probably going to have to get used to being with a woman from whom he couldn't hide. He pushed his hat back and smiled. There were worse things.

Miranda looked back down, gave Wendy some instruction, and then rose. He met her at the door. Light from inside spilled out along with the aroma of supper. So did Miranda's uncertainty. She stood there, hand on the doorknob, looking at him as if she didn't know whether to fight or run. He sighed and pushed his hat back farther.

"No need to worry. I'm over my mad."

Her smile was shaky. "Good."

Despite her words, the tension in her shoulders didn't ease. A wisp of hair fluttered around her cheek, an irresistible lure. He reached out and tucked it behind her ear. When she flinched, he slid his fingers around the back of her head, resting his palm against her cheek, cradling her head in his hand.

"I'm not a violent man, Miranda."

She looked at him as if he had just sprouted a second head. He couldn't blame her; about all she'd ever seen from him was violence.

"And especially not toward my wife."

"We're not married."

"After tonight we're going to be."

She blinked.

"Blade explained it to me. You've proclaimed me your mate. I gave my life for your child. Once we come together, it's a done deal. Even the council can't tear us apart."

She made a noise. It might have been a sigh or a curse. He couldn't tell and didn't care.

"You were hoping to get out of it?"

She shook her head, smoothed her skirt, sighed again, and this time gave him the truth.

"I was hoping you weren't aware of the law."

"Why?"

She shrugged and glanced back at Wendy. "If down the road I wanted to claim we weren't married, you could just walk away."

"Uh-huh." He leaned against the jamb. "But until then you're just planning on using me?"

For the first time that night her gaze skirted his. And she didn't answer. He took advantage of her distraction, pulling her a little closer, stroking his thumb down her cheek. The stroke provoked an answer.

"Yes."

"I can't fault you for that."

Her gaze snapped to his. "You're not mad?"

He shook his head. "No, it's good to know my partner has got a level head on her shoulders. There'll be times, probably, when you're going to need it."

She didn't flinch or pretend to misunderstand. He liked that.

"You have a lot of enemies?"

"I've ticked off a person or two."

"A few Reapers also."

He nodded. "Yeah."

She stood there, neither leaning in nor moving away. Just accepting his touch. Waiting, he realized, for him to take the lead.

"Are you going to invite me in for supper?"

She blinked. Her energy flickered with uncertainty. "It's your home now, too. You don't need an invite."

That was generous, but he didn't want her feeling completely out of control. Yet. "I'd prefer it."

She stepped back. His fingers glided against her smooth skin as she retreated. On the next step he dropped his hand to his side, but he didn't let go of that satiny sensation. He memorized it, rubbing his thumb against his fingertips, imprinting it on his memory. She'd probably be that silky smooth all over.

She waved him in. "Supper's ready if you're hungry."

He was hungry for a hell of a lot of things, but the way she was nervously rubbing her hands on her skirt, she probably wouldn't appreciate hearing about any of them right now.

"Good, I'm starving."

She nodded.

Wendy looked up just then and motioned eagerly for him to come over.

"Look, Cole! Look what I can make."

He didn't have any choice but to go. As he turned his attention to Wendy, her energy struck him, stronger even than Miranda's, but all little girl and innocent. He looked down at her bent head and the soft shine of her neatly braided hair. The hairs on the back of his neck stirred. They were going to want her for sure. His hands clenched to fists. Feeling Miranda's gaze, he forced them to relax and admired the chalk drawing on the wooden table.

"Now, that's a right nice letter *A*."

Wendy grinned up at him, revealing her missing tooth and fairy-child charm.

"Mommy says I'm very smart."

He ruffled her hair. He'd never let them near her. "Your mom has the right of it."

"I'm going to learn the letter *B* tomorrow."

"You are?"

She nodded. "*B* is for bumblebee, you know."

He couldn't remember when he'd ever had such innocence. "It is, is it? What's *A* for?"

"Apple." She drew a circle and added a leaf. "I like apples." Not glancing up from her drawing, she added, "An apple took my tooth, you know."

"Stole it dead out of your mouth?" He put his hand on his gun. "Am I going to have to have a talk with this apple?"

Her eyes grew wide. She looked at the gun, then she looked at him. Her gaze fell to the corner of his mouth where he could feel a smile tugging, and she giggled.

"No."

"Sure? Because I'd be willing."

She shook her head, setting her pigtails to bouncing as she colored in the last section of the apple. "No need."

"Why not?"

She set her chalk down with a satisfied plop. "Because I ate it."

"I guess that would settle things."

"Get a wet rag and clean off the table, baby," Miranda interrupted. "We're going to have supper."

"All right."

Wendy hopped out of the chair, carefully gathered up the materials, put them back in her little wooden box, and brought it over to her bed, sliding it underneath.

Her bed. Cole looked at the little bed tucked on one wall and the bigger bed tucked on the other, "bigger" being a relative term. No way would that hold them both, which led to another problem. How the hell was he going to consummate his marriage with an all-ears six-year-old a few feet away? Shit.

Miranda followed his gaze. The twitch of her lips surprised him. She ducked her head before he could comment. He strolled the whole four steps it took to get to her side. Her skin drew him like a moth to the flame. He couldn't resist grazing the backs of his fingers down her cheek. She didn't pull away.

"Seems likes we're going to have to make some arrangements for tonight."

"Oh?"

A tendril of hair draped over his fingers, binding them together. "Unless you want an audience?"

Her eyes grew big and that grin disappeared.

"No." On a defiant "And neither do you," she turned back to the fire, blocking him physically and mentally. That he didn't like. Closing his fingers against the urge to grab her arm and turn her back, to make her open to him as she'd promised, he forced himself to walk calmly back to the table.

Miranda stood over the stew pot, bowls in hand, and took a breath as Cole moved away.

I'm not a violent man.

The bowls rattled as her hands shook. He might not be a violent man, but just then something powerful had ahold of him. Something scary and deep. Maybe she should have taken Clark after all. He might be a brute, but he was predictable. With Cole, she could never foresee which way he was going to jump. It bothered her. No, she admitted, as she willed her hands to stop shaking, it scared the living daylights out of her.

She'd wanted a husband she could control, but controlling Cole would be like trying to control the wind rushing down the mountain. He did everything with a sense of purpose, including stepping through her door tonight. She didn't know what had been said or happened during the day, but she knew that up until the moment when he touched her cheek, he'd been debating something, and then when he touched her and the energy had arced between them, he'd made a decision.

"You need help over there?"

She jumped and the bowls rattled again. She hated the betrayal. "No, I've got it."

She put the bowls down on the little table beside the fire and scooped stew out of the pot.

Behind her she could hear Cole talking to Wendy. There was no impatience in his speech when he conversed with her. No impatience in his manner as he watched Wendy clean the table with a six-year-old's careless attention to detail, scrubbing at one spot, missing the rest. Miranda expected him to take the rag from Wendy or to lecture her, but instead he just chatted about *A* is for apple, *B* is for bee, and then some rambling speculation on what *C* could be for, letting Wendy do her best and just seeming to enjoy her. What was Miranda supposed to do with a man so darn scary and likable?

All too soon the bowls were filled. She carried two over to the table. When she would have headed back for the other, Cole shook his head and held the chair out for her.

"Why don't you have a seat and let me get that for you?"

She blinked.

"You've had a long day," he added a bit gruffly, as if he wasn't any more used to extending such courtesy than she was to receiving it. It was oddly endearing. She rubbed her hand down her skirt.

"So have you."

"It's my wedding night."

It was for all intents and purposes hers, too. The ceremony might not happen until tomorrow, but coming together tonight would make that ceremony superfluous. In the eyes of the council, and in her soul, tonight was the night that mattered.

"All the more reason I should serve you."

"That the way it is in your culture? Among Reapers?"

She really had no idea. "It's just the way it always is, in any culture."

"Well, this is our house, and I'm the head of it, and I say I want you to sit down and take a load off and let me get the rest of dinner."

And that was that, Miranda realized. She did as she was told, smiling at Wendy, who poked her finger in a bowl to test the temperature. Miranda was so nervous; she didn't even bother to correct her daughter.

Wendy leaned forward. "He's a big man, isn't he, Mommy? Almost as big as Uncle Isaiah."

Cole wasn't that big, but she imagined to a six-year-old he was huge. She nodded. "He is, but he's nice, too."

"Not like Uncle Clark."

She hated for her daughter to call that man "uncle."

"You don't have to call him uncle anymore."

Wendy looked up at her, sucking in her lip. "Won't he get mad?"

Miranda just shrugged.

"If he gets mad," Cole said from the fire, "you come tell me about it, and I'll have a talk with him."

Wendy's eyes got big. Her mouth pursed and then a beatific smile crossed her face.

"Truly?"

Miranda rolled her eyes at Cole. Wendy was a spirited child. "You really shouldn't have told her that."

Cole came back with the basket of biscuits and the last bowl of stew. "Why not? It's the truth."

"Because now she'll think you're a weapon she can throw at anyone."

He cocked an eyebrow at her. "So?"

"Well, that's not . . ."

He cut her off as he set the biscuits on the table. "That's the truth." He took his seat. "You hear me, Wendy? Anybody threatens you, anybody touches you, you let me know, and I'll handle it."

Wendy licked her lower lip the way she did when she was scheming. "Anyone?"

Cole nodded and plopped a biscuit on her plate. "Anyone."

Miranda sighed, took the biscuit, and broke it in half. "You really don't know what she'll do with that."

He met her gaze not one wit concerned. "There is no harm in a girl knowing her dad's got her back."

Wendy perked up again. "Daddy?"

Miranda groaned and smiled weakly. She'd been going to ease into that subject gently.

Cole showed none of her hesitation. With too much ease for Miranda's peace of mind, he said, "Your momma and I are getting married."

Wendy picked up the biscuit and took a bite. "Honest?"

"Don't talk with your mouth full."

That got Miranda a look from both Cole and Wendy.

"Honest. How do you feel about that?"

Wendy looked at Cole. "And you'll be a daddy like I used to have?"

"I don't know what you're used to, but if you mean, will I help you and protect you and make sure you have food to eat and clothes on your back?"

"Uh-huh."

He nodded. "Yeah, just like that."

"And no one can hurt me?"

"I'll kill anyone who tries."

He said that entirely too calmly. Wendy was enthralled. Miranda was appalled.

What on earth had she gotten herself into?

WHAT had she gotten herself into? Miranda asked herself the question again as Cole closed the door behind him after dropping off Wendy at his cousin's house.

The bar fell in place with a soft thud. Her stomach dropped with the same velocity.

"Was everything all right?"

He nodded. "Addy had just baked some cookies."

"She's a wonderful baker."

"Yes, she is; she used to have a very successful shop back home."

"You allowed that?"

He grimaced and took a step farther into the room, taking his hat off his head, revealing the smile in his eyes. "Believe it or not, Addy can be a bit headstrong."

Miranda licked her lips. So could she. Or rather she used to be. She touched her fingers to her cheek, feeling the scar's ridges against her sensitive fingertips.

She didn't know what had happened to that woman. Somehow over the years, through all the changes, she'd disappeared, but she wanted her back. If it wasn't too late. She lowered her fingers to the locket she wore around her neck. Inside it was Wendy's umbilical cord. She'd been so idealistic when she'd put it there. So damn innocent.

"Isaiah indulges her."

"Isaiah took her away from her life."

That piece of bitterness flicked across her conscience.

"Like I'm taking you away from yours?"

"Yeah, I'm having trouble with that."

"I didn't know you had Reaper blood."

"But you knew how to convert a person. You knew a second bite was a start."

He was mad at her, and by human law and Reaper law since she was his, he could do whatever he wanted to her and she would have no recourse.

"I wasn't thinking." At the time.

She took a step back, bumped into her chair. He took a step forward.

"I know."

Her stomach plunged to her toes, and for a second her heart felt like it stopped beating. His gaze never left her face as he took another step. She looked around for a weapon, but she'd done the dishes, and the knives were sitting over in the corner of the room, and she knew no matter how fast she was, he'd be faster.

She licked her lips. "I didn't know what I was doing."

His gaze dropped to her mouth. Heat flared between them. "I know that, too."

His fingers grazed her cheek, tracing over the same scar that she'd just touched.

"I'm pissed as hell at you, you know."

She nodded. His head tipped slightly to the side.

"You're shaking."

What was the use of denying it? "Yes."

"You're scared."

She nodded.

His eyes narrowed. "I'm not fucking Clark."

If he were Reaper, she'd swear he'd just growled. She swallowed hard and nodded. It was her turn to say, "I know."

He could be so much worse.

"I don't want to be Reaper."

She nodded. What else could she do?

"Hell, for all we know, maybe I'm not."

She knew how it felt to lose that sense of self. She didn't want him to think that there was nothing left of him. "Maybe."

She wished the word back as soon as it left her lips. His gaze sharpened. His thumb came to rest just at the side of her nose. His fingers slipped back, the pinkie touching the nape of her neck. She'd seen Blade snap a man's neck from almost that same position.

He took a half step until his big body was pressed up against hers. The top of her head came to just under his chin, and if she tilted her head just a little bit forward, she would be resting against his chest. She remembered how good that felt with her husband. In those moments when her husband, Carter, would hold her in his arms and she'd rest her cheek on his chest, she'd naively felt so safe.

She sighed at the much younger and much more naive woman she'd been then. Carter had seemed so strong compared to her, but he wasn't, or maybe he just hadn't been strong enough. It was hard to know, to remember. They'd married so young.

Cole's hand slid down the side of her face in a gentle caress, slipping through her hair to her nape, to her shoulder blades, and down to her back. His other arm slid up her hip, across her bottom, making her jump. He chuckled and did it again. She didn't jump again, just stood there stiffly, wondering what he was up to.

"Miranda?"

"What?"

"When a man hugs you, it's a good thing."

The breath she hadn't known she'd been holding escaped in a sigh.

"You're angry."

"As hell."

"At me."

"At life. There's a difference, and if you put your cheek on my chest, you might feel it."

"I don't understand."

"Try it and see."

She shook her head. "I can't."

"Why?"

Because if she relaxed that little bit, she might just fall apart. She'd been relying on no one but herself for so long, trying to keep her place, to protect her daughter. Some nights she'd felt like she'd scream. Others she had been too exhausted to scream, but always she'd known, she had to protect herself and her daughter. Always she'd known there was no one left but her.

Cole's voice softened, his arms tightened, coaxed. "It's only an inch, maybe two. How much harm can there be in two inches?"

She didn't have a defense for that, and then he didn't give her a choice. His hand came up again and pressed until her cheek met his chest. She let her breath out in a shuddering sigh. As the last bit of breath left her, she heard it, the slow, steady beat of his heart. Heard it pick up speed as her hand touched his forearm. Felt inside that insidious melting, that false sense of safety. And she just relaxed into it.

His hand stroked over her hair. "We're going to be a team from here on out, Miranda. You can trust me."

She'd heard that before, and she had done as her instincts had said then, too, but at the end of the day she'd been alone.

"You might not always be around."

"I'll be here."

"You're not invincible."

"Close enough."

She shook her head. Men always thought they were invincible. They always thought it was close enough. Then they took these stupid-crazy risks, and they died, and they left her alone. Her father with his desire to break the stallion that had thrown him off and snapped his neck. Her husband's desire to tame the Wild West had left her raped and scarred and beaten.

"My father said the same thing. So did my husband."

"Yeah? And where are they?"

"My father is dead."

"Your husband?"

"Gone, too." She expected him to let her go, but he didn't. He just stood there, his fingers rubbing between her shoulder blades in small, light circles, his heart beating strong and steady under her cheek.

"How?"

"He killed himself . . . after. He couldn't live with the shame."

"I'm sorry."

"It was his choice." She had to believe that. That there was nothing she could have done to stop him.

The heat of Cole's body wrapped around her with the same strength as his arms.

A hug was such a dangerous thing. Such an insidious way of weakening a woman's will. She could have fought him if he'd grabbed her, would have if he'd hit her, but this, this insidious comforting was just diabolical.

With a soft sigh of surrender, she slipped her arms around his waist. "You are a very clever man to seduce me this way."

She felt his smile against her hair. "Thank you, I try."

Heat and muscle slid under her palm. "Dangerous even."

"To some."

He wanted her to know he wasn't a danger to her, but he didn't understand what she feared. He was a man, how could he? Everything worked in his favor. Nothing worked for her.

"Are you going to bed me tonight?" she asked.

She felt the slight start under his skin, could feel the hum of tension under his muscles. She glanced up. His expression was unchanged. If she hadn't been touching him, she wouldn't have realized a thing.

"It's what married couples usually do."

She licked her lip "We can just pretend."

He tipped her chin up, looked into her eyes, and that was definitely a twitch in the corner of his mouth.

"I've been told Reapers can tell when a couple mates. There is a change in the scent. Got a way to fake that?"

She shook her head. She hadn't known that. She searched his gaze, looking for the truth of it. There was no sign that he was lying.

"If this mating isn't believed to be real, Clark has a claim." He didn't have to say any more. She reached for the buttons of her shirt. He cocked his eyebrow at her.

"Can't say I find any fault in a woman eager for bedding."

She snorted.

He moved her back, forgetting she was so close to the chair. He caught her before she could stumble and fall, pulling her back against him as she pitched toward the floor. His front to her back, his strength to her weakness, his determination to her hesitation. He was always saving her. Standing within his embrace, she went back to work on her buttons.

His hands came over hers. The sides resting on top of her breasts, just a slight pressure that seemed to take on so much more significance the longer they lay there. And that tension, that fine tension that always whispered between them, increased to a hum.

Her nipples peaked, and in between her legs moisture gathered.

There was something about this man that was so irresistible. He scared her; he excited her. He was inevitable.

"Miranda?"

"Yeah?"

He moved her hands away from the buttons and turned her around so she rested against him. So he could see her face, she realized as he tipped her chin up.

"I'm not going to hurt you."

"I'm not a virgin. I know what to expect in the marriage bed."

"Well, you're just determined to kill the mood, aren't you?"

"We have a mood?"

"Not yet but I'm working on building one."

"I'd prefer you just get it over with."

"Well, this is my first wedding night, and I'm kind of thinking I want to make it memorable."

"Why?"

"Because someday I'm going to be old, and I'm going to be gray, and my knees are going to kill me, and my hands aren't going to work too well, and I'm going to look across the table, and I'm going to see you there, and I'm going to think of this night. And I want to know that the reason I'm there with you, when I'm old, is because we started out right."

She could see that. She could picture that. She could feel that as strongly as she could feel the softness of his energy wrapped around her. A hug so much more intimate than his arms, and the truth just spilled right past her lips.

"I want that, too."

He took her hands and moved them up to his shoulders.

"Then maybe it's about time we start it right."

⇥ 15 ⇤

HE WANTED TO COURT HER, COLE REALIZED. A WOMAN like Miranda deserved soft kisses, moonlight dances, and all the trappings a man laid out for the woman he chose. His options might be limited on the "all" but he could offer her a dance.

Miranda stumbled against him as he took the first step in a waltz. It was the most natural thing in the world to slip his hand down to her waist to steady her. She looked at him, clearly confused, as he moved them around the small space.

"Haven't you ever danced with a beau?"

"Not in a long time."

"Then you're overdue."

She didn't have anything to say to that, but she didn't protest when he started humming. If anything, her energy focused. He smiled at the determination. "Dancing is supposed to be fun, you know."

"I don't know this dance."

"Just follow my lead."

She did, getting the hang of it right up until the first turn. Then she stumbled again. He caught her, using the moment to pull her against him too tight to be proper. She blinked, catching her mental balance. He felt the flicker of her energy wavering between passion and confusion. He squeezed her hand and repeated.

"Just trust in my lead."

She looked down.

"No." He tapped her chin with their clasped hands. "Watch my eyes."

He liked that she obeyed immediately. He liked a lot of things about her. He liked the wave in her hair, the softness of her mouth, the fullness of her breasts, the heat of her passion that slid over his so deliciously. Everything about her fit him well, like she'd been made for him.

"What are you doing?" she asked.

"Haven't you ever waltzed before?"

"That's a scandalous dance."

"For a scandalous woman."

"I'm not scandalous."

He smiled. There was one thing he knew for sure: she wasn't conventional. A conventional woman would have caved long ago.

"You're a fighter."

She stumbled again. It just gave him an excuse to hold her closer.

"I'm not denying it. I'm just saying I'm not much of a dancer."

"That's because you need to trust me."

"You keep telling me that."

He tried a turn. "I'm waiting for you to start doing it."

Her nails bit into his upper arm.

"I'm not a trusting person."

"You need to be with me. There's likely going to be a few hiccups down the road where it's going to get dicey."

She didn't deny it. He liked that about her, too. She didn't run from the truth.

"And in those moments . . ."

He spun her in a circle, smiling at her little gasp, enjoying the feeling of her breasts pressing flat against his chest as she leaned into him.

"You're going to need to do what I tell you, when I tell you."

She caught her balance and looked up. "Just like that?"

He nodded and spun her again.

"Just like that."

This time she was ready for him, moving easily without stumbling, without falling, just staying with him. He found he liked that better. His partner. This time when he spun her, he felt that little surge of confidence when she kept up with him. She was enjoying the dance. He added a couple more intricate steps, inordinately pleased when she followed easily.

He could feel her mind touching his. Normally that was an intrusion, but from her, fuck, it was hot as hell. She'd feel everything when they made love, his passion, his lust, and he'd feel hers reflected back tenfold. They'd be connected in a way never possible before. In a way, he realized, he'd always yearned for. "You think you're going to keep up with me, china doll?"

She smiled. "Do your worst."

"A dangerous invitation for a man like me."

"How do you know I'm not dangerous?"

"Oh, you're very dangerous."

He did a quick sidestep around a chair; there really wasn't much room for dancing. There wasn't much room for anything. He looked at the bed, but he'd make it work.

On the next spin, he pinned her against the wall. Hip to hip, belly to belly, chest to chest. She gasped. He leaned down and took that soft expulsion as his own, fitting his mouth carefully to hers.

Her fingers curled into the back of his hands. She moaned, and he realized he was pressing her too hard. He eased up, and she moaned again at the separation. He didn't miss the regret in her eyes. She was soft to his hard, patience to his anger, strength to his strength. He relaxed his mind, letting her energy flow through him. She held him tightly in a feminine, soft, seductively hot grip. It was his turn to moan.

Her lips parted beneath his, just a little, just enough to tempt and tease the passion within him. He traced that slight opening with his tongue in little flicks, teasing back in return. She responded with everything he could have wanted, her mind, body, and passion. Fuck.

Her eyes opened, and he felt the start in her energy as he lost the hold on his. He'd have to be careful. This tuned in to him, she could feel overwhelmed and he didn't want that.

He smoothed the hair off her cheek, keeping his hand against her face when he was done. Another connection. He wanted to build many of them with her. With his thumb under her chin, Cole tilted Miranda's head back just a little, adding that little bit of tension that spiked her desire. Her lips parted farther.

He studied her face, the flush on her cheeks, the shadows in her eyes. Felt the flow of her desire as completely as if he'd had his hand between her legs. She was wet already and ready for him. He didn't have to touch her to know that. And he was hard and ready for her, and he bet she would have known that even if he hadn't been pressed up against her. He'd never had a lover so in tune with him. It was hot. Erotic. Perfect.

Inside him a wildness started to pulse, following the lust in his blood, firing it. His muscles itched under his skin, and the desire to take her increased. From deep within his chest came a growl. He felt the spike of her wetness as that growl shivered through her. She gave him a little growl of her own.

"You have too many goddamn clothes on," he muttered.

She just smiled. He grabbed her blouse.

His nails pressed against her skin. Another shiver shook her from head to toe. Another growl rose from somewhere deep inside. His senses sharpened even as the world narrowed. He memorized her scent, her sigh, as her lust poured over him in debilitating waves that stripped his control. The material tore, and he took her gasp into his mouth. Holding her breath as his own. His. She was his.

It wasn't enough. He felt pressure against his chest. He looked down. Her hands were pressed against him, the fabric of his shirt keeping her touch from his skin.

"Tear it off."

She just stared at him and shook her head. "You don't have another."

He didn't care. His hand slid down to her throat, closing around it, keeping her face to his as he slid his knee between her legs.

His "You don't tell me no" was a guttural statement of fact.

Her eyes widened, her lips pulled back, showing him her canines. The growl rippled from her throat, shivered down his spine all the way to his cock.

She was ready to fight him. He shook his head and kissed her hard, smiling at the thought of pinning that little body against his. Pulling up, he brought thought to action. He groaned or maybe she did. Those beautiful breasts melted into his chest. Her mouth into his. Running his tongue over those canines she liked to flash at him, he muttered, "My hot little doll."

Her claws bit into his chest. "I'm not a doll."

No, she wasn't. She was all woman. Desirable. And tonight she was his. "But you are mine."

It irritated him that she didn't agree immediately. Catching her lower lip between his teeth, he bit gently.

"Open."

She looked at him, gaze questioning, breath catching.

"Wider."

She did, and he fitted his mouth to hers. Teasing the sensitive inside of her lip with his tongue, making her jump and quiver.

"Yes. Just like that, baby. Give me that."

He kissed her until she was soft and compliant against him. He kissed her slow and deep, drawing out each caress, each shiver of sensation. He kissed her until her fingers were stroking rather than pressing and her breath came in soft little gasps that buffeted his lips. Kissed her until she was fighting to get to him rather than away from him.

"Tear my shirt off," he repeated.

He felt the prick of her nails as she curled her fingers to obey. Heard the rip as the fabric gave. Felt the blessed coolness of the air against his heated skin and then the bliss of her palms spreading over his chest.

Hot, cold, woman, wolf. She was all that and more. Another growl and he didn't give a shit what she was, what they were; he just knew they had to be together. He pulled her up, or maybe he leaned down, who the hell could tell? He had her beneath him, her soft thighs sliding along his as he ground his hips into hers, his cock straining to be closer still, needing her.

She cried out. A bit of the haze lifted, and he swore. He had to be hurting her, but when he checked, all he saw was the passion-drugged expression on her face, the red-hot glitter of desire in her eyes.

"Did I hurt you?"

"No. Yes." She moaned and drew her pussy along his cock. Even through two layers of clothes, the sensation buckled his arms. "Who cares?"

"Spread them. Give me room." With a knee he nudged her legs apart. She shifted, and he claimed the space as his own. Anchoring his fist in her hair, he tipped her head back. He needed to know she heard this. "And for the record I care. I want you screaming with pleasure, not pain."

He expected her to flinch from his gaze. Most people did when he put that much of his personality behind a statement, but Miranda just nodded, skimmed her palms up his chest until her hands were around his neck. Holding his gaze she pressed her nails into the back of his neck, pulling him back into the kiss, back into her, her tongue twining with his, inviting him deeper.

"More."

The whisper or thought, he wasn't sure which, spread into his mind. Yes, they both needed more.

He grabbed her by the shoulders and pulled her away from the wall, scooping her up in his arms. It was only three steps to the bed. Three steps that stretched like an eternity. Three steps that tested his patience, his resolve. Three steps that heightened his passion to the critical point before, with another irreverent curse he laid her down upon the bed. The smile she offered him was pure witchery. The shift of her body pure enticement. Instead of accepting the invitation, he took a moment to look, just look at all the perfection that was his wife.

"You're beautiful."

"I'm not."

He cocked an eyebrow at her. "What'd I tell you about telling me no?"

She closed her mouth on whatever it was she'd been about to say. "Not to do it."

He brushed the hair off her temple. "Good girl."

She smiled tentatively, a tremulous quiver of her lips showing the uncertainty banking the passion. He didn't want that.

"You are a delight, Miranda Cameron. On every level. In every way, you are beautiful to me."

And she was, lying there, a sensual goddess waiting to be taken, her full breasts rising from the tatters of her shirt. Her nipples, hard and pink, topped each white mound like candy on a confection. He very badly wanted to taste them. His cock throbbed and strained as he imagined doing just that. Lust thickened his blood. Damn, he wanted those nubs more than pink. He wanted them wet, red, and aching from his mouth. He wanted to feel them slide along his cock, his balls, and then back up. He wanted to tease and torment them until she was writhing and begging. He wanted . . . her.

He glanced up, and all that chugging lust slammed through him in a control-stealing wave. She was watching him watch her. That soft smile on her lips as she saw his pleasure raised all kinds of hell with his control.

"You like the way I look at you?"

She nodded. "I do."

Tapping that smile with his fingertip, he traced a path from her lips, down the side of her neck, over the ridge of her collarbone, to the hollow between her breasts. Goose bumps trailed in the wake of his touch and raced ahead, climbing the rise of her breast. Her nipples pulled tighter. It was his turn to smile. "Good."

Slowly reaching over, giving her all the time in the world to anticipate his touch, he took the right nipple between his finger and thumb, pinching it lightly, increasing the pressure gradually until she moaned and shifted, arching up. He held the tension there.

"Right there, doll?"

She nodded and closed her eyes. "Oh, yes."

Her legs shifted on the mattress, invisible to him beneath the skirt. Inside him a reckless power surged, tightening his muscles, heightening his passion. He wanted to see her do that naked. Wanted to see the moisture gather on her pussy. Wanted to see her spread her legs in wanton invitation. Wanted to gather her moisture on his tongue. To taste her. Shit, he needed to taste her.

"More."

He released her nipple reluctantly. Her nipples just sat there, pert and sweet, just begging. Before he could help himself, he gave them both a little slap. As if struck by lightning, her eyes flew open, and she arched higher. His breath stopped. So did hers. She gasped his name. Son of a bitch. She liked that. His smile broadened. Well, so did he.

He did it again. No different, just the same light contact, just enough to tease, to snap her nerve endings to attention.

"Cole!"

Her fingers dug into the sheets. There was a ripping sound as her nails cut through the material. He liked that, too. He grazed the back of his own nails down her stomach, smiling when the muscles sucked in. When he got to the waistband of her skirt, they both stopped breathing. He popped the threads on the first button at the waistband, holding her gaze as the second one followed the first. She didn't look away, but she still didn't breathe. He smiled, knowing what she wanted. He brushed her hair off her face with his free hand, feeling the dampness of her skin, the heat of her passion. His senses sharpened on a surge of energy.

Her scent surrounded him. Spicy, sweet, sexy woman. His cock pounded in his pants. He'd tell her to free him except if he did, he'd be in her so fast that it would be over before it began. And he didn't want it over yet. He wanted to explore all the options with this woman. Wanted to see how high he could take her before he satisfied them both. He slipped his fingers under the loosened waistband, gliding them over the cotton of her drawers. Still holding her gaze, he shook his head.

"I don't want you wearing these anymore."

He found the slit. His finger naturally slipped inside. She moaned and bit her lip.

"I can't go naked."

"What did I tell you about telling me no?"

"But . . ."

"I want you available."

Her energy flared in a convulsive ripple of delight. "They have a hole!"

"So do you."

He teased her with his fingertip, circling lightly, once, twice. Her muscles clenched. He did it again, harder. "A silky, tight one."

She bit her lip and groaned, whether from his words or from his finger parting her folds, he wasn't sure, but she was wet, deliciously wet. He dipped his fingers into her juices, coating them, watching her squirm as he did, deliberately not touching her clit. Just as slowly he withdrew. Watching her watch him as he brought his fingers to his mouth was one of the hottest things he'd ever done. With a slow flick of his tongue he tasted her. The growl came from deep within, torn out from the depths of his soul as the taste spread through his mouth. Sweet, spicy. His.

She shivered. He swore that same shiver snaked down his own spine. She reached up and touched his cheek. The barest hint of contact. The impact sliced through his defenses like the hot edge of a knife, searing the open wound on his soul he'd learned to live with, cauterizing the bleeding but leaving an ache. A bone-deep ache that was somehow harder to bear. Until her fingers feathered over his lips. Then it just seemed right.

"Yes, my little china doll. Feel what I feel as I make you squirm and scream."

Slipping her fingers between his lips, she drew him to her with the slightest of pressures. Chest to chest. Mouth to mouth. So close when he exhaled, his was the breath she drew in. Perfectly primal. Just—he groaned—perfect. Fuck waiting.

He went to tear open his pants, but her hand was there before his.

With a grin, that almost made him spill, she murmured, "Let me."

"Worried about the sewing you'd have to do after?"

A widening of her grin was her answer. Her other hand joined the first. Unbuttoning, brushing. Squeezing. It was his turn to groan. Her turn to smile.

She liked him like this, Miranda decided. Impatient and needing, wanting what only she could give. Wanting her. Not for what she could bring him. Not for status, but simply because she made him hunger. She unbuttoned the last button. His cock fell into her palm. So hard and thick. She measured its length in a series of squeezes. And boy, he was big. Her pussy throbbed and clenched.

"Damn, that feels good, china doll."

Yes, it did. And right. He forgot to say right. In a way it never had before. She felt a pang of guilt at the comparison to her husband. But he had been more boy than man, chasing dreams without substance. And she'd followed him. Been loyal to him. But she was a woman now with a woman's needs and understanding, and Cole was a man. All man.

"Your man," he growled, thrusting his cock through her fist. She shivered as he pulled back and the rim caught on the edge of her hand. A stroke of her thumb found the broad head wet. It was her turn to taste and his turn to curse.

"Fuck."

He did swear too much, but right in that moment she didn't care. She had the taste of him on her tongue, salty sweet and spiced with the essence of Cole. Everything Reaper in her went wild with the demand for more. She wanted him. Not for the short time she'd have with him as a human, but all of him. For a Reaper's lifetime and beyond.

Her canines itched and lengthened as his scent, that addictive scent, grew stronger. Beckoned and drew. Tempted.

She put her hand over the mark of her previous bite. It would be so easy, so easy to take the final step that would bring him into her world. Into her life.

She looked up. "Don't let me bite you."

His gaze searched hers. And while everything inside said hide, she didn't. She just lay there, her mark heating under her skin, and she let him see the battle inside, the good and the bad. The need. His hand covered hers. Immediately the chaos settled to calm.

"I won't."

He didn't sound any more sure than she did. But it was a start. And when he came over her, it was another. A blending of souls as skin warmed skin.

"Mate."

The word whispered from deep within.

"Wife," he answered just as fervently. Two different words from two different people but only one meaning.

"Mine."

Cole shook his head and feathered kisses over her forehead. "You've got that backward, china doll. You're mine." His knees separated hers. Her legs spread easily, naturally. He felt so right.

"Every delicious inch of you."

She arched her back, opening. Offering. "Yes."

His cock fell hot and heavy against the pad of her pussy. Her senses drew up taut, focusing on that point of connection.

She grabbed at his shoulders. "Cole."

"Yes, baby?"

Her fingers slipped on the fine sheen of sweat glistening on his skin. She tried again. Even Reaper, her strength was nothing against his. The knowledge just spiked her passion further.

"I need you."

"Fuck." It was a curse and a plea. "I need you, too."

She tugged harder, her nails digging slightly. He growled and tucked his arms under her knees, pulling her legs high and wide, pinning her with his strength. His desire. His lust. Oh God, she loved his lust.

"Don't let me hurt you."

He couldn't. "You can't."

She lifted her hips higher. Arched her back. The wet heat of his mouth closed around her right nipple in a burning consummation echoed in her pussy as his cock tunneled into the tight folds, claiming her inch by inch. It'd been so long. Too long and never like this. Everything in her opened as she took him, body, heart, and soul. Everyone said it took three bites to make a Reaper. Three bites to make a mate, but in that moment when Cole's cock stretched her beyond capacity, while she breathed and struggled to manage the sensation, the knowledge that wasn't the truth sunk deep. All it took was the right man and the right woman coming together. Nothing more, because that was enough. Almost too much.

"Too much?" he asked, in a voice gone guttural with the same emotion buffeting her.

She squeezed tentatively or tried to. And within her the flames burst forth. It was too much. Unbearable. Perfect. But at the same time she needed . . . With a twist of her hips she whispered, "More."

"Yes, more. All." He ground against her. "Jesus, baby, I need you."

His expression was hard and tight with desire. It wasn't enough. She needed more. She wanted to see his face softened with repletion, wanted to feel his come soak her pussy in a rich explosion, to know that she'd drained him, emotionally, physically. In every way. To know that they were one.

"Take me. All of me. Please."

He needed no more encouragement. With a growl that spiked her lust to a fever pitch, he pulled back, his cock dragging deliciously on the delicate flesh within, stretching her again as he drove back in, harder, deeper. Every stroke building on the last, giving her more as her plea repeated itself in a primitive litany.

"Please. Please. Please."

Over and over she begged, and over and over he gave her what she wanted until she couldn't hold on and he couldn't hold back. Until she was so raw and sensitive just the pulse of his cock, just knowing he was about to come, threw her into orgasm.

"Fuck!"

On a thrust so hard she felt it in her womb, he flooded her spasming pussy, filling her as she rippled around him, reveling in every pulse, every drop. She squeezed harder when he released her legs and collapsed against her, milking those last drops of come from him, letting his shudder reverberate through her, feeling the depth of his pleasure.

"Greedy woman," he muttered, shivering again, his cock giving a little jump inside her. Her teeth itched to bite. To mark. Oh Lord, she wanted to mark him again.

Pushing up on his elbow he smoothed her hair off her face. "You all right?"

She nodded. "You?"

She would have been offended by his chuckle if he hadn't kissed her right then. She closed her eyes as his lips met hers, and she felt him inside and out. She'd never been kissed so tenderly before, so deeply. Never been so utterly and completely owned in one moment by one man. It scared the crap out of her.

His lips grazed her eyes, her nose, the corner of her mouth. "Just relax, baby. I've got you."

She had to believe, Miranda realized, because sometime in the last few minutes she'd given herself away. Wrapping her arms around Cole's neck and her legs around his hips, she whispered, "Don't let me go."

He held her just as closely with one difference. There was no fear or uncertainty in his voice when he promised, "Never."

⊰ 16 ⊱

FOR A MAN WHO'D BEEN LOOKING TO RUN, HE SURE hadn't gotten very far, Cole thought the next morning, tying the last knot in the rope he'd braided around the limb of a big tree out behind the house. He might not be able to give Wendy much right now, but he could give her a swing. Every child should know what it felt like to almost fly.

"Is it done yet?"

He looked at Wendy. She was so full of excitement she was about to pop out of her skin. "Just about. You wouldn't want me to tie it wrong and have you come crashing down just as you were about to touch the sky, would you?"

She shook her head, sending those braids to dancing. "No." A pause and then, "Will I really be able to touch the sky?"

"Yup." He smiled down at her. It was a small untruth that wouldn't even matter once her imagination was set free. She grinned up at him with that gap-toothed smile of hers. He'd made the swing simply because it bothered him that the little girl had nothing to play with but dirt. Almost as much as Miranda's defensive declaration this morning after the glow of lovemaking wore off.

When push comes to shove, you'll leave, and it will just be Wendy and me.

She'd said that over leftover stew and biscuits as if bringing it up over something as normal as a meal somehow made it normal. If Wendy hadn't bounced in right then, he'd have blistered Miranda's butt, and not in a good way.

He yanked the knot tight. How the hell the woman could say that to him after being so close his breath was hers, her thoughts were his, their scents and energy blended, he didn't know, but she had. Somehow, somewhere along the line, she'd learned not to depend on anyone to survive, and she was trying to push him away.

He tugged the rope, testing the soundness. That was going to change, because come hell or high water, that woman was going to learn to depend on him. People had made marriages work on a lot less than the compatibility they had.

"Is it ready now?" Wendy asked again.

He looked down. She was pretty much dancing on her toes, her often-repaired dress blowing in the breeze, her eyes big with anticipation. He couldn't believe she had never had a swing. The girl was made for the mental adventures that went hand in hand with swinging high on bright sunny days. "Yup."

By the time he climbed down off the tree, Wendy was already scooting her butt back onto the wooden board he'd made into the swing. She gripped the ropes with white knuckles, looking up at him with uncharacteristic caution.

"You won't push me too high?"

The uncertainty was too reminiscent of her mother's. "I'll only push you as high as you want to go."

Her feet dangled above the ground. She bit her lip. The wind blew her hair off her face. She looked very small, very scared, and he remembered how she'd hung on for him in the barn. There was a lot of fight inside that little girl. But also a lot of hurt.

"You know I'd never do anything to hurt you, little one." He needed to say it to her for the simple reason he didn't think she'd heard it enough from enough people.

She nodded and took a breath. And before his eyes that grit he admired in her settled into place, tightening her expression and narrowing her gaze. When her tongue poked out the corner of her mouth, he had to smile.

As soon as he stepped behind her, she looked over her shoulder. "Just a little one, all right?"

He nodded. "It's always best to test the waters before you go pulling the trigger on something new."

He couldn't see Wendy's face now because she'd turned around, but the nod of her head was tight, indicating all the fear inside her, but she was still sitting on that swing, still ready to go. The kid had guts. His brothers were going to love her. He put his hand on the ropes. She jerked.

"Just a little one," he reassured her.

Again that stiff nod. He gave the swing a gentle push. She squealed as if he'd sent her sailing to the moon. The squeal brought back memories.

Addy used to like to go sailing to the moon. Her skirt would fly up, and her petticoats would flash. Reese would tease her about showing her ruffles, and she'd squeal again and try to hold her skirt down with one hand or catch it between her thighs. Reese would only push her harder then, just to see that laughter in her face. She'd lost so much laughter, and Cole hated to admit it, but with Isaiah she seemed to have found it again. Cole resented the hell out of the fact that she'd found it without him. But he understood. And he was glad. Like Wendy, sometimes he had to test out an idea before he could pull the trigger on it.

He fits her.

Reese's words came back again. Cole sighed and gave Wendy another little push. Goddammit, he was getting tired of Reese being right, but Isaiah did seem to fit Addy, filling those holes that Cole, as her cousin, couldn't fill, understanding her in ways that he hadn't been able to. Addy just might have known what she was doing when she'd started feeding Isaiah.

Cole gave Wendy a third push. This time she didn't squeal, but he felt the excitement start to replace the dread in her energy. She was a bold thing under all that caution. He pushed her again and again, keeping his promise, not sending her any higher, just a nice gentle rhythm that she was comfortable with, building her trust. It saddened him that she needed him to build that trust, but he was used to it; this was a hard country. Hard on humans, hard on Reapers, and maybe, he decided, especially hard on humans living with Reapers.

"Do you like it here, Wendy?"

She nodded. "It's much better than moving all the time."

"Why is that?"

She cast him a quick look over her shoulder, her knuckles still white on the rope. He had an impression of resignation. "I couldn't have a swing if we kept moving."

"Fair enough. What else would you like to have?"

"A puppy." She was surrounded by wolves, and she wanted a puppy? "What else?"

She kicked her feet, making the hem of her dress flutter. "A pretty new dress like Milly Sandoval had."

"Who is Milly Sandoval?"

He could feel the walls close up around her. Whoever Milly was, she'd hurt Wendy. Cole hated that. Hated the thought that anyone would dim that bright, glowing spirit.

"A girl in town."

"Which town?"

She shrugged. "I don't remember, but she had a pretty yellow dress. She looked like sunshine."

"Did you like Milly?"

There was a silence while he pushed her two more times. Finally she muttered, "She laughed at me."

Cole had the overwhelming inclination to dislike Milly Sandoval. "She did, huh?"

Wendy nodded. He could guess why. Wendy's clothes were serviceable but screamed poverty.

"Must be she was jealous of how pretty you are. So pretty you didn't even need a yellow dress to make you shine."

She turned. "That's what Momma said."

"Your momma is a smart woman."

"Not about everything."

And her daughter was a smart girl. Too smart to be corralled into a blanket assertion that might not work in her favor down the road.

Cole hid his grin. "But she was right about this."

Wendy's "maybe" was sullen. He knew right then he was going to find the prettiest material he could from somewhere and Wendy was going to have a dress so beautiful it would put all the other girls' dresses to shame.

"I guess we'll have to see about a shopping trip."

Wendy looked at him out of the corner of her eye. "Mama needs a new dress, too."

Yes, she did. This time he didn't hide his smile. "We'll have to see about that, then, too."

Another look over her shoulder, less hesitant this time, more secure. "She likes blue."

"I'll bet her eyes look pretty when she wears blue."

Wendy nodded. "They look just like the best chocolate."

"Chocolate is my favorite thing."

Wendy licked her lips. "Mine, too."

"Duly noted." He pushed her higher. "Next time we go to town, we're going to have to find some chocolate and some dress material, yellow and blue."

Wendy shook her head so hard her braids didn't know which way to fly. Up and down with the swing or side to side with her head. "I don't want yellow."

"No? I thought we were going to outdo that town girl?"

"I want red."

A bright, cheery color, scandalous on an adult and not too proper for a child. Miranda was probably going to fuss at him. "Then red it will be."

"Mom said red is a scandalous color."

Ah, so the subject had already been addressed. "On anyone else but you, maybe. You'll look as pretty as a strawberry in a patch."

She nodded, satisfied. "I think so, too."

This time when he pushed, she kicked her feet.

"You want to go a little higher?"

"Yes."

"A lot or a little?"

"A little." That caution still lurked in her. He liked it. Caution wasn't a bad thing in a girl.

This time when she got to the peak, she giggled. A happy sound he heard from her too seldom.

"Now that was pretty. Sounded like music on the wind."

"What?"

"Your laughter. I don't think I've heard you laugh like that before."

She frowned at him. "I laugh all the time."

Not like that. Like nothing could touch her. "I'll have to pay more attention."

She enjoyed the swing for a while. Not chattering, just riding the curve. If Cole hadn't been paying attention, he would have missed the tightening of her energy. But he was. She was building to something.

"Are you going to stay with my mommy?"

He looked at her. That was out of the bushes. "I'm planning on it."

They hadn't heard back from the council yet, but he wasn't expecting trouble in that department. Not with the union consummated.

"Jenny says it's not your decision."

Jenny was Clark's stepdaughter, he remembered. "Jenny doesn't know everything."

"Whose decision is it?" Wendy asked. "Clark's?"

"Clark doesn't have a say in anything you do anymore." That needed to be clear.

"That's what Mama said."

"But you didn't believe her?"

She shook her head. "He's a big man and mean."

"I'm meaner."

"It doesn't make any difference how mean you are if you're not going to stay."

"I'm not planning on leaving."

"Then why isn't Mommy smiling?"

He didn't have an answer for that he could share. "Life is sometimes complicated."

This time it was a glare she threw over her shoulder. "You like her."

"Yes, I do."

"She likes you."

"Yes, she does."

"It's simple, then."

It really was from a child's perspective.

"Your mom and I are different."

"Because you're like me?"

"Like you?"

"Not Reaper."

She was awfully young to grasp that difference.

He gave the swing a maintenance push. "Does it bother you not to be Reaper?"

She nodded and swung her feet. He took his cue and pushed her a little bit higher.

"Why?"

"Because I'm weak and it bothers everyone."

She'd picked up on that well enough. He wondered if Miranda knew.

"Do you know why it bothers them?" she asked.

He wasn't sure how to reply at first. It seemed trite to say she was a woman and didn't need to worry about being strong, but people, whether Reaper or human, could be like chickens picking at the color red when someone different sat in their midst. And that had to eat at a child as perceptive and sensitive as Wendy.

"People tend to worry at things that are different. Doesn't mean that thing's bad, it just means it's different."

"So they're worried about me?"

"Yes."

"Oh."

From the sound of that "oh" she wasn't entirely convinced. Thank goodness she didn't know that she had potential as a mate; she was too young for that kind of nonsense, but soon enough it was going to be a factor in her life. And when that day came, she was going to need someone strong to stand for her.

"You know if I'm not around and you need him, Isaiah always has your back."

She nodded, but she didn't look soothed. He gave her another push, sending her a bit higher.

"You don't seem comforted."

"He's not always here."

The way she said that gave him pause. "And when he's not here?"

She shrugged but wouldn't say. He pressed harder. "How is it different when Isaiah isn't here?"

"Everyone changes."

He bet they did.

"They talk and they fight."

He imagined so. The Reapers were new to each other. Their society was new. It only made sense they'd jockey for power. "Then you need to tell him about it when he gets home."

She shook her head. There was only one reason he could think of why she wouldn't tell something to Isaiah.

"Are you worried about getting hurt if you say something?"

"No."

"Are you worried about your mama getting hurt?"

There was no misinterpreting the kind of stillness that took Wendy over then. He stopped the swing. She jerked her head around as it jostled to a stop. He wanted to hug her, but he wasn't sure if he should. Sometimes she seemed so fragile, this little girl who had withstood so much. She looked so much like her mother, he just wanted to shelter her from everything, but there was only so much he and Miranda could do. And only so much room Miranda was willing to make for him in Wendy's life right now.

Wendy blinked, and he realized those were tears she was holding back. Fuck Miranda's limits.

He squatted in front of her, holding the ropes of the swing so it stayed put. She wouldn't meet his eyes. He didn't let it stop him. "I'm going to make you a promise right now, Wendy. A Cameron promise, and everyone knows a Cameron doesn't break a promise."

Her gaze snapped to his. Deep inside him the last brick in a wall he didn't know he had crumbled. "For real?"

"You ask Addy if that's not for real."

She nodded and waited.

"I'm promising you right now that no one's ever going to touch your mom. Or you."

The "as long as I'm alive" he left unspoken. Wendy didn't need contingencies. She needed something to believe in.

"Do you believe me?"

She bit her lip and didn't answer.

With the back of his fingers he brushed her hair off her temple. "You wondering if that promise is any good?"

She nodded.

"You know your aunt Addy?"

She nodded yes.

"I made her a promise a long, long time ago that if anyone ever took her, I'd come get her, no matter what."

She blinked. "No matter what?"

He nodded. "And that's why I'm here now. Mister Isaiah took her."

"But he loves her."

"I didn't know that, not for sure. So I've been following her for two months."

Her eyes widened farther. "That's a long time."

"Yeah, it was snowing when I started out."

"It's warm now."

"Yup."

Another fear entered her energy, marred her expression. "Are you going to take her away?"

Cole smiled wryly. "I don't think Isaiah would let me."

She shook her head. "No. They're only happy when they're to-gether."

From the mouths of babes. A few weeks ago Cole would have mocked that as romantic silliness, but now, after being with Miranda, he had a whole new perspective. He didn't know if he could be content without Miranda by his side.

"I agree. So I guess I need to leave her here, but as far as my promise goes?"

She looked at him.

"I want you to understand something. I won't abandon you or your mama. Ever. You're mine now, a Cameron. And that means something."

"Like being Reaper?" she asked, hope lightening her expression.

He nodded. "Just like being Reaper, being a Cameron is a forever thing, and if something happens to me, you've got uncles that will come for you, too."

Hope fell flat. "But they don't know about me."

"I'll see that they do, just as soon as I can."

"Will they like me?"

"They'll love you." Of that he had no doubt. Those big brown eyes, that elfin face, that spirit, they'd be wrapped around this little one's finger in a heartbeat.

"I'd like to swing higher now." If there had been any enthusiasm in her voice, Cole might have taken that for relief, but she said it the way of somebody who needed the distraction, like she wanted to escape.

He pushed her a little at a time, inching her higher, letting her confidence build. Little girls were delicate, fragile, and needed to be protected. Whoever Wendy's father had been, he'd failed her mis-erably.

Cole pushed her higher than before just to see how far she was willing to go to hide what she didn't want known. If he expected her to back down, he was mistaken. He could feel her fears, old and new, overlapping each other, and it tore at his heart the way it had when Addy had come home broken. She'd been full of fear and without hope, and he'd given her that worry stone to hold on to. The rituals she'd built around it had made her whole. He still had the worry stone in his pocket And in that moment he knew what he had to do.

He stopped the swing again. Wendy looked up at him with those big brown eyes that just tore at him. He took her hand. Reaching into his pocket, he pulled out the stone, feeling like he was giving up the past and changing the future. He put it in her hand. Her fingers naturally curled around the stone. Her thumb and forefinger found the smooth surface the same way Addy's had. She frowned at him, not understanding. And how could he expect her to without knowing the history?

"A long time ago," he began, "I gave this stone to another little girl who had been very scared of things that had happened and worried about things that might happen again. It kept her safe."

"It did?"

He nodded. "It kept her safe for a very long time until she didn't need it anymore."

"What happened then?"

"She gave it back to me."

And that's precisely what Addy had done when she'd left that stone behind, Cole realized. Nobody had picked it up because it wasn't needed anymore. Addy had saved herself and Isaiah had become her security.

"She left her stone?"

"She knew there'd come a time when someone else would need its magic."

Wendy held it between her fingers, studying the dull gleam of sunshine off the facets contained within the amber stone. "Is it magic?" she asked, hushed awe in her tone.

He nodded. "Yeah."

It wasn't a lie. The magic was there for those with the need to believe.

"Is it magic for anyone?"

He shook his head. "It finds its owner. It finds the one who needs it. When it came back to me, I didn't know what I needed to do with it, but I held on to it through everything. I think it's been lonely."

Wendy looked at him, those eyes going big again in that way that just tugged at his heart.

"No one should be lonely."

"No."

Then, "Do you think it will like being mine?"

He closed his fingers over hers, pressing the stone into her palm. "I think it was waiting for you."

Her expression earnest, she asked, "What magic will it do for me?"

He shook his head again. "That's between you and the stone. Only you and the stone will know that. It's your secret, but when you're worried or you can't figure out what to do, just rub that stone between your fingers and think, and you'll find your way."

"Promise?"

"I promise."

It was an easy promise to make because he was never going to leave her alone where she'd have to stumble and rely on a rock for guidance. She had a mother who loved her, Jones and Addy, and all the damn Camerons he could throw at her. But knowing that was a rational thing. And sometimes the only thing that would get a body through was a touch of magic.

Her expression went intent as she rubbed the stone.

"Can you feel it?" he asked. "Do you feel its power?"

She frowned. "It's warm."

"It's saying hello."

She licked her lips. "I think it's talking to me."

"Well, don't tell me what it says. That's just between you and it."

She nodded. "A secret."

"Your secret."

She carefully put the stone in her pocket. Time flickered as he remembered Addy doing the same thing. He knew Wendy wasn't Addy. Wendy was very different, but many of her struggles were the same, and in her own way she'd become a part of his life he couldn't do without. If the stone gave her something to believe in, he didn't see the harm in it, and as her pocket bulged ever so slightly, he knew Addy wouldn't mind that the worry stone had been passed on. She would likely even approve.

Standing, he asked Wendy, "Are you ready to go extra-high now?"

Face set in a determined expression, she nodded and grabbed hold of the ropes. "I'm ready."

"You know," he said as he started to push her, watching her feet swing naturally as the swing went up and tuck back as it came down. "If you get real good at swinging, I bet you'll be able to reach up and pluck the sun from the sky."

Her laugh let him know she thought he was full of shit but didn't care. The sun was shining, and for this moment, she was a kid learning to fly.

He smiled. Now if he could just get her mom out here, he might be able to clear up a few other misapprehensions.

❧ 17 ❧

IT WAS TOO MUCH TO HOPE THAT HE WOULD BE ABLE TO get back to Miranda without interference. These Reapers made the biddies at a church social look uninvolved. What was a surprise was who it was that accosted him halfway back to the house after dropping Wendy off at Addy's.

Cole nodded to Blade. "Afternoon."

The enforcer grunted and matched Cole stride for stride. The sheer nothingness of Blade's energy told Cole whatever was on the man's mind was weighing heavily.

"Word is that you're planning on leaving?"

"You don't strike me as the type to listen to gossip."

"It wasn't gossip."

Cole tipped his hat back. "Just what exactly is your interest in my comings and goings?"

"Everything involving this set of Reapers involves me."

"Really? Last I heard you weren't even part of this pack."

"I'm here, aren't I?"

"You seem to be in a lot of places." Cole folded his arms across his chest. "And from what I'm told, everyplace you show up, so does trouble."

"You think I bring it?"

"It's a possibility."

"Maybe I'm just warding it off."

"Only God can tell what's going to happen before it happens."

"True, but a man with enough information can make an educated guess."

This time there was no mistaking the touch of the enforcer's mind. Cole slammed his shut. The enforcer smiled and cut through Cole's defenses like a hot knife through butter. The touch was light, but it said all that Cole needed to know. There would be no secrets from this man. Cole growled under his breath.

Blade growled right back. "You need to make decisions, human."

Cole stopped and faced Blade. "You say 'human' like it's a bad thing."

"Only because you're mated to a Reaper capable of producing children. The mother of a child likely capable of breeding. Keeping them both yours, keeping them both safe, is going to be a full-time job."

"And you don't think I'm up to it?"

"I don't think any human is up to it."

"I've already taken out four of your Reapers at one time."

"Then next time they'll send six."

"You're saying the pack won't protect Miranda?"

"I'm saying you need to make a choice, either pack or human, but you can't live straddling both worlds."

"Why not? Seems whatever I am now, it's a nice compromise."

Blade shook his head. "It's not enough. Not in these times."

Cole folded his arms across his chest. "So you're saying they'll no longer be pack if they're with me?"

"I'm saying you're going to have too many enemies from within the pack and out. It's not like Clark's going to disappear. He's been ostracized but he's still lurking around. Haven't you felt his energy?"

Cole shook his head. Truth be told, he hadn't felt much besides Miranda.

Blade snorted, "Young lust."

"Young? You're close to my age."

Blade looked at him and smiled an enigmatic smile. "So you think."

"You saying you're older?"

"I'm saying there are a lot of things you haven't considered. Like the fact that Reapers don't age the same as humans, and if you stay human . . ."

Knowing he would age and Miranda wouldn't tore him up, but it wasn't something he was going to tell the enforcer. "I'll cross that bridge when I get to it."

Blade shook his head. "What I'm trying to make you understand is you're already standing at the foot of it. You don't have a choice anymore. You need to decide where your loyalties lie."

"My loyalty is always Cameron."

"And where does that leave Miranda and Wendy?"

"They're Camerons, too."

"You're one stubborn son of a bitch."

Cole smiled. "So I'm told."

"You're going to get yourself killed, and then what's going to happened to them?"

"Again, are you telling me they are no longer pack if they are with me?"

"It's more than pack. Mates are for life and then some. Miranda's life is going to stretch a long time, and it's tough to be lonely for a long time."

Something flashed in the other man's energy. Cole looked at

Blade more closely, but it was gone as fast as it had appeared. There was nothing soft about Blade, dark eyes, dark hair, dark energy, and an expression as tough as rough-hewn steel. Had to be the human in Cole, but he had a nonsensical thought that maybe the man was lonely.

"Considering we don't even know what I'm capable of now as this 'something different,' I'm not feeling a rush to go all in. This may be enough."

"One more bite and all doubts go away."

"You don't know that."

"It makes sense."

It did, but making sense didn't make it so.

"The Rogues won't keep hunting Miranda and Wendy if I convert?"

"No, they'll hunt them."

"Pack won't want to try to take them from me?"

"Yeah, they'll want to."

"Then how will my problems go away?"

"Because you'll have the power to stomp them into the ground."

"What makes you so sure I don't have that power now?"

Blade smiles had a definite edge. "Ask me again when you're Reaper."

"I'll never take that step. I'm a Cameron, I'm human, and that's just how it is."

Blade growled under his breath, "You don't know what you are doing."

"Maybe not, but I'm doing it anyway."

"Stubborn fucker."

"Takes one to know one."

Another snarl.

Cole looked down the path toward his house, the little one-room shack he shared with his woman who made it feel like a palace. There wasn't anything he wouldn't do for her except this one thing.

"And that's the only thing she needs from you."

"Stay out of my head, Enforcer."

"Wake up before that woman and that little girl pay the price."

This time it was Cole who snarled. Why the hell did everything have to be so complicated?

Could you live without her? The thought entered his head.

Cole jammed his hat on his head, before sending back, *No*.

He was halfway to the house when Blade asked one more question.

Do you want her living without you?

He didn't give an answer because he didn't have one.

When he got to the house, Cole's mood had definitely turned sour. He opened the door without preamble. The scents of venison stew and fresh-baked bread surrounded him. Even though he knew Miranda had heard him when he entered, she didn't turn around. He wondered if the others had been working on her as hard as they'd been working on him. He wondered what effect they'd had. Their romance had been more like a tornado sweeping across the plains than a slow, steady affair. Nobody trusted a tornado. Maybe she didn't trust him.

Setting his hand on the back of the chair he said without preamble, "I had a talk with Blade."

The spoon banged on the side of the cauldron. Miranda's shoulders tensed. "You're leaving?"

Why the hell would she think that? "Turn around, and I'll answer that question."

He wanted to see her eyes, feel her energy. Despite her promise, she still tried to hide from him sometimes, but she never could when he was looking into her eyes.

Miranda laid the spoon carefully on the shelf by the mantel and turned. She'd unbuttoned the first two buttons of her dress in deference to the heat, revealing the hollow of her throat. He could see her pulse pounding under the soft skin, a few beats too fast to be normal. She was nervous. He couldn't blame her.

"I'm turned," she said, arms folded under her breasts, boosting those delicious mounds into prominence. He wanted to unbutton each of the remaining buttons, one by one, tasting her skin as he did, until he hit the barrier of her arms. The nerves under his skin tingled.

"We can't stand at war with each other."

She raised her eyebrows. "I wasn't aware we were."

"I know what you want."

"You do?"

"You want me to take that third bite."

Sighing, she brushed her hair off her forehead. "What I want to be is human, but I can't be changed back."

"Whatever I am now is as far as I'm going, Miranda."

He wanted her to understand that.

She nodded. "I understand." Rubbing her hands down her skirts, she repeated, "Believe me, I understand."

She said that so fervently. So honestly. Which made what she'd done make no sense. Passion could account for some of it, but Miranda was a strong woman with strong convictions. And she didn't believe in tricking someone without good cause, which could only mean one thing.

"There was another reason you bit me, wasn't there?"

He could feel her building a lie, shielding her thoughts.

With a slice of his hand he cut through the pretense. "The fucking truth, Miranda, for once let's just have it between us."

There was a long pause in which her anger lashed at him and her fear.

He didn't care anymore what had bound them together, but he wanted that bond set in the truth, not in some prettied-up farce. "Why?"

"Wendy's human."

"You said that before. Now, finish it."

The words burst from her as if they'd been dammed up too long. "You're human with family, a home. A future. If anything should happen to me, I want her to know what it's like to go to a social. I want her to know what it's like to play with little girls, to have hopes, to have dreams. I don't want her growing up alone as a Reaper. I don't want her facing men who think they can take her just because she has the potential to mate. I want her to know love. I want her to know happiness."

It all made sense then. "You want her to have everything you lost."

She nodded.

"One question."

She looked at him.

"What makes you think I'm ever going to let you die?"

The smile she gave him was sad, as if she had knowledge she couldn't share.

He took a step closer. "If push came to shove between the two of us, me being human, I'd be the one going first."

She smiled again but didn't respond, and he knew, son of a bitch, he knew what she thought, why she was holding him at a distance. Why she was all right with him not taking that third bite, and it had very little to do with his wishes.

"You think they are going to come for you, don't you?"

"They will. If not Clark, somebody like him. Or a pack like him or one of the fanatical Rogues who believe that I'm unnatural and a temptation away from the path and need to be burned at the stake, like the witches of old."

"There're that many sons of bitches out there?"

She nodded. "This pack isn't big enough to fight them all, and eventually they will have to make a choice."

She'd thought it all out. "You or them?"

"Yes."

"And you're going to surrender, just like that?"

"No, but no matter how I fight, I'll eventually lose." She took a breath and added, "And die."

The knowledge lay between them. Cole took a step forward; she stiffened. He took another. Two more was all it took to get to her side. Reaching out, he ran his fingers down the scars on her cheek.

"It takes a heck of a lot to kill a Reaper."

She nodded. "But you need to promise me something."

"I'm not making blanket promises."

"This you need to promise me."

"What?"

"If we're in a spot and it doesn't look like we're going to get out, you take Wendy, and you run with everything in you, and you take her home and give her what I can't."

"Normal."

"Yes, normal."

Son of a bitch, just the thought of her in a fight made his gut twist. Leaving her behind to face rape or death? It would never happen. "China doll, there is no way on God's green earth that I could ever walk away and leave you to fight my battles."

Her fingers circled his wrist, and her eyes sought his. There was passion in her touch, but there was also desperation, a mother's love for her daughter. Her belief that this could work. Her need for him to believe it, too.

"I've had my life."

"Your life is just beginning."

She shook her head and repeated, "I've had my life, and if my dying means that Wendy gets hers, then that's a choice we have to make."

"Like hell."

"Promise me."

He couldn't promise that. "Fuck."

"Promise me."

"I can't make that promise."

She didn't let go. Wouldn't let it go. Her nails dug into the back of his hand. "Promise me."

He growled at her as the scent of his blood tinged the air. "I promise you I'll make sure she is safe."

She growled right back. "Even if it means you leave me behind."

"Fuck." He didn't have any choice. She was right. He had to promise. If he was the only hope, he had to save Wendy. The words came out harsh and angry. "Even if it means I leave you behind, if there's no other choice, I'll save our daughter."

But he would never allow it to come to that. He would never, ever let her make that choice.

Miranda rested her forehead against his chest. "Thank you."

They weren't done. With a finger under her chin he lifted her face to his. "Now you make a promise to me."

She nodded.

"It's my choice to stay human, or whatever the hell I am now, no matter what."

She nodded.

"If I'm down and I can't speak for myself, I want you to make me a promise. No matter what, you don't change me."

Tears welled in her eyes, and she blinked. "I won't."

He wanted her to understand he understood. "Blade went into deep detail to explain to me the difference between Reapers and humans. He's a persuasive S.O.B., but I've thought this through."

"I promise. I won't let anyone take your humanity from you."

"Thank you."

He slid his fingers across her cheek, hooking them behind her head, pulling her closer.

"Where's Wendy?" he asked.

"She's with Addy."

"They're going to start thinking she's theirs."

"You know Addy loves kids."

"I know."

"And having Wendy around makes her smile."

"I know."

Cole pulled Miranda closer, until her toes touched his and her breasts grazed his chest. "And having you in my arms makes me smile."

He ran his finger down her throat, chuckling when she swallowed hard.

"What makes you smile, china doll?"

Her hands locked behind his neck. "You."

"Good answer." With his thumb he tipped her chin up. When he lowered his head, she was ready for him, her lips parting, her breath mingling with his. She accepted his dominance and his desire with a shuddering sigh, taking his next breath as hers.

"It drives me crazy when you do that," he told her.

"Do what?" she whispered against his lips.

"Go all soft and compliant in my arms. You give me that silent permission to do anything I want to you."

"I'm your mate."

"That just makes it sweeter." He looked over to the fire. "How long has that stew got to cook?"

"About an hour."

"More than enough time."

She shook her head with a smile. "You made love to me this morning."

"That was this morning. I find I'm hungry all over again."

"You'll create a scandal." Despite the words she was rubbing her hips across his.

"Don't tell anybody."

"But how will I brag if I don't tell?"

He stopped midkiss. "You brag on me?"

She smiled softly. "Just a little."

He decided he liked that.

"What do you go telling the women?"

"I just let them judge how happy you make me by the width of my smile."

"That's why you've been grinning ear to ear?"

She nodded. "That and because I've been happy."

He stroked his fingers from her temple to her chin. She was smiling at him now, lips slightly swollen from his kiss. His china doll, all happy and soft and warm and teasing. Such a big change from the woman he'd met just a few days before, the one who'd looked at him with fear and trepidation.

As natural as breathing, his hands went to the buttons on her dress, and as they slid free, one by one, he followed his fingers with little kisses, until the depth of her cleavage was displayed in a sultry invitation. In a moment of silliness, he buried his face between and blew a raspberry. He felt stupid as soon as he did it. She laughed and clutched his head, and when he looked up, he realized stupid was the right thing to do. Because now she looked as carefree as he wanted her to feel. Like the girl he wished he had had a chance to know before life had scarred her.

He could give her peace, he could give her tenderness, and he could give her freedom from the worries that plagued them. Not forever but for the next ten minutes, and sometimes ten minutes could carry you into forever if you played it right. If you remembered it right.

The memory of his mother's last smile flashed before him. She'd waved him off from the window of their home. It was the last time he'd seen her in a recognizable state. Before the Comancheros had wiped out everything, changed everything, taught him about impermanence. The next time he'd seen her, he'd been burying the charred remains of her body and wondering what the hell he was supposed to do now.

Blade's words came back to haunt him. *Do you want her to live without you?*

No. He didn't want that for Miranda. This time her fingers touched his cheek. He looked up.

"What is it?"

He shook his head. "Just a ghost skipping across my grave."

"I've always hated that expression."

"Then I won't use it again."

She shook her head and opened her mouth. He shut her up by picking her up in his arms.

"Hold that thought."

She frowned at him as he dropped her on the bed. "For how long?"

"Until it doesn't matter anymore."

He didn't want that part of his life touching her.

He came down over her, pinning her with his weight, pressing her hands beside her head in the way he knew she liked, tucking his feet around hers, using his knees to edge hers apart.

"I can't give you forever, Miranda, but we've got now, and I can make now pretty damn good. Will you let me?"

She nodded, and her softly whispered "Yes" stoked his desire as he realized she really would let him do anything he wanted with her, and there were a lot of things he wanted to do. More than anything, he wanted a lifetime in which to do them, too. A Reaper's lifetime. But he was a Cameron; he'd been born that way, and he'd die that way. Human. At least in his heart. So his lifetime maybe wasn't going to equal hers, and she was going to have to go on without him eventually, but he'd send her off rich with memories of them to carry her until she found someone new. The thought of someone new ripped a snarl from his throat.

Another whispered "What is it?" and another shake of his head.

"Just come here, china doll." He bent down, and she leaned up. As always, her thoughts were in sync with his, her energy stroking along his, her passion fueling his. Her lips bit at his. He slid his hand behind her head, holding her still, gentling the kiss, easing her back. The passion always took them so hard. It was wild and wonderful, but it wasn't what he wanted this time.

He remembered Wendy on the swing, her hair flying around her as she looked at him uncertainly over her shoulder and the joy on her face when he told her he was staying. She believed he could work miracles. He wanted to work miracles for Miranda, too.

Her tongue licked across his lips, and he smiled. "Impatient?"

She nodded.

"Get used to it."

She raised her eyebrows at him. "Why should I?"

"Because I want you slow tonight." He threaded his fingers through hers. Raising her hands, he pinned them to the mattress above her head, stretching his torso along hers, giving her a bit of his weight, catching her gasp in his kiss as his cock snuggled against her pussy through all the layers of clothes.

"What's wrong with hot?"

"Not a damn thing, but tender's better." He pushed her legs farther apart with his. She moaned. A flex of his hip and his cock slid up along her pussy, and even through clothes, the shock was electric. He did it again and again, a slow, easy seduction to a passion already roaring out of control. It was bittersweet. It was good.

She tried to rush him, pressing her mouth harder against his, but he leaned back, keeping it slow and easy, nibbling along the edges of her lips from one corner to the other, from the top around to the bottom, stroking with his tongue. Her mouth opened immediately, and he took possession not with the hard thrust she was expecting but with a gentle glide, for once in his life letting his soft side out. She moaned, and her nails dug into the back of his hand.

"Easy."

"I don't want easy," she protested in a soft exhale.

"I do. Sweet, easy, and slow. A memory between us."

Her eyes opened. This close it was hard to miss the darker flecks among the brown. Chocolate eyes, delicious eyes, eyes that could steal the soul, eyes that had stolen his the first second he'd seen them, eyes that watched his expression as he pushed her dress off her shoulders with one hand, as he slid his fingers down her arm and back up, as he dragged his hands over her shoulder until he could cup her breasts in his palms. The cool flesh heated immediately. The nipples hardened into points.

He smiled. "You've got the sweetest little breasts."

Her thank-you was a bit off expulsion of sound. She didn't know what he was doing and was cautious. It didn't matter; he'd show her. Leaning down, he followed the path of his fingers with his lips, coasting over the soft white skin until he reached that pink tip, brushing it with his lips before kissing it a little harder, opening his mouth, bringing her nipple into the heat, rubbing the hardening nub with his tongue before flicking it. He knew he was doing it just right when her nails dug into the back of his neck and she tugged him to her.

He smiled down into her eyes. "Pay attention now. I want you to feel what I feel. Know what I know."

He let his mind open a little, just a little. Letting her feel the passion, the desire, the want. He sucked a little harder on her nipple, experiencing the jerk that went through her, her energy wrapping around him, her lust taking hold of his, and just below that a softer emotion. She loved him. He heard the whisper in his head, felt the echo in her touch. Fuck, he wished he could say he loved her, too, but he didn't know what love was. So he cherished her with his mind, with his hands, with his mouth. It had to be enough.

Peeling the clothes from her body, revealing the perfection of her form, he moaned when she was fully naked. She was so beautiful to him. As usual her hands went to the scars on her face and her stomach. He moved them aside.

"You're beautiful, china doll. So fucking beautiful. You make me forget how to breathe."

He meant what he said, Miranda realized. With his mind touching hers, there was no way she couldn't know the reality of his feelings. When this beautiful man looked at her, all he saw was beauty.

She took her hand away and put it on his shoulder, reveling in the muscle, letting his mood lift hers. As he'd done to her, she unbuttoned his shirt one button at a time, caressing the flesh as it was revealed, feeling his breath catch, his passion spike. She smiled, pushing the material off his shoulders. With a growl he stood, shrugging out of it while she dragged her nails down the muscles of his abdomen. Hooking her finger beneath the waistband of his pants, she gave a tug. Growling, he shoved her hands away.

"I do love your growl," she whispered, watching him strip with brisk efficiency. She would have lingered a lot longer over the task, nipping and teasing. When his pants hit the floor, he stood back, hands on hips, his heavy cock straining forward. Cupping the thickness in her palm, she admired the man who was her husband. Broad shouldered and lean hipped with the well-developed muscles of a man in his prime, he had scars of his own. A knife wound on his shoulder, a bullet crease on his side. Other scars she couldn't so easily identify decorated the hard planes of his body, reinforcing his humanness and his frailty, but also that rock-hard core of toughness that was so much a part of him. More than he was human, he was Cole, and he was hers.

"Does it bother you?" he asked.

She must have been thinking too loudly "No, I wouldn't have you any other way."

He came down over her, and she welcomed the heat of his body, wrapping her legs around his hips, her arms around his shoulders. She pulled him to her, and his arms were around her, holding her as tightly as she held him. For a moment they were Reaper and human, man and woman, lovers.

"It's going to be all right," she told him.

He didn't respond, just held her tighter. Brushing his lips across her cheek, he found her mouth with his and kissed her with the soul-deep tenderness that was so beautiful it made her want to cry. Wiggling her hands free, she cupped his face between her palms and stroked her finger over his eyebrow, memorizing the lines of his face, the hint of crow's-feet at the corner of his eyes, the strength and the passion there. He was such a hard man she never expected him to display tenderness so blatantly, but he was now, and she had to wonder why.

Before that thought could form into words, he was kissing her again, stroking his hands down her sides, tugging her bloomers down, stealing the last of her control. He had such wonderful hands; rough yet tender, they drove her crazy as they glided over her skin and teased to life nerve endings she'd never known she had. When he patted her hip, she lifted, and he whisked her bloomers off and across the bed. His fingers brushed across her skin, stroked between her legs, and found the center of her passion. She braced herself for the onslaught that didn't come. With a butterfly touch he slid his finger across her clit, centering her attention. Her breath caught in her throat. Her pussy clenched. With the utmost delicacy he stroked, tempting her passion rather than driving it. The shiver started at her toes as his fingers just grazed, then just pressed, and then lightly, ever so lightly moving in a gentle rotation that coaxed her passion higher.

She didn't know what to do with this Cole, how to handle him, so she did the only thing she could and laid back and let him have his way, moaning as his teeth nibbled on her skin. His lips brushed across her breast so gentle, so sweet, so like nothing she'd ever experienced before. She realized it was fire and passion blended with tenderness and caring. He was telling her the only way he knew how that he cared. Tears welled in her eyes; she blinked them back, not wanting an explanation to ruin the moment because she'd never been cherished like this, as if there were nothing more important in the world than her smile and her pleasure.

He looked up at her from between her legs, his breath teasing her pussy as he moved down. "There isn't."

The words trapped in her throat were lost forever as his tongue skimmed her clit with the same delicacy as his touch, snapping nerve endings to attention, leaving her straining upward against his hands and wanting more. Desire pulsed and throbbed under her skin. Her breasts swelled; her canines split her gums. She was Reaper, and she wanted; he was human, and he was giving. It shouldn't work. It couldn't work, but at the next stroke of his tongue she knew with blinding clarity that it did. Perfectly, wonderfully, just the way they were, two imperfect beings coming together. They worked, and she wouldn't change a damn thing.

Another stroke of his tongue sent her thoughts skittering. There was so much she wanted to enjoy, so much of this man she wanted to experience. She'd seen his strength, felt his lust, but this, *this* was so much different. This was loving.

She closed her eyes and spread her thighs. She couldn't help but smile as he said, "That's my girl."

She had to dig her claws into the bed so as not to rake his skin as he laved her over and over, top to bottom, bottom to top, circling, prodding, nibbling, easing her to orgasm, holding her with his hands and his energy as her world exploded. His mouth and mind whispered incoherent praise, soft words that melted into her skin, into her heart, into her soul, and anchored her through the chaos.

And when it was over and she was still shivering and weak, he came over her, his eyes holding hers as his body merged with hers, slowly, inch by inch. Until there wasn't a breath of space between them, not a speck left to be filled. Until all the empty want and need had been squeezed out, and there was only him and her. Until it was perfect.

⇥ 18 ⇤

"YOU KNOW I HATE LAUNDRY DAY," ADDY SAID, WIPING her arm across her forehead before grabbing the soap and pouring it into the cauldron of water set over a banked fire.

Miranda nodded and grabbed up the wooden paddle. "What's to like? It's hot work, it's hard work, and I about catch myself on fire every time I do it."

"It doesn't help that it's hot enough to fry an egg out here." Addy shoved the layers of cotton that made up their dresses and skirts into the water. "It'd be so much easier if we could wear pants."

Miranda gave the clothes a stir. "I don't see why we can't."

"Maybe because, rather than getting anything done, our men would be standing around us all day, running off all the other men trying to ogle our posteriors."

Miranda laughed. "You think?"

"I think."

An echo of laughter came from the right. Miranda looked over to where Wendy was sitting on the swing that Cole had built for her last week, inexpertly trying to make her legs move in time with her body in order to get the swing going. She remembered Cole exhausted from a day of training, braiding that rope so her daughter would have the swing. She remembered Blade telling her Cole would be even more special if he'd take that third bite. She remembered as Cole had stood before the council, holding her hand as he slipped on the etched metal he'd made into a ring, promising her forever without a hitch in his voice. Miranda shook her head and rubbed her thumb on the ring. Cole was special just as he was. She would never let them change him.

Addy followed her gaze to the ring.. "Cole's a good man, isn't he?"

Miranda nodded. "But you already knew that."

"Hard not to. After my parents died, he took me on, and he was only a young man. And when the Comancheros captured me, he came and fetched me home."

"Fetched me home." Such an innocuous turn of phrase to describe how hard it must have been to not only find Addy but to get her back. "He's a stubborn man."

Addy smiled softly. "He'd argue that."

"He argues everything."

"That he does. Does he plan on staying?"

Miranda shrugged and stabbed the pile of laundry floating in the cauldron, doing its best not to get wet. "I don't know. But if he leaves I know he's not planning on taking you with him."

She hoped her smile didn't look as forced as it felt.

A touch on Miranda's arm had her looking up. "He wouldn't leave you."

She wasn't so sure. In the week since they'd married, they'd talked about a lot of things: their favorite colors, their enjoyment of each other, how fast Wendy was growing, the emptiness of the council's approval . . . everything but what mattered. Their future. "Thank you."

Addy sighed. "You should know Isaiah and Blade are talking to him now."

"About him changing?"

"Him being human is a weak link in our chain."

Miranda stabbed at the air bubble keeping the clothing afloat. "There isn't anything weak about Cole."

"Nope." Addy put her hands on the small of her back and stretched before glancing at Miranda out of the corner of her eye. "But that's not going to stop them from putting a lot of pressure on you to convert Cole with or without his permission."

"I've already felt it." It seemed everyone had a little hint to drop.

"I'm not surprised. Having a human among us is a weakness. Cole being your mate, but not being Reaper, creates a lot of tension, a lot of competition."

"It can't be helped. Cole doesn't want to be any more Reaper than he is."

Addy nodded. "I know. Cole's always been proud of who he is, where he came from, and how he made it to where he has without a hand up."

Miranda poked down a fold of petticoat, watching the off-white color slowly darken as the water swept over it until all that remained was a small, stubborn peak. "That's what makes Cole, Cole."

"Cole would be Cole no matter what."

Did she really believe that? Miranda looked over at Addy and saw the stubbornness in her expression and realized how hard it must have been for her to leave everything secure in her life, to leave her family, when she decided to go with Isaiah. Stirring the clothes, Miranda asked, "Was it hard for you?"

"It should have been." Addy shrugged and poured a bucket of water into another cauldron. "It might have been if I'd had a choice."

Miranda knew the story. All the Reapers of their pack did. Isaiah had been living with Addy in town, had taken on the role of baker—

baker!—when the Reapers the high council had sent out had found them. They'd almost killed her. "And when you healed and found out what Isaiah had done?"

"Did I hate him, do you mean?"

Miranda nodded.

Addy sighed and stuck another piece of wood under the fire. "No, but I think Isaiah wanted to hate himself."

"Why?"

"Isaiah always ran from who he'd become, fought the power, never explored it. He felt as if a beast lurked inside. Something that had to be exorcised."

Miranda's own abilities were so weak, she'd never seen as much of a benefit to being Reaper as others.

"Cole would fight it always."

Miranda knew that in her soul. As much as she longed to have him forever, as much as the thought of holding him in her arms while she was young and he was old, of watching his life force slip away frightened her, making Cole into something other than what he was would tear the heart from him.

"Maybe," Addy said, "but over time he'd get used to the powers and understand how they'd enable him to protect you and Wendy, to keep you safe, because, trust me, you two are the most important things in that man's life. He'd be happy for it."

No, he wouldn't, but Addy didn't want to hear that. Miranda settled for, "Maybe."

Addy sighed and conceded, "Yeah. Maybe."

With a last thrust Miranda pushed the fabric down and held it below the surface, not giving the sheet any choice but to soak up the water. Being Reaper never brought her the confidence or strength it brought others. In many ways she felt like she'd been sold snake oil when the rest of the world had been handed a magic elixir.

"Look, Mommy!" Wendy squealed.

Wendy had finally gotten the knack of pumping to make the swing go. She wasn't going high, but she was going.

"I knew you could do it," Miranda called back. And she had. Wendy might not be Cole's daughter by blood, but they shared a bone-deep stubbornness.

"That girl doesn't know the meaning of quit." Addy smiled.

"No, she doesn't."

"She'll lead some man a merry chase some day."

Not if that man was Reaper. A Reaper wouldn't risk losing her. But if he were human . . . Miranda stirred the laundry hard, working the dirt out, working her fears out. She moved the heavy weight until her arms ached and determination settled around her resolve. Her daughter would have a choice. "Yes, she will."

COLE took off his hat and wiped the sweat from his forehead. His mood was not at peak, seeing as he'd just spent an hour discussing his options with Blade and Isaiah. Options. He wanted to spit. In their eyes there was only one. His disagreement didn't seem to make much of an impression. When he'd felt the unease coming from Miranda, it'd been a convenient excuse to end a conversation he was leaving one way or another. He was not turning. He'd been born a Cameron and would die one. Period.

Even though the anxiety coming from Miranda didn't ease the closer he got, a lot of the tension inside Cole did. The last of his worry disappeared when he cleared the back corner and had Miranda in view. Whatever was upsetting her, he would deal with it. Not having her in arm's reach? That was a whole other animal. In a very short time she'd become integral to his contentment.

If the number of sheets and items hanging on the line were anything to go by, he'd say she and Addy were almost done with the laundry. Had it been up to him, he'd have left the chore for a less blistering day, but when he'd suggested it, both women had looked at him as if he'd sprouted two heads. There'd been all sorts of reasons from the scheduled rotation of the only set of laundry cauldrons, to the dirt level of the sheets. Personally he'd have put up with the dirt, but he knew how Addy felt about dirt, and he was learning Miranda was of a similar mind, so he'd done the only thing a wise man could do in the situation. He'd thrown up his hands and backed slowly away.

But he bet if he put forth the suggestion now, it wouldn't be so virulently rejected. He'd never seen two women drooping more around the edges than Addy and Miranda. Frazzled didn't begin to describe their energy. He tried not to feel sympathy. He'd told them it was going to be a scorcher, that doing laundry today was going to be nothing but torture. If they were suffering now it was their own fault. The problem was he didn't like to see Miranda suffering.

Just as he was about to call out, Wendy hopped off the swing and ran over to her mother, tugging at her skirt. He saw the flash of impatience go across Miranda's face as she moved her daughter away from the coals, felt it in her energy. A split second later he felt the love she felt for Wendy. But hot on the heels of it, impatience simmered again. The woman was on her last nerve. She needed a break.

Miranda wiped her hand across her forehead. The braid she'd so meticulously worked that morning had long since given up the ghost. Long brown strands stuck to her sweaty face, which was paler than normal. A few more steps got him within earshot. He heard Wendy asking to go swimming. He couldn't blame the little girl. He'd like to go, too. It was that kind of day. Miranda's shake of the head wasn't a surprise. The woman wouldn't let herself have fun until the work was done.

"Afternoon, ladies."

"Cole!"

Wendy came running. Cole caught her up in his arms. She smelled of grass and dirt and little girl sweat. She squeezed his neck.

"Hello, little one. How are you this fine day?"

She promptly pouted. "Mommy says we can't go swimming."

"I said not this minute," Miranda sighed. "I need to finish up the laundry."

"Same thing."

"No, it's not."

Cole tread carefully. "Well, that seems sensible—"

"No, it's hot!"

Miranda frowned at her daughter. "You, young lady, are about on your way to a nap. Remember to whom you're speaking."

"I don't want a nap," Wendy snapped, glaring at her mother from his arms. "I want to go swimming."

Little sizzles of temper reached out from Miranda to him. She didn't like being manipulated. Neither did he, but she couldn't expect a six-year-old to understand the call of work when the pond was so temptingly near.

"I don't care about stupid work," Wendy added for good measure.

"Wendy!"

If he didn't do something soon, the child was going to dig a hole for herself so deep there'd be no option but to just throw dirt on top and call it a day. Cole gave her a jostle to get her attention.

"Your mom's got a point. Work's got to be done before you can play."

"But it's hot now!"

"I can see your point, too."

Miranda crossed her arms over her chest. That deliciously full chest he'd nibbled on that morning. Licking his lips, he imagined he could still taste her.

"Don't encourage her, please."

"I'm not encouraging her," he explained calmly, catching the frayed edges of her energy and smoothing them. "I'm working on a solution."

Addy chuckled. "Have you been keeping your diplomatic side a secret, cousin?"

He cut her a glare. "You're not too old to spank, Addy."

Wendy gasped. Miranda looked like a spider had landed on his shoulder, and Addy, well, Addy just smiled and handed the shirt she'd wrung out to Miranda to hang.

"I think that threat lost its oomph about six months after you started issuing it fifteen years ago."

"Da—darn." He ruffled Wendy's hair. "I guess I need new threats."

Miranda snapped out the shirt. "What's your solution?"

Irritation, exhaustion, confusion, and . . . fear? All came off her in waves, pricking at him, drawing him. He didn't like her upset. He walked toward her.

"How about . . ." he hooked his hand behind Miranda's neck, tilted her head back, pulled her to the right around the dying fire, and kissed her softly on her lips, her nose, her cheek before pulling her in for a hug. She melted against his free side. Her energy calmed. And oddly enough so did his.

"That's your solution?" Miranda asked again, looking up at him from the hollow of his shoulder.

"Well," he said, "I'm also thinking that maybe I could take over your job at the laundry, and Wendy and you could go down to the pond and catch a quick dip."

"Oh, yes." Wendy bounced and kicked. "Let's, Mommy."

Miranda just blinked. "Laundry is women's work."

"Work is work, and it's not like Addy and I haven't done laundry before. It will be like old times. Won't it, Addy?"

"Of course."

The look she sent him said she knew what he was up to, and it would cost him. He didn't care. There were a lot of things he didn't understand about the situation he was in, things he needed to know. A fresh perspective would help.

Wendy was all for the idea, bouncing in his arms, pushing against him, trying to get down, he realized. He let her.

Miranda said, "I can do my work."

"Yes, you can. So can I, and"—he pushed the hair off her face—"a little bit of freshening wouldn't hurt you."

That snapped her head up, as he'd known it would.

"Are you saying I stink?"

He raised an eyebrow. "There's a distinct scent of bluing about you."

For a second she fluttered as if she didn't know whether to hug him or push him away. She settled for the latter. He allowed her a couple inches before stroking his thumb over her cheek. "Go have some fun with your daughter."

"I can't go play in the water in the middle of the afternoon with work still undone."

"The work will be done."

"By you?" She set her hands on her hips. "And who will be doing your work?"

"My work is done for the day."

"Then why don't you go splash in the water with Wendy?"

"Because I'm not the one who's been standing over the fire on a hot day, whose temper is worn to a frazzle, who's worried and hot and miserable, and who's longing to jump into that pond but stubbornly refusing to go because she thinks I'll somehow think less of her."

She blinked at him.

"Do I have it about right?"

"You don't always have to be right," she pointed out disgruntledly.

"I know. But I enjoy it." He pushed her toward Wendy who was impatiently dancing in place. "Go have some fun."

Miranda walked away. Slowly.

As soon as they were out of earshot, Addy said, "So, what about me? Don't I look hot and sticky?"

She did. "That you do."

"And don't I deserve a cooling break?"

"Yes, you do."

Arching her brows at him, she asked, "But?"

He smiled. "But I need some questions answered first."

Addy nodded. "I figured as much." She handed him the stick for dragging the sheets out of the pot.

He held it up. "Gonna cost me, huh?"

She nodded again and went and sat on the stump next to it. "As you said, it's hot, and this is heavy work, and you clearly have more muscle than me."

"You're a Reaper."

She shrugged. "You're human. Are going to fight over the semantics? Work is work."

He smiled and fished out a sheet and dropped it into the rinse cauldron.

"You know I'll always make things easier for you if I can."

"I know; it's one of your more endearing qualities."

He watched as Miranda stripped Wendy down to her bloomers and chemise and hung her dress on a bush.

"I know you want to make things easy for Miranda and Wendy, too," Addy said softly, her gaze following his. "That's not as easy as taking over the laundry."

"Maybe it's not supposed to be."

"There's always a price for happiness, Cole."

"And you think I need to pay it?"

Addy shrugged. "I think you're deciding whether you want to pay it or not and until you do, no amount of argument will persuade you."

"If the price is turning Reaper, the answer is hell no. I am who I am, and if that's not good enough, then I need to take my family and move on."

He dragged a sheet out of the cold water. Addy stood up. He shook his head.

"It takes two to wring that out."

"No, it just takes one person willing to get wet." He smiled at her. "And it's a damn hot day."

He wrestled the sheet, folded it in half, and started twisting it from the top. Water spewed over him, and even lukewarm it felt good, soaking his pants, dripping into his boots. Hell, he hadn't thought of that. He took a second to sit down, kicked one boot off, then the other, until he was barefoot in the dirt. Now the water could drip all it wanted.

"I wondered if you were going to save those boots."

"You knew I would."

"I remember when you got them."

"So do I. The Christmas before Isaiah came."

"He was actually already here on Christmas."

"You just didn't know it."

She nodded.

He chuckled and shook his head "And here I thought the 'Harry' you were leaving food out for was a stray cat."

She smiled. "Well, he was a stray, and I did bring him home."

"Are you happy, Addy?" Cole had to ask even though every bit of her energy and every bit of her life force said she was.

"I am."

"And you don't mind that you're Reaper?"

"I don't mind it a bit. I was scared for so long, lost to myself for so long. I had my rituals, but they were all I had, and it all just felt so fragile." She raised her hands and dropped them in her lap. "Do you understand what I'm saying?"

He understood because he'd been there, and he'd seen the tenuous thread that held her to sanity. Everything always had to be perfect; everything had to be done just right. Always clean, always neat, always on schedule.

"With Isaiah it's okay to be me. He doesn't mind my rituals."

He tossed the sheet over the line. "I never minded your rituals."

"I know you didn't mind them, but to you it was never right that I needed to have them. You always felt so guilty."

"I should have been there."

"And maybe I shouldn't have been where I was, who knows? Things happen, life changes us, and we go on. And I like this change. I'm happy."

He fished out another sheet. "What changed Isaiah?"

"I was wondering when you were going to ask that." She came up and grabbed the other end of the sheet. "Don't fuss, it will go faster if we do it together. And it's easier for me to work when talking about difficult things."

"I know."

"I don't know everything that happened. I know his memory of his life before he was changed is sketchy, but he wasn't happy. He was alone, and he was hurting, and he was angry."

"All the Reapers seem angry."

She nodded. "I think that was the criteria when they were chosen."

"And how did they know to make them Reapers?"

"I don't know. He doesn't know, either. No one knows."

"Blade implied there might be others. Older, more established Reapers."

"That makes sense. The blood that they used to change them had to come from somewhere."

"They didn't just change their blood though, did they?"

She shook her head. "No. They tortured them to break their minds, then they re-created them as monsters."

Her expression sobered. "I think for a while there wasn't much to Isaiah beyond the monster they wanted him to be."

"So what happened?"

"Another awful thing. He was imprisoned at Andersonville during the war. They kept him in a hole in the ground, and he went crazy."

"Crazy or crazier?"

"I don't know. His energy when he talks about that . . ." She shivered. "In his mind there are violent flashes of all kinds of stuff. Past, present. Whole streams of emotions. I can't read it. It's just chaos."

"Damn."

"What you never understood about him, Cole, is he is who he is, but that person is based on what he's built. Not on a foundation of faltering memories."

"Fuck."

"What?"

He sighed. "I'm trying not to like the man, you know."

"I know, but he's a good man."

"Yeah. But he's a mean son of a bitch."

"Not to me."

"Good."

"Somehow in that craziness, when he was locked in that dark hole with nothing but bugs and dirt and mold, he found himself." She looked at him. "That's the impression I get, by the way. When he thinks on it. Bugs, dirt and mold, and the walls closing in."

Cole knew how that felt. "He still doesn't like dark places."

"I know."

"Doesn't stop him though."

"Would it stop you?"

He smiled and twisted the sheet, waiting as the water dripped. "Not a bit. And thanks."

"For what?"

"For making me feel important in that mighty shadow Isaiah casts."

"You are the man against whom I always judged all other men. You know that. You might be my cousin, but you were like my big brother, the one who made me feel safe, the one who came for me when nobody else would, the one who never gave up."

"Reese and Ryan didn't give up, either."

"I know, but they might have eventually."

"No, you underestimate them. They are happy to let me do the managing when I'm around, but when I'm not, they're Cameron to the core."

"Probably, but Isaiah is like that, too. What's his stays his, and he'll die protecting it."

Cole looked around the ragtag settlement of huts and tents. "And all these people are his?"

"Yes. And the dream. He wants normal. They might not have had a choice about being Reaper, but they have a choice about being normal."

"Reaper law is pretty absolute."

"But the people within it are so different." She nodded. "When they thought they couldn't have children, when they thought they couldn't change at will, when they thought they were at the mercy of this demon that had been put inside them, they made laws to save the world from themselves."

"And now they're finding out those laws don't work."

"Yeah, but there are fanatics. You don't know . . ."

He filled in the blank. "I'm guessing you have people who want to use the power for good, people who want to use it for evil, and people that just fear it or use it to hurt others."

She nodded. "Even the ones that want to do good hurt others. I don't know. It's like anything else, Cole; it's got its good side and its bad side. Being Reaper, it doesn't change who you are."

"Bullshit, it changed you."

"No, it brought me back to me, and that's a good thing."

"It's not something I want."

"I know."

He looked at her. "Ever."

"I know."

"I want you to promise me, no matter what happens in the future, you won't let them change me."

She bit her lip, and again he saw the shattered girl he'd brought back from her captivity with the Indians, but then in a heartbeat that little girl went away and in her place was the woman she'd become since meeting Isaiah Jones. He'd been as good for her as she'd been for him. They were a match, Cole realized.

As he took the sheet from her, she pushed the hair off her face with her wet hand, the wet strands making a funny bump on her forehead. Any other time that would have made him smile, but this wasn't that time.

"I want your promise, Addy. I've always lived my life as I wanted. That doesn't change just because Miranda is a Reaper and all of you want another rooster in the henhouse."

She rolled her eyes. "You make it sound like there's a campaign going on."

"Isn't there?"

"I'll admit a lot of people would feel much more comfortable if you were one of us. No question. No doubt."

"You one of them?"

"I thought so but . . ."

"I've convinced you otherwise?"

"No, Miranda did."

That was a shock. "Miranda?"

"She has a funny notion that you should always stay you, no matter what."

Because he'd made her promise, and she was keeping her promise to back him in this. But he knew in her heart she wanted him to be Reaper.

"She knows what it's like not to have a choice."

"Yes, she does, but she also knows how easy it is to live with a different choice."

"Easy? Have you seen the scars on her face, the fear in her eyes?"

"She's a woman alone. Life is difficult for any woman alone with a child."

"She's not alone; she has me now."

Addy nodded. "For how long?"

Because he chose to stay human and mortal if that were still possible. He got the point. "You have a nasty way with words, Adelaide Jones." It was the first time he'd ever used her married name.

She smiled, acknowledging the concession. "Facts are facts. We live in a dangerous world, and this little corner of it, right now? It's downright treacherous, but I'm not going to interfere with what you and Miranda decide is right. The same way you didn't interfere with Isaiah and me."

"I grumbled a bit."

She nodded. "But you left me to be happy."

"Sort of."

"I know you, Cole. I knew you'd come. The last time you'd seen me, I was dead for all intents and purposes, and then Isaiah took me away. It was too much like before for you to leave it."

"So why didn't you stop me?"

"I don't know. Some things people have to see for themselves, and maybe I needed to see that I could be happy as this new me before I stopped holding on to you."

"Damn." He tossed the sheet over the line. Addy tugged it straight on the other side.

"That is the last of the laundry, and I'm thinking that pond looks mighty inviting right now."

He looked over in time to see Miranda toying with the buttons on her dress. "Fuck."

"I wish you wouldn't use that word."

"I know. I'm working on it."

"All we need is for Wendy to start running around saying it."

"I don't say it around her."

"You don't always know when she's around."

"True enough." He was going to have to modify his language along with a lot of other things.

Miranda had her fifth button undone. Was the woman thinking she was going to swim unguarded in her chemise and pantaloons? When wet, she'd be all but naked. Addy followed his look. She didn't say anything, but he felt her laughter stroke along his anger.

"It's not the first time she's gone swimming, you know."

He didn't take his gaze off Miranda. "Uh-huh, but she's a Cameron now."

She laughed. "And what's yours stays yours?"

"Yep." He headed toward the pond, grabbing a sheet off the line and tossing it over his shoulder as he went. "And covered up, too."

⁅ 19 ⁆

AS ALWAYS, MIRANDA FELT COLE'S APPROACH BEFORE SHE saw him. Ankle deep in the water, she turned. She had a brief glimpse of his face and a flash of something white before she was enveloped in it. She looked down.

"I just washed this sheet."

"Uh-huh, and I just made love to that sweet body, but it's not like I want the whole world to see it."

"I was just going to cool off."

"Mmm-hmm. While everyone around you heats up."

"Everyone does it."

"Not my woman." He ran his fingers from her shoulder, down her back, to the hollow of her spine, his hand opening over her ass, pressing gently, spreading the cheeks ever so slightly, sending shivers of arousal through her. Her knees went weak. He chuckled and pulled her close. "This is for my eyes only."

Wendy turned, saw them, and giggled. Cole moved his hand to safer ground.

"You told us to swim and cool off; this is the only place we can go."

"There is another pond farther upstream."

"No one is allowed to go there without an escort."

He kissed her. "Consider yourself escorted."

"Are you sure it's safe?" She frowned.

"You're with a badass Cameron, how much safer can you be?"

It was hard to argue with that. "Not much." Turning to Wendy, she called, "Get your things, honey. We're moving to a better spot."

Wendy splashed toward them. "Are we going to the big pond?" she asked excitedly.

"Yes."

Wendy surged out of the water and up onto the shore; she was twenty feet ahead of them before Miranda could get a breath. "I can practice my swimming, then," she called back excitedly.

"How far along on the practice is she?" Cole asked, scooping Miranda's dress off the bush and holding it over her head.

"She can paddle quite well."

When she would have let the sheet drop, he ordered, "Keep that sheet tucked around you."

She felt obliged to point out, "This is going to be awkward."

"Not if you tuck that sheet well and do as I say."

It was going to be awkward even then, but she was finding sometimes it was easier to humor Cole than fight with him. Especially in his possessive moments.

"Now, hold your hands up."

Holding her hands up like a child, she waited while he dropped her dress over her head. It was bulky and, as she predicted, wouldn't fit over the sheet.

"At some point I've got to unwrap this thing, you know."

"Hold on."

It wasn't like she had much choice. She felt him tugging and pulling at the skirt.

"It's hot in here."

"Hold on."

He tugged some more. She grabbed the sheet, yipping when he pulled a bit of her hair.

"Sorry."

"This isn't going to work."

"It's working fine, just hold on."

"Where's Wendy?" She had visions of her halfway to the big pond on her own.

"Right here, Mommy."

Another tug and Cole said, "Okay, now you can let it go."

She peeked at him through the crack in the bodice. "How am I supposed to do that?"

His eyes warmed with that humor that she enjoyed so much. "A bit tied up, are you?"

She tried to get her hand out of the sleeve, but the elbow got caught in the waistband. "A bit."

He chuckled.

"I think I like you like this."

His fingers stroked her cheek, then down over her neck, his knuckles discreetly brushing her breasts.

She gasped as a shiver of awareness went through her. Passion pushed the laughter from his eyes. "I do find I'm liking you like this."

When she could see his eyes, the laughter still lingered there, and she liked that. He had been so serious before, but now, with her, there was laughter, too. It was a good thing.

"All tangled up?"

Passion weighted his smile. "Helpless."

His knuckle pressed her breast again. To onlookers it would be nothing, but the contact was lightning to her, streaking from her breasts to between her legs and then back up again, leaving her wet and aching with her breath caught in her lungs.

"I'm going to look a little silly if I try to walk like this."

"I know. I'm just contemplating the possibilities."

She licked her lips, telling herself as a decent woman, she shouldn't be wondering about those possibilities, but she was wondering, hard.

"You like that, don't you?" he asked, that stern mouth of his soft with desire.

What was the point of denying it? "I do. I find you're a very inventive man."

His fingertips separated her lips. "And I find you a very receptive woman."

"That's good, right?"

He leaned down and kissed her gently, his hands sliding up under her skirts, giving the sheet a tug so it fell to the ground. "Very, very good."

"That's far enough, Wendy," he called, "wait for us."

"Hurry, then."

Miranda closed her eyes at the blatant disrespect.

"Shades of her mother," Cole grinned.

"Are you saying I'm bossy?"

"I'm saying you know what you like. As long as you continue to like me, I'm not going to have an argument with it." He caught her hand and dragged her forward. "Now come on."

"What about the sheet? We can't just leave it there in the mud."

"Sure we can. It's not like anybody else is going to claim it."

"Sheets are rare."

"Muddy ones need cleaning. Trust me, it will be there when we get back."

She supposed he was right. There was enough hard work around the camp that no one was going to pick up extra. The sheet could wait. She pinched Cole's butt.

She turned and skipped backward ahead of him. "Then what are you waiting for?"

His fingers squeezed hers, and one of his rare smiles spread across his face, a real smile, the kind that brought the sun out inside her.

Catching up with her, he kissed her quickly. "Not a goddamn thing."

THOUGH Miranda had never told anyone, she'd never liked the big pond. She didn't know why. The walk through the copse of trees was pretty shady and picturesque, and it could have been the subject matter of any painting hanging in any of the fancy homes back East, but every time she walked into these woods, a ghost walked over her grave. Wendy skipping ahead, whacking the trees as she skipped passed, didn't feel any of her mother's unease. Neither did Cole, but no matter how she tried to focus on the beauty, the sense of unease wouldn't pass.

The pond was barely an eighth of a mile from the campsite, secluded by this little strip of woods. It wasn't far enough away to be scary, but it was far enough away to be isolated, which, based on the squeeze of Cole's hand on her ass, was part of its appeal for him. What he thought they could get up to with her daughter running around she had no idea, but if there was something, a shiver of arousal went down her spine, she was sure Cole would find it.

When his hand dropped to his side, she slipped hers into his, feeling his start of surprise. And she realized rather sadly, she didn't touch him that much. She'd have to fix that, because he was always touching her and it always made her feel good. And he deserved to feel good, too. If this was going to be more than just a now thing, then she had to start acting like it.

Leaning over, she bit his upper arm. The growl that rumbled from his throat found its way to her. She closed her eyes briefly as the sound sank into her consciousness. He was as affected by her as she was by him. They were, she realized, vulnerable to each other, and there was safety in that, comfort in that, security in that.

She hugged his arm. He pulled it away, and for a minute she thought she'd gone too far, until he put his arm around her shoulder and tucked her into his side. That bit of unease that had haunted her as soon as she stepped in the woods slipped away. The storm that threatened wasn't here yet. She had now, and it was good.

He dropped a kiss on the top of her head. "You worry too much."

"Some things just bring the ghosts walking over my grave."

"I don't want you having bad thoughts."

"You can't stop them."

He cocked an eyebrow at her. "I could order you not to have them."

She smiled. "And I could promise not to let you know."

"Hurry up, hurry up," Wendy called.

Cole sighed. "We'd better hurry before she gets out of sight."

Her heart sank. "Do you think there's trouble?"

"No, but there's no telling what that girl could get up to. She's got a spirit of adventure about as big as the sky."

"I know. It scares me."

He looked at her. "Why?"

"Because I don't think she'll be content being in this world."

"You mean the Reaper world?"

She nodded.

"There's nothing to say she has to stay with the Reapers."

"They won't let her leave."

"It's not their choice."

"You don't understand."

"I understand. A lot of people want a lot of things. A lot of people want diamonds. A lot of people want gold. Wanting it doesn't make it possible to have it."

"But what if she falls in love?"

"With a Reaper?"

She nodded.

"Then that's the man she'll choose, and that's the life she'll choose, but I'm thinking any man that tries to tame that spirit is going to know what he's getting into, and he's probably not going to be the kind of man who wants to smother it."

"Do you think so?"

He looked down at her, and again there was that assessing look in his gaze that always made her wonder what he was thinking. "Not all men want to crush what they can't control."

She licked her lips and asked the question that often haunted her. "Do you want to control me?"

"This isn't the place for that conversation."

She supposed he was right. Wendy was likely to come back any second wanting their attention. She didn't have many playmates, and Cole was a new force in her life. She seemed to be jealous of his time. Miranda hoped that would lessen, but she wasn't sure.

"But, no" he said, catching her attention as they reached the edge of the water. "I don't want to control you. Not like you're fearing."

She supposed that was some consolation, but his statement left a large area of conjecture as to just what he wanted to do with her, and she hated that instant of fear that whipped through her. Flashes of her attack snapped into her mind, mean faces, hurting faces, claws tearing at her skin.

"Miranda." Cole's voice called her back. She realized he was cupping her face in his hand, and his breath was soft on her skin. As he leaned in, his lips touched her in the gentlest of caresses, and within the slight contact she felt the promise. "No one's ever going to hurt you again. Not as long as there's breath in my body."

She knew that was supposed to make her feel better, and it was quite the promise from quite the man, but her first husband had made her that same promise, and she'd watched him struck down as if he was nothing, and then she'd been left alone without protection. But all she said to Cole was "Thank you."

He shook his head. "That was supposed to make you feel safe."

She said, "I know."

His fingers traced the scars on her cheek. "But you know how easily promises can be wiped out."

She nodded.

"How about if I teach you how to protect yourself?"

She looked up, her heart skipping a beat. She'd asked Clark to teach her, and he'd told her that he would show her later, but later never came. When that failed, she'd tried to teach herself to shoot a gun, but she never quite got the hang of it. And when she'd asked for Clark's help again, he'd put her off and never seemed to have time—there was always so much to do. "I'd like that."

"Then we'll start tonight."

"Tonight?"

"No time like the present."

"Yes."

Because he didn't believe a future was necessarily always going to be there, like her. It should have made her nervous, but for some reason it made her feel secure.

Wendy started splashing into the water.

"You sure she can swim?"

Miranda nodded. "She took to paddling so fast I think she's part fish."

"Can you?"

She nodded. He cocked an eyebrow at her. "Like a fish?"

And she chuckled, "Yes."

"Good." His thumb stroked over her lips, the rough surface catching erotically on the damp flesh.

"It's going to be all right, Miranda."

For the first time, when somebody told her that, she actually believed it. It was probably the sweetest gift he could ever give her. She stepped into his arms, sliding her hands up over his chest, ignoring his start of surprise at her making this move.

Using his own technique, she pressed her nails into the back of his neck, urging him down to her. He bent so easily, this man who was so strong but wasn't afraid to give her what she needed. As his lips met hers, she whispered, "Thank you."

He took her thanks and her mouth with a thoroughness that she'd come to expect, bringing forth passion and emotion. Lust flitted through her right along with love, she realized. She loved this man. She had sworn to never love anyone again, to never be vulnerable again. But she loved him, and she couldn't stop kissing him. As the realization swamped her and the floodgates opened, the woman she'd been hiding for so long came to the fore.

One of them moaned. Him, her, she wasn't sure. The kiss took fire, or maybe it was just her, who could tell? His hands slid down to her hip; her thigh slid up his, her ankle wrapped around him, pulling him closer; her arms tightened; his growl rumbled in his chest, vibrating against her nipples, making her more aware of the differences between them and the potential if only they were alone.

"Mommy."

But they weren't alone. They had to stop. She couldn't, but he found the strength. He was always finding the strength that they needed. He was a man to trust. Everyone had told her that. She didn't know why she hadn't listened earlier. His lips parted from hers, the pad of his thumb pressing against the softness of her lips, rubbing gently, keeping her attention focused on the tingling there.

"Later you can tell me what that was all about."

She nodded. Later, she'd tell him a lot of things, and the most amazing thing was she wasn't afraid of the prospect. His gaze softened, and his lips pressed against her forehead, just once, but so much was said in that gesture. She didn't think anything she'd be telling him would be a surprise. He had to suspect most of it. That was good.

"Right now, let's go play with our daughter."

"*Our.* Such a pretty word." Catching his hand, she tugged him along.

"Race you."

She took off before she finished the challenge. She didn't have a prayer of beating him, but when she looked over her shoulder, she was. A second look told her why. His eyes were locked on her hips. She didn't run faster and he didn't catch up. When she reached Wendy, she gave in to the mischievous impulse and bent over on the pretext of pulling up Wendy's pantaloons and tying the knot. They tended to stretch when they got wet. And as she bent, she wiggled. He growled and swatted her butt. She jerked and gave him the squeal that he wanted. Her gaze met his, finding in his eyes the smile that matched hers.

And inside her more ice shattered under the warmth of the sun, the heat of his gaze, the perfection of the moment. She would never forget this day.

"Mom, hurry up! I want to go on the rope."

"The rope?" Cole asked.

Wendy pointed over to where a rope had been tied to a large limb.

"I like to swing out."

"Nice. You ever do a flip off that?"

"Oh my gosh," Miranda gasped. "Don't get her started."

It was too late. Wendy's interest was caught. She perked right up. "A flip?"

Cole started taking off his boots. "I'll show you."

That just made Wendy tug harder, which made tying her drawers impossible.

"Hold on a minute. I can't tie this knot if you keep dancing."

With a puff of exasperated breath Wendy stood still. Miranda tied the knot.

As soon as she was free, Wendy was in motion. "I'll race you to the rock!"

Cole looked down at Miranda. "Figures, the first time you let your guard down with me we'd have company."

"But at least I let my guard down."

His expression softened. "There is that."

"Come on!" Wendy called impatiently.

Cole looked over at the pond. There was a rock way out in the center. It actually wasn't a pond. It was big enough to be a small lake, which was good. "I think your daughter intends to beat me."

"She has big ideas."

"Nothing wrong with big ideas."

"No, there might not be." That was quite a concession on her part. Whatever had happened in her past made her reluctant to spread her wings, but he liked that she didn't want that for her daughter.

"I'd best get to shucking the rest of my clothes or else she's going to take off without me."

She licked her lips. "Yes."

He eyed her. "I'm shucking to swim, not to pleasure."

"You can do whatever you want."

"And you're going to do whatever you want?"

"When it comes to picturing you naked, yes."

"I'll be leaving my long johns on."

"Not in my mind."

He shook his head and undressed. The woman was a caution.

"Are you going to let her win?" Miranda asked.

"I'm a Cameron, what do you think?"

It pleased him to no end that she said, "I think you're going to build her confidence. I think you're going to let her beat you to the rock."

"Now why would I do that?"

"Because you're a good man."

"You keep talking like that, and I just might let you beat me to the mattress tonight."

She shivered, and he smiled. There was a lightness in his soul that he wasn't used to but he'd be happy to grow accustomed to it. He kicked off his right boot and then the left. "You going to come swimming with us?"

She shook her head as he tugged off his socks. "I think I'll just get the makings for a fire here."

"It's a hot day."

She nodded to the clouds. "But with the breeze coming in off that storm, it's going to get cold."

"And?"

"And if you two decide to go fishing, there'll be lunch to cook."

He shucked his shirt and unbuckled his belt, taking his time as her gaze clung and she licked her lips. He liked knowing he aroused her. "Putting us to work, are you?"

She wrinkled her nose. "It can't be all fun."

He laughed and dropped his pants. "We'll see about that."

He had to race Wendy to the big rock three times before the girl wore out. He couldn't remember if there had been a time in his life when he had that much energy but there must have been. They floated in the cool water, leaning up against the rock and catching their breath.

"You're a strong swimmer, Miss Wendy," he complimented. It wasn't a lie. For her age, size, and skill level she was strong.

"So are you." She pushed her hair off her face. "You almost caught me that last time."

He smiled and wiped the water out of his eyes. "Well, that was quite a bet you laid out. I didn't want to end up having to do your chores for a week. I have enough of my own."

She giggled, another happy sound in a happy day. It had been a long time, a real long time, since he'd felt this carefree, but he liked the feeling the way he seemed to be liking a lot of things lately.

Leaning his arm against an outcropping of the rock, he let his body float, catching Wendy when she tried to imitate him and slid off the rock. When he propped her back up, she mimicked his position right down to what he imagined his expression looked like. And that just made him want to smile wider.

"Your mom said we need to catch some fish if we want to eat lunch."

"How we going to do that? We didn't bring the hooks."

"Well, I'm thinking she'd think it was funny to watch us try to catch them with our bare hands, but I got a few tricks up my sleeve."

"Like what?" She was all eyes and anticipation.

"Figure if we take some of those sticks over there and make a couple of spears, we might be able to stab us a few over there by that shady rock while they're snoozing."

"Spear them?"

He nodded. "It's hard to do, but if you learn the technique, it's a way to keep yourself fed when you don't have much else going on."

She was clearly fascinated. The sun went behind a cloud. A shadow chased over the lake, covering them.

"Might be that storm blowing in," he said.

"Now?"

"Not till tonight, I don't think."

A cold wind chased the shadow. Wendy shivered. Bad energy chased the wind. A chill crept up Cole's spine, a chill that had nothing to do with the temperature in the air. The hairs on the nape of his neck prickled. He looked ashore. Miranda waved, her long hair blowing about her shoulders. Beyond her in the bushes other shadows moved. Sinister shadows.

Fuck.

"Wendy!" he said very calmly. She turned to look at him. "Go on the other side of the rock, then swim for that deadfall on the shore. Stay down low. No matter what, once you get there, hide. Don't you peek over."

"What's wrong?" Her gaze followed his. Before he could block her, she saw what he saw, wolves—Reapers—closing in on her mother. She opened her mouth to scream a warning. He slapped his hand over her mouth, holding her tight, giving her no place to look except at him.

"We don't want them to know we're here," he hissed. "Now, get over there behind that rock. I'm going to get your mother safe, but while I'm doing that, you need to hide and stay put, understand?"

She nodded.

"Then do as I say."

She slipped around the rock, face pale, expression terrified when seconds before she'd been laughing.

A scream came from shore. Wendy whimpered. Cole glided into the water, watching as the Reapers jumped out of the bushes. Miranda grabbed up a stick from the fire and swung it at them. The flame was too new, it didn't hold. She backed up toward the pond, holding the stick like a club. Cole didn't wait to see any more. Slipping beneath the surface, he swam with all he was worth toward the shore. Hoping Wendy was doing as he said, hoping Miranda could hold her own long enough for him to get there.

Her next scream was so loud the echoes reached him underwater. Miranda's terror ricocheted along his nerves. A growl built in his throat. His mind teemed with all the possibilities that could have brought about that scream. He swam harder. His lungs burned. His heart pounded. When the cold calm of rage wrapped his senses, he embraced it. And when that high-pitched scream cut short, for the first time in a long, long time, he prayed.

"God, get me there in time."

⊰ 20 ⊱

MIRANDA TOOK ANOTHER STEP BACK INTO THE POND. Cold water closed over her ankles. It had nothing on the terror choking her as the Reapers approached, fangs exposed, jowls dripping, hackles up. This was it. Her foot slipped on a wet rock. She caught herself. There was nowhere left to go. Tightening her grip on the stick she'd grabbed, she looked into the leader's eyes and borrowed Cole's favorite expression.

"Fuck you."

If she were going to die, it wouldn't be cowering or begging. No one was ever going to make her beg again.

The Reaper leapt. She lunged to the left. His claws dug into her shoulder as he overshot. Scrambling on her hands and knees, she made it back onto dry land. Before she could spring to her feet, another Reaper hit her from the side. Pain exploded in her ribs. She heard him cough a laugh. Smelled his scent. Clark. Rolling onto her back, she snarled right back. Seeing him like this, she remembered him. Remembered how he'd laughed all those years ago as she'd begged for mercy, begged for death. He'd been behind the attack on the wagon train. And no one had known.

"Fuck you!"

Clark leaned down, teeth bared. His saliva dripped on her face. His breath stung her nostrils. She was going to die. Here. Now. With the sun in the sky and her daughter splashing in the water.

Inside the panic blended with prayer. She closed her eyes, not brave enough to watch it happen. *Don't let them find Wendy. Please, not my little girl.*

And to Cole she whispered, *Remember.*

There was a roar, real or in her head she didn't know, but she'd recognized that punch of energy that surrounded her like a shield anywhere. Cole.

And in that moment, the killing blow came, not to her, but to the complacency that she had adopted since her change. Cole had come for her. Against common sense, against his promise to save Wendy, he'd come. She opened her eyes and saw Clark's vindictive smile as he jumped back and yipped a command. The wolves were inching in, tightening their circle around her. She saw Cole square off to the right, drawing them away from her. They'd tear him apart if she sat on her butt like she had for the last four years bemoaning her fate, too scared to do anything. Paralyzed by a choice she'd never made.

Springing to her feet, she shook off the dizziness and reached for her beast. For the first time she rejoiced in the sensation of her canines tearing through her gums, her nails stretching to claws, her muscles hardening. Letting that wild part of her she always suppressed surge, she welcomed the strength and the power. Welcomed the anger.

She leapt for the Reaper heading for Cole's back. She recognized him. Traitor! Past, present, snarls, roars. What did they matter? She threw her all into the fight, clawing at the man's face in a fury, biting at this neck, both horrified and and elated at the taste of blood.

Run.

The order exploded into her mind. She ignored it. This was her home. This was her man. She wasn't leaving either.

The Reaper spun and reached back with wickedly curved claws. She heard Cole's yell, saw the Reaper in front of him go down, and then Cole was there, knife in hand. Unbelievably quickly, he slashed the Reaper's throat. The wolf staggered beneath the combined assault.

"Get the fuck off," Cole ordered.

She did, leaping aside as the Reaper went down, landing on her feet with an agility that astounded her. She had known the beast was inside her, but she hadn't known it was capable of this. That she was capable of this. Hate and fear blending into a ferocious rage, she snarled at Cole. He snarled right back.

"Get out of here!"

She shook her head. He would have said something else, but there was no time because the rest of the Reapers were on them. She howled, summoning the pack. Four Reapers jumped Cole. She managed to block one. The second threw her aside. She watched as Cole went down under their claws, saw Clark smirk as he landed a blow to Cole's side. She screamed as the Reapers piled on. It was happening again. She couldn't stop it, had never been able to stop it, but this time she wasn't going to passively let it happen with her screams her only defense. This time she was going to fight for her daughter, for herself, for Cole. They couldn't kill Cole.

Reaching out she found Cole's energy and his determination. Her world narrowed to a single focus, saving Cole, and this time it was her teeth tearing and her claws ripping flesh as she jumped on the men piled on Cole, and she ripped her way down to him, screaming his name in a hoarse parody of a voice whose words made no sense but echoed with an unearthly timbre. From far away she heard answering howls. Help was coming.

She bit the back of another neck but never tasted the blood as it spurted, never felt the bones as they crushed. She bit harder and shook her head. She felt blows hit her body, but they were distant echoes. The only thing that mattered was getting to Cole.

She released the wolf's neck. He fell to the side, and there beneath her was Cole. She saw a paw descending, the claws viciously curved for the back of his neck. She threw herself over his body, taking the blow herself, wrapping her arms around him, and screaming louder. As his flesh rent and his energy faltered.

He isn't dead. He isn't dead.

That was the only thought she held on to.

Down as she was now, there was no fighting, no resisting. All she could do was wrap her legs around Cole's limp body and cling when they pulled. They would have to kill her before she'd let him go. She wasn't losing another husband to this senseless violence. The first had been expendable, but Cole was her life, her soul, and she hadn't yet heard him tell her he loved her.

His energy wavered again. She clung to it with her mind as tightly as she clung to his body. The scent of his blood was terrifyingly rich in her nostrils, so strong. She moaned. So much of it. How much he could afford to lose when he'd already lost so much.

Live, she ordered. Changed as she was, she couldn't voice the words, but she could express the thought, and with everything in her she shoved it into Cole's mind, past his resistance, past his pain, past everything, digging it in so deep that even if he wanted to die he wouldn't be able to. *Just live.*

She could feel her own blood dripping down her side, her own life force slipping. She would heal, but he wouldn't. The thought was unbearable. She felt the unease slip through the wolves around her. She looked up, saw Clark backing off. She'd know him anywhere.

She'd memorized his face in all forms. A hundred years from now when she met him again, she wanted there to be no mistake. He'd done this to her, to them, because he believed being a monster made him above the law.

She snarled at him. He didn't look impressed. She didn't expect him to. He vanished into the woods with the rest just as reinforcements arrived. No one saw him, she was sure. No one knew he'd been there. Except her.

Blade and Isaiah reached her first.

Again there were hands tugging at her. "Let go, Miranda."

She shook her head. She was never letting go.

"We've got to see what we're dealing with."

She shook her head again.

"Is he alive?"

"The stubborn son of a bitch is alive," Blade said. "I can feel his energy."

"How is he?" Isaiah asked sharply.

"Dying."

No, he wasn't dying. Miranda wouldn't let him die, ever. Fingers touched her cheek. She'd recognize them anywhere. She opened her eyes again. Cole. He was looking at her. Seeing her like this. She closed her eyes. She never wanted him to see her like this.

With a shudder she forced her wolf back, finding it harder than she expected, but finally she succeeded, and there was nothing between their skin except the tatters of his long johns and her dress. Miranda clutched Cole's cold hand, squeezing it to her cheek, pressing a kiss into his palm. The faintest of tremors shook his fingers.

"We need to get him back," Blade said at the same time Isaiah told her, "Miranda, you need to move."

She shook her head. There was blood on his face, bruises forming on his skin, and more scary, a slash across his throat. She pressed her finger to the laceration, trying to stop the drip of blood.

"It's not an artery," Blade said almost gently. "The blood's too slow."

She looked at Blade. "Thank you," she whispered, but she kept her fingers there. Even one drop was too much. Cole's lips shaped words. She shook her head. "Save your energy."

He frowned. She felt the push of his mind against hers, and now that the danger was over, her first instinct was to resist.

Don't.

The word came to her mind as clear as day. *No.*

"What is it?"

He licked his lips and tried again. Words didn't come out.

"Miranda, we need to get him back."

Whatever they thought they needed could wait. "What is it?" she asked Cole again.

His thumb stroked over her mouth the way it always did, but while there was a connection, there was no rush of sensuality. His touch was cold, foreign, as if he'd already left her. She blinked the tears back from her eyes and waited. She felt his presence in her mind like a subtle poke that grew stronger until it became pressure. The pressure built until it became a shove. So harsh, such a strong presence. She wanted to lean back, but she needed to stay because she could feel his urgency. A picture of the deadfall on the other side of the pond formed in her mind.

"Wendy. You left her there?"

He nodded and his fingers fell from her cheek. She caught them and brought them back, pressing him to her.

Don't leave me.

Even as she held on to his energy, she felt it slip away.

The scream came from her soul, "No!"

"HE'S not a goddamn Reaper, Miranda. We don't have the luxury of time. You need to do it now."

Miranda sat beside the bed where they'd laid Cole and touched her fingers to his cheek, still clutching his energy to her heart, feeling it get fainter with every beat. The sheets around him were stained red with his blood. She wanted to change them.

"You need to stop the bleeding," she whispered.

"We've done everything we can to stop the bleeding. He's too hurt. Cut in too many places. He's too injured," Isaiah said gently.

"The only thing that will save him is you," Blade added.

She couldn't. Miranda's fingers trembled on Cole's collarbone. A smear of blood just to the left marred the tan of his skin. She didn't know if it was her blood or his. There was just no telling. Using her thumb, she rubbed at the blood.

If it was hers, it didn't matter. She would heal. She was already healing. She could feel the power surging through her, but Cole was dying, her Cole, her might, the man who'd given his life for her and her daughter. And she had to sit back and do nothing.

"I can't bite him."

"Then we'll take a chance, and I'll do it," Isaiah said.

"It won't work," Blade said.

"What do you mean it won't work?" Isaiah snapped.

"Feel his energy, taste his blood. Both are thin. If you bite him, he'll die anyway. He's too weak."

"The hell you say. What is the difference between me biting him and her?"

"He's already tuned to her. You know he would have to adjust to you, and he just doesn't have the strength for it."

"You turned me," Addy said.

"No," Blade corrected. "Isaiah turned you. For the same reason Miranda has to change Cole."

"Don't you want him to live, Miranda?" Addy asked, placing her hand on Miranda's shoulder. It was supposed to be a soothing touch, Miranda knew. She couldn't bear the weight of it.

More than anything in the world Miranda wanted Cole to live. She wanted him in her future. She wanted to laugh with him. She wanted to dance with him. She wanted to raise her daughter with him. But not as a Reaper.

"Yes."

"Then bite him now before it's too late."

"He doesn't want that."

"He wouldn't want to leave you alone, unprotected."

That was true, but it was her choice.

"Ask him," she told Blade. "Ask him and then tell her."

"I can't."

"You can do a lot of things that you don't tell any of us about. You know a lot of things that none of us know. Surely you can ask one unconscious man one question."

"And what would you have the question be?"

"Does he want to be one of us?"

I want to be one with you. She remembered him saying that when she'd ask him if he wanted to be a Reaper. One with her was not one with the Reapers. Cole was . . . She shook her head. He was Cole.

"He's my cousin. He saved my life. Now, goddammit, save his," Addy ordered.

"He wouldn't want to live that way."

"You don't know that."

"He told me." She looked at Addy. "I'm willing to bet he told you, too."

"He told you that when it was theory. This is reality. If you don't change him, he's going to die."

Miranda looked at Isaiah. He nodded, confirming what she already knew. What they all knew.

"He's lost too much blood to live without changing him."

"Maybe."

"There's no maybe. Just fact."

Then what was she supposed to do? She knew what it was like to have the choice taken from her, and if she did this, there was no changing him back. Or was there?

She looked at Blade. "Is there a cure for being Reaper?"

"Don't you think I would have tried it if there were?"

She shook her head. "No, I think you like being who you are."

"Smart girl, but if there's a cure, no one's found it yet."

"So if I bite him, it's forever." Forever was a long time.

A long time to be without him, she heard Blade whisper in her mind. It was a low-down trick.

"There's something else you're not thinking of," Addy said.

"What?"

Addy nudged Isaiah. He sighed. "We talked."

"Who's we?"

"The council, Blade, Gaelen, Dirk, and me."

"And?"

"If you don't change him, he can't stay here, and you'll be alone anyway."

"Why?" Good God, did they think any of this mattered?

"We're having a hard enough time as it is keeping people together. Him being human is a weakness we can't afford, and him being here disrupts the unity we need."

Miranda stroked her fingers down Cole's chest, skipping the jagged edges of an open wound, trying to ignore the grisly sight of his ribs showing through the tear. Placing the third finger of her left hand, her ring finger, over his heart, she felt the sluggish beat. He was slipping from her when she had just found him, leaving her alone again. She'd been alone so much. To lose Cole . . . Just thinking about it was like tearing the flesh from her bones, the soul from her heart, the will from her life. Cole. She felt a jag in his energy. Cole. Stubborn, loyal, honorable, passionate, loving. Cole. Who'd sacrificed himself for her.

Oh God, she wanted to turn him. Her teeth ached, and her fingers shook; her talons extended out of her fingers, pressing into his flesh, making tiny indents that would be so easy to replace. To lean down, to put her mouth on that spot, to replace her nails with her teeth, to bite, to bind forever. It was such a tempting prospect.

"Do it, Miranda," Addy pleaded. "Do it now."

The pressure was incredible. Four minds shoving in on hers, pushing her toward what they wanted, pushing her toward her heart's desire. Cole loved her, and he'd forgive her one day. She knew that. The words might not have been spoken between them, but they were mates, and mates did what was right. She looked up.

Addy bit her lip and whispered, "It's time someone thought of Cole first."

Miranda nodded and leaned down, pressing her lips to the faint marks left by her fingers in a lingering kiss. She had to do what was right.

Forgive me. Please.

⊰ 21 ⊱

IT HAD BEEN TWO DAYS SINCE MIRANDA HAD MADE THE decision to not change Cole. Two days in which nothing else had changed, either. Cole still lay there, a shadow of himself. She tried to take heart in the fact that he hadn't grown weaker, but he wasn't stronger, either. Maybe she should have bitten him. It had to be better than this hell.

Better for whom? her conscience asked.

A small hand slipped into hers. "He's going to be all right, Mommy."

Miranda put her arm around Wendy's shoulder and hugged her tight. "I hope so." The reassurance was weak, even to her own ears.

Wendy's face set in that stubborn expression. "He is. He promised he wouldn't leave me."

"There are some promises people can't keep."

"Cole keeps his. He told me so."

How could she tell a six-year-old that the man she worshipped and who'd put his life on the line for them wasn't going to make it?

That sacrifice didn't always result in good? That while God answered prayers, sometimes the answer was no?

Wendy tugged at her skirt. She looked down. "We just have to pray harder, Mommy."

Yeah, they did. "All right. Then that's what we'll do. We'll pray."

"Together?" Wendy asked forlornly.

Miranda knelt down and cupped her daughter's shoulders in her hands. "I've been hard to talk to the last few days, haven't I?"

Wendy bit her lip and nodded. Miranda shook her head. She'd sworn never to let anything come between her and her daughter, but she'd surrendered to her grief.

"I've been sad."

"Me, too," Wendy said, tears filling her eyes. "I'm sad, too." She wiped at her cheeks. "But we just have to be patient. Cole says patience is important. No one ever wins a hunt if they can't stay still."

It was obviously a quote. "Then we'll be patient."

Wendy looked up, her eyes big and round. "And pray."

"Yes, we'll pray."

"Now." Wendy knelt at the side of the bed. Miranda knelt with her. Just then the sun burst out from behind the clouds, and a narrow beam shown through the window and spread over Cole.

"See, Mommy," Wendy whispered. "The angels see him."

Before Miranda could contradict Wendy, there was a knock on the door. Wendy's eyes went wide.

"The angels."

Miranda stood, ignoring the protest from her tired legs, and opened the door. Hardly an angel.

"Hello, Blade." She didn't care that her tone sounded unwelcoming.

"May I come in?"

She held her ground. "No, but if you came to check on Cole's condition, it hasn't changed."

"I've got to admit, I'm kind of surprised. I thought he would have gotten worse."

"Me, too." If only he would get worse, she wouldn't have to fight the constant temptation to bite him.

"Biting him now would do nothing."

"How do you know? You thought he'd be dead already."

"Some things don't take guesswork."

"I think you're just doing your own brand of wishful thinking."

He cocked his eyebrow at her. His tone was as stern as his expression; he entered the room. It immediately felt smaller.

"I don't indulge in wishful thinking."

She did, all the time. Every hour, every minute, every second of the last two days she'd done nothing but wish.

Wendy stood and squared off against Blade, her chin jutting out belligerently. Catching her daughter's slight shoulders, Miranda pulled Wendy back against her.

"What brings you here, Blade?"

"You're wanted by the council."

"Tell them I'll be there later."

"This can't wait."

"What can't wait?"

He touched a finger to Cole's hand. "Clark has renewed his claim."

Clark. Her lip lifted in a snarl. "I won't have him."

"It's not your call."

"The hell it's not. I have a mate."

"That's Clark's argument. He says your mate can no longer protect you."

"Maybe I don't need protection." She turned slightly, reaching under the edge of the mattress, feeling the blade of her dead husband's sword, so sharp still that it cut her finger at the slightest touch. She'd carried that sword around like a talisman, but maybe she'd been carrying it for another reason, one she hadn't understood till just now.

"There's no point in me going to this meeting. I won't have him."

"You know Reaper law. If the council decrees it, it's as good as done."

She set her jaw. "I won't have him."

"Either way it's best you come to state your case."

"I'm staying with Cole." She didn't want to leave him.

"You can't be worried that anybody's going to get past me."

She cut him a glare. "Maybe I'm worried about you."

"If you hurt my Cole, I'll hurt you," Wendy threatened, her fists bunched at her sides.

Blade's tone softened. "I won't hurt your Cole."

"Promise?"

"I promise."

Wendy narrowed her eyes and then held up her pinky finger. "Pinky swear."

For a second Blade look taken aback, but then he crossed fingers with Wendy. "Done."

He looked over at Miranda. "Now that that's taken care of . . . ?"

"I have a right to stay by my husband. I have a right to grieve if he dies. I have a right to rejoice if he lives."

"I agree with you."

"Then why do I hear a 'but'?"

"The council doesn't. You know how they feel about unrest."

"And how they feel about Cole being human?"

He nodded. "There are more than a few that are looking for an excuse to break the bond."

There was no breaking the bond between Miranda and Cole. Why didn't they understand that?

"Tell the council I'll be there when I'm ready."

"That will be seen as a sign of disrespect."

She looked over at him, feeling oddly detached. "Then they would have read my mood correctly."

With a half smile, he touched his hand to the brim of his hat. "I'll pass your message along."

Beside her she could feel Wendy tremble as the door closed behind Blade. Miranda put her hand on her shoulder. "It's all right."

Wendy shook her head. "The council does bad things to people who don't listen."

"I'm listening."

A sob caught in her daughter's throat, and the shaking didn't stop. Miranda knelt and gathered Wendy in her arms, holding her daughter tight. "I won't let anything happen to you, baby."

Wendy's arms crept around her mother's neck, and she clung. "I don't want anything to happen to you."

"It won't."

Miranda ran her hands down Wendy's hair, hugging her back just as tightly. Pressing a kiss to her forehead, Miranda whispered, "I promise you, baby; when this is all over, we're going to leave here."

Wendy's eyes went big. "You mean it? We can be real people again?"

Miranda pushed the hair off her face. How could she not have seen for all these years that desperate desire inside her daughter? "Yes, I mean it. When Cole's better, we'll go."

Wendy's face fell. "The council won't let us."

"They will."

"How do you know?"

Miranda's fingers grazed the sword again. She changed her mind. She was going to that meeting after all. Shielding her actions with her body, she tucked the sword into the folds of her skirts. It felt good in her hand, as if her husband's energy still clung to it—

the sword with which he'd taken his life because he'd felt he'd failed her. Maybe tonight they'd get a bit of that honor back. "Because I'm going to make them."

THE council appeared exactly as she'd expected it to. A bunch of men frowning at her, their energy hitting her like a wall as soon as they came in the room. They were united in their decision, whatever it was. To the front and to the right stood Clark, his hands folded behind his back. He looked like a general surveying his troops. They couldn't be so stupid as to be in the palm of his hand.

Blade sat in his own chair at the council, three left of center. There was no expression on his face, and when her eyes met his, he offered no comfort. She kept her mind blank and tightened her grip on the sword. She'd never realized until she embraced her wolf how easy it was to read others' emotions. They thought they could intimidate her. That she'd be easy. They were wrong.

"Good evening, gentlemen." She didn't keep her eyes down, not anymore. Those days were done.

A none-too-happy Gaelen started the proceedings "Clark has petitioned the council for the position of your mate."

There was a time she would have been shaking if called to stand in front of the council to have her fate decided by so many strangers. She would have been swallowed up by the feeling of helplessness, of being caught in a system that she couldn't fight. But not today and not for a long time, she realized looking back on it. She was a woman grown. She had a daughter and a husband and wants and desires of which they knew nothing

"I'm already married."

"Clark has petitioned to have that union set aside."

"No."

"Excuse me?"

"I said no. The union will not be set aside."

"The council is not unsympathetic," another of the council members spoke up. Miranda didn't know much about him aside from his name. Noah Kinder. He was older in appearance. And a bit pompous. "It was decided that upon the death of your current mate, we would consent to the mating with Clark. I know it seems abrupt, Mrs. Cameron, but Clark has agreed to give you a time of mourning before instituting the rights of mating."

"It's so kind of him to decide to wait to rape me."

Noah snorted. "There is no rape in a mating."

She looked at him, at all of them, as if they were out of their minds, because they truly were. Her free hand clenched into a fist. "You have no idea what you do to women with your rules. You think you're so much better than the ones who maraud and rape and steal, but all you do is dress it up prettier, because in the end the woman still has no choice."

There was a rumble of disapproval from all the men except Blade and Gaelen. The latter nodded.

Noah cleared his throat and frowned at her. "Do you wish to speak against this mating?"

"I don't need to speak against it."

"Then it's settled."

"I've already refused it."

She could feel the council's flinch.

Blade asked, "Why?"

"He's a brute, a bully, and he's a traitor."

"The hell you say, woman." Clark took an angry step forward.

She turned to face him, lifting her chin, standing her ground. "And right now, he intends to beat me because I told the truth."

"Do you have any proof of this?" Gaelen asked.

"He was there when Cole was attacked, and I think he was there when I got these." She touched her scars.

"That's a lie!"

"Do you have proof?" Blade asked.

"Only what I saw."

"Then it's your word against his," Noah said as if that settled everything. And she supposed in his eyes it did.

"It's the truth."

"No one believes you."

She looked Clark in the eye. "I won't marry you, and if you touch me, I'm going to hurt you. Before God and the council, I swear I will."

"Enough," Noah cut in. "The council understands it must be hard to think of taking another man before your husband is dead, but these hysterics won't change anything."

She growled deep in her throat. No one paid her any heed.

"The decision has been made. There are signs of renegade Reapers. You and your daughter need protection. Sitting in the middle of the pack is not enough. Clark will claim you."

Tightening her grip on the sword Miranda repeated, "I am claimed."

"A dead man can't protect you."

She jerked her chin in Clark's direction. "Neither can he."

"Enough," Noah snapped again while the rest of the council watched her, like an amusing bug pinned to a board. "We don't have time for your foolishness."

"Then don't waste your time preaching the impossible," she snapped right back. "I won't go with him. I won't mate with him. I won't be with him." She turned to Clark. "And if you take a step closer to me, I'm going to kill you."

Clark just smiled and kept coming, victory dripping from his gloating smile. "The council has spoken."

He shouldn't have smiled. She might have held on to her control had he not smiled, but she'd seen that smile before. She'd seen it as

Cole went down, his blood staining her hands. She remembered the blood so well. It bled into her heart, into her soul, into her anger until red was all she could see.

Clark took another step. Before he could take a third, she whipped the sword around, her aim true. She was braced for the force of hitting a tree, but his head severed from his body with surprising ease. Blood sprayed in a warm rain. The council snarled and gasped. Blade chuckled as Clark's body fell to the floor. Taking a step back, Miranda turned in a slow circle to face them all, blood dripping from her outstretched sword.

"Clark raped me when I was changed. He ordered the attack on my mate. He struck my child, and he struck me. If I were a man, you'd be surprised I hadn't killed him long before, but I have news for you. I may be a woman, but I'm Reaper to the bone, and I deserved justice, not a forced marriage."

"Kind of a moot point now," Isaiah pointed out.

"It always was. It was only your inflated opinion of yourselves that made you think you had a say otherwise."

"You go too far," Noah growled, standing.

She brought up the sword. Other members of the council stood, Blade and Isaiah among them. She didn't care. She was just . . . done. "I'll honor your laws, every single damn one of them that's fair to everybody, but I won't be forced to marry, and I won't be forced to bear children I don't want."

"The law is the law."

"Then the law needs to change, and you need to change it. Or you can anticipate a heck of a lot more bodies lying about."

"She's got a point," Blade said from where he stood, calmly rolling a cigarette.

"The hell she does." Noah slapped his hand on the table. "She just killed a man in front of us all."

"The woman's crazy," she heard someone mutter.

"Can't say that I blame her." Blade lit his cigarette and took a draw. "The man needed killing."

Miranda looked at him, feeling the weight of the sword in her hand. "Why didn't you?"

He blew out a stream of smoke. "You were doing all right on your own."

Yes, she realized, she had been.

"The council had spoken. She had no right," Noah said again.

Isaiah took a step forward. "The council was wrong."

That set off a whole new furor. No one seemed to care about Clark lying in the middle of the floor, pumping blood into the dirt. They were caught up in the argument. None of the discussions revolved around the right and wrong of her killing Clark. All of it had to do with who should have what power.

Blade motioned toward the door. "Now might be a good time to leave."

Miranda couldn't agree more. When she stepped outside, the women gathered around the door stepped aside, clearing a path for her to walk through. All except Cindy, Clark's wife. She just stood there at the end of the small gathering, pale and quiet as always, a fresh bruise on her cheek. Miranda didn't know what to say to her. Clark had been a brute, but he'd been her husband. Miranda settled for a completely inadequate, "I'm sorry."

For a long moment, there was silence. Then Cindy wiped her hands on her apron. "Don't be. The man needed killing."

As if that was all she needed to say, she turned and walked toward her house.

Miranda could only watch her go. She heard someone say, "Amen," and then the applause started, small claps that built. The women of the Reapers weren't many, but they were united in this moment. And all it'd taken was killing a man. She sighed.

"Don't follow my example; they're probably going to kill me come morning."

The clapping stopped. She didn't. She needed to get back to Cole. Someone touched her arm, and she turned. It was Addy.

"You can't go back like that. You'll scare Wendy."

Miranda blinked and looked down. She was covered in blood. Her stomach heaved.

"You women fetch some water. We need to get her cleaned up." Addy took her hand. Her voice gentled. "You come with me."

Like a puppet, Miranda followed Addy into her cabin. It could have been minutes or hours before the bath was ready. Everything was so out of focus. Miranda sat through the bathing, that numbness still holding her, the sword clutched in her hand. After one attempt to take it, Addy left it, working around it.

"Where did you get your sword?" she asked finally as she handed Miranda a clean dress.

Drifting as she was in that uncaring sea, Miranda struggled to form the answer. "It was my husband's."

"I didn't know you kept it."

"No one pays much attention to what I do."

"They will now."

Addy started buttoning the dress. Miranda saw again the light flash against the sword's blade, Clark's expression of horror. She'd been fast, so fast, and he hadn't expected it. No one ever expected bad things to happen. The horror of what she'd done finally sank in.

She looked at Addy and whispered, "They're going to kill me, aren't they?"

"No, they're not going to kill you."

"How do you know?"

"Because I won't let them."

"You're a woman."

Addy huffed. "As you've proven, women have a lot more power

and a lot less patience than these men think, but Isaiah won't let them kill you, either. And neither will Blade or Gaelen or Dirk."

Miranda pushed Addy's hands away and took over the buttoning. "Blade didn't say a word, the whole time. I thought he was with them."

"You never know what that one's thinking."

"Do you think they'll take revenge?"

"On you? No."

"On Cole?" Ice settled in Miranda's gut. He was alone and vulnerable. "Oh my God, I've got to get back to him."

"Cindy and Bebe are with him, keeping guard.

"They won't be any match for the council."

"Bebe has a gun."

"Bebe has a gun?" Bebe was sweet and gentle, and she never bucked the current. Her surprise must have shown.

"I don't think there is a single woman here who doesn't feel exactly as you do. The laws were written before the Reapers had women, but the laws have to change. Whether they think they are protecting us or not, they have to change."

"Change takes time."

Addy nodded. "I know." She handed Miranda a brush. "Has there been any improvement at all in Cole?"

Miranda shook her head and yanked the brush through the snarled ends of her hair. "No, it's like he's dead but won't accept it."

"You think it's just a matter of time?"

Miranda wouldn't think that way. "I think it's in God's hands."

"And you trust God?" Addy asked.

Miranda knew Addy had her own experiences that put doubt in her voice. "I think God's the only hope I have."

Addy nodded. "Then we need to get to praying."

"I don't have time right now. I have to get back."

Addy nodded. "You go ahead, then. I'll arrange it."

"And if the council comes for me?"

Addy smiled. "They'll have to go through our prayer circle to get to you."

Miranda paused. "You believe faith will deter them?"

Addy's smile grew harder. "If that doesn't," she patted her hip pocket, "Isaiah has given me a few things that will bring them to their knees."

"You can't confront them," Miranda gasped.

Addy looked at her, showing the iron side Isaiah bragged on but Miranda had never seen. "They have a choice. They can accept us or fight us, but either way, you're safe here."

"You're declaring war?" Miranda couldn't comprehend it.

"In a manner of speaking." Addy's smile softened again, this time with amusement. "However, it's not that bad. We're talking husbands and wannabe husbands of a pack selected by Isaiah for their character."

Miranda handed Addy back the brush. "They're pretty set on their precious laws."

Addy took it. "True, but since every man knows a happy wife makes for a happy life, I'm not anticipating a prolonged fight."

And Miranda understood. In a confrontation every mate would be forced to stand by his wife. Every man hoping to have a wife wouldn't touch a woman with mate potential. The men's hands were tied from the get-go. That had never occurred to Miranda, she'd been so cowed by the circumstances surrounding her change. She just looked at Addy and shook her head. "I hope Isaiah appreciates the brilliance of you."

"He does, and though he likely won't appreciate the timing of this, he'll come to understand the why eventually."

"He's a good man."

Addy nodded, handing Miranda a rawhide tie for her hair. "He's the best, and so is yours, and it's time you got back to him."

It was. She bound off her braid and flipped her hair back over her shoulder. "Thank you."

"Thank you for getting rid of Clark. Isaiah's hands were tied, though he was considering alternatives." Addy turned and rummaged in a chest at the side of the table. "If it's any consolation, you would never have been forced to marry that bastard," she said from the interior.

Miranda picked up her sword. "Why did no one tell me?"

Addy straightened and turned back. "Suffice it to say we had a plan."

"And now?"

Addy placed a mean-looking revolver on the table. "I think you improved upon it."

IT was exactly as Addy had said it would be when Miranda got back home. Bebe and Cindy sat outside the door. Propped on the wall beside Bebe was an old-fashioned rifle.

As was happening a lot lately, Miranda didn't know what to say. When they stood and greeted her as if nothing out of the ordinary was occurring, Miranda followed suit. With a simple "Afternoon," she entered her home.

It took a second for her eyes to adjust to the dimmer light. Everything was as it should be. Cole was still lying as he had before with no change to his position. Wendy sat by his side, patting his chest, talking to him about her day, Addy thought, until she heard her end on a flourish only a six-year-old could conjure, "Then Mommy cut off his head."

Oh dear heavens. Miranda stood the sword against the wall. It slid to the side until it hit the doorjamb. "Don't be telling him that."

"Why not? It's true, isn't it? Bebe said it was true."

She didn't have any choice but to nod. Outside she heard female voices murmur greetings.

"I'm telling Cole why he has to wake up," Wendy explained.

"Why?"

"Because now that you've made the council mad, we really have to go. And he has to go with us."

The child was entirely too perceptive. Outside voices rose in prayer. A little of the tension inside Miranda eased, but not much. They were only safe for the moment.

"Yes, we do." She just didn't know how she was going to do that. How she was going to take her daughter away to be safe but leave Cole behind to be vulnerable. She reached out and touched his energy. It might have been her imagination, but there was a flicker. Or not. She sighed.

She heard footsteps at the door and turned. Blade and Isaiah stood in the doorway, blocking out the light. She grabbed the sword in both hands and sprang, putting herself between them and Cole.

"Mister Isaiah!" Wendy cried out happily.

"Stay back, Wendy," Miranda ordered harshly enough that Wendy obeyed out of surprise.

Isaiah shook his head and sighed. "You wouldn't even get half a swing in before I took that from you."

"We'll see."

"I don't want to take your sword from you, Miranda."

"He killed my first husband, attacked Cole."

Blade cut her off with a slash of his hand. "You don't have to go into your reasons. Just answer this. Do you swear your accusations against Clark to be true?"

What were they up to? "Yes."

"Then that works for me."

"And me," Isaiah echoed, leaning against the wall and folding his arms across his chest. He looked amazingly nonchalant for such an intimidating presence.

"And the council?" she asked.

"Nobody has a problem with you killing Clark. Deep down they all kind of thought he needed it."

"Yet they would have married me to him."

Blade shrugged. "It was the easiest solution to the biggest problem."

"So what is their problem now?"

"You told them to go to hell."

"They have no right to do whatever they want to me or to any other women under their protection."

"I got to say, I agree with you," Blade said. "The laws are weighted in the wrong direction, but change isn't going to happen overnight."

"I know that. What is their verdict?"

"They don't have one yet. They're still busy fighting among themselves over how much disrespect was shown. They're also a bit distracted by a bigger problem."

"They are?"

"Addy and some of the women are blocking the council entrance from the inside and out."

"What are they doing?"

It was Isaiah who answered, "Praying."

Miranda smiled. "Addy is a woman of strong convictions."

"Their support for you is quite visible," Blade continued.

"Council's about fit to be tied," Isaiah explained. "Can't rightly go hanging all the women."

She touched her neck. "Hanging?"

"Figure of speech."

Maybe it was; maybe it wasn't. Again Miranda felt that flicker from Cole. She turned and put her hand on Cole's cheek, hoping to find life but only finding that bare pulse of nothingness. Her mind was playing tricks on her.

"There has got to be a reason he's still alive," she whispered.

Isaiah dropped his hands and stepped closer. "Too damn stubborn to die, I imagine."

She glared at him. "I need him to be stubborn enough to live."

"He lost a lot of blood. Even if he survives, he may not be right in the head."

This time she glared at Blade. "Why do you have to be the voice of doom?"

He shrugged. "My nature I guess."

She shook her head, the weariness she'd been holding off for so long overtaking her. "So the council's not coming for me tonight?"

Blade's expression softened. "They'll leave you be."

"Good. Then you need to leave. I need to rest."

When they got to the door, it was Blade who looked back before closing it. "I always knew you'd be a force to reckon with once you found your feet."

"Is that approval?"

He didn't answer, just closed the door.

She lowered the sword. Damn irritating man.

MIRANDA sat on the edge of the narrow bed. There was just enough room, if she clung to Cole, to make a space for herself. She lay down and put her head on his shoulder, the slow beat of his heart her only security.

Wendy climbed over Miranda and then over him. She couldn't even lecture the child for maybe disturbing his wounds. When Wendy reached the other side, she wrapped her arms across Cole's chest, her fingers stroking Miranda's upper arm. connecting them.

Miranda smiled at her daughter's solemn face. Wendy smiled back. They fell asleep that way. Shielding Cole between them, arms wrapped around him, holding on to the hope.

SOMETIME later a soft tremor of sensation woke her, and her smile took form before she remembered there was no reason for its birth.

"Did you really cut off his head?"

The voice was dry and raspy, but oh my God, so familiar. "Cole?"

The whisper of his lips across her forehead came again. "I'd better be the only man in your bed."

On the other side, Wendy still slept.

"Oh my God!" Just as quickly she changed it to, "Thank you, God" in her mind. She tried to stand, but his arm kept her anchored.

"Don't make me fight you, china doll, I'm feeling a bit peaked."

Even weak, he still had enough force to keep her put; thank God for that blessed strength of his and that stubbornness.

"Did you really cut off his head?" he asked again.

"You heard that?"

He nodded. Arching a brow at her, he repeated, "Did you?"

"I was annoyed."

The other brow arched to match the first. "Annoyed, eh?"

She nodded.

"I'll be hearing that story later, but right now, you're going to tell me what the repercussions are."

"I don't know. Blade said they wouldn't bother me tonight."

"Is it still night?"

"You can't see?"

"I can't tell if it's dark in here because you've got the curtains drawn so tight or if morning's just coming."

"Morning's coming."

He went to get up.

She placed her hand on his shoulder. He looked at her. "Don't," she whispered, "just don't."

Just then Wendy woke. "Cole!" She jumped across his chest and hugged him tightly. Miranda didn't have to be connected to him to feel his pain.

"Careful, Wendy."

"Hey, little bit." He gave her a stiff hug and kissed the top of her head. "You been waiting on me?"

"Forever and ever," Wendy sighed, hugging him again.

"Well, good thing you waited and prayed. It kept me going."

She propped herself up. "You heard me?"

He nodded and moved her elbow over a bit. His gaze met Miranda's over Wendy's head. "I heard you both."

And he'd stayed with them. Miranda shoved her fist into her mouth, trying to hold back a sob. Reaching over, Cole caught her hand and tugged. Even broken and weak, he was stronger than her. And she went because she needed that hug as much as Wendy.

"I thought I'd lost you."

"I told you, I'm not so easy to kill." He sighed. "This is good. Both my girls in my arms. Well worth waking up for."

"We missed you," Wendy whispered fervently.

"I told you I wouldn't leave."

"Mommy said some promises can't be kept."

He chucked her chin and wiped a tear from her cheek with his thumb. "Well, now you know I'm keeping that one."

Wendy nodded hard. He eased her off his chest. Miranda scooted over to make room. She ended up kneeling on the floor.

Cole kept hold of her hand. "Could you get me some water from the well, little bit?"

Wendy jumped up. "There's some in the pitcher."

"Cold water would be better."

She paused, thought about it, and then nodded. "'Cause of your booboo there?" She pointed to his throat.

He nodded. "Thank you."

Wendy was off in a flounce of skirts and pigtails. Miranda stopped her before she reached the door. "But don't tell anyone Cole's awake."

"Because of the bad ones?"

Miranda hated her daughter had to know that. "Yes."

"I won't tell." The door slammed behind her.

Cole touched his throat, felt the scab through the bandage. "I must look a sight."

Miranda could only nod through the tears choking her. He was going to be all right.

His thumb stroked over the back of her hand. "I'm glad you killed the son of a bitch."

So was she. She eased back up onto the bed. "I made more problems."

"You did what you had to. There comes a time when the people in charge need to realize there is an end to their power, and that's usually right about the point where people can't take any more."

She stroked her fingers down his cheek. His skin was warm, his energy vibrant. "You weren't even dead."

He frowned. "When did all this happen?"

"Two days ago."

He went still. She didn't care. She couldn't stop touching his face, his lips, his eyes. She couldn't stop kissing him, couldn't stop shaking, couldn't stop crying. Oh God, he was alive.

"Miranda?" he grunted.

"What?"

"Your elbow is killing me."

"Oh my God." Her elbow was digging into his side. "I'm so sorry." She started to cry harder.

Cole sighed, tucked her against him, and stroked her hair. "You can stop crying, china doll. I'm going to make it."

"I can't help it. You just look so good."

"I look like I've been drawn through a knothole backward, rolled in the mud, and tossed in the sun to dry."

"But still good."

He chuckled. Wendy came back with the cup of water. Miranda sat beside him and propped him up. She felt his distaste at his weakness. She didn't care.

"Sip it or you'll vomit."

He did, drinking slowly.

Miranda took the opportunity to pull Wendy aside. Kneeling down she pushed the soft brown hair off her face. "I have a job for you, baby."

She had the child's full attention. "What?"

"I want you to go find Mister Isaiah. And this is very important, baby. I want you to walk like you're just going over for a piece of cake. I don't want anybody to know that Cole is awake."

She nodded, eyes getting big again. "You think they'll hurt him?"

Brushing Wendy's hair off her face again, Miranda forced a smile. "I just want this secret between you, me, and Isaiah. Can you do that, baby?"

Wendy nodded. "Yes."

"Then go."

Wendy turned, stopped, and before Miranda could catch her, darted back and hugged Cole so tightly the breath left him in an "oof."

"I'm glad you're back, Daddy."

On that she sprang up and ran for the door. It banged behind her as she left. Cole stared after her.

"Shit."

"I'm sorry, she didn't mean . . ."

"Yes, she did. And rightly so. The kid had the guts to do what I should have done."

"What was that?"

"Claimed you both in a way no one could misunderstand."

"You did."

He shook his head. "No, there's a difference between playing a role and staking a claim, Miranda. I staked my claim on you, but I left her dangling. I'll be making up for that."

"Why? She doesn't care."

"Because it's right."

It was Miranda's turn to shake her head. "You're as bad as the council."

Tugging her over, he kissed her softly before finishing up the water.

"When it comes to you, baby, I'm worse than the council." He held out the empty cup. "Now, please, get me another drink of water?"

"Why?"

He grabbed the sheet in his hand. "I'm getting dressed."

"You can't even get up."

He threw the sheet aside. "Watch me."

He wobbled. She fretted, but in the end he was up. Pale, unsteady, and gritting his teeth, but he was up.

"I don't know why you're insisting on this," she muttered, handing him his clothes. "You should sit down before you fall down."

"Because it's time to go."

"To where?"

He looked at her, hooked his hand behind her neck, and drew her in for a hard, lingering kiss. A kiss that contained all the emotion she wanted to feel. All the words she wanted to hear. A kiss that was over long before she could bear, and then he said one word.

"Home." He stroked his thumb over her lips, rubbing it across the moist surface as he smiled that smile that made her heart skip. "I'm taking my girls home, Miranda."

⊰ Epilogue ⊱

MIRANDA STOOD ON THE CLIFF LOOKING BACK OVER THE mist-shrouded valley from which they'd fled. It looked so peaceful in the cool, flat light of predawn. The low-hanging clouds hid its secrets and its flaws. Miranda leaned back against Cole and took it all in with a sigh.

"I came here with such hopes."

On the horizon the first fingers of sunrise tinted the sky. Behind them Dirk, Cindy, Jenny, and Wendy waited. A ragtag group of refugees fleeing the past, moving toward hope.

Cole wrapped his arms around her. She loved it when he held her so tightly within his embrace, cradled in his energy. She felt so safe and cared for. It didn't matter that he didn't say the words.

"And now?" he asked.

She smiled and reached back, stroking his beard-roughened cheek. She could feel his worry. And his impatience. He wanted to get on their way, but she'd needed this time. Leaving this valley . . .

she was leaving a lot more than just a house. She was leaving friends, hopes, dreams, people like her. Security. Some good-byes were necessary. Even if they were from afar. Taking a breath, she let it all go. "I'm leaving with more than I came with."

Cole turned her around, fisting his hand in her hair, pulling her head back while he held her close and safe. Those too-perceptive eyes of his searched hers. "Even if the Rogues believe you dead, there will always be risks out in the world, Miranda."

Blade had spread the rumor that after the council meeting she'd died of wounds sustained in the battle the day before. It was a weak ploy, but the pack would propagate the rumor. The others' absences would be explained away through the by-product of dissension. They, like she, only needed the perception of believability.

"I'm not afraid."

His fingers touched her cheek not with their usual arrogance but with a delicacy that reached all the way to her soul. He had her full attention.

"I am."

"Why?" She turned her face into his palm. "I want this. For us and for Wendy."

"Time to go," Dirk prompted impatiently from behind them.

"In a minute," Cole responded, not taking his gaze from hers.

"We don't have that many to spare," Dirk countered with his usual bluntness. "If those Rogues catch our scent, all those sweet nothings you're spouting will be for nothing. Especially as you're not at peak."

"Shut up, Dirk." Cole stroked his thumb across her lips. "This is important."

Yes. It was. Miranda could feel how important it was to him. His energy stroked along hers, whispering things she so wanted to hear. She couldn't catch her breath.

"What scares you?" Her voice was a breathless wisp of air. She didn't care as his head tilted ever so slightly to the side and his mouth softened.

"Waking up in the morning without you. Wendy growing up, and young men sniffing around her." Another stroke of his energy, this one poignantly tense. "Losing you."

She touched her fingertips to his jaw. They were trembling. She didn't care about that, either. There was no hiding from Cole. "You won't ever lose me."

His lips pressed together. "But you will lose me."

He was referring to the difference in their life spans. She didn't care about that, either. "Life doesn't come wrapped in a bow, Cole. I want what we have for as long as we can have it."

He rested his forehead against hers. "And then?"

There would come a day when she'd have to say good-bye to Cole and Wendy, but that day wasn't now. Now was a beginning. She curved her fingers over his, holding him to her. She didn't look away. "And then I'll have the memories of something so special it will sustain me until we're together again."

For a brief second his eyes closed, and when they opened—oh Lord—when they opened, it was all there. Every emotion he felt. The good, the bad. Just . . . everything. "Goddamn, Miranda Cameron, I fucking love you."

The tears came unexpectedly, dripping down her cheeks, spreading around his hand, binding them together. Sorrow and hope. Faith and love. So much love pouring over her in strong, deep strokes. Cole giving her all the love she'd ever longed for. "I love you, too."

His eyes narrowed. "Then why the tears?"

"I never thought you'd tell me that."

Cole sighed and tipped her head back before placing his mouth over hers gently, easily, almost reverently. Taking the tears and her sob as his, holding her close as their breath mingled. "I want it all, china doll. I want you in my bed and in my life. I want breakfast and lunch and dinner. I want to kiss you awake in the morning and hold your hand at sunset. I want to watch Wendy grow up. I want to give her suitors hell and her children piggyback rides." He rested his forehead against hers. "I want us."

She eased her fingers through his hair, pulling him closer still. "I do, too."

They stood like that for a moment, two people with one heart. Dirk cleared his throat. Cole stepped back and held out his hand. His smile was more beautiful than the sunrise. "Then let's go home."

From behind them, Dirk muttered, "About damn time."

Yes. Miranda smiled as she took Cole's hand and turned her back on the valley. It was.